THE
DARK
ARMADA

A Project Waypoint Novel

L. S. Roebuck

SHADOWLANDS PRESS
El Paso, Texas

The Dark Armada
© 2020 L.S. Roebuck

ISBN 13: 978-0-9986090-4-1

1.2.1

Published by Shadowlands Press
5528 Last Waltz Dr.
El Paso, Texas 79932
www.shadowlandspress.com

For my children: Max, Maggie, Xander and Millie.
God put the stars out there for you.

With gratitude to Jerry Goldsmith, Bear McCreary, Michael Giacchino, Hans Zimmer, James Horner, Daft Punk, Jack Wall, Arlon Ober, Thomas Newman, Sam Hulick, Martin O'Donnell, Ulpio Minucci, John Williams, Claude Debussy, Tracy Manos, Hagood Hardy and Peter Schilling, whose music stirred the wonder of the cosmos in my soul during the hours I wrote the Project Waypoint series.

Special thanks to Johanna "Merwin" Musgrave for her insightful edits.

And with love to Cherissa, who supported me with infinite love as I traveled to the waypoints over this seven-year writing adventure.

PROLOGUE

ARMADA (N) – A SPANISH NAVAL INVASION FORCE
SENT AGAINST ENGLAND BY PHILIP II OF SPAIN IN 1588;
A FLEET OF WARSHIPS PURPOSED TO DESTROY

*The M.S.S. Normandy, 32 hours out from Waypoint Magellan,
en route to the Spencer Belt, January 26, 2596*

Kimberly Macready looked out the viewport, her eyes drinking the light of a million stars.

As a young girl on her home planet Arara, those stars called her into space. After decades of disenchantment, Kimberly now longed for home.

Reclining in the pilot station of the Valkyrie-class runabout *M.S.S. Normandy*, Kimberly's husband, Alroy, checked the magnetic resonance screen for the estimated arrival at Sonnet.

Alroy enjoyed the silhouette of his bride against the starfield beyond the viewport. Kimberly was his definition of beauty, her raven-dark hair falling over pale skin. Framing her button nose were intensely powerful eyes, full of life, a gateway to an intelligence he could not begin to understand.

He loved her.

But he did not trust her.

"Ten minutes till we arrive at Sonnet," Alroy announced, scratching his fingers through his thick, short red hair. Then he addressed his virtual intelligence construct, currently loaded in the memory banks of the *Normandy*. "Jules, go ahead and switch to manual. I'd like to bring us in."

More than 100 kilometers in diameter, Sonnet was the largest of the thousands of lifeless rocks in the Spencer Belt's distant orbit around stellar object HB 2343453, Spencer Minorum.

Kimberly remained silent and distant. Alroy frowned.

"We should make Sonnet before Fuentes Station slips into night. You are setting up radiation trackers, aren't you?" Alroy asked too knowingly.

Kimberly, a leading researcher for *Waypoint Magellan*'s Science Corp, did not acknowledge her husband. Alroy considered her stoic look and thought about their 16 years of marriage. He remembered when he first met Kimberly, not long after she arrived at *Waypoint Magellan*. Her journey from the colony planet Arara to *Magellan* took three years for even the fastest deep space ships to complete.

When long-voyage ships arrived at *Waypoint Magellan*, the celebratory spirit was intoxicating. Fresh faces and fresh meat mixing together after years trapped on ship and station created a social cacophony.

Alroy was captivated by Kimberly's energy and her genius; she truly was unlike any woman he had met before. She challenged the pilot in novel ways. He knew she was his intellectual superior, but then again, Alroy imagined few, if any, played on the mental level that Kimberly did.

On the other hand, Alroy loved the gift of life. He did everything he could to share that love with everyone he encountered. He had a certain faithfulness and capacity for love that gave him an incredibly compelling *soul*.

This characteristic was unexpected for Kimberly. She had been through many men before she met Alroy. All inferior, they bent to her will like cheap flatware. Men had their uses in her secret cause, but she had no respect for the masculine gender. She had originally thought Alroy, like so many before him, would fold in submission to her charismatic potency. She would use him for what he was worth, and then discard him.

But he would not be molded. His spirit was powerful. And that power attracted Kimberly in a way she had never been attracted to a man before. And then Alroy showed her true love.

She had commanded the slavish devotion of men before, screwballs who were addicted to her pleasures and praises, who worshipped in her wake and obeyed her with a cultish fanaticism. They did horrible things for her, debasing themselves for a wink or a nod. But when Alroy was kind to Kimberly, it was not transactional. It was not for the promise of a drip of attention or an intoxicating hit of Kimberly's magnetism. He did it selflessly, *just because.* No manipulation. No submissive fetish. No quid-pro-quo.

Kimberly, despite all her superior complexity, had fallen for a simple and pure love. The leader of her revolutionary conspiracy, the Chairman, would be furious if she knew that Kimberly had begun to build a family in her undercover role as a researcher.

Against the advice of his religious friends, Alroy married Kimberly, a somewhat outspoken atheist.

Kora was born soon after. And then came baby Amberly. Since then, their relationship had been one of fire and ice. Currently, the temperature was frigid.

Kimberly looked over at her husband, a sadness covering her thoughts like morning dew on the Lewis Island grasslands. *He is so naïve*, she thought. He loved their two daughters in the same selfless way that he loved her. The men of the conspiracy, the men of Chasm, were often driven by selfish focus on personal pleasure and petty ambition, not true devotion to common good. That made them weak and easy to manipulate.

But in the final analysis, Alroy's selflessness was misplaced, Kimberly believed. His focus on the family, on the tribe, instead of the common good of society as a whole, disgusted her. *The family is the enemy of the state*, Kimberly recited the Chasm truth in her head. Perfecting humanity required the elimination of tribal family in favor of the communal state.

This was the day she would start to eliminate her accidental family.

Literally.

Kimberly eyed the swagger stick clipped to Alroy's belt. He could weaponize it. She fingered the stun weapon she had tucked in the fold of her flowing khaki robe. She thought about the Chairman, and even though she was more than a light year away, Kimberly felt her dark, seemingly iris-less eyes gazing on Kimberly in harsh judgment.

"There's no research equipment, is there?" Alroy asked again, snapping Kimberly out of her deep thoughts.

"You *know* then, Roy?" Kimberly responded with a question of her own.

Alroy looked away from his wife. The time had come for confrontation, and he feared what was to come.

"Your sensor boxes are full of emergency rations," Alroy replied. "That was the most recent clue. But also, the encrypted messages. Verne could only crack headers and subject lines. Who is Raven One? And what is Chasm?"

"Verne? That virtual intelligence program you bought for Amberly? Not a gift for our daughter, but a tool to spy on me?" Kimberly's eyes went wide, and in an instant, she threw off her robe, revealing her black jumpsuit and her stun gun. She leveled the weapon at her husband's chest. "Not so naïve then, husband?"

Her eyes lit with a blast of understanding.

"It was *you*," Kimberly smiled, impressed. "I always had a sense I should not underestimate you. Järvinen thought it was that runt dock worker, John Tyler, who had figured out who I really am. But it … was … you."

Alroy abandoned the pilot's chair, standing in an athletic stance with his abnormally long swagger stick in hand. The smooth, black stick was about a meter in length, had a brush-like tail, and was otherwise completely ornamental in function. Alroy enjoyed fidgeting with the stick, a gift from his late friend, *Magellan* Marine Officer Murray. He would twirl it rapidly like a in a drill program to delight his daughters when they were younger.

"Who are you, Kim?" Alroy asked, as he slowly sidestepped around the small bridge, simultaneously closing the gap between him and his wife and trying to stay out of the gun's firing line.

"I am Raven One. Leader of the Chasm triumvirate on *Magellan*, chosen by the Chairman for glory."

"Chairman? Glory?" Alroy was confused. "I thought you were a disciple of science. A seeker of knowledge, of truth?"

"Indeed, I am. The truth is that humanity can never improve as long as we are shackled to the evils of Earth. Endless wars. Racism. Latent misogyny. Inequity. We must break away from that to engineer a perfect society. The Chairman has a grand plan for perfection. I wish you could live to see it. Then you would understand," Kimberly said. As she spoke, she matched Alroy's rotation so as not to be flanked by him. Clearly, he meant to disarm her, and if he did, though she was in top physical shape, she knew that Alroy could overpower her.

"I never meant for us to be. I'm sorry. It's over for you, love," Kimberly said, the taste of remorse hanging on the back of her tongue. Alroy could see tears forming in Kimberly's eyes.

"I love you. Let me help you," Alroy said. "We can figure it out. Help you escape this… Chasm."

Kimberly's face was sardonic. "I don't want to escape. Don't you see, *I* am the harbinger of perfection. And now my family is in the way. This family," Kimberly choked out, tears now streaming down her soft cheeks. She pointed to herself and then to Alroy. "Our family. The Macready family. It wasn't supposed to happen. It was a *mistake*. And now it's a liability. And Chasm does not abide liabilities. It cuts them off, swiftly. Decisively. *I* cut them off. I am *Chasm*."

"Kora and Amberly are not mistakes," Alroy said, anger filling his words as he took a step toward Kimberly. She retreated, her back now against the cool steel bulkhead. "My love for you is not a mistake."

"Stop!" Kimberly insisted and she raised the gun with the intention to shoot. Alroy did as he was instructed. "I don't expect you to understand. You are so *luminous*. After all this time, I still don't know how. I am sorry to extinguish your light from the universe. But it is for the greater good."

Kimberly pushed the gun out again, and Alroy saw murder in her eyes. But he also saw hesitation.

He side flung his swagger stick at the gun; Kimberly balked, not pulling the trigger. The impact of the stick knocked the gun out of her hand, sending it sliding portside. Alroy immediately stepped forward, pinning Kimberly to the wall. His nose was pressed toward hers. Her pupils were dilated, full of fear and passion.

"Kimberly!" Alroy said as he pressed his dry lips into her moist ones. He grabbed her head, running his fingers through her raven black hair. She returned the kiss, running one hand down his lower back and snaking her other arm toward the swagger stick.

She pushed him back forcefully and unexpectedly, and he stumbled but stayed on his feet. She brought the stick around with all the force she could muster and caught Alroy on the forehead with a cracking smack.

Alroy hit the floor hard, and he struggled to remain conscious. Kimberly recovered her gun and stood over her husband, his head bleeding from a severe laceration.

"Goodbye, Alroy."

"Wait," Alroy said firmly, seeing his end. "Tell Amberly and Kora that I love them. Promise me."

"I promise," Kimberly said, tears returning to her piercing eyes. "I'm sorry, Alroy. But you must understand we all must sacrifice for the greater good."

There was no escape. Alroy knew his next words would be his last. "I love you, Kimberly Macready. And I forgive you."

Raven One juiced several stun bolts into Alroy's prone body.

"Aaaaaugh, dammit," Kimberly cried out as she hit her bleeding-out husband again in the head with the swagger stick. "I'm so sorry." Kimberly dropped the stick and brought her hand to her cheek to wipe a tear.

"Proximity warning," Jules, as the installed VI in *M.S.S. Normandy,* alerted Kimberly to potential danger. Kimberly snapped her head in the direction of the pilot's station. She hopped into the seat to see *Normandy's* penetration of the edge of the Spencer Belt — and an imminent collision with a rock roughly the same size as the runabout. Though she knew how to pilot a ship, she wasn't experienced.

"Engage the autopilot," she shouted at the VI. But when the ship shuttered violently from the impact of asteroid, she knew she was too late.

The interior of the ship sparked and several gas lines ruptured, pumping pure oxygen into the hull.

"Critical damage," Jules reported. "Recommend abandon ship."

Kimberly knew the whole interior of this ship could become a fireball at any second, so she decided against retrieving the extra supply rations. Fuentes Station was well stocked, though she might have to be especially frugal on her consumption, depending on how long it took her comrade Joti to complete his mission.

She looked at the unconscious Alroy, a large, lacerated lump on his head emerged where she struck him, but otherwise resting peacefully on the floor.

"Extreme fire danger," Jules warned again. "Recommend abandon ship."

Kimberly leaned over her Alroy, kissed the crown of his head. "I loved you, too."

She hurried off the bridge, headed aft to the escape pod.

"But Alroy is not aboard. We must wait for him. Please go and recover him," Jules said through the ship's internal PA. "I will keep the pod ready for launch."

"Sorry, Jules. Roy is staying."

"I will not permit you to leave without Alroy," the VI insisted.

"I don't have time for this," Kimberly said as she punched in an administrative code into the command console just outside the escape pod hatch. "Override protocol. Jules, please erase all your data and disable your ship access."

"As you wish," Jules complied. "Goodbye, Kimberly. Goodbye, Alroy. Beginning memory purge."

Kimberly slid into the escape pod. She punched the door shut, and then expanding gas shot the life capsule off of the *Normandy*. As the pod cleared *Normandy's* artificial gravity field, Kimberly felt the effects of weightlessness. The pod was designed to carry six individuals, so as sole passenger, Kimberly had space to float over to the pod's one viewport. She looked out and saw the damaged *Normandy*, with a rip in the hull where it had collided with an asteroid. The safety systems had probably sealed off that room, one of the crew quarters, Kimberly surmised. Then she saw a second asteroid hit the *Normandy*.

The ship ricocheted from the impact, and began to spin wildly away from the asteroid field. She noticed *Normandy* was venting smoke or some other gas as it moved out of Kimberly's view.

I'll miss you, Roy, Kimberly thought as she began to use the pod's limited thrusters to navigate to the abandoned Fuentes Station. *It would have been nice to have you during the long wait, but I don't need you. I don't need any man.*

***

February 12, 2596, on board the unregistered deep space freighter Butch Cassidy, en route to Waypoint Cortes from Waypoint Gilbert

First Officer Scott Klungy was a little stir crazy. More than a year had passed since the deep space ship *Butch Cassidy* left *Waypoint Gilbert*. And the fact the pirate ship could not dock at

Magellan meant another year would pass until he could step foot on a waypoint again. He so desperately wanted to enjoy even a week of shore leave, away from the rust bucket that was his current home.

It wasn't that the *Butch Cassidy* was cramped. The freighter was huge with plenty of open cargo holds not laden with lucre. The crew of the *Cassidy* had a basketball court and a baseball diamond, though the diamond was hardly regulation. If you hit the ball 60 meters into the "outfield" wall, a simple sensor built by the ship's engineer declared a home run.

But the food was mostly vita-paste, and the water from the ships filter always tasted toxic (though the ship's science officer, Dr. Fields, assured everyone it was perfectly safe to drink). Occasionally, the captain would allow them to dip into the cargo for something a little tastier – dried fruits and other preserved natural foods. But those times were few and far between, because Captain Timothy Paul was opposed to his crew literally eating his profits.

Klungy rubbed his hands through the thinning brown hair that capped his Nordic-shaped face. Frankly, he was sick of his crewmates, and he thought meeting some new people would be nice.

His journey to a life of crime had been a strange one. After a boring two decades on *Waypoint Vespucci* as a procurement clerk for the largest multi-waypoint retailer, the thought of joining a black-market pirate ship seemed thrilling. Captain Paul was pleased to sign on someone who had the business acumen to help his enterprise remain profitable.

But space life was hard on Klungy, who could only play so many waypoint simulators on his infopad before feeling the fingers of insanity tickling the edge of his brain. Klungy had named his infopad's VI Riggy, after an old family cat that had died years ago. He had paid a small fortune to find someone with basic taxidermy skills to preserve the animal, which now sat as a trophy in his windowless office on the *Cassidy*.

Captain Paul, Dr. Fields and First Officer Klungy were playing cards in a dark corner of an empty cargo hold. Isabella Deanza, the ship's only medical doctor, walked into the dimly lit corner.

"Deal me in, boys," Isabella said. She pulled up a chair and sat down on the vacant side of the square table.

"What do you have to play with? There's no way you have any hooch left," Klungy asked.

Deanza smiled a perfect white set of teeth and batted her deep brown eyes. Then she produced what appeared to be a full bottle of Finian's Irish whiskey.

"Where the hell did you get that? Is that from Earth?" the captain asked.

Klungy saw the bottle and instinctively licked his lips.

"Don't get too thirsty, Scott," Isabella quipped, "You won't be winning any of this tonight."

It was worthless to bet money on the deep space ship; when they arrived at the colony planet Arara in a few years, they would all be worth billions of credits. Till then, money could rarely be spent – except when they put into a waypoint. So halfway in the two-year journey between *Gilbert* and *Cortez*, the only thing worth betting was one's share of the ship's dwindling supply of liquor.

Dr. Fields pointed his infopad at the Finian's. The infopad scanned the bottle, and then flashed a green indicator.

"Authentic. 2512. A good year. Sit down, my dear, sit down," Dr. Fields said. "I'll deal you in."

As the science officer dealt the cards, Klungy thought about how that bottle could help him with his rotten nights until they made it to *Waypoint Cortes*. Such a long time till shore leave. He desperately wished they would stop at *Magellan*.

"Are you sure we can't pay off the dock master at *Magellan?*" Klungy asked as he peeked at his pocket cards, a seven of clubs and a two of hearts. He folded.

"Look, F-O, we've spent about 30 percent of our gains on buying off dockmasters. And I'm good – I usually make it worth our while with black market trades. But I know the Marine Commander at *Magellan*. Anderson. If he catches us, no amount of credits, no unique bottle of booze will be able to keep him from throwing us in the *Magellan* brig and confiscating everything we own. It's not worth it," the captain said. He looked at his pocket cards and smiled – suited jack and queen, in spades. "I'll raise two grams." Dr. Field's infopad heard and recorded the captain's bet.

Klungy grunted his acknowledgment. "I know, I know. Too much risk. But why do we have to fly so close to *Magellan*? Such a tease."

The captain didn't bother answering the question for which his first officer already knew the answer. First, if they did have a critical emergency, they could call for help and *Magellan* may be close enough to respond. Second, like its namesake, *Cassidy* was a train robber, so to speak, and there was always a chance it could find a small ship in the vicinity of a waypoint to pirate. Specifically, *Magellan* always had mining ships running between the Spencer Belt and the waypoint. Paul thought they could catch one unescorted if they were lucky. If they were really lucky, they would get one with a full cargo of minerals and a crew.

They had already captured a number of smaller ships on their journey. Three they had scrubbed off IDs and kept, the others they stripped for parts to sell on the black market.

"The tease is you folding, Klungy," Isabella said as she thought about her pocket cards, a pair of fives. Two grams was a high bid, but she thought the captain was overplaying his hand on the first round. Ten years of playing cards with Paul, and she knew all his tells.

Dr. Fields looked at his pocket cards, frowned and pushed them in.

"Just you and me, captain," Isabella smirked. The captain ignored her.

Dr. Fields flipped over the flop: seven of spades, two of diamond and two of clubs.

"Of all the dirt-licking..." Klungy said. "What are the odds?"

The captain shot Klungy a scolding look and reached down to the table to peel his cards up for another look.

A klaxon sounded. The alarm hadn't gone off in years, and Isabella, startled, jumped out of her chair, knocking the table and causing her bottle of whiskey to go crashing to the dirty, rusted floor. Klungy instantly felt bad for her, though his sorrow for the lost alcohol was greater.

"Noooo!" Isabella gasped. "Dirty hell!"

The captain tapped the infopad strapped to his wrist, calling the crew member on the watch, Abieyuwa, a mid-twenties woman who had just joined the *Cassidy* a year ago at *Waypoint Gilbert*.

"Yuwa, I hope this is good," Paul said as he rubbed his salt-and-pepper beard, "because you just made Deanza break the most valuable bottle of whiskey this side of *Waypoint Coronado*."

Abieyuwa's excited voice replied through the infopad, "I found a ship! Valkyrie class! It's listing out of control. And here's the good part: No emergency beacon broadcasting."

Now all the officers were standing up. The captain looked at his first officer. "Out of control? No call for help. Hmmm… You said you wanted some excitement, F-O. Send out the corvettes and see if we can catch this thing. Maybe this will make up for the sting of the lost booze."

Isabella, still in a bit of shock from the broken bottle, opened her mouth to respond, but the others were already on their way to the bridge.

Several hours later, the captain and first officer waited in hangar control of the *Butch Cassidy*. The roomy bay housed a half-dozen smaller ships, mostly corvettes, but had enough space to carry complement twice that size. The space door closed as two corvettes, both stolen from *Waypoint Vespucci*, towed the smashed-up Valkyrie into the hanger.

"F-O to engineering," Klungy spoke through the ship's internal comms. "Please re-pressurize the hanger." New deep space ships equipped with small vessel hangars enjoyed atmospheric control from the same deck. But the *Butch Cassidy* was more than 100 years old and nearly every major function had to be executed from the bridge or engineering. Most ships were upgraded to newer technology as it became available. But most ships weren't illegal black-market traders. Though *Cassidy* had been back to Earth several times in the last century, putting into space dock for retrofit would almost certainly end up with the *Cassidy* impounded.

"I hope everyone is dead on that ship," Paul said.

It was easier when everyone was dead. If they weren't, then they would have to find some way to coerce the survivors to keep quiet. Usually the threat of death along with the promise of riches once *Cassidy* reached Arara was enough. Rumors had circulated that in the past, the captain had airlocked individuals who would not make a deal.

Klungy and Paul left the control room and entered the hangar once it was filled with atmosphere. Both men had pistol-laden holsters and served as their own security team. The deck crew locked down the two corvettes and the runabout they had captured. Klungy looked at the ship – it was pretty beat up, but probably salvageable and not meant for scrap. Klungy figured the ship had twice the range as any of their other small vessels. He saw the registry painted just above the three bridge viewports: *M.S.S. Normandy.*

That it was a *Magellan* ship was no surprise, given their proximity to the waypoint.

Klungy moved to open the main port of the *Normandy*, and Isabella walked up behind him, with her portable medical kit in hand.

Just as Klungy was about to see if the hatch was locked, it hissed open. Lurking in the doorway was a disheveled man with dark red hair and a matching beard. On his forehead was a blood-caked indentation.

"Thank you for saving me," the man said, as he stepped out of the ship. "I couldn't get control of my ship." The man walked over and hugged Klungy. "Thank God you saved me. I was all alone."

"What happened?" Klungy asked, instinctively stepping back from the smelly man.

"I… I … don't know… I can't remember," the redhead said.

"Who are you?" the captain asked.

"I'm sorry," the man said, rubbing the scar on his head. "I've been trying to remember who I am for … weeks … months. I remember how to, um, fly a ship. A few days ago, I started to remember how to read — it's coming back slowly. My VI's memory is blanked and … ."

"Are you from *Waypoint Magellan*?" the captain asked.

"I'm sorry," the disheveled man said. "*Magellan*. That's a waypoint? Maybe. I … can't remember."

The captain looked at Klungy and smiled. He couldn't believe their good luck: a pilot with amnesia after some sort of space collision, probably with asteroids from the nearby Spencer Belt. Even better, the ships VI and logs already seemed to be clean.

"I think I need medical help," the man said, shrugging and

yawning.

"That's what I'm here for," Isabella said. "I'm a doctor. Have you been eating? Drinking?"

"Oh yeah, I found a huge supply of rations," the man replied. "I'm not sure who put them in the ship, but they certainly came in handy. My head hurts. Maybe I should go back inside and lie down." The man turned to go back inside *Normandy*.

"No, let's get you over to my office and check you out," Isabella said, putting on her best bedside manner. "Hold my hand. Come with me."

After Isabella had taken her patient out of the hangar, the captain clapped his hands with a joyful smack, and turned to his first officer. "What good luck. I want this ship scrubbed of all ID. Make sure the VI is really wiped. Also, wipe the logs, wipe the navigation computer. Scrape off the exterior letters, the works."

"What if he gets his memory back?" Klungy said. "The *Magellan* Marines may be looking for … Red."

"Red? You want to call him Red? We'll worry about him getting his memory back when it happens," Paul smiled. "In the meantime, let's put as much distance between us and *Magellan* as possible. And let's start building a new life for our amnesiac pilot. We have plenty of credits to make him rich as Midas when we get to Arara. His ship alone will fetch a king's ransom."

"Hopefully, if he does remember his past life, it was a miserable one," Klungy said, as he remembered his own pre-*Cassidy* monotony.

L.S. ROEBUCK

CHAPTER ONE

December 24, 2606. Waypoint Magellan, 49 months after the battle of Magellan, 24 months after the battle of Marquette.

Amberly Macready, 23, hero of the *Battle of Magellan*, commander of Fuentes Station, daughter of the infamous Raven One, was red-in-the-face.

"You *owe* me," she gritted, sitting in a chair opposite of Marine Commander Rita Moreno. Behind the commander's desk was a floor-to-ceiling window, making the great void of space an imposing backdrop. "Dek should be pardoned from exile. So should Sparks. You can't keep them off *Magellan*."

"Amberly, I think the world of you," said a large, gentle man standing in the shadows of the dimly lit office. Governor Thor Rillio was not a puppet of Commander Moreno, but he gave great deference to his military counterpart. "You are the future of *Magellan*. But we have the rule of law."

"Then convene the tribunal again," Amberly said as she stood up, the suddenness of her motion tossing her red locks. "I *demand* it."

"Sit down, Mission Commander Macready," chided Moreno, a sharp-featured, olive-skinned woman in her 40s. "The governor and I have defended you, promoted you, trusted you, and so far, that trust has brought us great dividends. But don't think for a minute that you are so special that you can come in here and dictate terms, Amberly. I am your ally and friend, but don't ever cross me. You will regret it."

"We all have our place," Thor added, though with a grandfatherly tone. "And all of us are expendable. Even you."

"You are not the *only* person owed. Look down that wall. All the good women and men that we lost at the hands of Chasm's attack," Moreno pointed to the wall on her right. Dimly lit portraits of Marines Anderson, Jindal, Snyder, Twig and a dozen others who had died during the Battle of *Magellan*. "As you know, a few people think you belong over there –" and Moreno pointed to the left wall, with portraits hanging upside down and stained in red, "along with Kimberly Macready, God rest her soul, and the other *Magellan* traitors we executed or killed in combat."

Amberly felt suddenly small and young. She sat down again, and Thor sat in the empty chair next to her.

"What happened to the girl we sent to Fuentes Station not even two years ago?" Rita sighed. "What you did at Sonnet was *tour de force*. Because of your efforts, we routed out another Chasm saboteur – one on the *Magellan* council, no less – and now with Fuentes Station operational, we have the resources to prepare for the Chasm attack. It will come. That's not to mention what you did before Fuentes Station. You brought critical information about the Chasm conspiracy during the insurrection. You even shot your own mother, traitor that she was, to save us all. So yes, you've earned a lot. A seat at the table."

Amberly leaned back in her seat, the flushness of her previous fury draining from her cheeks as Rita talked her down. Moreno also reclined, pushing back her worn faux-leather chair. She closed her eyes and rubbed her temples. The tribunals held four years ago were a necessary evil, she believed, and she did not want to reopen them. Sparks and Dek were supposed to never return. She remembered the words of her friend, Captain April Eaton, another victim of the Chasm conspiracy. *Leadership is confronting what is not supposed to happen and helping your followers to cope with it.*

"Now that we are clear, my dear Amberly, for you I will reopen the tribunal. It's against my better judgement to rip open old wounds — your friends were lucky to get away with their lives. The mob wanted more blood. The tribunal denied them," Moreno said. "That tribunal had three members: the governor, myself and North, who's a full commander himself now. North will be here soon. Until then, if Mr. Tigona or Sparks set foot on *Magellan*, they will be shown an airlock. Do I make myself clear?"

"Yes, Commander," Amberly said, resisting her nervous habit of twirling her fingers in her hair, holding her emotion in check. She had always been broadly supported by both the governor and commander. Resistance from them was new. Perhaps she had misjudged the situation. But at least Sparks and Dek would get a hearing.

She had returned to *Magellan* six months ago from Fuentes Station via the *American Spirit*, hero a second time over for bringing the raw resources needed to fortify *Magellan* to resist the expected second Chasm attack. The *American Spirit* was now commanded by Dek Tigona, who like Sparks, had betrayed Chasm at a critical moment. Dek's betrayal was prompted by his love for Amberly, who manipulated Dek to thwart Chasm's attempt to destroy *Magellan*. A worthy deception, but a deception all the same, and it haunted Amberly.

After the battle of *Magellan*, Dek was exiled on *American Spirit*. When deep cover operatives known as Chasm Hawks sabotaged the *American Spirit*, not long into its decades-long voyage back to Earth, *Waypoint Magellan* staged a rescue flotilla to save the deep space ship. Damaged, the *American Spirit* returned to Fuentes Station, reuniting Dek and Amberly. Dek still loved Amberly, but he had come to accept he could not fully win her heart. Still, their friendship had grown in the months they had been working together to fortify *Magellan*.

Amberly stood up to leave. "I have to get ready for Ship Day and the arrival of the *Magnus*, as I am sure you both do as well. Thank you both for graciously agreeing to reconvene the tribunal. And Merry Christmas."

"Merry Christmas, Amberly," Moreno said, as she watched the young woman pace out of her office. *She's had to grow up so fast to survive all this adversity. I fear there's more to come,* Moreno thought.

***

December 25, 2606. U.S.S. Magnus, 24 months after the battle of Marquette, one day out from Waypoint Magellan

Sparks pushed herself so hard she thought her lungs would explode. Sweat soaked her natural strawberry blonde bangs, which flailed over her dark green eyes, as the 33-year-old raced along the workout track. She wore dark, tight-fitting-but-flexible carbon polymer clothes, designed for intense physical activity.

As she sprinted along *Magnus*' kilometer-long running loop, she saw two black nondescript barriers, one about a meter high, and a second about two meters high. *North thinks these can slow me down?* thought Sparks as she smirked. On the approach to the first barrier, she sprung up, hurtling the padded box with nearly a half-meter to spare. In the two paces between the obstacles, she flipped herself up, catching the top of the two-meter high barrier with her outstretched arms, using them to powerfully fling herself over. She came down hard, breaking her fall with a low crouch before bouncing back into her sprint.

Her muscles burned in a hell fire. She ignored the pain. Sparks had spent most of the last year too injured to walk, and she was determined to never go back to such weakness, no matter how much it hurt.

Just a dozen meters from the end of her circuit, she smiled through her sweaty tears as she saw North standing at the finish line. Even though he was the *Magnus'* executive officer and Marine commander, North looked the part of a transient. He wore loose fitting sweat clothes, and he had let his brown hair and beard grow out. The locks of his hair covered most of his ears and the back of his neck.

Sparks ran past North before slowing down and leaning over her knees to catch her breath. A wave of nausea threatened to overcome her, but she focused her body to calmness.

"Not bad," North said, as he leaned against the track wall and folded his arms approvingly.

"Congratulations, Sparks," a synthetic voice emanating from North's infopad piped in. "You beat your previous record by 1.3 seconds."

"Even with North's little surprise, Condi," Sparks said to the VI, but with a look that burned through North.

"Oh, come on," North said, smiling sheepishly. "You like an unexpected challenge."

"It was *annoying*. It was no *challenge*," Sparks said as she wiped sweat from her scarred face with a white towel. The left side of her head was severely burned when the *Magnus* was hit by a nuclear warhead during the Battle of *Marquette*. Radiation exposure also had riddled her body with cancers. Tumors were removed, but trauma from the extensive surgery had initially made her unable to walk anything longer than the shortest of distances. She had spent every free moment of the last two years working to regain her strength. North had been with her every step of her recovery.

"I believe it was no challenge," North said. "What I still can't believe is how well you have recovered. I'm proud of you."

"Let me go get cleaned up," Sparks returned North's smile, "and then maybe we can go grab lunch at the mess?"

"Sorry," North hemmed. "I have to review ... docking protocols with Captain Obadiah."

"Lame excuse," Sparks said as she returned the sweaty towel to her gym bag. North was declining her again, and Sparks cynicism turned on like a switched light, her luster now smothered in the half-darkness of bitterness. "You don't want to be seen with me in public now that we are days away from being back with your 'one true love' on *Magellan*."

"Don't do this, Sparks," North said. "You know I am busy. You know *Utopia* is coming. You know Chasm won't give up the fight for *Magellan*. ... You know this isn't about Amberly."

"Isn't it, though?" Sparks quipped, standing up and heading for the corridor in the direction of the quarters she shared with Junior Grade Lieutenant Rhodes. "When you found out my sister hadn't taken up with Dek or the Hawk Skylar, when she asked for your forgiveness, and when you knew we were heading back to *Magellan*, not to Arara, things got chilly over here."

North ignored Spark's 'sister' comment; she had come to regard Amberly Macready, daughter of her deceased Chasm mentor, as a spiritual sister of sorts.

"That's not fair," North's voice got quiet, his frustration obvious on his face. The pair stood facing each other for a moment. "We've been through too much for you to use that against me. You are my friend, one of the best I have. Don't make this about Amberly ... let's not have this conversation *again*."

North was correct; Sparks knew this conversation well. She retreated.

"I'm sorry, North," Sparks looked down and spoke in a muted tone. "I'm jealous. I'm bitter. Can you blame me?" Sparks offered an empty laugh.

North didn't respond, so Sparks continued. "You don't owe me anything. You've never promised me we'd be anything more than friends."

"But good friends..."

"Too bad I want more. We had dreams of beating Chasm and

then retiring to the Lewis Islands. But instead of winning at *Marquette* and going onto victory at Arara, we tucked tail and ran back to *Magellan*. I know where this is going, North. Fate made me an ugly bitch and is putting you back into the arms of the perfect Amberly."

"I don't know what's going to happen with Amberly," North said, sadness creeping into his eyes. "And ... I'm sorry I can't give you what you want, Sparks. I'm not there. There was a moment, you know as well as I, before the Battle of *Marquette*, but — "

Sparks interrupted the Marine. "I get it, North. I know." She took several quick paces toward the exit. "I need to go."

"Wait," North called out, "I have something for you."

Sparks complied, and North pulled a 10-centimeter by 10-centimeter wooden picture frame out of his bag and handed it Sparks.

"Merry Christmas, friend," North said, powering his charming smile back into the on position.

Made from the flesh of trees, the frame was rare and quite valuable. North had purchased the frame from *Magnus'* Chief Operations Officer Alicia Blight, who had collected an impressive assortment of Earth trinkets during *Magnus'* 8.5 light-year journey that touched 17 waypoints.

But what grabbed Sparks was what was in the frame. It was a painting of her, North, Rhodes and the toddler Nora. Nora was the sole survivor of the destruction of *Waypoint Cortez* at the hands of Chasm. The painting must have been based on a photograph taken during one of the many picnics the foursome had in *Magnus'* greenhouse observation deck. North of course was looking as handsome as ever, and his arm was wrapped around Sparks' back. *I don't look too bad, either*, thought Sparks as she looked at her likeness. In the painting she wore a simple red kimono that had belonged to the Chasm spymaster Ryder, another casualty in the Battle of *Marquette*. In the picture, she also wore her white half-mask. Covering the left side of her face, the mask had an eyehole, but otherwise concealed the most scarred areas on her head. It was held in place by a two practically invisible poly carbon garment wires: one connected to a choker necklace, and the other wrapped around her left ear. Chokers had been popular for women in the middle of the 25th century, and they were making a fashionable comeback in the last decade, at least on the *Magnus*.

In the painting, Rhodes had her arm thrown around Sparks' shoulder on the opposite side from North. Little Nora was holding Rhodes' free hand and looking off to the side.

"Where did you get this?" Sparks softy asked, as she fought becoming misty-eyed. Since she betrayed Chasm, these were the people that she loved. This was her family.

"I commissioned Ballab from engineering to paint it," North explained.

"She's dirty good." Many on deep space voyages became skilled artisans, often as a result of having thousands of hours of downtime through the long and lonely waiting for the ship to traverse light years of space. "Well, Merry Christmas," Sparks said, somewhat unfamiliar with the old Earth holiday. "Thanks for this." Then she slipped out and made for the sanctuary of her quarters before she lost it in front of North.

Rhodes stomach was tightening into nauseating knots. The 20-year-old junior officer wasn't sure if the topsy-turvy was from the thrill of arriving at *Magellan* after the four years of being cooped up during the deep space journey, or if it was just the effects of the inertia dampeners during the rapid deceleration from half-lightspeed. The *Magnus*' powerful computers calculated the precise slowing of the ship to optimize the soonest arrival time, efficient energy usage, and preventing the passengers from becoming splatter. Even with inertia dampeners, slowing the *Magnus* to a relative stop with a waypoint took weeks of hitting the breaks.

Rhodes was sitting on her bunk – the top one – studying her bridge assignments for the final docking with *Magellan*. The officer's steward just dropped off the laundry: freshly cleaned outfits for both Rhodes and her roommate, Sparks. Rhodes spread out her dress uniform, white with blue trim on her bed. She hung up Sparks' red kimono from the bottom of her bunk.

"Laundry is here," Rhodes called out to Sparks, who was taking a shower in an adjoining bathroom. On *Magnus*, the officers' quarters were outfitted with private bathrooms, unlike the enlisted and Marines quarters, who had shared facilities.

Sparks wasn't technically an officer, but due to her heroic actions during the Battle of *Marquette*, she had been afforded many of the officers' perks.

Sparks, along with Dek Tigona and Captain Järvinen, had been the Chasm triumvirate running the conspiratorial operations on the *American Spirit* during the Battle of *Magellan* four years earlier. At the climax of the battle, Sparks betrayed Chasm by aborting a kamikaze run that would have annihilated *Waypoint Magellan* using the *American Spirit* as a missile. Because of her actions, her sentence of death for treason was commuted. Instead a military tribunal exiled her from *Waypoint Magellan*.

North conscripted Sparks to join the *Magnus* in its quest to put down the Chasm rebellion, figuring that Sparks could provide critical enemy intel. Sparks fought valiantly alongside North when *Magnus* brought the battle to the Chasm-controlled *Waypoint Marquette*. But Chasm was ready for the warship with its own instrument of destruction, the incredibly powerful *Utopia*, equipped with anti-ballistic technology that seemed like magic. Missiles and other projectiles dissolved on approach. Defeated, *Magnus'* Captain Obadiah decided to live to fight another day, and the *Magnus* retreated to regroup with Earth-loyal forces at *Magellan*.

Now they were nearly back at North's adopted home waypoint.

Sparks walked over to her bed in her underclothes, hair dripping wet. She toweled her head, took the kimono and wrapped herself in the traditional Japanese garb. The petite, powerful, broken woman sat down at the small vanity one the opposite wall from the bunk beds and began to fix her hair.

"Are they going to let you on the waypoint?" Rhodes asked, looking up from the task list on her infopad.

"No," Sparks said flatly, as she strapped the half mask on her face. "The chief magistrate was clear that the terms of my exile mean that I am not allowed to disembark on the waypoint. If I do, it's a long walk out a short airlock."

"What a dirt licker! In what waypoint is that fair?" Rhodes fumed. "Don't they know what you have done for us? They just expect you cool your jets indefinitely? Surely North will –"

"North has other more important concerns besides my freedom," Sparks remarked, as she adjusted the choke collar. She stood up and faced Rhodes. "How do I look?"

"Sexy. Great. I wish I could wear something besides my stuffy uniform for Ship Day," Rhodes grumbled.

Sparks seemed to ignore Rhodes, lost in her own thoughts. "I remember the last time I arrived at *Magellan*. I was on the *American Spirit* observation deck. So much has changed... Do you have enough time to come and watch the approach with me before your official duties start?"

"I wouldn't miss it," Rhodes said, scooping up her freshly pressed uniform.

Condi, North's VI currently installed on the *Magnus* bridge computer, identified the first visual of *Magellan*. It indicated the small speck of light on the main viewport. The bridge officers had all assembled in preparation for arrival. Captain Obadiah looked up from the head of the tactical table where he stood discussing logistics with Operations Chief Alicia Blight, Lt. Commander Cho and Commander North.

"Great hair, Alicia," North smiled at the operations chief. She had shaved her dyed red hair off and was sporting a bald look. She was already pale, but her pallor and lack of hair contrasted significantly with the dark skin and dreadlocks of her husband, Chief Petty Officer Bollard, who ran engineering for *Magnus*. Faced with the reality of their own mortality after the *Battle of Marquette*, the pair confessed their mutual attraction and were married in a quiet ceremony by Captain Obadiah. A year later, Blight gave birth to baby Tanisha.

"My honey is looking good, isn't she?" Bollard nodded, beaming his bright smile as his dreads swung around his head.

"Where's Rhodes?" North asked the captain.

"I gave her permission to watch the approach from the observation deck with Sparks," the captain said. "She'll be along shortly."

Magnus was still moving thousands of kilometers a second, but the retros were easing off. As the ship slowed down, the five-kilometer long *Magellan* became more than just a speck of light. Soon *Magnus* would be at a full-stop relative to *Magellan*.

"ETA *Magellan* sync, four minutes," reported Ensign Wilmott from the navigation station. Sporting a white goatee, the middle-aged Wilmott was significantly older than most who held the rank of Ensign. He was in his late 40s as a finance analyst on *Waypoint Estevanico* when in a midlife crisis he quit his job and signed up as crew for *Magnus*, bringing his wife with him. On the journey to Arara, he joined the officer training program, recently promoted to work on the bridge. His propensity toward numbers made him an excellent navigator.

The main bridge portal opened, and Rhodes walked to the table where the officers were gathered. Normally, she would have taken her post without comment, but today, on a Ship Day, everything was more formal, more dignified. "Junior Grade Lt. Rhodes, reporting for duty."

"Cutting it a little close, aren't we?" the captain smiled. "Establish a secure comm with *Magellan* command, let me know when you have confirmed docking protocols."

North caught Rhodes' attention as she left the table for her workstation. "How's Sparks?"

Rhodes knew enough that she didn't want to get in the middle of that spat. She hmphed and shrugged. She turned toward the viewport, and her heart leapt at the sight.

Magellan was close enough that detail in the waypoint's superstructure could be seen as the grey disk slowly rotated. The city in space was wide awake. Viewports across the floors twinkled with glorious artificial light. Several Valkyries and corvettes were moving around the station in a flurry of propulsion streaks. Some of the small ships were tagged for escort, but most were just filled with residents of *Magellan* who wanted to get the best seats to watch the arrival of *Magnus*.

"Home sweet home," North offered a slight smile, brown eyed fixated on the sublime waypoint. Long dormant emotions awoke in his chest — joy at the homecoming, mixed with apprehension. The innocent North that loved Amberly before Chasm was gone, but so was the broken North that bitterly condemned her when he left his home four years ago. *What will she think now?* North worried.

Rotating with the waypoint like an appendage, hard connected to the gangway, was the massive *American Spirit*.

"I never thought I'd see that ship again," Rhodes said. "So much for going to Earth. What did they do with the exiles?"

"Most of them are in the brig," the captain replied. "Except for Dek Tigona. They've gone and made him master of the *American Spirit*! I know why you spared him at the tribunal, North, but no ex-Chasm should be commanding our ship. I don't care how many times he's been the hero since. No amount of good deeds can wash away the blood on his hands."

"Yes, sir," North agreed. "As soon as we are on *Magellan*, I intend to discuss this with Moreno and the governor. Still, I bet we'll be glad to have the *American Spirit* when Chasm comes for us."

"*Waypoint Magellan* space control, this is the *U.S.S. Magnus*, requesting clearance for final approach and docking at gangway 2-J with standard 100 meter connect. Roll, 24 degrees. Pitch, 36.5. Yaw, 182. Please confirm," Rhodes said into her comms. The request was mostly for show and a final check; docking instructions had been dispatched and confirmed weeks ago.

The bridge speakers crackled to life with a familiar voice. "*Magnus*, on behalf of Governor Thor Rillio, welcome back to *Magellan*. Protocol confirmed. Permission granted for Captain Obadiah's advance party to board upon hard connect," replied Skip in the transmission.

"Skip!" North said a smile beaming on his face.

"Commander North, we're glad to have you back." A small laugh escaped his throat before he could quell it.

"It's good to be home, old friend. First drink's on me."

"I already have a table reserved at Rick's."

The captain and North stepped out of the gangway, onto the main deck of the *Magellan* hangar. A flash of memories flooded North. He remembered how Amberly Macready looked in her emerald green dress when she boarded the *Claire De Lune* on this very deck for years ago. He could still see her standing there: The dress was modestly cut, though it accentuated Amberly's natural curves. Her short hair was pulled up into a single tight bun with Oriental sticks holding it in place.

He took her to the dazzling Shard Caves to profess his affections; she painfully rebuffed him. A few days after that date, *also at this very spot*, he remembered, he would accidentally shoot Amberly when she was a hostage of her mother Kimberly.

Governor Thor Rillio, wearing a sharp black vest over a grey, long sleeve shirt, reached out to take the hand of Captain Obadiah. *The governor lost a lot of weight*, North thought, suddenly self-conscious about his own appearance. As soon as the men shook hands, a squad of Marines snapped to attention.

North stepped towards Commander Moreno, who was standing at Rillio's side. "Commander North, reporting for duty," he beamed as he snapped into a salute at his former commanding officer. North was more than a few dozen centimeters taller than Moreno, and at least twice her weight, but Rita's presence still seemed larger. She stepped forward and embraced North, and to his surprise, she was crying. "My God, North, my God." She took his arms and stepped back a pace and looked him up and down, as if to reaffirm that it was really North. "Thank God you guys survived. Now we fight together."

The governor spoke in a loud voice he reserved for official declarations. "Welcome to Waypoint *Magellan*, Captain Obadiah, and the honored crew of *Magnus*! Permission granted to come ashore."

The assembled crowd cheered and an eight-piece band started playing the American and *Magellan* anthems. The ranks broke and the captain's party – about a dozen officers and crew from the *Magnus* – began to intermingle with the *Magellan* welcome party, hugs, tears and laughs filling the large space to capacity.

North spotted a scrawny communication officer and ran to him. "Skip!"

"North!" Skip sported a rare ear-to-ear smile under his bowl-cut black hair. "Happy Ship Day."

"Happy Ship Day, buddy," North pulled his friend into a brief embrace.

"You'll never believe the adventures I've had when you were gone. My old boss, Skylar Triggs? Traitor! I smoked him out and captured him single-handedly," Skip exaggerated.

"That's not the story I heard," North laughed. "But I bet it sounds legit after a few shots at Rick's."

"Hate to break it to you, but the grog at Rick's has gone to piss since the Chasm coup," Skip lamented, putting a hand on North's shoulder. "But it will still buzz you, I suppose. Might as well get smashed while we can. We'll have plenty of time for sobriety once Chasm gets here."

The mention of the enemy drained North's mood. "Skip, I saw her. I talked to her. The Chairman. The leader of Chasm. Sparks actually took a shot at her. Unloaded a whole clip. She's soulless ... powerful. Her eyes, dark with evil. We *cannot* let her win."

"Easy, man," Skip said. "She won't. We'll get her. You'll never believe what we've built here with the resources Amberly gathered."

"Amberly," North pulled Skip further away from the crowd and spoke in more muted tones. He figured correctly that she would not join the welcome party and resolved to be patient, but could no longer do so when Skip brought her up. "How is she now? Where is she?"

"All work. She's up in her lab, already pulling stellar and navigation data over the hard line from *Magnus*," Skip brought his voice down to match North's. "I don't know what you are expecting from her. She was pretty messed up after her fiancé... um... after we tossed Skylar out the airlock. She wanted to love him. She's obsessed with her work now, I mean, she's always been obsessed with work. Now it's multiple times more than she used to be."

"I see," North said, not knowing what to say.

"North, you should have seen her running the show at Fuentes Station," Skip continued. "She really whipped the Sonnet operation into shape. I never thought of Amberly as the take charge type, but, man, the redhead lined us up and made it happen."

"I'm proud of all of you," North said, glancing up at the view port on the far side of the hangar that shared a wall with the *Magellan* Science Corps lab, where Amberly was director. With the Spencer Belt mission complete, Amberly resumed her leadership of *Magellan's* public labs.

North's ache was heavy. After so much time, Amberly was so close now. North resisted the urge to sprint out into the corridor that connected the Marine base, hangar and science labs to find

what his heart desired. *Patience*, North thought. *All in good time.*
"So, um, how are you and Lydia?" North asked.

"We're over," Skip said. "About a year ago. But it was a good run."

"I'm sorry," North glanced up toward the labs, unsuccessfully trying to get his mind off Amberly.

"Why don't you just go see her?" Skip said.

"First you should tell me about what happened between you two," North replied with a little bit of confusion.

"Not Lydia," Skip sighed. "Go see *Amberly*. You remember the way?"

"Right," North said, as he straightened his Marine dress uniform and headed in the direction of the labs.

"See you at Rick's. Don't forget! Twenty-three hundred hours," Skip called out after his best friend.

The stellar radiation lab was dark, mostly abandoned this morning as the scientists were out and about celebrating Ship Day. In the far corner, the light of an infopad screen cast a silhouette around Amberly Macready, deep in her analysis of potential dangers to her home waypoint. From behind, the light of the screen pushed through her long, full red hair, creating a crimson alpenglow. Silently, from across the lab, North studied Amberly's profile, her soft face, button nose. North didn't think himself overly sentimental, but in this moment his heart melted. This reunion wasn't supposed to happen. Try as he may, he could not put her out of his mind during the flight of the *Magnus*. He thought he would never cross paths with Amberly Macready again.

Now he was unsure. He felt himself faltering. He was a broken man. What happened to him at the Battle of *Magellan* scarred his soul. What happened to him at the Battle of *Marquette* left him even worse, barely escaping with his life, walking with Sparks through her recovery, seeing the Chairman defeat Arara's best hope to escape the certain oppression of Chasm's perfect society. He felt snapped. He held onto sanity because he must, for the sake of Sparks and Rhodes. Even little Nora was counting on him now.

He stepped toward her again, but hesitated as he saw

Amberly in a different light. He remembered her betrayal's kiss, how she used him to bring her evil mother to *Magellan* at the peril of all. He saw before him a likeness – no, more like a phantom – of Kimberly Macready, great betrayer that she was. North had first-hand experience to prove Amberly had learned the ways of Raven One well, rationalizing the use of weaponized lies to achieve some so-called greater good. Amberly's actions, of her own free will, driven by her selfish curiosity, led to the deaths of so many.

North stood silently in the darkness as he saw Amberly absentmindedly twirl her fingers through that famous red hair. She was no longer the 19-year-old girl he had left when he joined *Magnus*' crusade four years ago. He could see that she was fully woman now, and from the little he knew about Amberly's journey since he left, he wondered how she was shaped by her life trials. Who was she now? Was it possible the forge of life purified all that was good in Amberly? Was she like him, disenchanted and muted from the joy of his former life? If so, could he bear to see that Amberly?

What will be, will be, North thought, and he walked over behind Amberly and put his hand on her shoulder.

L.S. ROEBUCK

CHAPTER TWO

December 26, 2606. Waypoint Magellan, 24 months after the battle of Marquette.

After four years, Amberly didn't know what to do.

She ached to race to North, to throw herself into his strong arms, to give him what he wanted at the Shard Caves when the waypoint seemed so much simpler. Before Chasm. Before Dek. Before North's stinging condemnation at the tribunal.

With only a few hours until *Magnus* arrived, Amberly found herself back in her apartment, deciding if she should be there for North when he arrived. The uncertain feelings mixed with her fuming over how the *Magellan* authorities continued to punish Dek with exile. Amberly sat at her vanity, working a brush through her hair. Her older sister Kora sat on the bed behind Amberly, quietly listening while filing painted nails that matched the Kora's hair.

"I dreamed of the tribunal last night," Amberly told her sister. "It was horrible. All those people we airlocked. And when North, when he … you know. It was so vivid."

"You could see a counselor," Kora suggested, "if you are still dealing with that horrible day."

"I prefer the older sister discount."

"Don't get all sweet on me," Kora laughed.

"It's silly. I want a do over on the Shard Caves," Amberly said. "If I knew then what I know now…"

"But you didn't. Don't dwell on what you can't change. Now is not the time to wax romantic. Now is the time to allow your head to guide your heart," Kora advised.

"Who are you and what did you do with my sister?" Amberly turned her head and smiled, though her eyes seemed anxious to Kora. "What if North avoids me? Maybe he hasn't forgiven me."

"Amberly, stop. North is a good man."

"Is he? A lot has happened since that tribunal. So much has changed. Oh, Kora. What if he hates me? What do I even feel for him?"

"Hey," Kora turned Amberly to face her. "No matter what,

North is your friend, and friends don't do that unforgiving thing," Kora smiled softly. "And he's your friend because you love him."

"I don't even know what that means."

"Simple," Kora said. "It means that you'll choose to put his needs before your own. Think of it like Chasm's greater good, only on an individual scale. Sheesh. I thought you were supposed to be the smart one."

"I *am* the smart one," Amberly leaned back.

"I'd give up everything for Trot and little Alroy," Kora said. "That's how I know I love them. Has nothing to do with my heart. I learned that *after* I married my lawman. How much do you love North? Do you love him at all? Just ask yourself how much of who you are would you give up for his sake? Just a little? Just friends, then. Everything you are? Get hitched."

"I used to say I would never change for a man," Amberly said. She had grown less trusting of the progressive orthodoxy on male-female relations, especially after seeing her mother's true nature, but she was *not* a traditionalist. "Then Skylar proved I would. Bloody dirt! I want to undo that… unlearn that. I want to be in a place again where I will stand strong and not change who I am."

"I understand. But from that place, you will never truly love," Kora said. "The beautiful thing is when two people love each other, they *both* change into their best selves."

"Do you really believe that, Kora?" Amberly gently took the brush from Kora's hand and set it down. "I've seen you and Trot fight worse than mom and dad."

"Most days I do," Kora said. "Marriage is hard, and it's not for everyone. But even on our hardest days, I'm better because Trot is in my life. His love for me brings out the best in me. Of course, you don't have to be married to show someone love."

"Or be in love to be married," Amberly quipped. "I don't want marriage. I dodged that bullet with Skylar. I guess it's nice for you —"

"Oh, but 'marriage is the best garden for love,'" Kora hummed the words to a romantic ballad popular in the late 2500s. "Amberly, look me in the eyes. Tell me now, once and for all, no more wishy washing, do you love North?"

"I thought so when I sent him that message. Now, I don't know. So much has happened since then," Amberly sighed. "After

Dek. Skylar. Forget about *who* I should be in love with, Kora. *I don't even know what love is anymore.* How in the waypoint would I know if I *love* North?"

"I see," Kora said, smiling and pushing her pointing finger up to her lip. "Hmmmm. Good thing he'll be here *today*. You can find out."

Amberly decided against the hangar deck for the arrival ceremonies. After her conversation with Kora, she figured she didn't know how either she or North would react when seeing each other. She would have to face North eventually, and she wanted to face him, but she reasoned it would be better in a controlled, private environment. So, she retreated to her lab for the present.

The *Magnus*, like all deep space ships, collected zettabytes of stellar radiation data in her travels. This data was transferred upon docking to *Magellan*. The scan files were processed by powerful computers in the Science Corp lab to see if any cosmic radiation plumes posed enough of a threat to warrant moving the waypoint.

Amberly excelled in stellar radiation analysis, and she often spent lonely nights reviewing thousands of potential threats the computer algorithm tagged. The monotonous work would be yawn-inducing for most, but it calmed her mind like a Zen meditation. Now, she welcomed the excuse to hide. She left the light off; the darkness adding to the illusion that she could hide from the world. Verne served up flagged anomalies on Amberly's infopad, and she spent a half minute or so verifying that there was no threat, before moving to the next one.

She leaned forward in her chair, closer to the light of her infopad, and without thinking, as was her habit, started playing with her hair.

She felt a hand on her shoulder, and her heart jumped.

"Amberly," North said, looking down on her.

Amberly stood quickly from her chair, infopad falling to the floor, and threw her arms around the Marine. He put his arms around her and pulled her close. She could feel his strength, and she melted into him, resting her soft face on his firm shoulder. The floodgates opened and her green eyes filled with tears.

"North, North," she sobbed, waves of release crashing over

her. "It's been so hard."

"Amberly," North repeated, words escaping him.

After a few moments, Amberly pulled her head off his shoulder, took his hands and stepped back.

"Let me look at you," Amberly said, fumbling to turn her desk lamp on. She saw his familiar scar, and *a few lines of gray* in his otherwise dark brown hair. His body was solid, and in his Marine dress uniform, he looked even more formidable than she had remembered. He smiled brilliantly, but it was not his youthful, playful smile. Time had worn it at the edges, and it had a mature, bittersweet flavor.

She wanted a taste.

Indulging her whim, Amberly pushed herself forward on the balls of her feet, and slipped her pale right hand behind his solid neck. She pushed her soft lips on his while pulling his head to hers. She gently pressed against him, before taking his lower lip between hers and slowly pulling away.

She suddenly felt like she had been exceedingly foolish, or made a terrible misstep, and looked intently at North for a reaction. He wore the same bittersweet smile as when their eyes locked. She saw weariness in his eyes, and she saw pain.

"Amberly," North repeated, the intimate kiss catching him off guard. "It's been a long time."

North could see a slight terror forming in Amberly's eyes. He collected himself and moved to reassure Amberly.

"That was certainly the best Ship Day kiss I've ever had," he joked, then shifted into a more serious gear. "Hey, Red, we'll figure this out. Time has passed. You have to know, I'm not the same man that left *Magellan*. But I am glad to be home. And I *am* so happy to be here … with you."

"Of course," Amberly said, as she slipped her hands out of his, instead choosing to rest her left hand on hand on his right forearm. "I'm glad you are back. We need you here on *Magellan*. You *are* good news."

"I wish it were so; the return of the *Magnus* is bad news," North said, leaning back against a cabinet. "It means defeat."

"No, we're together now," Amberly said. "I've been working hard. We all have… Skip, Lydia, Moreno, Thor, Wong, Boro. We've upgraded *Magellan*. With *Magnus* and *Magellan* standing strong together, we can stand our ground, we can fight back. We can–"

"Amberly, the Chairman is coming," North interrupted Amberly. "She has this powerful ship, *Utopia* — it put *Magnus* to shame. We barely damaged it at *Marquette*. They nearly had us all."

"But she didn't," Amberly said. "And we've rebooted Fuentes Station. We've taken the materials and crafted better defenses and–"

North interrupted Amberly again. "Amberly, the Chairman is coming for you. Don't you understand? She had dedicated the force of Chasm to getting revenge on you."

"Me?" Amberly said, confused. "Why me?"

"She blames you for the death of your mother," North said. "She knows everything. She has spies everywhere. She knows you shot Kimberly, that you thwarted her precious Raven One. Apparently, your mom was someone very special to her, someone she loved dearly — if someone so soulless is capable of love. And she is hell bent on making you suffer for ending Kimberly's life."

"My mom is still such a mystery to me." Amberly suddenly felt a little sick. "How do you know all this?"

"I saw the Chairman. I spoke with her on *Marquette*," North said. "She had me in a trap. Amberly, she is evil in the flesh. How she moves, how she speaks. It's like she's a phantom or a demon or something. Fortunately, Sparks rescued me. … Sparks took a bad hit during our retreat. Physically, Sparks is back in top form, but she got the bad end of a radiation blast, and it left her, well, disfigured. Her face. She usually keeps it half-covered."

"Oh no. My poor sister," Amberly sat back in her seat, taking it all in.

"You too on the sister thing? I have no idea why – whatever," North shrugged, figuring he would never understand the link between Sparks and Amberly.

"We were really thankful for her warning about the Hawks," Amberly said, now sitting back down in her chair and looking up at North. "Though it was too late for April Eaton. Two Hawks were able to sabotage the *American Spirit*. I assume you have been briefed about that."

"Yes, Commander Moreno covered that. Such a loss. I didn't

know Captain Eaton well. She was a good friend to your parents and Moreno. Everyone's been marked by this war."

"We think there is still a Hawk in deep hiding here on *Magellan*. Apparently, they worked in pairs." Amberly paused and looked away from North. She continued, her tone muted. "We got the other one, and I put him out into space."

"I'm so sorry about Skylar," North said, pulling up a chair and sitting down, facing Amberly. "I have to admit, when I got your message, I was surprised to hear you were engaged."

"Maybe I've changed, too, North," Amberly said. "Or maybe not. I don't know what I was thinking."

"Yeah, I got that impression." The aftertaste of old pain lingered on North's words.

"Please don't," Amberly said, standing up and turning her face away from North. "I was alone. I couldn't feel your prayers anymore."

"I didn't know you believed in prayers."

"I don't know what I believe," Amberly snapped. "Sometimes I feel like my dead mother mocking me from an afterlife, as if she orchestrated the whole Skylar affair just to teach me a lesson."

"Skylar Triggs," North absentmindedly sounded the name out loud, thinking about what he knew of the man. Amberly suddenly felt indignant.

"And why not? Why shouldn't I have had a relationship with him? Dammit, North. *You* left me." Amberly's face grew red. "Through all my growing up years, you had always been there for me and Kora. And then you slapped me hard and left us! When we needed you *most*."

"Whoa, it's not like that," North said, also standing up, face to face with Amberly. "I was going to fight for *Magellan*, for my home, for everything I love. So, you could stay back here and... and…"

"And what?" Amberly demanded. "Look, I'm sorry that I misled you. I've paid and I'll keep paying for the mistake I made helping Chasm. But you were leaving on a one-way trip. Are you trying to say you wanted me to wait for you? For what? Why would I? Why would I even think that you wanted me to? You didn't even say good-bye."

"I'm sorry."

Amberly took a deep breath, then spoke.

"Taking on the Fuentes command, it was… I mean, I was 21. I was scared, North. Skylar was always there and so supportive and … well, he was an incredible actor. He knew exactly how to play me. And you made it clear what you thought of me at the tribunal."

"Amberly, I…"

"I had to move on, North. And surely you did too. You weren't coming back. Don't sit there and tell me you were pining for only me as you flew off to war."

"Well, Sparks wanted to —"

"Sparks? Are you kidding me?"

"Sparks wanted us to be something," North confessed. "And for a while, I thought maybe that God made us for each other, two people broken by war, hurting and trying to find some peace."

"Well, perfect," Amberly was uncharacteristically sarcastic. "A literal match made in heaven. I'm sure that she played you like a true Chasm agent would."

"I don't know, Amberly," North tried to keep his growing frustration from simmering. "Why don't you tell me about it? If anyone knows what it's like to be played by a Chasm turncoat, it's…" North choked back his words before he said something he knew he would regret. *This is a woman I love,* he rebuked himself for his selfishness.

Amberly sat down again, put her head in her hands and started to cry. They both said nothing for a few moments.

"I'm sorry, Amberly," North apologized again, now standing behind the seated Amberly, his hand lightly resting on her shoulder. "Maybe I should have stayed here with my friends. With the people I love. With *you.*"

"I *wanted* you to stay," Amberly said softly.

"You know, after we left *Magellan*, you were right. I prayed for you every day. And then, when we found *Cortes* destroyed, I felt ripped away from everything holy and good. Someone would have to be absolute evil to destroy a waypoint. Where was God? I prayed less and less. I wondered if God could hear my prayers. I doubted my faith. Deep doubt. Chasm had taken me away from everything I loved. I only wanted to destroy Chasm with a burning vengeance. I figured I would be the guy who does the horrific things, the necessary things, so everyone else can keep their hands clean."

Amberly reached over to her shoulder and placed her hand on North's.

"I thought maybe I'd die fighting Chasm on Arara. I never thought that we'd lose at *Marquette*. I barely escaped with my life. Sparks saved me. And she barely survived, maimed and diseased. If Sparks didn't need me, I would have probably allowed myself to despair. Who knows, maybe the toss-yourself-out-an-airlock despair."

Amberly stood and turned, sniffled, and took North's right hand.

"I cared for Sparks like she was my own family. But every time I thought about giving her what she wanted, about being with her, I couldn't get you out of my head. She knew it. She knew as long as *Magnus* was heading back to *Magellan*, she and I could never be. I didn't want to believe it, but she was right. And then I got your message. And your forgiveness. And I started to heal. And pray again. Sparks saved me. But you saved me, too. If it's worth anything, I forgive you, and I'm so sorry I didn't forgive you sooner."

Amberly took a deep, sobbing breath. The grace felt real. She knew she and North needed to say these hard things to each other, to air these ugly feelings. She sighed and smiled. Being around her old friend was going to be good.

"I'm glad we talked about this," Amberly said. Then suddenly, she frowned.

"What?"

"Poor Sparks. She must hate me," Amberly mused.

"No, she doesn't blame you or me. Just fate, or God, or the universe or something. She wants us to win. She has no more love for Chasm. She even tried to assassinate the Chairman. She's actually very protective of you, her sister. I hope Kora isn't the jealous type."

"Kora would love to have another sister," Amberly said. "Besides, Kora is too busy raising little Alroy to be jealous. He's nearly four, quite a handful."

As Amberly described Alroy, North thought about Amberly's innocent nephew, and then about the danger Chasm posed. He felt protective.

"Sparks is worried about more Hawk activity. She's worried the Chairman may be trying to reach her agents on *Magellan* to target you," North said. "Whatever you guys have prepared could already be compromised. The Chairman didn't know everything about *Magnus*, but she knew enough."

"We've been looking for the potential fourth Hawk for two years now. We might have had a chance of finding her if she didn't know we were looking, but now we all suspect the Hawk knows and has gone to ground. At least we can be reasonably sure that we have all external communication closed off, so the Hawk cannot be communicating with the Chairman. I'm hoping Dek and Sparks can help us smoke her out, but right now Dek and Sparks are still exiled, as I'm sure you know, stuck on their respective ships."

"Dek Tigona." Even saying the name left quite the distaste in North's mouth.

"Dek is a hero," Amberly defended the ex-Chasm leader. "He saved the *American Spirit*, twice. He saved me."

"He could be your leak, Amberly," North said, concerned. "How can you be sure you can trust him? Wait. You and Dek–"

"No, no," Amberly said. "Just friends. *Good* friends. North, he's sort of turned into a religious freak. My dad's old preacher has become his new mentor."

"Ramos? I thought he retired."

"Let's just say he started a prison ministry."

"I don't care if Dek had a prison conversion," North argued. "He isn't the first jailbird to claim God to get grace from man. How can you let him command the *American Spirit*?"

"North, I don't have to justify my decision to you," Amberly said coolly, releasing North's hand. "Dek has proven himself to me a dozen times over. I'd gladly put Kora and even little Alroy's life in his hands."

"I hope you know what you are doing," North said.

"North, you have to vote to commute the exile of Sparks *and* Dek," Amberly said, taking a step closer to North and looking hard into his eyes, as if she could will him to agree.

"You know I can't talk about that," North replied, inching back a bit to get some relief from Amberly's intense gaze. "Don't corrupt the tribunal."

"The integrity of the tribunal will mean nothing if we're not ready when Chasm shows up. We need them both on *Magellan* to help us. Think of what they have both already given us. You know if Chasm gets them, they will suffer immensely."

North sighed, then smiled. "Well, you are right as usual, Amberly Macready. But I am more worried about you if the Chairman gets you. And she wants you. So, if Dek and Sparks can help protect you, then welcome aboard, ex-Chasm traitors."

Amberly beamed with gratitude, and threw her arms around North for a second time. She whispered in his ear. "Thank you."

Condi beeped North's personal communicator. "Commander, Captain Obadiah is looking for you. He has requested your presence at Commander Moreno's offices immediately."

"Speaking of tribunals," North shrugged as Amberly released him from the embrace. "Duty calls. Amberly, this… us. I know we may have to work through stuff, but we're good, right?"

"We're good."

"You should go visit Sparks," North said as he looked to make his exit. He stopped at the lab's exit portal and took another long look at Amberly. "Skip and I are meeting at Rick's tonight, 26 hundred hours. Please come. Bring Kora; it will be just like old times."

Amberly smiled. *Everything is going to be alright*, she thought.

North had forgotten how dramatically the Marine Commander's office was furnished. The room was already unusually long, with dim theatrical lighting. At the far end was a desk and several faux-leather guest chairs. Behind the desk was a floor to ceiling plexiglass viewport into space. The infinity window made it feel like you could step out into the great void.

On the right facing wall as one entered was a shrine of sorts to the *Magellan* Marines who gave their lives defending the waypoint from Chasm. Twenty-three photographs were hung on the wall, each individually illuminated with honor. North recognized all of the fallen, and his heart broke again at the loss. He remembered his shock when, in this very office, he saw Commander Anderson and Wing Commander Jindal gunned down. The feeling made vengeance cloud his vision.

On the opposite side of the office, the portraits of 37 *Magellan* citizens that were Chasm conspirators were hung upside down. Each had a splattered red strike across the face. The room was designed so this wall was in perpetual shadow, and only with enough ambient light so a passerby could recognize their faces. North knew many of them and again felt the wound of their treachery. And in the center of them all was Kimberly Macready, mother of his love, architect of his misery. Even in her failure, what she was able to accomplish was sobering, and North resolved to be clear-eyed. The Chairman was more formidable than Kimberly.

Between the entrance and the several meters to the commander's desk was a conference table. A half-dozen people had surrounded the table, buzzing with aggressive discussion. Captain Obadiah noticed North first, and waved him over. Commander Moreno was standing at the head of the table. Next to her was Trish Moreton, Moreno's Chief of Staff. Alecia Bright, *Magnus'* operation chief and third in command was debating with Governor Thor, who had brought the new commander of his civilian police operations, Trot Wilder, Amberly's brother-in-law, to the meeting. North saw Lieutenant Boro, once sympathetic to Chasm, who had saved North's life, was leaning quietly against the wall while the debate caught fire. Boro was now XO on the *American Spirit*, appointed by Dek Tigona.

North's face lit up when he saw his fellow Marine and he paced over to him and embraced his old friend.

"Boro!"

"North, my friend," Boro, who matched North in stature, said in a booming voice, smiling a brilliant white smile. "I feared we would never meet again, but fate has brought us together. We are survivors. We are Marines!"

The commotion from the rest of the group died down and attention was drawn to the reunion.

"Commander North," Moreno said. "Good, I'm glad you are here. Let's convene the tribunal then."

"What? Here? Now?" North was confused. "I thought the tribunal was tomorrow at the William James Theater?"

"The governor and I decided that there was no profit in

having another show trial. After the Battle of *Magellan*, we needed the cathartic release provided by public executions," Moreno explained. "But now, they would just serve to inflame passions best left dormant."

"Things are calm now, stable," Thor explained. "Sorry we didn't loop you in North, but even if you objected, Rita and I are a majority vote."

"So, it seems," North quipped. "But how can we have a tribunal without the accused and representation?"

Rita stepped aside so North had a clear view of her desk at the end of the largest office on *Magellan*. Sitting in one of the guest chairs was Sparks, wearing her red kimono she "inherited" from the deceased Chasm agent Ryder and her white half-mask, covering the scars on her face.

"Hello, sexy," Sparks winked at North with her uncovered eye.

North looked at the second faux-leather chair, and his blood pressure increased as his eyes fell on its occupant.

"Captain Tigona," North said through gritted teeth.

"Commander North," Dek acknowledged North as he stood. Dek's hair was cut short, and he had a neatly trimmed dirty-blonde goatee to match. He still wore pedestrian civilian khaki clothes, but they were sharply tailored. When North fought Dek in the Battle of *Magellan*, he was surprised because his slight build hid the cohort-bred's true strength. In the years since North last saw Dek – the tribunal where North spared Dek's life – Dek had disciplined himself with intense exercise, and he looked much more formidable now.

Sparks read North's reaction to Dek's physique. "I know, right?"

"What is he doing here?" North fought to be civil. He knew sooner or later he would have to confront Dek, but he hadn't prepared himself for the flood of emotions this encounter would bring.

"You know perfectly well why he is here," the governor said. "Now, I know you two have some bad blood, but..."

North was conflicted. North may have granted grace in the court of law, but Dek was still the man who tried to destroy *Magellan* and personally shot and stabbed North multiple times.

He remembered their mano-a-mano skirmish near the climax of the Battle of *Magellan*. After North had given Dek a reprieve, the Chasm operative took advantage of the situation to drive his knife into an existing wound on North's arm. North slipped into shock as Dek pulled the blade out and stabbed North's torso beneath the left rib cage, only to pull the blade out and stab North's injured arm again, leaving the blade piercing the wound. Even after traveling a light year and back, the memory was fresh and scars remained.

But that was war. He was more furious at Dek because he directly guided Amberly Macready into Chasm's deadly plans. North was forced to condemn her, outvoted that he was, at the last tribunal.

As North fumed, Dek's blood also started to boil. He had promised Ramos, his spiritual mentor, he would remain calm, but North's disdain infuriated him. Giving in to temptation, Dek stepped toward the table in a fashion that made Boro and Trot both feel for their sidearms.

"The real question, North, is what are *you* doing here?" Dek asked. "You were supposed to be defeating Chasm."

North stepped up so he was face-to-face with Dek. "That information is not something we share with Chasm saboteurs so you can pass it onto the Chairman."

"The Chairman?" Dek scoffed. "You are insane. I defied her. I even defeated her Hawks. You should have never left *Magellan*. Never left her."

"Here? Her? What?" Again, North was confused.

"You had the choice to stay. I didn't have a choice. I was exiled."

"You *are* exiled."

"You left *Amberly* here. You should have stayed with her. You should have protected her. Some traditionalist. You left Amberly to the mercy of the Hawks. They almost had her."

"I didn't know about the dirty Hawks," North countered.

"Then it was a good thing that I came back when I did," Dek shot. "First you shamed Amberly. Then you abandoned her. You —"

North pulled back his fist to deck Dek. The rogue threw up his arms to protect himself.

"Whoa," Thor shouted. Before North could finish his punch, Boro grabbed him with a bear hug. Moreno had jumped in the middle as well, pushing North back.

Sparks leaned back in her chair. "What a waste. We could have sold tickets to that show."

"Like you said," Moreno said, "you can't have a tribunal without defendants. If we can cool off, that would be helpful at this – well, this is more of a sentence revision hearing."

With a calm but firm voice, Thor spoke. "Let's get to business, shall we. I call this tribunal in session. We have one order of business. Several years ago, this tribunal condemned Sparks and Dek Tigona to exile from *Magellan*. Mr. Tigona was placed under arrest on the *American Spirit* to be returned to Earth. Miss Sparks, allowed to travel in the custody of Commander North on the *Magnus* as an intelligence asset in our fight against the Chasm rebels."

Moreno spoke next from a script. "Amberly Macready, as commander of the Fuentes Station mission, petitioned this body to request clemency for both Sparks and Mr. Tigona. The extraordinary circumstances of sacrifice on behalf of this waypoint on behalf of both being duly noted, and the fact that Mr. Tigona had won the confidence of the Earth-loyal crew of the *American Spirit* to serve as captain, we are here today to consider her petition."

North was a little upset that he seemed to have been cut out of the loop. Still, he knew that if there were to be any commutation, waypoint law required unanimous agreement from the tribunal.

"North do you have anything you wanted to say?" Moreno looked at her fellow officer.

"Sorry, I guess I didn't do my homework," North said.

"I have done my homework," Thor inserted, not missing a beat. Thor wanted this tribunal dissolved and done, and its work kept as quiet as possible. The altercation between Dek and North already threatened that outcome. "I am prepared to render a judgment on the petition."

"Wow, that's fast," North mused.

"I am also prepared to render judgement. North, do you require further briefing?" Moreno asked.

North felt cornered. He knew the basics, and he already knew in his heart how he was going to vote. "I guess I know what I need to know."

"Good," Moreno said in a formal tone. "We will give the exiled an opportunity to make a statement before we vote on Miss Macready's petition. Both exiles had waived the right to counsel. Mr. Tigona."

Dek had calmed down. He stood, smiled, remembered a favorite scripture Ramos had suggested he commit to memory: If God is for us, who can be against us. *Well, I hope God is for me,* Dek thought. He spoke, "I appreciate the tribunal considering Amberly's petition. You have my gratitude. Otherwise, I think my actions speak for themselves. Thank you." Dek sat back in the comfy guest chair.

"Indeed, they do," Thor interjected, tipping his hand to no one's surprise.

"Miss Sparks," Moreno continued. "Do you have a statement?"

Sparks stood and slowly removed her mask. The exposed scars on her face were deep and repulsive. North and the other members of the *Magnus* crew had seen these before, but the others had not. Trish let out an audible gasp.

Brilliant way to illustrate her sacrifice, Thor thought.

Sparks put her mask back on, and everyone could feel the tension in the room drop. "Nope. No statement. I was just curious to see how you would react." She chuckled to herself and sat back down.

North had to suppress a laugh. The outcome of this tribunal was clearly a forgone conclusion. Once he realized that fact, he became much more interested in getting over to Rick's as soon as possible. "Let's vote. I move to commute the sentence of exile for Dek Tigona," North said.

"Aye," Thor said.

"Aye," Moreno said. "Dek Tigona, effective immediately, your sentence of exile from *Magellan* is commuted. The witnesses gathered will now notarize the decision by confirmation on your infopads. Congratulations, Dek."

The officials gathered round the table did as they were told. Thor offered the next motion, "I move the same thing for Sparks."

"Aye," Moreno said.

"Nay," North said. For an instant, it felt as if the room had depressurized. No one had expected North to deny Sparks. "Just kidding. Aye. Sparks is no longer exiled."

"That was not funny," Sparks scowled at North.

"Sure was," North winked at her.

"The witnesses gathered will now notarize the decision by confirmation on your infopads. Congratulations, Sparks," Moreno said with a wry smile. "This hearing is adjourned."

"Great. Time for a beer," North said as he shook hands around the table. Dek walked up to North and offered his hand.

"Thank you, North," Dek said. "I'm sorry I lost my cool."

The image of Dek stabbing him flashed in North's mind again, but he pushed it out.

"We have common cause, Dek." North couldn't bring himself to an apology, but he did search for something charitable to say. "I understand your frustration. We won't fail Amberly again. I swear it."

"As do I," Dek said, making hard eye contact with North.

"I hate to interrupt this bromance," Sparks said, giving Dek a peck on the cheek and then turning to North, "but I think you owe me a drink. Come on, I want to see this Rick's joint you keep talking about. Why do you think I wore this ridiculous dress? Let's party."

CHAPTER THREE

North and Sparks stepped off the Tube, *Waypoint Magellan's* pneumonic public transit system, at Lincoln Station in the President Quarter. The clock in the station read a quarter till 26 hundred hours.

The pair paced three-tenths of a kilometer down the arterial corridor towards Rick's. At this late hour, most everything in the retail district was closed. Every place they passed on the way brought on another wave of nostalgia for North: the bakery where her remembered buying Amberly a birthday cake for her 14th birthday, a year after she believed she lost her parents; the arcade where he and Skip would battle at Tog, and where he still held the high score on Forest Hunter III; the coffee shop where he would play poker and swap tall tales with the old men, like Alroy and Ramos; and then finally Rick's — his favorite watering hole on the waypoint.

Rick's had no exterior portals or other windows, and the entrance looked dark as Sparks and North approached.

"Wow, that place is the famous Rick's? Looks dead as an asteroid. I thought there would be lines weaving out the door, especially on a Ship Day."

"That's strange, no bouncer," North noticed. "Maybe they don't staff that anymore. I dunno, cutbacks after the Chasm attack?"

North walked up to the door and pressed the access button. In less than a second, a light blinked green to indicate pressure on both sides of the door, and it slid open.

It was completely dark inside.

"What in the waypoint?" North said as he stepped through the portal. "Maybe they moved Rick's to somewhere else? This isn't the hot nightlife I remembered. Hello?"

"Man, I'm going back to Chasm if this is the best party you can find on *Magellan*," Sparks threatened.

The lights suddenly popped on, and a crowd of people shouted in unison, "Surprise! Welcome back, North!"

North looked around at the standing room only crowd in the 20th-century themed-bar and smiled as he recognized dozens of the people he cared about most.

"Yes," Skip said, "Surprise pulled off. Kato, start pouring the drinks!"

North's eye was quickly drawn to Flora Dillington. She was wearing a low-cut dress and showed off legs that seemed to go on forever. Flora had been a friend of North's for a long time, and was also a rival of Amberly's in both love and science. Next to Flora in his Marine dress uniform was her brother, Mac.

"I've been waiting four years to give you a Ship Day kiss," Flora said as she stepped up to the brawny Marine and went for full-mouth contact. Some already intoxicated revelers started whooping.

Hidden from North in the back of the room, Amberly unsuccessfully tried to keep her eyes from rolling as the kiss seemed to her to linger just a bit too long.

Sparks saw her roommate Rhodes and went to give her a celebratory hug. Rhodes hugged her back, but kept her focus was on the North-Flora lip-lock. North had his hands up and open, but Flora leaned in and stole what she wanted.

"Definitely some chemistry there," Rhodes said. Sparks slapped her on the back of her head half-in-jest. Sparks wanted North for herself, but if she couldn't have him, he certainly wasn't going to be joined with someone as unworthy as Flora. Amberly and North getting together was one thing Sparks could abide, but Miss Dillington was out of the question.

Flora withdrew, flush and fluttery. "Whoa. We should have Ship Day more often."

As soon as a surprised North pulled away from Flora, who smiled seductively as she wiped a bit of saliva off her lower lip, he made eye contact with Amberly giving her a that-was-not-my-idea shrug.

He didn't acknowledge Flora's quip, staying focused on Amberly as he moved in her direction, leaving Flora flustered. His beeline to Amberly was interrupted by Pastor Ramos. The old friends shook hands, and North made a joke about his balding head. Ramos introduced him to Midas, a burly, blonde older delivery man and confidant of Amberly.

Then North saw his former Marine subordinate, Eli Wong. North was sorry when he heard Eli had been run out of the military after his misguided attempt to airlock Dek. If North had stayed, he knew things would have been different. North reached out and grabbed Wong in a full hug. Wong was crying.

"It's so good you are back," Wong said into North's ear, trying to keep himself from openly sobbing. "You can make things right. They've gone too far. Amberly's gone too far."

"We'll talk soon, my friend," North said, wondering exactly what Wong, once his most loyal Marine, meant about Amberly. Behind Wong was Leo, another Marine who had served under North during the Battle of *Magellan*.

"Commander!" Leo said as he snapped into a salute.

"We're at Rick's, Leo," North said, laughing. "In here, it's just North."

"Rick's has changed since you've been gone, sir," Leo said, extending a hand that was accepted by North. "I've actually been banned from this place, though that pansy Kato made an exception for your party."

"Banned? Why?"

"A long story best saved for another time," Leo smiled a tired smile. "But don't be fooled. Things are much worse than they seem. Aww… never mind. Don't you worry now. You're back. Let's celebrate this good thing."

Rhodes and Sparks pushed their way to North through the crowd.

"Commander, wow, you have a lot of friends," Rhodes, who had only known North during his time on the flight of the *Magnus*, sighed. "I never knew you were so popular. Any of your former Marines you might … recommend?"

"Rhodes, I don't think any of my former squad could handle your volume," North joked, though her unusually loud talking voice was actually helpful in the noisy bar.

Rhodes frowned.

"I'm kidding!" North smiled brightly. "Any of my old jarheads would be lucky to get a second glance from you."

A waiter handed North, Rhodes and Sparks shot glasses of a dark, synthetic liquor. North sent the strong brew down his hatch and handed the empty glass back.

"Well, aren't you a regular pop star covered in famous sauce," Sparks jumped in. "On the other hand, I hope the Marines here don't recognize me, or they might give me a personal tour of the airlock."

She was joking, but North immediately feared the truth in her words.

He pulled her head to his and whispered through her half-mask. "If anyone even looks at you with revenge in mind, send an emergency locator signal to Condi, and I will be there."

North's pledge of protection made Sparks feel good, feel loved. His masculine instinct to protect was so attractive, though she thought it should have the opposite effect. But the good feelings quickly evaporated as she caught Amberly in the corner of her eye. Sparks knew she and North would never be, and it hurt, like a slowly twisting knife.

"You worry too much, North," Sparks covered up her feelings, downing her shot. "Mmmmm. I can take care of myself." To prove the point, Sparks patted her upper outer thighs.

"You're packing?"

"And now that you've commuted my sentence, they're not even illegal."

"Well, don't shoot anyone tonight."

"No promises. At least, I didn't bring my sword, so there definitely won't be any neutering or even old-fashion beheadings. That sword is *so hard* to sneak by security," Sparks winked her uncovered eye at North.

Kora ran up and threw her arms around North.

"North you sonofagun, you made it back," Kora was elated. "Someone, give us a drink!" Two full shot glasses were passed to Kora and North. They clinked the glasses together. "Bottom's up!"

"There were a few times I wish you were around to patch me up, Kora," North laughed, his breath smelling of fake whiskey, "but I survived."

"Oh, I am sure the orderlies on *Magnus* were lining up to be your nurse," Kora laughed in return. "I'm glad that you've started to make out... I mean... make up with Amberly."

"Never mind that," North said stepping out of Kora's embrace. "Let me look at you. You're married! Wow. You have a kid now?"

"Guilty. I can't wait to introduce you to little Alroy. He has red hair just like his grandfather and his auntie."

Sparks took a side glance at Kora's dark hair and round face and immediately saw the family resemblance to Raven One, Kora's mother and Sparks' former mentor. Sparks took Kora into a tight hug.

"I'm so sorry for your loss," Sparks said. "Kimberly Macready was the closest thing that I ever had to a mother."

"Okay then," Kora said, pulling halfway out of Spark's hug. "You are Sparks. I remember you from the tribunal. Thank you. I choose to remember Kimberly when she was a loving mom."

"Well, I'm glad you two have met," North said awkwardly.

Lydia joined the group, with Amberly in tow. "But I haven't met," Lydia said, sticking out a hand to Sparks. "I'm Lydia. Pleased to meet you."

Sparks shook the outstretched hand, nodded and smiled sincerely.

"Wow, Lydia, you clean up well," North said. Lydia was wearing a fun, sexy cocktail dress, which was the exact opposite of the utilitarian grab North was familiar with her wearing four years ago when he left *Magellan*. The dark dress contrasted with her bright blonde hair. "So, you and Skip. What–"

"I don't want to talk about it," Lydia frowned.

"Right, sorry."

"Speech!" Skip, who was already on his third beer, shouted from across the room, as if on cue.

"Yes, please give a toast," Kora suggested.

North pulled a chair out from under a nearby table and mounted it, standing tall and holding his arms out. Kato handed the Marine a shot glass full of a foul-smelling liquor. North held the glass forward.

"Dear friends, both old and new, thank you so much for having this celebration in my honor. I am sorely undeserving –"

"You can say that again," someone shouted from the crowd, which responded with laughter.

North continued, "– but I am grateful. But first, let us toast the real heroes of the Waypoints. The ones who are no longer with us. Anderson, Jindal, Twig, Snyder, Kim, Franco, Ioder! Honor them with me! Honor their sacrifice. Hu-rah!" North threw one fist in the air and with his other arm, he threw back the shot. The crowd responded with appropriate noise.

"Wait, I'm not done. Kato, another shot!"

"Someone better open a tab," Skip shouted and the crowd chuckled.

"There is a dangerous enemy out there! I've met her. She has eyes of evil and a heart of stone. She wants to steal our future and erase our past. But the Marines will stop her! Do you hear me, Chairman, whatever the hell your name is, come and get us! We're ready for you. The *Magnus* is going to blow up your ass!" North downed the next shot as Kato handed him another full glass.

"Hear, hear!" Rhodes shouted and the crowd agreed.

"Now listen to me. I have something hard to say. Some of the people here have done bad things. They counted themselves with the enemy. But I've done bad things, too. We all have. My point is, we can waste all our ammo shooting each other over what has been. But if we do, then the Chairman will win. We need all the allies we can get. To all who now pledge your life to *Magellan*, I pledge my life to you! A toast to our new allies, you ex-Chasm bastards! I'm looking at you Dek Tigona, wherever you are. And you, Boro, my good friend! Well, he's not here either. Huh. Sparks is here! Anyway, here's to our new cannon fodder!"

Groaning and chuckling echoed through the crowd, as North slammed the next shot.

"Kato, another round," North shouted. "I have one more toast!"

"You better sit down before you fall down," Kora said.

"I'm fine, I'm fine," North smiled. Then, in a quick motion, he reached down and pulled Amberly up on the chair with him. She instinctively tried to resist, but quickly gave into North's powerful charisma. As much as she hated being the center of attention, she was attracted to this strong, cheerful man. She saw a lot of the old North she once knew. Amberly smiled nervously as she attempted to balance on the chair with North and not fall into the crowd. North held fast, pulling Amberly close and tight.

"Hello, Commander," Amberly attempted a sultry cadence. "Quite the view from up here."

"Hey Amberly, give him a Ship Day kiss," someone shouted. The crowd cheered in agreement.

North put the hand that wasn't wrapped around Amberly's waist out palm down to calm the crowd.

"You guys missed that show," North said, and then he faced Amberly but spoke to the crowd. "Sorry, Red, one per customer."

"I want to tell you about this woman, Amberly Macready. I was wrong about her. I said some horrible things –"

Suddenly Amberly realized where he was going. Her face reddened; she didn't want to do this, here, in public.

"North, you don't have to… you've had a few too many shots, I think –"

"No, I need to make this right. Everyone needs to know how wrong I was. Everyone needs to know–"

A sudden, large commotion near the front door drew everyone's attention from North and Amberly.

A squad of Marines, flanked by Dek, Boro and Moreno pushed into the crowded bar.

"We need to see Commander North? Where is he?" Boro said.

Dek kept a straight face as he pointed to the chair in the center of the room that North tightly held Amberly. Dek made eye contact with Amberly in a way to ask "what the hell is going on?"

Amberly slipped off the chair quietly and North raised a hand. "Commander Moreno! So glad you can make it to the party."

"All non-military and police forces, clear the room," Moreno countered. "This is an emergency."

The crowd started to grumble. "Aw dirt! The party just started," Skip protested.

The rabble didn't seem like they understood the gravity of the situation. Boro stood on a table. "Go home, now! Or you'll go to the brig. If you are stationed on *American Spirit* or *Magnus*, you are being recalled."

The crowd became a bit testy when Boro said "recalled." Most of the *Magnus* crew had only been off ship for a few hours after having been confined to *Magnus* for nearly four years.

Amberley looked at Lydia. "You better get going. I'll message you when I get home. If this is what I think it is, we'll need to get started on converting the lab for battle analytics." Her friend agreed and slipped into the exiting crowd.

"Thank you," Moreno looked at Boro as he dismounted.

The squad of the Marines started actively pushing people out.

North stepped down from the chair and wobbled a bit, and Amberly reached over to steady him.

"Rita, he has five… six shots in him," Amberly told Moreno. Along with Amberly, Dek, Kora, Sparks and the Rick's service staff were the only non-Marines remaining as the place emptied.

"I'm fine, Red," North said.

"I'm not sure," Moreno said, taking a pitcher of ice water from Kato. She walked up to North and in a sudden move tossed cold sobriety onto North's face.

"Mother of a dirt licker!" North swore as he swung his hands in front of his head.

"Sorry, but you have to sober up, quick."

"Long range scanners have picked up *Utopia*," Dek explained, "Just a few minutes ago. Cencomm estimates around eight hours till weapons range."

"Great!" North shouted, a little too loudly. "I've been waiting two years for a rematch."

"North, she's not alone," Moreno said. "There are three other ships."

"Four *Utopias*?" North looked puzzled.

"Apparently, the Chairman has built an armada," Dek said.

"She's sending them to Earth," Sparks said. "She must be."

"That would be a suicide mission," Skip surmised. "Earth's defense grid would take them out."

"Maybe," North said as he wiped back his dripping brown hair. "They almost had us at *Marquette*. If there are four ships as powerful as *Utopia*…"

"We don't have time to discuss this," Moreno said with a commanding voice. "The governor and I have consulted with Captain Obadiah. We are going to evacuate as many non-essential personnel from *Magellan* as we can on the *American Spirit*, which will make a sprint for *Waypoint Gilbert*."

"Evacuate? No! We can't run again," North's heart beat a little faster. "We can figure out something…"

"North, we might have had a chance against *Utopia*, based on the intel you provided. Against four, we must think about saving the lives we can."

"Then this is it, then isn't it?" Skip said. "This is the end of *Waypoint Magellan*."

"No! We must stand and fight! I won't abandon my home now… not again!" North shouted and pounded his fist on an adjacent table, knocking several abandoned synth-beers to the floor. Amberly took North's hand. She felt the same defiant spirit in her heart. *Magellan* was her home; in an instant she had already decided there was no evacuation for her. She was ready to die for *Magellan*.

"North, pull yourself together," Moreno said sternly. "You are an officer. Act like one."

"Yes, ma'am," North straightened up. Amberly released his hand.

"We don't know if it is the end of *Magellan*," Dek explained. "Chasm may try to capture the waypoint – use it as an early warning gentry in case Earth sends a force against Arara."

"Dek's right. The cat's out of the bag," Sparks added. "The Chairman knows we'll send a warning to Earth, and she'll find a way to use *Magellan* as a buffer if she can take the station. Maybe as some sort of trap."

"She likes those," North said, embarrassed that he had personally fallen into a trap the Chairman laid for him in the hours before the *Battle of Marquette*.

Kato, the manager and barkeep of Rick's, had been picking up the half-empty glasses of booze while listening in to the impromptu meeting of the extended *Magellan* leadership. "Excuse me. Sorry to interrupt. I don't mean to sound like a coward, but if we really care about saving lives, maybe surrender is the best option. If we can't stop this evil Chasm armada, what are our choices? Some of us might survive a twenty-year trip to Earth on a crammed deep space ship? Maybe we can negotiate some favorable terms if we don't put up a fight. I know you guys are mostly military, hard wired to fight. But… pacifism has its advantages, and one of them is we get to live."

Moreno was annoyed at Kato, partially because the barkeep didn't belong in this senior officers' conference, but mostly because there was some truth in what he said. She chose to ignore him.

"If you guys surrender, at least let me have my sword," Sparks sighed. "Once Chasm finds me, they are going to take me to the Chairman for a short life of torture. I'd rather go down fighting."

"And the Chairman personally told me she wanted revenge on Amberly," North said. "I would never just turn her over."

"Rita, I know you have a plan," Amberly looked desperately at the olive-skinned woman. "You could beat my mom at chess; you can figure out a way for us to win this."

"My dear Amberly," Rita smiled sadly, "we should have had more teas together. I fear now the supply I was hoarding I may never get to enjoy."

"We're just giving up?" Skip asked plainly.

"No, we just have to define what winning looks like," Moreno explained. "If we congregate our forces – *Magellan, Magnus* and the *American Spirit*, I fear we'll just make it easier for them to wipe us out. The *American Spirit* isn't a warship. It has almost no defensive armor and just one plasma gun. So it's the life boat. We've prepared for all sorts of scenarios. Even the possibility of an overwhelming force."

"We've run simulations," Dek agreed, thinking of the monotony of the thousands of training activities the Marines had forced Dek into over the past year.

"Your crew is ready. The ship is provisioned. Captain Tigona, time to get to your bridge. Governor Thor is already triaging civilians and preparing 3,000 of them for boarding. It will be tight, but the chances of survival are immensely greater. It's not likely, but maybe Chasm will stop at *Magellan* and leave Gilbert alone."

"That leaves about 7,000 people here on *Magellan*," Amberly said.

"We can get about 1,000 of them onto the *Magnus*," North said. "But it would be waste for us to run. Let's load our nukes and see if we get a good first hit."

"That simulation was not promising, Commander," Moreno told the wet Marine. "I've spoken with Captain Obadiah. The *Magnus* will retreat to the Spencer Belt and Fuentes Station. Hopefully, you'll get one or two of those battleships to follow you. Those would be much better odds. Obadiah is hopeful *Magnus* can pick off any pursing enemy vessels, and then circle back around and possibly flank the remaining ships in the Chairman's armada. It's a long shot, but it's the best shot. Either way, people will be safer on *Magnus* than *Magellan*."

"Our mission is to defend the waypoint, not run away," North protested.

"We're not totally defenseless anymore," Moreno smiled. "Thanks to Amberly's good work, we've been able to upgrade. We have some tricks we can punch back with. At least enough to buy us some time for *Magnus* to thin the enemy numbers and come around and hopefully save the day."

"That's a crazy plan," Sparks cracked, squirming in her kimono. "I love crazy plans!"

"Captain Tigona, XO Boro," Moreno looked at the two former Chasm operatives who now were responsible for the *American Spirit*, "you should get back to your ship, spool up your antimatter generators, and prepare for shove off as soon as possible. Even four hours of lead time will make it harder for Chasm to track you if they see you escaping. Dek, we'll have a final briefing for executives at two-hundred hours. I'll call you on your bridge."

Dek looked at Amberly. The last year working hand in hand with Amberly had been one of the best in his life. Deep in his heart, he still longed for her, but he would never act on that now, for fear of damaging the friendship they had built. He also believed pushing this issue would ultimately be futile. And then there was the brawny North.

"North, Sparks," Moreno was almost barking orders now, "you'd better get back to the *Magnus*."

"But if the fighting is here, I want to be here," Sparks protested. "I want to pay the Chairman back for this." Sparks tapped her white half-mask.

"You are a member of the crew of the *Magnus*, and you would be a distraction here," Moreno was annoyed with Sparks' resistance to orders. "Too many of my troops still want to shoot you out the airlock. You did destroy our garden, remember? I have forgiven you, but I can't spend my time worried about vigilantes now. Get to the *Magnus*. I am sure Captain Obadiah will put you to good use in the fight."

"What about Amberly?" North asked Moreno, but looked right into Amberly's green eyes. After so many years, he had only been with her for a few hours. The thought of having to leave her again made his stomach turn. "She's not safe here. I'm going to stay here and protect her."

"North, you are XO on the *Magnus*," Moreno said. "We need the *Magnus* to be at 100 percent for this plan to work. You have to draw some of that armada off, and then defeat whoever follows you. The odds are already unfavorable. We need you on our ship."

"I can stay behind, then," Dek stepped up. "I will make sure Amberly is safe."

"What in the waypoint?!?" Moreno snapped. "Dirty hell, you two! That would be worse than Sparks staying. Dek, you are Captain of the *American Spirit*! You have to think about the greater good now — the real greater good."

"Dek, North," Amberly looked at the one-time rivals. The bravado would have annoyed her if she didn't understand it was an expression of selfless love from both men. She knew they both only wanted to protect her, but she was her own woman, and she was ready to do her part as well. "I can take care of myself. I am needed here–"

"No, the Chairman is coming for you," North said. "She means to do it. She's focused on taking you. Come with me. Be safe on the *Magnus*. If the Chairman gets you, then…" North didn't want to complete the thought.

"I won't let it come to that," Amberly said. "Also, have some faith in Commander Moreno and her Marines. They will fight to defend this waypoint."

"Come with me please," North said. "*Please*. Or … go with Dek."

"You know I won't, North. *Magellan* is my home. I'll never leave," Amberly's face radiated patient bittersweetness. "This place is where I belong. I was born here. I will die here. I'm not a soldier or a rogue warrior. But I will fight for my home. I will die for my home."

"That's my sister!" Sparks said.

"Um… that's *my* sister, weirdo," Kora said.

"Time is short," Moreno said with a sense of finality that ended the discussion. "To your ships. To your stations. We'll have a final briefing at two hundred hours. Godspeed to us all."

The *Magnus* officers' steward met North, Skip and Sparks at the gangway portal connecting the warship to the *Magellan* hangar. She was carrying two long, thin carbon fiber boxes. The steward handed them to North, saluted and returned to the ship.

"Hey, that's mine," Sparks mock-swiped at the box.

"You're not allowed to have this on station anyway," North said, drawing the box back. "Well, maybe..."

"Listen Skip," Sparks said, considering the scrawny man. "You look like you could use all the help you can get. If those Chasm shock troopers invade, you'll need something to take them out at close range. Something to get past their PDS—"

"PD-what?" Skip asked.

"Point Defense System," North explained. "Their magic armor."

"No fears. This baby will help you out," Sparks suggested.

"Whoa," Skip said, as North opened the box, revealing the katana owned by Ryder and then Sparks.

"Use that blade to protect my sister," Sparks commanded.

Skip looked confused.

"She means Amberly," North shook his head. "Don't ask."

"Okay, sure," Skip replied to both. The steel blade glistened as it reflected the intense hangar flood lights. Skip took the blade in his hands and swished it in the air.

"Careful," North said, as he stepped back a few paces.

"Take care of her, and she'll take care of you," Sparks said. "See if you can add to her kill count. I actually used that thing to hack off someone's head."

Skip was a bit taken aback as he imaged Sparks decapitating a Chasm trooper with the sword.

"He was a really bad guy," North reassured Skip, and then pointed to the other box. "Take this box and give it to Moreno. It's a javelin weapon I built for melee combat to counter the point defense. It has a little more reach than the sword, and the tip will jolt you with a pretty good charge. Hopefully, she won't need it. But you have to discharge a lot of bullets pretty fast to get past Chasm PDS. With this, one stab will do the trick."

"Thank you," Skip said, and he stepped forward and clasped North's right arm with his left, careful not to impale him with the sword. "We're going to win this, right?" Skip attempted to muster confidence, but he was afraid.

"I hope so," North smiled. "I'm proud to call you friend, Skip. When the time comes to stand, you'll do alright. Godspeed, until we meet again."

Skip gripped North's arm harder, then released it. He turned to Sparks and nodded a goodbye. He gathered his parcels and headed for the Command Center access portal on the far side of the busy hangar.

"This wasn't shore leave. This was *short* leave," Sparks complained and started down the gangway. She noticed North hadn't followed behind. "You coming, XO?"

"Tell the captain I'll be aboard shortly," North replied.

"Where are you going? You know there is a fleet of pain and destruction coming?"

"I need to say goodbye to Amberly," North admitted.

Sparks bit her lip to hide her disappointment. As much as she had come to feel kinship of sorts for Amberly, she fantasized about a scenario where the redhead didn't survive the coming conflict. Then North and she could settle on the Lewis Islands in peace. The island life would be boring, Sparks thought as she watched North hurry away. *But it would be worth it.*

CHAPTER FOUR

December 27, 2606. On the bridge of the Chasm warship Utopia, 24 months after the Battle of Marquette.

The yeoman was thin and bald. He'd decided to shave his head, leaving a shiny brown dome that made him look older than his 17 years of life. Three years ago, he was fortunate to be selected for Chasm's navy program. But to work as a yeoman on the Chairman's flagship was a dream come true. He looked sharp in his duty officer's uniform. The jumpsuit sported a bright blue pattern that was supposed to mimic the appearance of the oceans of Arara.

The bridge was housed deep in the primary hull of *Utopia*. The Chasm flagship, like the other three ships in the fleet, was remarkable for its dual-hull design. Unlike the *American Spirit*, *Magnus* and most deep space ships, which had a single, cylindrical hull, the Chasm warships looked like two long cans connected with a thick, metallic space bridge. The primary hull was twice the size of the secondary hull. Chasm engineers conceived the second hull as a protected location to house the antimatter reactor. Those reactors were typically housed in the dorsal fins found on ships like *American Spirit* – a safety feature, but the fin solution meant the reactor was exposed to attack. Chasm engineers also needed space to house the power-sucking PDS and signal jamming systems — similar to the one that Sparks had implemented on the *American Spirit*, only much more powerful.

"Admiral Björk," the yeoman saluted sharply as he approached the captain's chair. The bridge was a large cubic room nearly 30 meters high with expansive wall displays on all sides and ceiling. In the "front" of the room was a floor-to-ceiling display of the view from the bow of *Utopia*. The right and left walls of the bridge cube showed unimpeded views of the port side and starboard. "Yeoman Carnell reporting. I have a message from the Chairman. She orders you to report immediately to the command center."

Maja Björk despised the cheery young yeoman; she only tolerated him because he was a *pet* of the Chairman. Björk was the senior-most officer in the Infinite Order navy, and she used her pull to secure command of the flagship to satiate her lust for adventure and power. The Infinite Order was the name given by Chasm to its new government on Arara, now that it had wrested power from the loyalists.

Maja had worked hard for 50 years to earn her place as master of *Utopia* and admiral of the Dark Armada. She secretly signed up with Chasm when she was only 15 years old, bored of the farm life found on Arara's agrarian continent, Ingram. Her generation had sacrificed much and risked everything to build Chasm for this moment. The younger generation, kids like Carnell, didn't appreciate the sacrifices she and the other older Chasm adherents had made for them. *No matter*, Maja thought, *it is for the greater good.*

The captain's platform was a large pedestal in the center of the room, rising nearly five meters higher than the rest of the various navigation, weapons control, fight control and communications stations. From this position, the captain on a *Utopia*-class warship could offer orders to her underlings from on high and have a visual of the ship's surroundings.

Maja Björk, sporting her activewear uniform — a snug fitting bright blue jacket and dark blue loose-fitting pants – held both rails of the steep staircase to the captain's platform and slid to the bridge floor. Her officer's cap bounced off her head as she hit the bottom. Carnell picked up the hat, handed it to Björk, and then stood at attention. *For an old, white woman, Admiral Björk is pretty athletic*, he thought. Björk didn't even glance at her underling as she double-timed it to the Chairman's command center, two of her personal armed guards, silent as ever, in tow.

The command center was nearly four times the size of the bridge. The vast room was shadowy, with only a moderately illuminated elevated platform on the far side. Admiral Björk entered, and the eight members of the Chairman's honor guard snapped to attention. The captain of the guard, a short, thick man with an emotionless face and icy eyes stepped forward and offered a salute. Björk returned it.

"I hope this is important, Narlo," Björk said. "I have to give the final crew briefing before our arrival at *Magellan*."

Narlo snorted. "Admiral, are you suggesting that a summons from the Chairman would be frivolous?"

"No, of course not," Björk said, pointing an open hand toward the platform on the opposite side of the cavernous room. "Shall we?"

"Please have your guards stay here," Narlo pointed into the foyer outside the main entrance. Björk's two guards were put off by the request, even though no one could see any expression through their opaque face shields.

Björk nodded. Her muscle complied and left the room.

"Eight guards?" Björk asked, her alto voice thick with sarcasm. Ever since the victory at *Marquette* and the surrender of the Earth-loyal government on Arara, the Chairman had expanded her power base, sometimes extravagantly. "Expecting an invasion? Or does the Chairman think you too incompetent to provide security with the standard two?"

Narlo growled a non-verbal response as he led Björk across the command center. Hundreds of Chasm officers and civilian support staff sat or stood at dozens of round multi-station worktables quietly monitoring magnetic resonance screens. They were all sharply dressed; and, as the Chairman preferred, the members of her support staff were relatively young, few older than 25. The ambient light from the screens lit the faces of the staff with a cool, electronic glow.

If Björk didn't know better, she would have thought the Chairman surrounded herself with young people because they were easier to manipulate, and more likely to worship their leader with a religious fervor. Fewer and fewer in the Chasm leadership remember the revolution before the Chairman took power. Björk remembered. She had seen over the past few decades how the Chairman had rewritten history to glorify her role in bringing about the coming utopia. Perhaps when they had fully consolidated power and eliminated all threats from the homeworld, the Infinite Order Council of Comrades would see to it that the record be corrected. For the present, Björk realized the advantages of the rank-and-file devoted to iconic leadership, so the Chairman's embellishments served the greater good.

Björk and Narlo ascended the large marble-like stairs to the top of the platform. A small woman sat in a large metallic chair with several data stations attached via articulated arms. The arms, controlled by the nameless VI installed in *Utopia*, responded to the Chairman's requests. In a flurry of movement, as the information she requested was brought into her view when seated in the chrome-colored chair.

Björk stood at attention in front of the seated Chairman, who ignored her at first before looking up from one of the arm-suspended screens.

"Admiral."

"Chairman," Björk returned the curt greeting. The Chairman's face was bright with energy, her silver-white hair pulled back into what looked to be a painfully tight single pony-tail. Her eyes appeared to have no iris, which always wigged Björk out a bit.

The Chairman said nothing for a few seconds, then folded her hands together. "Good news. My remaining Hawk on *Magellan* has reported in. Raven One's old nemesis, Rita Moreno, is still in command of the condemned waypoint. They are aware of the fleet strength of our Dark Armada. Fortunately, my Hawk is well placed and knows the enemy's next move."

"Excellent," Björk said. "There were some on the Council who questioned the amount of resources you put into the Hawk program, but I knew the investment would pay off." Björk recalled many on the council who had objected to the program because the deep agents would be only known and loyal to the Chairman herself, not the council. Anyone who ever did the math – and Björk always did the math – would see a statistically significant number of those Chasm directors who opposed the Hawks were now among the honored dead.

"Did *you* believe in the Hawks, Admiral?" the Chairman said as she walked behind to flank Björk. "Or are you just flattering me now because you fear me? No matter."

Björk flinched almost imperceptibly when the word *fear* rolled eloquently off the Chairman's lips. The Chairman paused for only a second, then continued. "Moreno has constructed a worthy plan to maximize their poor odds. They will send the *American Spirit* in retreat, hoping in vain to spare the lives of civilians by getting them to *Gilbert* or even further from our reaches."

"How noble," Björk said. "What do you know of the enemy commander, this Moreno?"

"Raven One mentioned Moreno often in her dispatches," the Chairman said. "Kimberly described her as tactically brilliant, but emotionally soft."

"Interesting. Who is in command of the *American Spirit*?"

"Dek Tigona."

"The agent corrupted by Raven One's daughter? Odd. They made that traitor captain of their deep space ship?"

"Yes," the Chairman said as she stared at the empty space next to the Admiral's head. "What do you think, old friend? Shall we recover Dek for his due punishment for failing the revolution, or shall we just end him?"

"I think we should err on the side of mercy," the Admiral said. "I propose dispatching the *Red Hammer* to intercept and destroy the *American Spirit* and her captain."

"Destroy the *American Spirit*?" the Chairman raised her eyebrows. "Maja, you are not one to waste a good resource like a deep space ship."

"An unfortunate necessity, I am afraid," Björk said. "Although we have the upper hand, we cannot afford to be distracted by dealing with a hostile crew and payload of refugees. We must not fail at *Magellan* again. Let's eliminate the distracting variable. Moreover, our need for deep space ships has waned. Our current inventory should service Arara for centuries to come."

"I concur with your compelling logic," the Chairman said, standing up. As she did, the screen-arms gave way automatically, clearing her path as she stepped toward the Admiral and Guard Captain Narlo. "If my Hawk is correct, our greater concern is the *Magnus* and *Magellan*."

"I would not be too worried, Chairman," Björk said. "Cautious, yes. But even with the *Red Hammer* in pursuit of the *American Spirit*, we'll still have three *Utopia*-class warships to deal with *Magnus*. We almost had her at *Marquette*. The Dark Armada will achieve its mission, Chairman. You must have faith in your comrades. This fine fleet will extinguish all light between Arara and Earth."

"My faith in my comrades has been challenged all too often by their incompetence," the Chairman placed a hand on Björk's shoulder and looked down. "Even Kimberly failed. If she could fail, anyone could."

"This fleet will not fail you, I swear it," the admiral said. "There has never been a more powerful force in existence. As the commander of this armada, I will not fail the Infinite Order and humanity's greater good."

"Dear Maja," the Chairman smiled, and now had placed both her hands on the admiral's shoulders. She moved her left hand to gently run her fingers through Björk's long, blond hair. "I am so, so proud of this fleet we have built. And I almost wish I could go with you to Earth to finish this Dark Armada's mission."

The Chairman so named her fleet because the ships' design to minimize light leakage, running dark, so to speak, so that her enemies would not be aware of the oncoming utter destruction until it was too late.

"Sorry, my dear Chairman, that honor belongs to me," Maja smiled proudly. The admiral knew that the closer she brought the Dark Armada to Earth, destroying the waypoints along the way, the more likely her fleet would meet enough resistance to be destroyed. She knew return to Arara would never be possible in her lifetime if she was successful destroying the waypoints. This was a 20-year one-way mission. However, she did believe that it may be possible, however improbable, that the Dark Armada could subdue Earth itself.

Chasm had no interest in Earth, one way or another, only desiring to cut the connection between the home planet and its colony. Admiral Björk held secret delusions she could become the Empress of Earth with a warship enforced reign of terror.

"And *I* must guide Arara into the new era of human perfection," the Chairman said, as if the words themselves weighed her down. "But we digress. Listen. My Hawk reports that the *Magnus* plans to retreat to the local asteroid belt."

"No matter. I will dispatch the *People's Harvest* to eliminate *Magnus*. With *Red Hammer* dealing with the *American Spirit*, that will leave *Utopia* and *Xander's Mace* to subdue and capture *Magellan*."

"I think not," the Chairman objected. "While your distribution of our fleet may have the intended effect, Moreno knows it also gives her the only chance of success. Dispatch the

Red Hammer for the *American Spirit*, but do not pursue the *Magnus*."

"But Chairman, with all due respect, the *Magnus* is no match for *People's Harvest*. I don't see –"

"Yes, you don't see," the Chairman snapped. "You don't see. We defeated the *Magnus* at *Marquette*, but we had the element of surprise. They had little knowledge of our point defense system. In the last two years, they could have developed countermeasures either on *Magnus* or on *Magellan*. They also didn't know that we had weaponized *Marquette*. My Hawk tells me the tables are turned, and that *Magellan* has been weaponized as well. Apparently as a result of the handiwork of the bitch, Amberly Macready."

"Raven One's daughter, again. How did they accomplish such a feat out here?"

"We underestimate Amberly at our own peril. She is more capable than even she knows. She led a secret mission to Fuentes Station, at an abandoned base on an asteroid not far from *Magellan* to recover raw resources to build tech from Earth plans. My Hawk tell me his partner operative, Skylar Trigs, gave his life to try to finish the destruction of *Magellan* and subvert this plan of Moreno's. Trigs was another noble failure. I grow weary of noble failure. Amberly Macready apparently tried to corrupt him, like she did Tigona."

"Kimberly's daughter will not be a nuisance to Chasm for much longer. My strike teams are ready to secure Amberly once we take *Magellan*," Björk vowed.

"Captain Narlo will be seeing to that," the Chairman replied. "I do not trust your strike teams with such a delicate task. Narlo's team will be able to move quickly and be less restricted by … protocol."

"As you wish," the admiral said, slightly offended.

"The moment Macready is onboard *Utopia*, transfer your flag to *Xander's Mace*. Captain Niki will return *Utopia* and me to Arara to complete the great work. Finish the subjection of *Magellan*; and when that is complete, hunt down the *Magnus* if needed. But I expect that won't be the case. She will come to you as long as you hold *Magellan*. Once *Magnus* is dispatched, leave Governor Alif in command of *Magellan*, then proceed to extinguish the rest of Project Waypoint and make Earth suffer."

"I understand," the Admiral said. She would be glad to be rid of the Chairman, and be the master of her own ship – and her own destiny – again. "Soon we shall never speak again, dear Chairman. Please remember the Dark Armada in the coming glory."

"Indeed, I shall, Maja," the Chairman smiled, and grasped the Admiral's hand. "Indeed, I shall."

Amberly had been up most of the 28-hour day. *Magellan* was expected to be in range of the Dark Armada in less than five hours, maybe sooner. She pulled on her nightgown and flopped onto her bed. This may be the last time she would enjoy rest for a while.

She was 19 when the Chasm first moved to destroy *Magellan*. She was only 23 now, but she might as well have been 33 or 63, forced to mature beyond her years. And in her maturity, she knew rest, even a little, would benefit her before the coming storm. She looked out the small window from her dark bedroom into the great void.

The stars moved slowly as the station slowly rotated, and right now, her view was pointed in the direction of Arara. *The end is out there*, Amberly thought, as the stars twinkled her to sleep.

"Amberly," a familiar voice echoed in the sleeping woman's memories. "Did you do it? Did you become the waypoint's greatest scientist?"

"Mom," Amberly said, sitting up in her bed, in her 13-year-old body. "Not really. I'm not sure I'll even get the chance now. They're coming for us. North says she's coming for me."

"Who is coming for you, favored daughter," Kimberly smiled through the inquiry.

"The Chairman."

Kimberly Macready sat on the bed next to Amberly and she started to brush Amberly's straight red hair. "Mom?"

"Yes, sweetheart?"

"Why do we dream?"

"Some people believe that our dreams help us deal with our hardest losses," Kimberly said as she continued to brush.

"I'm sorry I shot you, Mom," Amberly said as she looked over her shoulder at her mom. Kimberly's long dark black hair is as striking as Kora's, Amberly thought. Just like I remembered.

"I deserved to be shot," Kimberly said.

"Why? Because you left me when I was 13? Because you killed dad?"

"I never said I killed your father," Kimberly said, her tone becoming sharp.

"You never said you didn't. Anyway, it doesn't matter. You are here now." Amberly turned and hugged her mom tightly. "I wish we could go back to the day before you left with dad. I would live that day forever and ever, over and over again."

"When you come join me in this dark night, you can," Kimberly said.

"I'm tired, mom," Amberly said. "I'm going to get some sleep."

"Someone is at the door," Kimberly said. "Maybe you should wake up."

Amberly sat up in a start, on the verge of tears and with the words, "I love you mom," on the tip of her tongue.

Verne's attention tone was sounding. Amberly shook her head to clear it and rubbed her eyes.

"What is it, Verne?" Amberly said to her VI. "Can't a girl get some sleep before the end of the world?"

"I'm so sorry. Dek Tigona is here to see you, and I thought you'd want to see him. The *American Spirit* embarks in just under two hours."

"Of course," Amberly said to her VI. She stood up and looked at herself in the vanity. *Decent enough.* "Let Dek in." Amberly stepped from her bedroom into the only common room in her apartment just as Dek Tigona entered.

"Captain Tigona," Amberly smiled. "What a pleasant surprise. And I fear pleasant surprises will be in short supply soon."

"Director Macready, sorry to come by at this hour, but I wanted to say goodbye."

Amberly leaned forward and hugged Dek. "Don't worry, I wasn't going to let you leave without saying goodbye. I was just getting a few z's before I went to my duty station. I get the feeling I'm in for another long day tomorrow."

"For a woman who is on a waypoint about ready to be under siege, you are remarkably calm."

"For a man who is the epitome of grace under fire, you seem

pretty anxious," Amberly said. She looked into his deep blue-gray eyes, reached out and caressed his face slowly. "You have been so good to me, Dek. I literally wouldn't be alive today without you. I am going to miss you so."

"I know we were never going to be anything more than friends –"

"Being good friends is a lot," Amberly said. "Don't discount it."

"I know. I agree. I care deeply for you. So, listen to me: You have to get off *Magellan*. At least for a bit. If you won't come with me on the *American Spirit*, then go with North. Go on the *Magnus*. Go back to the Fuentes Station. You were great there."

"*We* were great there," Amberly corrected, and then shook her head. "I'm sorry, Dek. I'm not going back. This is my home. I belong here. My soul is in the bulkheads, my song is in the gardens."

"Stubborn woman," Dek chided. "You don't have to die here."

"We all die sometime," Amberly said. "That's why life is so valuable. Look at you. You've lived your life to the fullest, on your own terms. You've embraced love. You've found your God. You've grown into the best you."

"Only by grace, from North, Moreno. From Ramos, from you," Dek thought of those who had spared him. He thought of those who had saved him. "In the end, faith in the ultimate grace — God's forgiveness — will make us perfect. God's work. Not human work. That's what Chasm doesn't understand."

Amberly looked at Dek with patient eyes. This was similar to things her father had explained to her a dozen years ago. She didn't want to understand what he was saying then, and she didn't want to understand what Dek was saying now. She accepted that religion was important to those men, and so she resolved to be tolerant. She took a deep breath.

"Dek, I am choosing to become the best me. You've helped me figure out what that is. You brought adventure into my life ever since that crazy bar fight at Rick's. You helped me reconcile with my mother. And when Skylar was killed, you were there for me. Staying here, defending my home: this is the best me."

"I don't want to leave you Amberly," Dek's voice cracked with emotion. "Not again. Let me stay. I want to make sure you will be safe."

"Dek, everything is going to be *okay*," Amberly started tearing up. She knew this was the last time she would see Dek. She chose *Magellan* over him once before, and fate gave them a second chance. To expect a third was absurd. "No matter what happens, I'm going to be okay. Listen. *I know* you would give your life for me. But you can't protect me, Dek. North can't protect me. I have to stand strong myself, here, now."

"That's your mother talking in you," Dek said with resignation.

"It's not about you and me. Those people on the *American Spirit* are counting on you," Amberly encouraged Dek. "They believe in you. You have nearly 3,000 souls trusting you to get them to a safe harbor. They need you now."

"Yes, but *I* need *you.*"

Amberly pulled Dek's head to hers, and kissed him fully. Dek's heartbeat accelerated, and he did everything he could to capture the moment in his memories.

"You believe in prayer now, right?" Amberly asked, as she withdrew from the kiss.

"Do *you*?" Dek said, perplexed at the question.

"I'm not sure," Amberly was honest. "But if you believe, then pray for me. That's the best you can do for me now."

"I will," Dek said, looking down at Amberly's hands which he had taken in his. "To Earth then."

"Mom always told me about the magic of where land meets the sea on the Lewis Islands. I hear the beaches on Earth are breathtaking, too. If you make it there, enjoy them for me."

"I will. Goodbye Amberly Macready, my dear friend," Dek smiled and stepped back toward the exit. "Godspeed saving *Magellan*."

"Bye, Dek."

The rogue slipped out her apartment door, and Amberly was alone again.

Warning klaxons blared. Eight corvettes and three Valkyrie had fired up their propulsion engines as precious atmosphere was sucked into holding tanks. This strike force of short-range ships would delay, distract, disable and provide reconnaissance on the four approaching Chasm ships.

When the hangar was almost a complete vacuum, the space doors opened, and one by one the strike ships maneuvered out into open space.

Many of the pilots were inexperienced, recruited to replace those killed by Chasm during the *Battle of Magellan*. The force was under the command, however, of Eli Wong, who was a combat veteran. Wong was dishonorably discharged from the Marines two years ago for his unwitting involvement in the attempted murder of Dek Tigona. After Wong's impassioned plea for redemption, Moreno allowed him to lead this very dangerous mission to preempt the coming assault of the Dark Armada.

"Strike Team Twig is clear of *Magellan*, and en route to intercept the lead enemy," Wong reported from the bridge of the *M.S.S. Firebird* to the waypoint's flight control. Wong glanced at the three-person skeleton crew manning his Valkyrie. Private Panya was the *Firebird's* gunner.

Like the two other Valkyries in the strike force, the *Firebird* had been equipped with a new gun based on Earth technology brought by the *Magnus*. The weapon was designed to bypass the point defense system by not relying on particles, bullets or other ordnance with significant mass. Instead, high powered radiation beams transferred searing amounts of heat to the target. If a beam could be sustained long enough, the hope was a ship could be damaged or destroyed by internal fires or life support failure from superheating.

Panya, just 17 years old, lost both of her parents in the *Battle of Magellan*. She had spent her teenage years hell-bent on revenge, no matter what it may cost her. Wong was all too willing to indulge Panya.

The navigation station was manned by Lt. Vilek Hudak. Hudak, like Panya, had lost family in the *Battle of Magellan*. His daughter, Nedda had fallen for the Raven One's promise of sanctuary on the *American Spirit*. Hudak had told his 23-year-old daughter to just stay home when Raven One's chaos-creating claims of the end of *Magellan* had been broadcast. but Nedda feared the death that Kimberly Macready promised. Nedda was trampled to death by a crowding mob on the *Magellan* hangar.

"Vilek," Wong said, "please put the aft view on the viewscreen."

An image of a receding waypoint appeared. "Goodbye, dear friend," Wong sighed. "I'll never see you again."

"Wong," Panya said, looking at an indicator flashing on her control screen. "Commander Moreno is on the comm for you."

From the command console, Wong activated the comm.

"Wong," Moreno's voice had a calming effect on her subordinates, making them feel a sense of security. "I want you to take a few pot shots, take a few vids, and then double-time it back to waypoint with your recon. When does your navigator estimate ETA with the enemy's lead ship?"

Wong looked over at Vilek.

"Just under two hours, sir," the bright blonde man reported.

"Intercept in two hours, commander," Wong said over comms to Moreno.

"Hold. Okay. Listen. I just got the calculations from Amberly's data processing group. The eggheads expect that you'll be in signal jamming range of the enemy fleet, assuming they are employing signal disruptors, within the hour, so remember that any recon you get is going to be worthless unless you can retreat to outside of interference range."

"Understood, Commander," Wong said.

"Godspeed then, to all of your ships. Give those Chasm bastards hell."

"You can count on that. Wong out."

When the comm channel had been closed, Wong looked knowingly at Panya and Vilek. They had previously agreed in secret that they would not be returning.

It was a little late, but considering her youth, Wong looked at the young, beautiful ebony face of Panya.

"Are you sure you want to do this?" Wong asked. "We could drop you out in the life pod now. I'll tell *Magellan* I ordered you out."

"No, someone has to make sure at least one ship survives. We all agreed. It's better that we've made the decision now who will cover the retreat. Please let me finish this mission with you," Panya pleaded.

"In the heat of battle is no time to decide who gets to make the honored sacrifice," Vilek added. "Panya knows this."

"Very good. Signal the rest of the ships to pace with us and accelerate us to point-10-c. If we can punch through their fleet and swing around on the back end, some of us may live to clear the jamming field and complete the mission. We'll make sure of it," Wong smiled. "It will be an honor to die with you both today."

Amberly Macready and her team in the Science Corp had been tasked with using the Corp's powerful computers to provide instant data analysis for the decision makers on the bridge.

Amberly's dear friend and co-worker, Lydia, studied several magnetic resonance screens with two other Science Corp analysts.

"No, that will take them too far from the path to *Waypoint Gilbert*," one senior analyst protested.

"But it will almost be impossible to trace the *American Spirit*," the other said.

"Let's just send the navigation chart to the bridge along with our analysis," Lydia suggested. "They can decide."

Lydia looked over her shoulder at two Marines guarding the door. Lt. Mac Dillington and Pvt. Jana Smith, who had been seriously wounded during the *Battle of Magellan*, were both laden with full combat armor and assault rifles. "Why are they here?"

Amberly motioned Lydia away from the others toward the large viewport at the end of the lab. Amberly looked out the window at the docked *American Spirit*, the red, white and blue of Old Glory prominently featured on its hull. "Moreno ordered them to protect me," Amberly whispered, not looking over to Lydia.

"Protect you?"

"Yes. Apparently, North believes that the Chairman is specifically coming for me."

"For you?"

"Crazy," Amberly said. "I am not important. But it made North feel better, so Moreno assigned me my own guard. I didn't tell our colleagues because I didn't want them to worry for no reason."

"Waste of Marines," Lydia, who was physically imposing, especially when juxtaposed next to the petite Amberly. "If anyone tries to mess with you, I'll pound them. Still, it's nice to have a pair of assault rifles at our beck and call. And Mac is looking good these days."

"You better get *that* off your brain," Amberly replied a bit too loud. Everyone in the room looked at the blond and the redhead. Amberly smiled sheepishly, turned back to the window, and continued in hushed tones. "So, you and Skip are really over forever?"

"Oh, Skip," Lydia said. "What did I ever see in him?"

"Well, he was a war hero, I guess."

"Just like you," Lydia smiled.

"And you," Amberly smiled back.

The door to the lab slid open, and the two Marines snapped to attention.

"Commander," Mac said, "it's an honor to see you."

"As you were," North grinned, and extended his hand first to Jana, and then to Mac. "I'm counting on you to protect Amberly."

"I would give my life to save her, sir," Jana said.

"I am sure you would," North said. "Thank you." *Let's hope it doesn't come to that,* he thought.

Amberly's smile broadened and her heart skipped just a bit faster as North's larger-than-life presence filled the lab. He always looked incredible in his dress uniform, but her heart dropped when she realized why he was here. He had come to say goodbye.

And then Amberly frowned. Flora Dillington had entered the room, wearing a form fitting yellow dress that accentuated her feminine curves and cutely matched her blonde hair.

"North, Flora, so good to see you again," Amberly choked out. *I need to stop being so juvenile,* Amberly thought. After all they had been through, she still was envious of her school days rival. Flora worked as a researcher for Waypoint Research Group, the largest private research firm on the waypoints, making her a professional rival to Amberly's Science Corps.

Flora nodded to Amberly, and turned to her brother, Mac. "I'm leaving. WRG is sending us all to *Gilbert*, hoping to save our research in case… in case…"

"…we lose *Magellan*," Mac finished his sister's sentence. "I'm not surprised. We knew this could happen."

"Come with me," Flora pleaded. "Aunt Johanna still lives on Gilbert. She'd be so happy to see you and–"

Mac looked uncomfortably to North and then back to Flora. "You know I can't, sis. I've taken an oath to defend this place. But you go, and be safe. I'll follow when I can. I promise."

Flora gripped her brother in a tight hug. "Thank you for being there for me, Mac."

"I love you, Flo," Mac said, fighting tears. "You better hurry or you'll miss your ride. The *American Spirit* shoves off soon, doesn't it?"

"Half an hour," Flora said as she looked around the room in sequence at Amberly, Lydia and Jana. "Take care of my brother, you guys." Flora grabbed North's hand and squeezed it. "Thanks for walking me down here."

Flora turned and left the lab.

"My ship leaves soon," North looked at Amberly. "Do you have time for a quick walk?"

Lydia piped in, "I'll cover."

Amberly nodded to North and the pair exited.

The main corridor that led from the Science Corps lab to the dining commons at Kepler Tube Station in the Science Quarter was almost chaotic. Hundreds were headed toward the main hangar, laden with luggage, preparing to board either the *American Spirit* or the *Magnus*. Others were going to where they could help for the expected siege of *Magellan* by Chasm's Dark Armada.

Amberly and North walked, hand in hand, against the crowd, as if oblivious to the chaos around them.

"I can't tell you how glad I am that you aren't going far," Amberly glanced at North. "You'll like Fuentes Station. Wait till you see what I've done with the place."

"Let's go into Chinatown," North pointed to the popular restaurant, which, like most shops and eateries, was closed as battle prep had begun. The couple hid behind one of the tall rice grass planters that checkered the Asian restaurant's dining room.

"You know it all started here," Amberly looked down at the shiny metallic tile floor. "My plan to trick you. To steal the access card. You were here with Flora."

"I remember," North smiled. "You were sitting over there with Kora and acting really strange."

"I'm so sorry, North," Amberly looked into his deep brown eyes. "I was so young, so naïve. You have to –"

North silenced her with a tender kiss, brushing his lips into hers. She buried her fingers into his thick brown hair and caressed his mouth with hers. She slowly pulled back and leaned into North's broad shoulder as he tightened his embrace.

"North, if we don't survive this – I mean, there's a good chance that one of us, or both of us–"

"Have a little faith, Red. Moreno has a good plan," North comforted Amberly.

"Do you really think it will work?"

"It's our best shot," North said. "We'll draw off one or two of their warships and take 'em down. Then I'll come back for you."

"Captain Obadiah is paging you," Condi piped up from North's infopad.

"I have to go," North said, his tender demeanor turning urgent. "*Magnus* shoves off soon. Listen to me, Amberly. Stick to Mac and Jana like a magnet. If the Chairman's forces do take *Magellan* … then hide in the safe house. I *will* come back for you, hopefully with the *Magnus*. But even if I have to come back alone—"

"North, you can't protect me," Amberly said, "I have to be able to take care of myself now. You are not responsible for me."

"Of course I am, Red." North leaned into Amberly and gave her quick, hard, closed mouth kiss. He fixed the image of her delicate, soft face and red hair in his mind, and then sprinted into the crowds heading toward the hangar. The XO was needed on the *Magnus*.

L.S. ROEBUCK

CHAPTER FIVE

December 27, 2606. Central Command, Waypoint Magellan, 24 months after the Battle of Marquette.

Skip, now the ranking communication officer on *Magellan*, looked to Moreno and with an official tone reported, "Tight beam message sent both to *Waypoint Gilbert* and long cast to Earth. It will take nine years, but Earth will know *everything* we know about Chasm's armada."

Skip scanned the room. The *Magellan* Cencomm was frenetic. Commander Rita Moreno, barked orders from her command station. Three round balconies of action stations were fully populated with Marines and civilians providing data and issuing orders across the waypoint.

Rita looked up at the large magnetic resonance tactical display projected in the center of the room. The three-dimensional image showed *Magellan* in the center, with large blue dots nearby representing *American Spirit* and *Magnus*. She could see that the *American Spirit* had already pulled away and was quickly putting tens of thousands of kilometers between itself and *Magellan*. Four red dots at the far side of the screen represented the Dark Armada, Utopia-class warships which clearly were intending to engage *Magellan* and were on rapid approach. Speeding toward the red dots was a small yellow triangle, Strike Team Twig, named in honor of the fallen *Magellan* wing commander.

"Estimated weapons range on the enemy fleet?" Moreno called to her ranking tactical officer.

"One hour and 30 minutes," the officer reported. "Three of the ships appear to be decelerating for waypoint rendezvous. One of the ships seems to be maintaining a cruising speed."

"Do they see the *American Spirit*? How would they know…" Moreno wondered out loud. She looked over at her Chief of Staff. "Trish, redirect Strike Force Twig to intercept the warship breaking off from the enemy fleet."

Trish Moreton pushed her dark bangs from her face, activated her comm and relayed the commands.

"Skip, open a channel with the *American Spirit*. I want to talk with Capt. Tigona again before we are jammed by Chasm."

"I have the *American Spirit* now," Skip said, business-like. "XO Boro is on the line."

"Lt. Commander Boro," Rita spoke cleanly. "We're worried that Chasm may try to pursue your flight. We recommend that you take the most evasive course, even if it lengthens your travel time. Boro, where is the captain?"

"I am the captain now," Boro replied through the comm.

"I don't understand," Rita said, furrowing her brow in frustration.

"Dek Tigona resigned his commission. He did not depart with the *American Spirit*," Boro said. Even though she couldn't see him, Rita could hear timidity in Boro's voice.

He should be afraid, Moreno thought. *I am pissed.*

"Well, congratulations, Captain Boro," Moreno said, concealing her displeasure. "We anticipate signal jamming shortly, so this may be *Magellan's* final sign off to *American Spirit*. We are uploading the latest flight analysis data now for the enemy ships. I have dispatched our flotilla to intercept the enemy warship. Hopefully, we'll slow them down. Keep your people safe. Godspeed and get the hell out of here while you still can."

"Wilco, Commander Moreno," Boro said. "We are running at maximum power. And commander?"

"Captain?"

"It was an honor serving under your command," Boro said. "Go easy on Dek. *American Spirit* out."

When the transmission ended, Moreno slowly swiveled to face her Chief of Staff and the tactical display. The *American Spirit* was almost off the display grid now, but one of the Chasm warships was clearly moving to intercept. That ship would be facing down Wong's group in minutes.

"Trish," Rita said evenly. "Have the MPs find Dek and arrest him. And have them pick up his buddies Ramos and Midas for good measure as well. Those clowns must have known Tigona was going to pull something."

"Where do you think Dek is hiding?"

"Dek's not going to be hiding," Rita said. "Just find Amberly, and I'd bet you my supply of Darjeeling tea you'll find that jackass."

Even though the bridge of the *Firebird* was temperature controlled at a perfect 22 degrees, Wong was sweating. He was anxious; the end was near. He was brave enough to die, but his courage only helped him overcome his fear — not eliminate it.

Wong leaned forward in the *Firebird's* command chair. "Hudak, send to *Magellan*, we have visual with the enemy. We're engaging the Chasm warship which appears to have a registry of *Red Hammer*."

"Comms are jammed, Wong," Lt. Hudak said what Wong expected.

"Well, I guess that means we can't ask them nicely to surrender," Wong smirked. "Perfect."

"That ship is running fast," Pvt. Panya spoke up. "If she gets past us, we won't be able to catch it."

"Very well," Wong said, "Flash signal to our ships to enter into chevron formation, weapons charged and free. Hit hard and run. We'll likely only get one shot to slow it down. Valkyries, let's see if we can heat up the ship. Corvettes run escort. Protect us as long as you can if they send their fighters out to engage us. Have all ships confirm."

Hudak programmed the message into the flash signal, which used direct line of sight light beams between the small fleet to transmit messages, avoiding electromagnetic jamming. Within moments, Hudak had received confirmation from all the ships.

"We're good," he said.

"Lock and load, gunner. I'll see if we can get into a parallel course," Wong said. "Let's send these Chasm traitors to hell. Panya, as soon as you are in range, open fire. Focus on the secondary hull of that ship if you can."

From the aft viewport they could see the *Red Hammer* now with the naked eye, a gleaming speck in the distance. Both the Strike Force Twig and the *Red Hammer* were traveling in the same direction, veering off from a return course to *Magellan*. The strike force was just under a thousand kilometers ahead of *Red Hammer*.

"If this ship catches the *American Spirit*," Hudak said, "every soul on that ship is dead."

"There's no way they can catch *American Spirit*," Panya

asserted, but it sounded more like a question. "They have too much of a head start."

"Whoever is calling the shots on *Red Hammer* clearly thinks they can," Wong said.

"Firing in three, two, one," Panya counted down.

The electrical systems on the *Firebird* flickered as what essentially was a giant heat ray drew massive power from the reserve cells.

"I've got a lock on the enemy," Panya informed her shipmates. "Ha ha! No point defense system block, as we expected. Maybe they won't even realize we're cooking them until it's too late."

At first Captain Ai'la'ausd was frustrated that he would not be taking the *Red Hammer* with the rest of the Dark Armada to the glorious subjection of *Magellan*. He already despised the power-hungry Admiral Maja Björk, and the fact the Admiral was sending his ship on this cleanup task to deal with the *American Spirit* was humiliating. He convinced himself he loathed Björk because she was not pure in heart, lacking a true zealousness for the coming utopia. Ai'la'ausd believed Björk's loyalty to the cause was just a means to her own selfish ends. Why the Chairman could not see this befuddled Ai'la'ausd.

In truth, his animosity for his commanding officer sprung from a deeper source. Nearly two decades earlier, after at first entertaining his lover's advances, Maja shunned Ai'la'ausd and used their affair to publicly manipulate him. He was humiliated back then, too, and he believed her kiss-and-tell ultimately cost him a place in the admiralty.

But now, with the prospect of the first skirmish of the Dark Armada in front of him, he was already writing the history of his glorious victory in his head.

The bridge of the *Red Hammer* was nearly identical to that of *Utopia*, and from high on the command platform, Ai'la'ausd could clearly make out the ships of Strike Force Twig.

"Three Valkyrie-class runabouts, escorted by eight corvettes," the junior tactical officer reported.

"Deploy our interceptors. Take out the corvettes first. Please tell the wing commander that if she loses any of her interceptors,

I'm going to toss her out the airlock. And tell her to capture a runabout."

Panya didn't know if she should be pleased or not. The longer the *Red Hammer* didn't realize that the runabouts were superheating its hull, the better. But they had to realize what was going on by now. Was it possible the ray wasn't working?

"We hit that thing with more than a billion joules," Panya said. "Something has to be cooked in there."

"Why haven't they fired back at us?" Hudak asked.

"Maybe they are worried about the risk of firing conventional weapons while traveling so fast?" Wong surmised. "But surely their computers can calculate the firing solutions, even at speed."

"Looks like they want to take us ship to ship. The enemy has launched corvettes," Hudak said, reading his instruments. "They are making an escort formation around the *Red Hammer*. The jammer is off, too!"

"Which means they can't communicate to their corvettes when jamming, either," Wong said. "Hudak, give a status update to *Magellan*. Put me on with the rest of the Strike team.

"Done."

"Wong here. Everyone, this is it. Corvettes, defend the runabouts at all cost. We've got to heat that thing up as much as possible if we are going to have any chance of slowing it down."

Hudak left the channel open.

"Weapons free," said a veteran *Magellan* Marine pilot. "Remember what Sparks said. I'm going to get in close behind Bogie Tango."

"Noooo... no I can't —" another pilot screamed. On the tactical screen, Wong saw two Chasm interceptors converge on one of his corvettes, and the dot representing his corvette disappeared.

"There are too many of them," a young woman pilot shouted over comms.

"Stay cool, Marie," Wong told her. "Remember your training."

"Our bullets, they just disappear," Marie said. "How can anything get past this point defense system."

"You are not close enough, Marie," Wong said. "You can do

this. Let the VI pilot bring you close."

"I'm in behind Bogie Tango," the veteran said. "On his tail, less than a meter, computer pilot on. Firing! Whoooo hoooo!"

Wong saw the dot representing Bogie Tango disappear. The open pilots comm filled with cheers.

"Help, I've been hit. I'm on fire," Wong heard Marie scream as her dot vanished from his screen.

"Damn it, cover your wings," Wong shouted.

"I'm lining up for my next victim. On his tail. No, you can't shake me, Chasm bastard," the veteran announced. Then a loud crunch filled the comms.

"Collision! Collision! Bogie hit the brakes. Canopy is cracked, it's going to give. Sorry Wong, looks like I'm checking–"

Another friendly disappeared from the tactical display.

"We're losing escorts fast," Wong shouted. "Anyone on the Valkyries have any idea if we are actually doing any damage to *Red Hammer*?"

Ai'la'ausd smiled as another enemy corvette was destroyed. "These loyalists are desperate. They must know this is a suicide mission. Tell the flack cannons to prepare for kamikaze tactics. Any chance they are hiding a nuke on one of those runabouts?"

"I am not seeing a radiation signatures, but they could be hiding it," the junior tactical officer suggested. "Why else would their three runabouts not be making any sort of attack? Clearly, their corvettes are positioned to defend the runabouts?"

The engineering liaison shouted from the base floor of the bridge. "Captain, we have several fires reported in the far forward decks. Damage control is on the scene."

"Fires? Fires! How?"

"Damage control reports 24 fatalities in the forward life support maintenance."

"Cause?"

"Some sort of life support failure? These people are … fried," the officer reported.

"Captain," the liaison called out. "Chief says they are hitting the ship with some sort of heat ray. They are super heating the secondary hull bow and everything touching it is melting or burning."

"What's the risk?" Ai'la'ausd asked. "Connect me directly to the Chief."

"Captain," the chief engineer's voice came over comms. "They've figured out a way to hit us a heat weapon. I think they could compromise the hull in minutes."

"Damnit! Wing commander, did you copy that? Take out those runabouts now!"

"We just lost the *Old Glory*," Hudak said, looking up from his instruments. "They are coming for us."

"The game is up," Wong said. "They were probably trying to capture us. No longer, now they realize we are a threat. Hopefully we've done some damage. All ships retreat. Retreat. Best speed back to *Magellan*." Wong disabled the ship-to-ship comms.

"Let's do what we came to do," Hudak said. "It's been an honor."

"I hope they can get away," Panya said. "Let's get closer to improve the effectiveness of the ray while we still can."

The *Firebird* shuttered violently.

"Critical hit," the VI announced. "Evacuate immediately."

"The hull's been compromised," Hudak shouted, as the trio heard the distinct hiss of air escaping into space.

"I'm hitting our breaks," Wong smiled. "Let's see if we can get them to smash into us and cause some real damage. To hell with these guys."

Ai'la'ausd smirked as, one-by-one, he saw the enemy craft disappear from his screen. Then he noticed the lead Valkyrie slowing rapidly.

"Evasive! Don't let us…"

The nose of *Red Hammer's* secondary hull punched into the *Firebird* at thousands of kilometers a second. The Valkyrie's bulkheads splintered into a million shards thrust into every direction. The energy released from the impact disintegrated most of the runabout, including *Firebird's* three passengers.

The collision ripped a hole in the *Red Hammer* nearly 20 meters wide. A half dozen members of *Red Hammer's* Alpha Damage Control team working to extinguish fires in the second hull's life support center were crushed by the blunt force trauma. Another half dozen responders were riddled to death with bulkhead shards. Of the remaining eight that weren't killed by impact, seven were sucked out into space. The sole survivor of Alpha Damage Control Team was Trident Lews, a paranoid Chasm recruit who always tethered and wore a vac suit when working near the ship's exterior skin.

The bridge of the *Red Hammer* was a whirlwind of chaos. Captain Ai'la'ausd pounded his fist on the tactical display. "Order! Everyone, calm down."

The nearly 80 people on the bridge stopped and turned their attention to the captain.

"Engineering? What's the damage?"

The engineering liaison read from his infopad. "Hull breach in secondary life support. Chief has switched both hulls to primary."

"What's the report from Alpha Damage Control? Good thing they were already in the area," Ai'la'ausd looked to his first officer, Gee Comisky, a cohort-born from Arara. Comisky was probably the most jovial Chasm officer alive, thus his ashen demeanor was something his colleagues had never seen before.

"Engineer Lews reports that she is the sole survivor and is requesting rescue," Comisky stumbled over the words.

"Twenty of our best Chasm engineers were in that unit," Ai'la'ausd cried out. "Curse the dirty loyalists. Damn them."

"Beta Damage Control reports they are *en route*," the engineering liaison shared.

"Comisky, increase our speed to maximum velocity, and make sure our computers calculate the first intercept opportunity once we locate the *American Spirit*. She can't be far."

"But sir, with the secondary hull compromised, stressing the engines could invite additional catastrophe. Let us inspect –"

"Silence, ingrate. Your risk assessment doesn't concern me," Ai'la'ausd pounded the table again. "The crew and passenger complement of *American Spirit* is more than 2,000 correct? They will pay us back 100 times in blood what they took from us."

The captain looked to his communication officer. "Send to the Admiral: We have totally vanquished their advance defenses and are now in pursuit of *American Spirit*. Please ask if the Hawk on *Magellan* has any additional data on the course of *American Spirit*. Until then, let's make our best guess."

Moreno felt like her teeth had been punched out. She stared blankly at the spot on her tactical display where her small fleet had been. "Can someone get me confirmation we lost the whole strike force?"

Skip spoke up. "I'm sorry, Commander. Chasm doesn't appear to be bothering to jam signals anymore. None of the *Magellan* ship transponders are pinging."

"Damnit," Moreno said under her breath. "Wong got his suicide mission, after all."

Trish looked up from her infopad. "Capt. Obadiah reports the *Magnus'* engines are at full spool and they are ready to speed out of here at your command."

"Great. We don't want them to leave too soon. If they don't draw off–"

A commotion at the far side of the bridge caught Moreno's attention. She heard voices arguing.

"No drinking on duty," said one officer.

"Don't you get it? This is the end of the waypoint," the other said. "Kato, give me a stiff one!" A third man handed him a shot glass, and the officer immediately downed it.

Anticipating Moreno's whim, Trish Moreton had traversed the dozen yards to the other side of the Cencomm to find Kato, bartender from Rick's, with a cart of liquor. And not the putrid synthetic stuff, but actual bottles of whiskey and vodka.

"Attention!" Trish said after she cleared her throat. The two officers arguing, Beck and Maxis, immediately snapped into form. "What the hell is going on here?"

Trish turned to Kato. "And who let you in here? And where did you get those?"

Kato looked a little sheepish, but had a sly grin on his face. "Well, I've been saving these for a special occasion, but now that Chasm is going to destroy the waypoint, I thought it my patriotic duty to not let these go to waste. Thought the Marines up here could use a little nip to lift their … spirits."

"I'm sorry, how did you get past security?"

"Well, it cost me a half-bottle of vintage *Waypoint Polo* brandy," Kato shrugged.

"You bribed a Marine with alcohol?"

"So what? Did you not hear me? It's the end of the waypoint isn't it? The *American Spirit* is gone. I didn't get a seat out of here. What are you going to do? Arrest me? There is no escape. Let's enjoy our last moments!"

Moreno and Skip walked up behind Trish's interrogation of Kato. Beck and Maxis stood motionless at attention.

"Kato?" Skip was surprised to see his favorite bartender. "What are you doing here?"

"Libations for the end of the world, friend," Kato said, indicating his service cart with an open hand. "Care for a shot?"

"Yes," Skip said, seeing the real liquor and then eyeing Moreno, "but I'm on duty."

Moreno turned away once she realized what was going on and headed back to her command station. "I don't have time for this; deal with it, Trish."

"Yes, ma'am."

Kato eyed two heavily armed Marines with MP designations on their combat packs walk in through the main door. "Wow, that was fast."

"They're not here for you, idiot," Skip said.

"But they will do," Trish said. She waved the MP over, and then noticed who the military police officers had in tow: Dek, Ramos and Midas. "I'll take these three to the Commander. Would you mind detaining this bartender and confiscating his booze?"

"Yes, ma'am," the MP saluted the Commander's Chief of Staff.

Dek caught Moreno's eye. She turned from him and back to Skip, who had returned to the communication station. "Get me the *American Spirit*. Make sure the channel is secure."

"Chanel secure. Not even Kimberly Macready could crack it. Well, maybe she could. But she's dead."

"Skip!" Moreno chided.

"Lt... er... Captain Boro is on," Skip said.

"Commander," Boro's deep voice resonated through the comms. "I didn't expect to hear from you aga—"

"We found your captain, Boro," Moreno scolded. "And if Chasm wasn't sending a warship after you, I'd make you come back and get him."

"I'm deeply sorry," Boro said with all sincerity.

"I'm not," Dek spoke up. Midas elbowed him. "Ow."

"No one asked you," Moreno said, then focused back on her comms chat. "Listen, Boro. Fortunately, the *Red Hammer*, the Chasm vessel pursuing you, seems to have guessed your heading incorrectly, as we planned. But Amberly's team is telling me, based on *Red Hammer's* current trajectory and acceleration, she could see you with high powered radar in about 10 minutes on your current heading. Recommend you divert to heading Magellan relative X, 33-degrees, Y, 210-degrees, Z, 12 degrees."

"But that will add months to our trip," Boro said. "Are you sure?"

"I supposed the real question is, do you trust Amberly's math?"

"I do," Boro said.

Kato spoke up. "Listen, I really need to go settle my affairs, Commander. I'm sorry to have bothered your men. May I go now?"

Moreno frowned, then nodded. Kato grabbed his cart, pulled the shot glass from Beck's hand, and left through the main portal.

Moreno studied the tactical. "Boro, if the *Red Hammer* finds you, you are all dead."

"I am aware," Boro said. "I must go and see to it that they don't. Thank you, Commander Moreno. Oh, and so long, Dek Tigona. I hope Rita doesn't throw you out the airlock." Boro let out a reverberating guffaw before closing the channel.

Moreno looked sternly at Dek.

"I don't think this is funny," Dek said.

"I'm glad to know that, Dek," Moreno said. "What am I going to do with you?"

"Assign me to Amberly's guard detail?" Dek suggested.

"Commander! We're being hailed by the *Utopia*," Skip said, and suddenly all the commotion around the bridge came to a stop.

"Secure the bridge," Moreno said. "Trish, everyone here have security clearance?"

"Except those three?" Trish thumbed over at Dek, Ramos and

Midas.

"Fine, I know Ramos can keep a secret," Moreno said. She sat down in the Commander's chair and took a deep breath. "Weapons control, bring all particle beams to bare on the lead ship. Time to firing range?"

The officer at the weapons control spoke up. "Maybe 10, 12 minutes."

"Prepare to fire the minute we can lock on target. Let's hope this plan works," Moreno said. "Trish, signal Capt. Obadiah, it's time to get the *Magnus* out of here. Hopefully they'll follow him. Dek, anything I should know before I talk to these traitors?"

"They believe their cause is just," Dek said, "just like I used to. If you believe you are correct, you are willing to sacrifice more. They believe they are on the right side of history."

"*Magnus* is away," Trish reported what everyone could see on the tactical. The dot representing *Magnus* started putting distance between itself and *Magellan's* dot.

"Good," Moreno said. "Okay, Skip, patch them through."

"*Utopia*, I'm connecting you to the Commander now," Skip said, attempting to hide his fear.

"This is Commander Moreno of the *Magellan* Marines," Rita announced. "Who am I addressing?"

"My name isn't important. But you know me as the Chairman," an icy voice said over the comms. "Kimberly told me so much about you, Rita. You are a smart woman. You know you can't win."

"Maybe I'm smarter than you know," Moreno barbed.

"I doubt it. I *am* getting *Magellan*. I'm sure you'll put up a fight with whatever slipshod weapons you installed on your magnificent waypoint in the last few years."

"Whatever do you mean?" Moreno spoke slowly. "The waypoints aren't weaponized. You know that."

"I choose to ignore your lie. Make it easier on yourself. On your people. If I must take *Magellan* by force, I may need to cleanse the waypoint of its residents. Surrender to me unconditionally, and I will spare half the lives of any *Magellans* who pledge fealty to me. Surrender Amberly Macready to me, and I will spare everyone's life. Life is precious and shouldn't be wasted. Don't you agree Rita?"

Dek could barely contain himself. His head filled with rage and fear for Amberly. *Focus, Dek, focus*, he thought to himself. *Calm down. You can't help Amberly unless you are cool. Collected.*

"Amberly Macready?" Moreno asked. "Who's she?"

"I chose to ignore your lie, again."

"Very well, Madam Chairman," Moreno spoke slowly, "Please know I understand the situation here perfectly. I understand the odds. Those odds are that the good people of *Waypoint Magellan* may not live to see another day. All things come to an end; it is the nature of universe. Whether by random happenstance or by divine design, I can't say, but the natural order will prevail over Chasm. Maybe not today, but someday. Your evil will not stand."

"Evil. Tsk. Tsk," the Chairman's voice came over the cencomm's speakers. "Commander, I am trying to uplift humanity. We are purging evil from human existence. The only good is the *common good*. We will eliminate war, racism, sexism, inequality, selfish individualism. All humans will work together, giving according to their gifts and taking only what they need."

"Equality at what price? At the price of our freedom. All our freedom. That price is too high," Moreno said. "We would be equal, true. Equal *slaves* of the state. No thanks."

"The freedom you cherish so much is an illusion," the Chairman countered. "Your desire for freedom is nothing more than your excuse to be selfish, to put you and your loved ones ahead of everyone else. Your freedom is chaos. We will provide a new order to purge the chaos. We will burn everyone who opposes us. Your fleet of fighters attacking *Red Hammer*, for example. You tossed their lives away needlessly."

The loss of Wong and his group was so fresh in Moreno's mind, she barely had time to process it. But it fueled a righteous anger burning deep inside her.

"Those men and women died with honor," Moreno said. "They gave their lives for what they believed in. You think Chasm is the only side that knows sacrifice? I swear to you, we will fight to the very last soul."

"Don't be a fool, Moreno. Don't sacrifice the children of *Magellan* so easily," the Chairman implored. "Give me Macready. Surrender. My resolve is stronger than yours. We will lay waste to

Magellan. Know this: my Dark Armada will not return to the glories of the new utopia on Arara. She will go to Earth, waypoint by waypoint, cleansing with fire, sending these monuments of old humanity out of existence. And when the Dark Armada arrives at Earth, they will inflict as much pain as possible in their sacrifice. The message to the corrupt people of Earth: to never, ever attempt to bridge the Chasm. Perfection doesn't need you. Perfection doesn't want you. Perfection will stand apart from you."

"You are insane," Moreno said. "You cannot edit out your humanity."

"Last chance. Surrender now. Give me Raven One's daughter and give your people hope to join perfection."

"Kimberly Macready made us the same offer. It didn't go well for her."

"Commander Rita Moreno," the Chairman said. "I will make sure the generations of Arara will know you for the cowardly villain that you are, who caused the deaths of thousands for her selfish vanity."

"If our choice is slavery or death, we choose death."

"So be it."

The Chairman leaned back in her throne-like chair, running her hands over her tightly bound, silver-white hair. Her über-dark eyes were moist, and a single tear rolled down her pale cheek.

"She died here," the Chairman said, looking into the vast expanse of space projected as the forward view of *Utopia*. Admiral Björk flanked the Chairman, standing and also looking out into deep space. Björk felt a touch of nausea from the inertia dampeners as the *Utopia* entered the final stage of deceleration. *Waypoint Magellan* would soon be in visual range. The Chairman turned and looked over her shoulder at the admiral. "Her body is floating out here, somewhere."

Maja almost gasped when she noticed the tear streak on the Chairman's face. "For Kimberly?" she asked.

"No, for the people of *Magellan* who will die on the pikes of Moreno's vanity. The time has come for you to take full command of the Dark Armada, Maja. As soon as we have Amberly, I will make haste for Arara. I grow weary of space and long for the cool winds of the Lewis Islands. When this war is over, I am going to build a grand retreat there for the leaders of Chasm to rest, reflect and transcend as we guide humanity toward perfection. I will name this palace after Raven One, who came to us from the Lewis Islands. I can picture every detail already in my mind."

"I'm sorry I won't be able to see it," Maja said.

"And I'm sorry I won't be able to see the fires blaze on every waypoint between here and Earth," the Chairman smiled at the thought.

Yeoman Carnell bounded up to the command platform. The admiral had to contain her revulsion at his presence. "Madam Chairman," Carnell saluted. "The bridge sends word that your *Magellan* Hawk has transmitted the new flight path for *American Spirit*."

"So, the drunkard is not a complete failure after all," the Chairman swiveled her chair to face Maja and the Yeoman. "Maja, order the *Red Hammer* to intercept and destroy the *American Spirit* with due haste. Go ahead and transfer your flag to *Xander's Mace* now. Captain Narlo's strike team will have Macready's daughter in hand shortly."

"As you command. Today will be a glorious day for Chasm, and a turning point in human history. Goodbye, Chairman."

"Success, Admiral."

CHAPTER SIX

December 27, 2606. The Siege of Waypoint Magellan.

Moreno studied the tactical screen. The Dark Armada was almost in firing range. The *American Spirit* was evading the *Red Hammer*. The *Magnus* was pulling far away from *Magellan*, accelerating rapidly, thousands of kilometers now between the two.

Come on, take the bait, Moreno thought.

Governor Thor Rillio had just entered the command center, with his chief of staff, Micha Gonzalez, a young, round woman with unremarkable features, in tow. "What's the status?" he asked as he stepped up to the bridge. Rita caught his eyes and just shook her head.

"Commander," a junior tactical officer shouted from his station, "the *Red Hammer* is changing course. It's on a direct intercept with *American Spirit's* flight path."

"How is that possible?" Moreno barked. "It's like they know the exact –"

"The Hawk is here," Dek interjected, starting to scan the room to see reactions. "We knew there was another Hawk. She must be here on the bridge."

"Or *he,*" Micha said, accusingly toward Dek.

"Skip," Moreno called her comm officer, "warn Boro!"

"Already done," Skip said, pulling a comm pod out of his ear.

"Dirty hell. The *American Spirit* is found," Midas said. "Now they know where to look. It's only a matter of –"

"God help them," Ramos, the itinerant pastor who stood next to Dek, bowed his head.

"Dek is clearly feeding his Chasm compatriots information," Micha said, loudly. "Commander, how can he be here on the bridge? We can't take the chance–"

"I am not a Hawk," Dek sighed. "We've already been through this. How could Skylar have been transmitting information to me on *Magellan* when I was with him on Fuentes Station?"

"And why would one Hawk – Skylar – order the death of another?" Midas reminded. "I saved Dek from Skylar's airlock."

"We don't have time for this," Moreno said. "Thor, get your staff in line or get her out of my command center."

The tactical screen blipped. "Dark Armada in weapons range," the gunnery officer informed from his station.

"Hit them with everything we got, heat and particle," Moreno clenched her fist.

"Fire order confirmed."

"Permission to go to the Science Corp labs?" Dek implored.

"Fine," Moreno spit. "Take those two with you." Moreno waved at Midas and Ramos. She needed to focus, and Dek and his compatriots were potential distractions. "If we survive this, I am going to bring you up on charges of dereliction of duty."

"I've been accused of worse," Dek smirked as the trio exited to find Amberly.

"Three Utopia-class vessels are heading for *Magellan* intercept," the tactical officer reported.

Thor nervously watched the tactical display. "No one is following *Magnus*. The Hawk must have disclosed our divide and conquer strategy. Call the *Magnus* back!"

"Captain Obadiah knows the score," Moreno said. "He knows our contingency."

"Based on their deceleration trajectories, I believe the enemy intends to forcibly dock," Trish predicted.

"It's going to be a ground war. Trish, distribute the Marines. Make your best guess where they are going to land. And Thor, make sure your police are enforcing the civilian lockdown. We're going to be shooting to kill."

"All weapons firing on the lead ship," the gunnery officer said.

Admiral Björk stood on the command platform of the bridge of *Xander's Mace*. She was glad to be finally out of the shadow of the Chairman, hopefully for the rest of her life.

"Admiral, point defense systems are repelling particle beams, but we're showing the secondary hull superheating."

"That's what *Red Hammer* warned us about," Maja replied. "Thruster controls, put us into a random wobble pattern, so we are not exposing the same part of our hull. All hands, all decks, prepare for forced docking and extreme maneuvers."

Maja sat in the command chair and strapped herself down. Across the bridge, other officers did the same.

"ETA *Magellan*, four minutes," the navigation officer spoke up.

The bridge began to sway erratically. Some of the officers reacted with whoops. The tactical officer regurgitated the meal he ate a half hour ago.

"Comms, put me on with the fleet," the admiral said, unfazed by the additional motion.

"Admiral, you're hot," the communication ensign confirmed.

"Heroes of the Dark Armada," Maja spoke, "today you are chosen. Chosen to make our Chasm permanent. Chosen for glory. This day, we master *Magellan*. We will make the waypoint a vanguard for Arara. Should Earth attempt to bridge our chasm to corrupt Arara, and our Chairman's Infinite Order, this waypoint will stand ready. We, however, will go on and burn Project Waypoint, station by station. We bring a message to the forefathers: *The child has supplanted the parent. We are the new beacon of humanity. Earth must die and make way for the future.* Comrades, remember, the Chairman is watching. She will return to Arara with tales of your bravery and sacrifice for the greater good. I look forward to celebrating our victory today. We are ushering in the never-ending age of human perfection. Björk out."

The bridge crew cheered, though the bravado was somewhat muted by the rotating ship movement.

"Chief reports wobble maneuvers are effectively distributing the heat. No one place is getting super-heated, but he's worried that she cannot vent heat fast enough. The whole *Xander's Mace* could be in danger," the engineering liaison explained.

"How long till we reach critical temperatures?" the admiral said, wiping her brow, not sure if the room was getting hotter or her perspiration was psychosomatic.

"Seven, eight minutes?" came the reply.

"Good. More than enough time. Strike commanders, prepare to board."

On rapid approach, the Dark Armada was now visible on *Magellan* to the naked eye. *Xander's Mace* and *People's Harvest* were out in front with a flotilla of support Valkyries and escort corvettes. Though they were close, the battle group was still difficult to spot. The ships were nearly black in color, and unlike most ships, had few exterior ports shining light. *Xander's Mace* appeared to spin like a wobbling top. The point defense system deflecting the ineffective particle beams created an unintentionally beautiful dazzling spectrum of sparks. *Utopia* had already come to a complete stop relative to *Magellan*, 50 kilometers away.

Both *Xander's Mace* and *People's Harvest* had two arm-like devices extending from their primary hulls. These siege gangways were designed with a boring head to cut through the outer hull of a waypoint and then create a hard seal, allowing Chasm shock troops safely inside.

The gunnery officer looked up at Moreno. "Ma'am, our weapons fire appears to have minimal effect on the *Xander's Mace*. And they are too close to the waypoint – we can't train our fire."

The tactical officer looked up from his magnetic resonance screen. "Looks like they will lock near the 170-degree point and 230-degree point, State and President Quadrants."

"Trish, you have your deployment orders. Get the Marines moving."

"Wilco," Trish responded and began to punch commands into her terminal.

A loud creaking sound reverberated shook the command center.

"They are here," Skip said. "They've locked onto us. Where's the *Magnus*?"

North looked at the tactical map at the command table on the bridge of the *Magnus*. "Dammit, turn this thing around faster!"

Blight looked at the XO. "North, the inertial dampeners are at full capacity. If we hit the brakes any harder, we will all be paste."

The captain looked at the tactical map. "We're not going back to *Magellan* yet."

"What!?!" North looked at the captain, confusion fueled the desperation burning in his brown eyes.

"We can't abandon *Magellan*!" Rhodes agreed.

The captain ignored his XO and his XO's protégée. "Navigator, lay in an intercept course for the *American Spirit*," Obadiah commanded. "If we go to *Magellan* now, it's three against one. We can save *American Spirit* if we catch the *Red Hammer* off guard."

Kora Macready Wilder watched through the exterior window of her apartment as the four arms extended from the two Dark Armada ships smashed into the hull. She saw the grinding teeth on the boring head shimmer in the starlight just before it began to chew through the carbon grey outer hull of *Magellan*. Fear froze her.

The sound of shredding metal reverberating through the bulkheads. The extreme shrieking noise terrorized Alroy, nearly four, as he woke from a nap.

"Momma!"

Kora stepped into Alroy's room and grabbed the boy's hand. The shrieking stopped, but was followed by a series of pops. Kora's info pad pulsed, and she saw that her husband was calling.

"Trot!" Kora shouted over Alroy's crying. "What is going on?"

"Kora, you and Alroy get over to Amberly's lab now! Chasm troops have boarded *Magellan* not far from you. Hurry. I'll meet you there. I'm trying to get them to send some troops to get you, but it's all crazy. We're going to try to get Amberly out on a corvette to *Magnus*. You're going with them."

"What?! What about you?"

"We'll talk about it when you get here. Move! Get out of there before the Chasm troops find you!"

In an instant Kora looked around the apartment that had been her home for her whole life. She and Amberly had inherited the place when her parents, Alroy and Kimberly were allegedly lost in space a decade ago. When she married Trot, Amberly moved out, and now Kora's young family made it home. The memories of mom and dad bringing her baby sister home from the medical center for the first time, of her long talks with Amberly about boys, of her nesting when she was expecting baby Alroy – they all flooded her mind in a second. *Will I ever see this place again?* Kora thought.

Then she heard gunfire.

She grabbed Alroy, opened the front apartment portal and peered down the thin hallway that terminated at her door. Chasm troops were going through the apartments in her row, one by one. She saw them pull out her neighbors three doors down, Mars and Maria Dino.

"Do you have any kids?" the masked Chasm trooper asked, gun pointed at Maria.

"No, we don't have any kids," Mars said.

"Are you sure?" the trooper insisted.

"Go to hell," Maria said.

The trooper pulled the trigger on his automatic rifle, the Dinos fell to the floor, dead.

"Maria!" Kora shrieked. The Chasm trooper, clad in blue-green armor, looked down the hall and saw Kora and Alroy. Two other troopers joined him.

"Hey, you, surrender your kid," the trooper, five yards from the front door to Kora's apartment. Kora pushed Alroy back into the apartment and followed.

"Bob, close the door!" Kora shouted at her apartment's VI. "And lock it!"

Bullets flew as the door slid closed. The door snagged a lock of Kora's long raven-black hair, pulling Kora's head painfully towards the now sealed portal.

Little Alroy was on the floor, confused and crying. "Don't worry, baby. Daddy knows we are here."

Bullets pelted the outside of the door as Kora struggled to free herself. "Alroy, baby, can you bring me a knife from the dish drawer?"

"Momma! No carrying knifes," Alroy whimpered the household rule.

"I know, buddy, but just this once," Kora smiled through tears of pain and fear. "Get the sharp one."

"Yes, momma," Alroy walked the few paces across the living area to the food prep station and found the sharp knife.

"Careful, but hurry," Kora pleaded, stretching one hand out towards Alroy while trying to free her hair with the other.

She noticed the atmosphere indicator, the red-green light on every portal in the waypoint that indicated it was safe to open, was flashing. The Chasm troops were hacking the door. "Bob, send a message to Trot. Tell him we're trapped by Chasm and in trouble."

Kora took the knife from Alroy and began sawing the thick black lock of hair caught in the door. She was pulling her head back as hard as she could with her neck, and when she had cut enough of the strands, the remaining ones ripped out of her scalp.

The door whooshed open, and the trooper stood in the portal, surprised to see Kora standing so close on the other side. She instantly drove the sharp knife into the neck of the Trooper, severing his trachea. He fell to the ground, gurgling a call for help.

The two troopers backing him up raised their rifles at Kora. "Give us the kid, and we won't make him watch as we shoot you," one said. "Drop the knife."

Kora raised her hands in surrender, the bloody knife clinked as it hit the hard, metallic floor. "You wouldn't dare kill me," Kora said.

"The hell we wouldn't," the trooper replied, while her partner rendered medical aid to their comrade with the lacerated windpipe.

"I am the daughter of Raven One," Kora announced.

"You don't look like the pics we have been given," the trooper said.

"Quit stalling; we have work to do," the other said. "She's obviously lying. Look at her hair."

"Oh, I'm not Amberly. I'm the older sister."

"I better call it in. Chasm Trooper Tango Beta Theta Two to command deck, we have–"

The two uninjured Chasm trooper spasmed and fell to the floor. Kora's eyes were wide.

"Praise God," she said, as see saw a squad of four marines down the hall, sprinting toward her, stun guns drawn.

"Mrs. Wilder," said Marcos DeLeon, the Marine squad leader, "are you okay?"

"Marcos, I'm so glad it's you," Kora gave the Marine a shaky hug. Both Marcos and Kora had been on the *Magellan* hangar deck during the Battle of *Magellan*, and the violence brought back the horrific feelings of that fight.

Kora called to her hiding son. "Baby, it's safe. These are the good guys. Let's go find daddy."

The red-headed boy popped out from and Kora hoisted him up on her hip. "Hold on as tight as you can to momma, okay? Can you show me your strongest muscles?" Alroy nodded, determined, and pressed his against in his mother's neck.

"Private, please escort Mrs. Wilder and her son to the Science Corp labs, and report to me when they are safe," Marcos ordered his subordinate.

"Yes sir," the Marine, Inon, saluted. She led the pair from the Kora's apartment on the waypoint rim, down the hallway toward the station interior. Inon figured if they could get to the Tube without running into anymore Chasm, they would likely be home free to the labs.

When the three had left the corridor, DeLeon holstered his stun gun and pulled out his pistol.

"We can't detain these guys; there are probably a hundred more on the ship," Marcos said to the other Marine on his squad.

Marcos put one bullet in each head of the two stunned Chasm troopers. He looked at the third, slowly suffocating. The trooper extended a shaky, bloody open hand towards Marcos.

"I'm sorry," Marcos said as he put down the third trooper. He tapped on his comm unit. "We've secured Trot's family and neutralized a Chasm squad. Waiting for next deployment orders."

Jana, Mac and Trot were double-checking their weapons, loaded and hot for action. Trot stood out from the Marine pair in his police uniform.

"Dammit, Trot," Amberly protested to her brother-in-law. "I am not leaving *Magellan!*"

"Sorry, Amberly. Decision's made. Commander Moreno and the governor have no intention of handing you over to Chasm. The *Magnus* is the last safe place left."

"This is my home. *This* is my life," Amberly waved her arm around to indicate the stellar radiation laboratory in the Science Corp headquarters.

"At least I got Moreno to agree to let Kora and little Alroy go with you," Trot implored. "Amberly, this is as much an attempt to save my family as it is to keep you safe. Please, for my sake, and

Alroy's, get to that corvette. There's no telling what Chasm will do to the survivors, if they intend to leave any."

"What about Lydia? Midas? The Dinos?" Amberly protested. "They just have to stay here and die? What about you, Trot?"

"Mars and Maria are already dead!" Trot was nearly shouting, then he lowered his voice and repeated himself. "Amberly, the Dinos are dead. Chasm is murdering everyone, only sparing children at this point."

"That's what Chasm wants — the children so they can indoctrinate them," Dek Tigona said as he stepped through the lab door along with his old shadows, Midas and Ramos. Midas and Dek carried stun guns, and a variety of explosive grenade-like devices on weapons belts. Amberly was not surprised to see Ramos dissimilarly armed: He carried a rare, worn paper copy of the Bible. She was, however, *shocked* to see Dek.

"Dek," Amberly ran to the rogue and gripped his right hand with both of hers. "I thought you were on the *American Spirit*."

"I went AWOL. I'll probably go back to the brig for that, if we survive," Dek looked at Midas and Ramos and back to Amberly. "They are coming for you Amberly. We are going to make sure you are safe, or die trying."

The old men agreed with affirmative grunts.

"Dek, we've been through this. I told you —"

"You don't understand. The Chairman tried to make a deal to spare half of the people of *Magellan* in return for handing you over to them. Moreno told the Chairman to go lick dirt."

"What? Take the deal!" Amberly said. "Are you all crazy?"

"No deal," Dek smiled sadly. "The Chairman doesn't make demands here. After all my years believing in Chasm, I finally realized that *every individual has value*. And when we are willing to harm an individual for the so-called common good, it diminishes us all."

"But I am willing to sacrifice myself," Amberly said. "Why can't you understand that? My dad would talk about 'no greater love' than to give your life for the people you love. Isn't that what you believe now?"

"She has you there, Dek," Ramos said half under his breath.

"Not helping, old man," Midas chided.

"Eli, Maria, Mars, whose next?" Amberly said. "I don't want

to lose anyone else."

"Amberly," Midas softly placed his large hand on her shoulder, "we don't want to lose *you*."

Amberly looked around at the faces in the room. Jana Smith was a true war hero, Purple Heart recipient from the Battle of *Magellan*. Lydia was a brilliant researcher and loyal friend. Mac was a loving brother and dedicated solider. Dek Tigona was a selfless, gifted leader and valued partner. Ramos had shepherded his flock for generations. And Midas' grandfatherly wisdom was only surpassed by his generous spirit.

"All this for me? I'm not special. This is insane." Amberly looked at the floor and spoke quietly.

"North said when he was captured by the Chairman, she wanted revenge," Ramos said, "for the death of Kimberly Macready."

"Revenge *is* a powerful motivator," Midas agreed.

"Could be more than that," Dek explained. "The Chairman took a special interest in your mother, partially because of her intellect. She had no equal. I saw her... brainpower first hand. And we know a child's intelligence is determined by genetics and training – nature and nurture. In the tube-born cohorts, rumors were Chasm operatives started secretly reviving illegal experiments with gene splicing. I'd bet a protein ration the Chairman wants to exploit your genes in developing ...I dunno...um... smarter people for her new order? You are the daughter of the Raven One."

"But I am not Raven One."

"Genetically, you are all that's left of her," Dek said. "You and Kora."

"Oh no," a frightening thought hit Amberly. "Does the Chairman know about Alroy?"

"With an active Hawk on board, there's a good chance," Dek frowned.

"All the more reason," Trot told Amberly, "you must go. Get all the Macready's off this waypoint. Take a corvette and rendezvous with *Magnus*."

Amberly knew Trot was right. Her heart wanted her to stay here with the people she loved and fight for her home. But in her head, she resigned herself to Trot's plan.

Lydia looked up from her terminal. "Tactical reports a sizable Chasm force is getting close to cencomm. Once they get to the command center, they'll have a direct path to us and the hangar, and you won't be able to escape."

"Kora will be here any minute," Trot said. "Once she arrives, Jana, Mac and I will escort you to the hangar. Jana is corvette rated. She'll be your pilot."

"We'll help with the escort," Midas said, referring to himself, Dek and Ramos.

"Of course, you will," Amberly smiled, resigned. "Thank you."

"Inon just signaled Kora's party is just past Chinatown," Mac announced.

"Okay, we'll meet them at the main hangar," Trot said. "Jana, you ready?"

"Locked and loaded," she nodded. "Let's get the Macready sisters off station. If we're lucky, we can share our bullets with the enemy."

Trot, Midas, Ramos and Dek headed into the hall. Trot and Dek gripped weapons.

The science lab overlooked the hangar, but there was no direct connection between the two facilities. Amberly's escort party had to exit out a capillary hallway that connected to the arterial corridor.

Lydia took Amberly's hand. The pair followed just a few meters behind Trot's group. Bringing up the rear of were Jana and Mac.

The group of eight spilled out into the wide corridor. Per curfew orders, the way was abandoned.

Amberly looked down toward Chinatown, the tubestop, the commons. The familiar breeze from the atmospheric cyclers blew against her face. Could she really leave *Magellan* in its darkest hour? She paused to take in sight, perhaps for the last time, when Lydia yanked on her arm.

"Amberly! Come on!" Lydia urged. "Chasm is coming!"

Amberly and Lydia ran after Dek and Trot, now just a dozen meters from the *Magellan* hangar main access.

Shots rang out from the direction of Chinatown.

Amberly saw Kora running towards them, struggling to

carry little Alroy.

"Kora!"

Private Inon and Kato, Rick's barkeep, raced along with Kora, both looking over their shoulders. Amberly was relieved Kora had backup. *Even Kato is risking his life to save the Macready sisters*, Amberly thought.

"Help! They're right behind us!" Panic filled Kora's gasping voice.

Inon turned and traded shots with their Chasm tail. Kato clumsily shot some cover fire at the enemy squad a dozen meters behind.

"That pacifist has no idea how to use a gun," Mac said, as he and Jana ran to assist Kato and Inon. "Come on!" Inon took another shot down the hall.

"Kora!" Trot burst into a full sprint toward his family, gun drawn, looking for a Chasm target. He reached Kora first, grabbed Alroy, and pulled Kora toward the hangar.

"You have to come with us. Please," Kora pleaded.

Trot stopped to catch his breath. "The governor did not release me from duty. I can't abandon my post. I will not die a coward."

"Damn your duty," Kora said. "Taking care of your family is not —"

Gunshot interrupted the conversation. Trot hoisted Alory over his shoulder and dashed. The hangar was close.

One of the Chasm troopers in pursuit took aim at Inon and ended her life. Mac and Jana's returned fire hit the target. The bullets vaporized in point defense armor.

"Don't let them get to the hangar," the squad leader yelled.

Suddenly, the leader stopped. Amberly noticed, and they briefly locked eyes.

"Dirt!" Amberly swore.

"Tell command I have eyes on Macready... *Amberly* Macready," the trooper radioed, and then shouted to his squad as he started to approach again. "Careful! If anything happens to the redhead, Captain Narlo will gut us! Get her. The rest don't matter."

Kato, Kora and Trot, carrying Alroy, had reached Amberly's group at the hangar door. Kora was heaving tired breaths. Her lungs burned from her race across the waypoint, and she was having difficulty recovering.

"Move! Into the hangar, now," Dek said as he ran back toward the Chasm troops. Bullets zipped over his head. Dek offered a grenade in return. Midas followed Dek's lead, and his toss made it a little farther. The grenade blast radius overwhelmed Chasm's point defense system. Chasm troops scattered. Explosions ripped up benches, planters and people.

"Put down some smoke," Jana yelled to Mac. Mac's tossed grenade filled the corridor with thick, white smoke.

Dek and Midas watched and waited. Midas peered through the smoke to see if the enemy was troubling the mists. After a few moments, no Chasm forces emerged, so Dek tossed another explosive grenade into the smoke.

The pair ducked through the main door, moving through the abandoned lobby into the hangar itself.

"Let's get Amberly out of here," Dek said as he came around a dividing wall into view of the *M.S.S. Misaka*, one of the few corvettes in *Magellan's* large hangar. Dek's eyes fell on the door on the far wall of the hangar which gave direct access to the command center — the same portal where North accidentally shot Amberly in his attempt to take down Raven One during the Battle of *Magellan*.

Kora shrieked.

Dek's eyes were drawn to Kato.

Instantly, Dek drew his gun and pointed it at the bartender. Similarly, Midas pulled a grenade from his bandoleer.

"Disarm the grenade, Midas," Kato smirked. "What, are you going to blow up this kid?"

Taking advantage of the chaos, Kato had snatched Alroy from Trot seconds earlier and now pointed his gun at the four-year-old's head. Kato looped his free arm around Alroy, clutching the boy tightly. "Dek, put your gun down. Now!"

"I don't think so," Dek said, his weapon's sights trained between Kato's eyes. "You better think about what you need to do to walk out alive."

"That's exactly what I am thinking about," Kato frowned.

"Kato, what are you doing?" Kora cried.

"Daddy!" Alroy looked up to his father as the boy tugged to

get free from Kato's grip.

Trot held his hands up. "It's going to be okay, Alroy," Trot reassured his only child. Then he looked to Kato. "Easy now. We'll get you what you need; just give me my son."

"The Chairman wants Amberly," Kato said, eyeing the researcher, "but I bet she'll take Alroy here. Time for me to cash in my chips."

"You bastard," Mac said, resisting the urge to also draw his weapon. "You're the Hawk."

"Right under your noses, all the time. You can't imagine the secrets people spill to their bartender. Now, no sudden moves," Kato said, as he walked backwards with Alroy toward the lobby. "Let's make sure Alroy lives. I'm sure the Chairman will make him a prince of Arara, like she intended for Amberly. Before Amberly committed matricide."

"Kato, you are our friend," Kora sobbed. "All these years. Please… give me my son."

"He's not your son. He's part of our great society now, part of the future," Kato preached. "But, you Kora are such an idiotic simpleton. You have no value to Chasm."

"Kato, just give me the boy and walk away," the plainly unarmed Ramos said calmly, walking slowly toward Kato and his hostage.

"Not another step, preacher," Kato snarled, pushing the barrel of his gun into Alroy's head. Alroy yelped. "Don't think I lack resolve! I've waited decades to fulfill my destiny. Do you know what it's been like, having to pretend to be one of you for years? Do you know how I've suffered!? The Chairman has finally come for her children. I'm going home with my gift for her."

"You'll never escape," Dek narrowed his eyes. "Another step and I put a bullet in your head. You're not getting out of here alive with Alroy."

"No, this boy here is my *only* escape," Kato snapped. "I must bring a suitable offering for the Chairman, so she will take me back to Arara. Don't you see? If you love this boy, this is the only way Alroy survives."

Dek tried to run through the scenarios quickly in his mind, ciphering a path to victory, the way Kimberly Macready had taught him. Let Kato leave and they would never see Alroy again.

Shoot Kato, and there was a good chance he would be able to pull the trigger before Kato went down. Could Dek signal one of his companions to make a distraction?

Amberly suddenly stepped between in the middle of the standoff. Amberly's presence seemed to grow exponentially. That she was taking command of the situation was clear to everyone on the deck.

"This is what's going to happen," Amberly said, pouring confidence into the room. Her face was resolute; her eyes even. "Kato is going to let Alroy go and take me instead."

"No!" Dek shouted, the situation changing too fast for him to control the outcomes.

"Yes, yes," Kato smiled, "a worthy trade. You can have the brat and I'll take the frigid Macready sister."

"Amberly, you can't! You have no idea what the Chairman will do to you," Dek implored.

"Decision's made. Mac, listen to me," Amberly said, "as soon as you have Alroy, you take him and Kora, and you get them the out of here. Promise me!"

"You can count on it," Mac replied with certainty.

Two more Chasm troopers rushed onto the deck, firearms at the ready. Pretty much everyone had weapons drawn in the standoff.

"Don't shoot," Kato ordered. "That's Amberly."

"Sir," the faceless trooper acknowledged the Chasm Hawk.

"Everyone, weapons down, now. Give us Alroy and I'll go with you, Kato," Amberly commanded.

The trooper looked to Kato. "Sir?"

"Do it, idiot. What are you going to do? Shoot Amberly?" Kato said through gritted teeth. Slowly, guns went down.

"No! Amberly! Oh, Amberly," Kora said, tears streaming down her face.

"Let's do this before Chasm backup arrives," Amberly as she slowly walked toward Kato.

"I love you, little sis," Kora said. "God protect you."

"We'll meet again," Amberly said.

Midas gave Amberly a look of reassurance.

"No matter what happens, you're dead," Dek growled to Kato. He then turned to Amberly. She looked into his blue grey eyes, a wave of grief overcoming her.

"Thank you, Dek, for everything," Amberly smiled weakly. She looked at her nephew, who was confused, but calm. She was now within arm's reach of Kato. He quickly took his gun off of Alroy and pushed it up against Amberly's head.

"Come to momma," Kora shouted, and the boy ran to her.

"Now don't do anything stupid we'll all regret," Kato said, as he backed toward the exit, pulling Amberly at gun point. "I don't want to kill Amberly. But I promise you, I am ready to kill her. I know you'll kill me, but if I can't make it out with her, I'm already dead. So, let's not be hasty."

A half dozen more Chasm troops rounded the corner.

"I have Amberly, fools," Kato screamed, moving away from the group, arm over Amberly's shoulder, hiding behind her with his gun pressed painfully into her side. "Kill them. Capture the other Macready daughter and the boy if you can."

Guns fired.

Jana had already retreated with Kora and Alroy to the *Misaka*, and she was handing Alroy up the lower access portal to his mother. Trot fearlessly stood as a shield in front of his family and unloaded his police-issue pistol at the Chasm troops. His fire had little effect, as the point defense systems transformed the bullets into poofs of molecular elements.

Chasm's ballistic answer hit the unshielded Trot a dozen times in the torso and the head, and all life escaped his body before he hit the floor.

"No! Trot!" Kora screamed, reaching for her husband.

Jana strained to force Kora back into the corvette and scramble inside herself. "You can't help him now; think about Alroy!" As soon as Jana had cleared the entry portal, she sealed the *Misaka's* lower hatch, bullets pinging off of the metallic surface.

With no cover, Midas made himself fall to the floor and let a grenade roll, trying to place it away from Amberly but in the radius of the enemy. The grenade exploded, catching one Chasm trooper in its blast and scattering the others.

Mac found cover behind an empty cargo crate and, popping his gun around the corner, discharged several rounds to no effect.

Dek, sprinting back towards the *Misaka* hoping to find some cover, took bullet spray in his right calf, and he fell flat on his face.

"Dek!" Amberly called out as she struggled against Kato's gun.

Two troopers joined Kato to secure Amberly. Enraged at seeing her brother-in-law and Dek take enemy fire, Amberly determined to call Kato's bluff — no way he would shoot her. She swung her arm into the head of the trooper on her left, causing the woman to fall. In the chaos, with adrenaline and vengeance filling her heart, Amberly put her foot on the trooper's neck and snapped it before Kato could stop her.

Lydia had avoided the attention of the Chasm fire up to this point and decided to charge the Chasm troops. She hit two of them with stun blasts in the armor, which had stun diffusers to absorb the electrical charge. The hits were still painful, and the Chasm troopers recoiled. She reached the first one and leaped on him, bringing the large trooper to the ground. Lydia ripped off his helmet and began to pound his face, before pushing her stun weapon into his temple and firing.

The second partially stunned trooper aimed his gun at Lydia, but was then distracted when the command center access portal at the far end of the room opened.

Skip charged out wielding the katana gifted to him by Sparks. Marines Macros De Leon and Leo Kendrick followed with stun guns blazing.

Behind them, Marine Commander Rita Moreno stepped into the battle, carrying the javelin North made for this occasion. *I prayed it would never come to this,* Rita thought. "Today is a good day to die," she uttered the ancient Earth battle cry under her breath. She looked for a target in the chaos.

She found one, and Rita charged with the javelin forward. Marcos provided some cover fire, charging beside her. The Chasm trooper saw Rita's attack and took aim with her assault rifle. DeLeon hit the trooper with a stun bolt, which didn't take the trooper down, but did disturb her aim as bullets discharged harmlessly away from the commander.

The Trooper screamed as Rita impaled her, and then removed the javelin, looking for her next enemy. Seconds later, Marcos knocked Rita to the ground, removing her from the path of an onslaught of Chasm weapons fire.

"Thanks," Rita said as she lifted her head and made a tactical assessment of the situation. On one side of the hangar, the *Misaka* sat, ready for escape. On the far side of the hangar, Kato and a few Chasm troopers were making an exit with Amberly. In the dozen meters between, a chaotic mix of melee and close quarters weapon fire claimed both *Magellan* and Chasm casualties. *Can't let them take Amberly. Not now*, Moreno thought as she willed herself off the floor and back into the fight. *I have to get to Amberly.*

Pain shocking his system, Dek rolled over in a pool of his own blood and saw Kato and an escort trooper about to round the lobby corner with Amberly. Dek raised his rifle, calmed his breathing and took a shot.

A nine-millimeter hole opened in Kato's skull. Blood and brain matter oozed out. Amberly struggled with her remaining captor as Chasm reinforcements arrived.

"*Magellan*... is... my... home," Amberly said, attempting to break free. And then suddenly her whole body lit up with the pain of a stun bolt. She looked desperately at the fallen Dek as her vision went dark. The trooper dragged the unconscious Amberly into the lobby and out of sight.

"Amberly!" Dek called out, trying to force himself to rise, but failing. A second bullet hit him, this time in the shoulder.

Amberly Macready was gone.

"No!" Dek shouted, his helplessness crushing him like a thousand kilo weight. "Help! Midas! Ramos! Get Amberly!"

"Retreat to the command center," Moreno shouted as she provided cover fire with stun bolts, slowing but not stopping the Chasm advance. "Go, go, go!" Moreno handed Mac her javelin, then he sprinted first through the door.

Midas tossed his last smoke grenade as he called for Ramos, who was still clutching his rare printed Bible and praying behind a storage container. Ramos tucked the Bible in his back pocket, and the pair grabbed Dek and dragged him toward the door under the cover of smoke, leaving a streak of blood along the cold steel floor.

"No, we have to go get Amberly!" Dek screamed.

"It's suicide," Midas grunted as he pulled on the younger man.

Lydia was grappling with a second Chasm trooper. He

pushed Lydia to free himself from her grasp, giving him enough space to aim his weapon.

"Auuuuuuugghhhhhh!" Skip screamed as he charged Lydia's assailant. The lightweight jumped and lunged, plunging the sword into the mouthpiece of the helmet. The sword came out the back of the trooper's neck, staining the trooper's armor crimson.

"Holy Dirt, Skip! What the hell is that thing!?" Lydia asked.

Skip's eyes moved from his sword to Lydia's face then back to the sword.

"How do I get it out?" Skip's eyes were still wide.

"Oh, for heaven's sake!" Lydia grabbed Skip's hand on the sword and ripped it out of the trooper's helmet.

"Come on," she shouted. "They have Amberly!"

The smoke started to clear. Through the haze, Skip made out dozens of Chasm troops. Leading this elite strike team was Chairman's guard captain, Narlo.

"We can't save Amberly now," Skip said rapidly, "We'll have to figure out something. If we don't fall back, we're dead!"

"Lydia, Skip, come on," Moreno shouted. "Move!" The pair sprinted for the open door.

Almost there, just a few meters, Lydia thought, as she saw Skip slip in her peripheral vision.

"Lord, no!" Lydia cried as she turned to see Skip fallen on the ground, riddled with bullet holes. Lydia fell to her knees next to her old beau. Bullets whizzed by Lydia's ears.

"Tell North ... I tried..." Skip choked, his eyes quickly growing distant.

"Skip, I love you," tears streamed down Lydia's face.

"Run... Lydia..." Skip offered his last words. Lydia's eyes locked on his as they became glassy and soulless.

"Come on!" Midas, who had returned after he and Ramos had slipped the injured Dek into the relative safety of the access corridor. Marcos and Leo threw down another round of stun bolts as cover.

Midas grabbed Lydia and hoisted her to her feet.

"No, no!" Lydia didn't care now if she lived or died. She'd lost Amberly, and she'd lost Skip. Her world was over.

"Let's go, Lydia!"

Lydia snatched the bloodied katana and moved with Midas.

It was too late. Chasm consoled the hangar now. Moreno was forced to seal the escape door to prevent Chasm from accessing the command center, locking herself, Lydia and Midas out. Losing the cencomm to Chasm would end the game. *You may have me in check, Madam Chairman, but this isn't checkmate*, Moreno thought. She dropped her stun gun, raising her hands. *Time for the sacrifice gambit.*

"We surrender," Moreno shouted. "As commander of the *Magellan* Marines, I offer unconditional surrender. I want to speak to the Chairman."

Captain Narlo couldn't believe his luck. Amberly was likely already on her way to *Utopia*. He had captured *Magellan's* queen, and he had the elder Macready sister and Raven One's grandson cornered in a corvette that couldn't launch in the sealed hangar. *The Chairman will be pleased, and history will most certainly remember my contribution to the greater good*, he thought.

"Hold your fire!" Narlo shouted orders to the Chasm forces. "Hold your fire."

As attention focused on Moreno, Midas exchanged a subtle glance with Lydia. She nodded, and he quietly led her toward the *Misaka*.

Moreno lowered her arms and stood boldly in front of her adversary's captain. Nearly 100 Chasm troops had flooded onto the hangar deck. Moreno knew this force would move quickly to take the command center – it wouldn't take them long to get in, using brute force if necessary.

"You are all humanity's brothers and sisters," Moreno shouted, flailing her arms, as she paid clandestine attention on Midas in her peripheral vision. "You must see that the Chairman is evil. Turn against her now." *Just a few more minutes, and maybe I can save a few more lives before I go*, Moreno thought. *Surely, these are my last moments.*

Several of the Chasm troopers assembled laughed out loud.

"That doesn't sound like a surrender," Narlo snapped. "What game are you playing?" He raised his rifle.

"Games?" Moreno smirked, "I used to play chess with Raven One."

The hatch to the *Misaka* popped open, and Lydia started scrambling up, drawing the attention of some nearby Chasm weapons.

Midas knew he had to create a distraction. He raised his gun, whooping, and ran from the *Misaka*. "I'll never surrender," he shouted as he aimed to fire into the gathering of Chasm troopers. More than a dozen guns trained on him and unloaded, and Midas fell.

The old man smiled as he saw Lydia pull the hatch shut. *It's been a good life*, was the penultimate thought to echo in his brain. *I hope Skip saved a seat for me on the other side.*

Several chasm troopers took aim and fired at the *Misaka* hatch.

"Stop it, you idiots," Narlo said, keeping his weapon trained on Moreno. "The Chairman will have your heads if you injure the spawn of Raven One. Cease fire and fall into ranks before you do something stupid."

A young Chasm attaché approached Narlo with an infopad. "I have the Chairman, captain."

"There is no escape," Captain Narlo smirked. "You should have surrendered earlier. You could have saved lives instead of wasting them." He handed Moreno the infopad, the Chairman's taught face filling the small screen.

"Chairman," Moreno spoke evenly. "I am honored again to speak with you. It seems you have us in check."

"I am told you are prepared to offer unconditional surrender," the Chairman's cool voice flowed. "Please give my captain access to the command center immediately to prove your sincerity, and we will stop this senseless bloodshed today."

"Very well, let me have my XO unlock the command access corridor," Moreno said. "Trisha, are you on this channel."

"Yes, Commander," Trisha's voice came on the line, her voice despondent.

"It's my time, Trisha. Godspeed to you," a calm confidence filled Moreno's words.

"I understand," Trisha said, with a slight waiver in her voice.

"What is going on Narlo?" the voice of the Chairman demanded.

"I can't believe Chasm fell for this twice," Moreno smiled and closed her eyes. "First Kimberly. Now you."

"What?" the Chairman demanded.

"Surely Kimberly told you about my penchant for the sacrifice gambit. Checkmate."

"Wait!" The Chairman saw Moreno's play now, but it was too late.

"Goodbye, Trisha. You're in command."

Klaxons sounded as the emergency curtain fell on the lobby side of the hanger, sealing Moreno, Captain Narlo, a company of Chasm's finest strike forces from the life-giving protections of *Magellan*.

"Warning! Safety measures have been disengaged," the generic *Magellan* VI voice spoke over loudspeakers in the hangar. "Space doors opening. Space doors opening."

Narlo cursed and spit at Moreno, as his soldiers scrambled in vain toward the sealed exits. Others ran to the *Misaka* and started pounding on the locked access portal.

Moreno calmly smiled. *Totally worth it. Still, I would have liked to enjoy a hot cup of Darjeeling one last time,* she thought. She looked toward the corvette's window, and knew she had saved little Alroy. *He is the future, not the Chairman.*

In the *Misaka*, Jana looked out of the starboard viewport at her heroic commander. Moreno's stall saved her, Lydia and the Wilder family. Sadness attempted to overtake her, but she fought back. *There will be time to mourn later,* she thought.

"Strap in," Jana instructed her passengers. "We are going to have to make a fast break to clear the firing solutions of the Dark Armada." Jana wiped at her stinging, moist eyes, and traded a glance with Moreno through the viewport. Moreno smiled sweetly, snapped a salute, and Jana reciprocated the gesture.

The space doors began to pull open. Commander Rita Moreno closed her eyes and was sucked into the cold void.

Bodies, alive, barely alive and already dead, bounced off of the *Misaka* as it floated clear of the *Magellan* hangar into open space. Kora pressed her face against the window, desperately looking for the body of her husband in the jetsam projected by the atmospheric evacuation. She quietly murmured through her tears, "Please, Lord. I just want to see him one more time." She did not. She held Alroy's hand, who was seated between her and Lydia. Lydia held little Alroy's other hand tightly, focusing on the boy's needs to overcome her own shock. Midas died for her. Skip died for her.

Time to find the Magnus, Jana thought, as she pushed the *Misaka* away with maximum safe acceleration. *Misaka's* passengers were forcefully thrown back into their chairs as *Magellan* disappeared from the rear view.

The Chairman cursed as she watched the mayhem from the still transmitting infopad, frozen in her dead captain's hand, his body spinning just outside the outer hull of *Magellan*. The loss of Narlo and his forces was regrettable, but for all practical purposes was not even a slight setback. Still, she let Moreno get the better of her, and the old woman's pride was hurt.

Just as soon as the hurt had surfaced into her conscious mind, the Chairman pushed it away. And then she couldn't help but smile at the glorious tactic. *Well played, Commander Moreno*, the Chairman thought, respectful of her expired adversary. *Enjoy your rest.*

Yeoman Carnell quietly but quickly stepped onto the *Utopia's* command platform and cleared his throat. "Madam Chairman," he said meekly.

"Don't cower, pet," she smiled thinly. "I don't mourn them. I celebrate their sacrifice for the greater good. We are all expendable for the *greater good.*"

Carnell forced a smile in reply. "Yes ma'am. I have confirmation that Amberly Macready is secure on the *Xander's Mace.*"

"Thank you, Carnell," the Chairman lit up at the expected, but welcome, news. She had what she came for. She stepped over and stood closely to the yeoman and reached up and pulled his head beside hers, holding it tightly. She kissed his ear, and whispered. "Tell Admiral Björk to have Raven One's daughter transported to the *Utopia* immediately."

The Chairman bit hard into the tall, young man's ear until it bled. The painful bite shocked the yeoman, but fear of the Chairman kept Carnell silent and still.

"I love the taste of blood," the Chairman cooed in Carnell's ear before shoving his head away from her. Standing near the Chairman's vacant command chair, Maldevia, captain of the *Utopia*, wondered if she was referring to the lives lost, or the literal taste. *Probably both*, Maldevia thought as she tucked her dark brown hair under her captain's cap. "Many have died. That is the price of perfection."

The command platform was silent for an uncomfortable moment.

"Run along, Carnell," the Chairman said. "Let me know the moment Amberly is on board."

The Chairman ran her hands over her white, tightly-pulled back hair. "Captain, set course for Arara. Let's go make a perfect world."

CHAPTER SEVEN

December 28, 2606, Command deck of the Red Hammer, two days out from Waypoint Magellan.

Chasm's *Red Hammer* had overtaken the *American Spirit*.

On the port view screen, Captain Ai'la'ausd could see the *American Spirit*, just a few dozen kilometers away, traveling on the same trajectory as his ship. The edges of the single-hulled *American Sprit* diffused the starlight bathing the vessel, creating a blue sheen surrounding the silhouette. The captain assumed that the darkness from the ship itself was a matter of standard stealth practice: if you don't want to be seen, turn out all the lights near your windows.

"Sir, if I may, the admiral said to destroy the enemy ship," First Officer Comisky looked across *Red Hammer's* bridge at his captain. "Asking them to surrender is not part of our orders."

Ai'la'ausd fumed at his first officer. "Do not question *my* orders."

"Yes sir, but –"

"We will pillage the ship, then destroy it," the Captain scowled. "I have no intention of disobeying your beloved admiral, Comisky. It the meantime, go bathe. You reek of ambition beyond your station."

"I don't know what you mean, sir."

"Of course, you don't," Ai'la'ausd sighed. "Communications, see if you can get their captain on the horn. I want to finish this so we can get back to *Magellan* and rejoin the Dark Armada. It's already going to take several days to decelerate and turn our boat around."

In its attempt to escape the Dark Armada, the *American Spirit* had managed to accelerate to .2c, one fifth of light speed, since leaving *Magellan*. Millions of kilometers of empty space now separated the *American Spirit* and the waypoint. The older ship would need another month of acceleration to reach its top cruising speed of .5c. The superior propulsion of the Dark Armada's *Red Hammer* allowed the warship to easily catch the deep space transport.

Engineer Lews stepped up to the command platform. "Captain, I've personally completed the quality assurance on the nukes. Everything inspected. Ready for arming."

"Excellent, Lews," Ai'la'ausd said. "Tactical, do you have any data on the whereabouts of the *Magnus*?"

A woman with short dyed-pink hair looked up from a magnetic resonance display. "I'm tracking a half dozen signal wakes that could be generated by *Magnus*, or they could be false positives. Only one wake poses any threat if it is indeed *Magnus*."

"Thank you, Renee," the captain acknowledged his tactical officer. "Everyone, keep a close eye out for *Magnus*. The main fleet at *Magellan* has not seen her either."

"Do you think she made for Arara?" Lews asked.

"More likely that ship is hiding out back in that asteroid field where *Magellan* established an outpost," Ai'la'ausd said. "The Spencer Belt, I believe."

The comm officer spoke up, "I have the master of the *American Spirit* on comms."

Captain Boro and his bridge officers stood around *American Spirit's* tactical table. The crew of the deep space ship knew that the *Red Hammer* had been in pursuit for nearly 30 hours now. The massive warship had set into a parallel course, an incredibly close twenty kilometers away. Traveling at even a fraction of light speed so close to another object meant that the error tolerance for navigation was essentially zero. Boro had ordered the ship's VI, Jefferson, to manage the helm in a desperate attempt to evade the *Red Hammer* without crashing into it. So far, the computers on the *American Spirit* were not a match for the navigational prowess of the mammoth Utopia-class battleship, and *Red Hammer* remained locked on identical course with her prey.

"We should open fire while we still can fire," Caddo, the ship's security officer. "Maybe it will have no effect, but maybe we can get lucky."

"We have no reason to believe our particle beams can penetrate the PDS," said Chief Engineer Kuuku Akachi. Akachi was a young engineer who had risen to prominence for her role on the rescue flotilla that saved the *American Spirit* after the Chasm Hawk sabotage. "Hell, I'm not even sure we can puncture

Red Hammer's hull. We're still alive, let's not provoke a battle we cannot win. Diplomacy gives us a better chance for survival."

"You may be right about diplomacy," said Elizabeth Hawkins, a sharp, petite 21-year-old blonde, who survived the terror of Skylar Triggs. "We don't seem to have any cards to play, except surrender." Elizabeth, who went by Betsy, served as the communications officer for *American Spirit*.

"We may have an ace," Captain Boro said, filling the bridge with his deep, resonant voice. "The *Mangus* will come. North will come."

None of the other bridge officers held the captain with much esteem. The first Chasm conspirator to defect, Boro rose from turncoat Marine to captain by being in the right place at the right time. When Dek went AWOL and *American Spirit* left without its leader, Boro, as XO, became captain. Not that the crew didn't like Boro, but the consensus was he was incompetent. Caddo was planning on calling for a vote of no confidence, but that was before the message from *Magellan* warned them *Red Hammer* was in pursuit.

"*Magnus* is running silent," Betsy said. "We have no idea where they are, if they're even coming."

"Captain, it's true that one of Commander Moreno's contingencies was for the *Magnus* to defend the *American Spirit* should the Dark Armada pursue," Caddo argued. "But that was one of 23 potential outcomes Moreno planned for. It would mean that either *Magellan* was lost or the Dark Armada was destroyed."

An alert flashed at Betsy's station, and the young officer activated her magnetic resonance screen. "Boro, the captain of the *Red Hammer* wishes to negotiate the terms of our surrender."

"Well, they have been teasing us for long enough. Let's find out what cards *they* have," Boro said as he indicated for Betsy to open the comm channel.

"This is Captain Boro of the *American Spirit*. Please disengage and allow us safe passage. We wish you well and mean you no harm."

"*Captain* Boro?" The voice of Ai'la'ausd piped onto the bridge. "Where is Dek Tigona? We were under the impression that traitor was master of your boat. The Chairman had a message for him."

"Dek Tigona is not on board," Boro said.

"I highly doubt that. Boro is it? You are covering for Dek."

"I tell you, Dek is not here. We left him on *Magellan*."

"I don't believe you, but we'll come back to Dek in a moment," Ai'la'ausd said, sounding rather amused with himself, voice full of a flippant confidence. "You must surrender your vessel immediately and unconditionally. Slow your vessel to 10,000 k.p.h. waypoint relative and prepare to be boarded. Any resistance, and we will destroy your ship. Our fusion warheads are armed and ready."

Boro looked over to Akachi, who had taken her station. She looked back up at Boro and nodded, to confirm without words what he feared: sensors detected radiation signatures of primed nuclear warheads.

North will come, Boro thought. *I just have to buy him time. If I am wrong, all is lost anyway.*

"We do not have a death wish, Ai'la'ausd," Boro said. "As a former Chasm conspirator, let me surrender myself to you. I am ready to submit myself to your judgment. But you have no quarrel with the rest of these good people. Let them continue on their journey which takes them a lifetime away from your utopia on Arara."

"Boro, you are at the same time both noble and hilarious," Ai'la'ausd chuckled. "Perhaps you do not understand the hopelessness of your situation. Once the *Dark Armada* has subdued *Magellan*, we will destroy the remaining waypoints. There will be no replenishment from waypoints. No ports for your ship to make berth. If you continue on your present course, even if we do not impede you now, you will all die when your resources run out light years before you'd ever reach Earth. Our fleet will outpace you. Consider your next move carefully."

Boro sat down in a chair at the head of the tactical table, placing his head down into his large, dark hands. He wished he had Dek's wit or Moreno's stratagems to help him. "I see the situation clearly now."

"Good. The Chairman has already passed judgment on the *American Spirit*," Ai'la'ausd said. "Nothing can change that now. However, you have one thing I want, that I am willing to negotiate for. Bring me Dek Tigona dead or alive, and I will spare the lives of the children under five years of age. Deny me, and we'll share a warhead with you."

"How is destroying us for the greater good?" Boro said. "How is all this violence for the greater good?"

"Your children will serve the greater good," Ai'la'ausd spoke slowly, impatience now coating each word. "This discussion is over, Captain Boro. Your time is shorter than you think. But you have a chance to save the children of *American Spirit*. No more lies. I need your straight answer now. Will you hand over Dek Tigona?"

"I will," Boro lied. "Give me a moment to have my security forces apprehend him for you."

"Very good," Ai'la'ausd said. "Have him placed into an escape pod and ejected. Once we have Tigona in our custody, we'll make arrangements to transfer the children to *Red Hammer* before we destroy the *American Spirit*."

"Understood, Ai'la'ausd," Boro said. "I will signal again before we launch the pod. *American Spirit* out."

Betsy nodded again to Boro, to confirm the channel was closed.

"Well, this is it," Akachi said. "Once *Red Hammer* realizes we are bluffing, we're all dead. Captain, you've bought us a few minutes. Thank you. Permission to go to my family now to be with them at the end?"

"No, Akachi," Boro said. "North will come! Have faith. Can we put something explosive in an escape pod? Maybe send them a bomb."

"As soon as thermal scans show there is not a warm body in the pod, they will take it out," Caddo said, eyes moist with emotion, but face steeled with resolve. "Someone has to be in the pod to sell it. ... I volunteer. Maybe they won't suspect anything until it is too late."

"No, Caddo!" Elizabeth objected.

"Betsy," Caddo smiled sadly, "we are all already dead."

"We might be able to cause some damage with some conventional explosives," Akachi said, "but nothing that would stop them from immediately retaliating with a nuke."

"Too bad we don't have one of those on board," Boro lamented.

"If they were going to nuke us, they wouldn't do it at this distance," Caddo said. "There would be danger they'd get caught in the blast. They'd have to clear some space. Maybe that would give us an opening for escape?"

"It would only take them seconds to do so," Akachi said. "There is no escape from that ship. It's too fast."

"We go down fighting then," Boro said. "Akachi, you and Caddo go make an escape pod bomb as fast as possible. We don't have much time. We'll open fire with our particle beams at the same time we bomb them. If we can't win, let's hurt them as much as we can."

"Should we inform the crew and passengers of the situation?" Betsy asked.

"No, Elizabeth, no," Boro said. "Everyone already knows death is a likely outcome. If people have not made their peace with that now, it's on them. No good would come out of a panic."

"What does it matter now?" Akachi said, anger pumping blood into her head. "Who are you to deny people the right to know they have only hours or minutes left? Let them settle up with their families, friends and gods."

"It matters because the *Magnus* is coming," Boro said. "I feel it."

"Akachi," Caddo said, placing a hand on her shoulder, "let's go do our job. The sooner we stuff me and a bunch of explosives in an escape pod, the sooner you can go be with your family."

"Get real. The *Magnus* is not coming," Akachi said.

The tactical display blipped.

"Captain! The *Magnus* just broke radio silence! Look," Betsy shouted and pointed to the table display.

The bridge erupted with spontaneous cheers.

"I stand corrected, captain. My apologies," Akachi said, blushing through her mocha skin. "So glad to be so wrong."

So, I was right, Boro thought. *But are they too late?*

"*Magnus* to *American Spirit* on emergency encrypted channel 234b. We're coming in on a hot vector to disable bogie," a woman's loud voice filled the bridge. Boro recognized the voice as that of *Magnus'* junior communication officer Rhodes. "ETA ten minutes."

"If *Magnus* pulls our ass out of the fire, I might believe there is a God," Caddo said. "Ten minutes. I hope we can stall that long. We have to launch an escape pod."

"*Red Hammer* will see the *Magnus* coming soon; they may already see it," Betsy said.

"Not likely. As soon as they see *Magnus*, they will kill us so they can engage the true threat," Boro said. "*Magnus* must still be undetected."

"The only way they could kill us fast enough is by nuke," Akachi said. "Too close, remember."

"Hawkins, please update *Magnus* on our status, and our plan to stall them with a life pod bomb," Boro ordered. "Make sure they know what they are walking into."

"Transmitting encrypted message now," Betsy worked her station.

"Come on, Akachi. Let's get to it. Boro, everyone," Caddo squared off and saluted. "It's been an honor. Please send all those Chasm bastards to hell for me."

Boro returned the gesture.

"God be with you," the captain called out, as Caddo exited the bridge. Akachi followed close behind him.

Captain Obadiah's heart was pounding. If *Magnus* was lucky, she would have one shot to take out the *Red Hammer* before the Chasm warship destroyed the *American Spirit*. To get into firing range with *Red Hammer* as soon as possible, *Magnus* would not even attempt slowing to combat speed, matching the velocity of *Red Hammer* and the *American Spirit*. They would hit the enemy with everything they had while shooting past the pair of vessels at sub-light speeds.

So close. Come on. Obadiah was second-guessing his moral calculus. The plan was to go after *Red Hammer* and save *American Spirit*, believing he could do nothing to save *Magellan*. If he failed to rescue the *American Spirit* now, this failure would be the defining moment of his existence.

"All tubes open; solutions loaded into the guidance systems," Suri, *Magnus'* gunnery chief, responded.

"I am ready to engage the heat and particle beams on command," Condi chimed in from the bridge speakers.

"That's a good VI," North said, and then turned to the

captain. "Marine strike force ready to board *Red Hammer* or *American Spirit* should the situation call for it. We're ready, sir."

North was geared up, dark gray assault armor covering his muscular torso, his javelin strapped neatly behind his broad shoulders. His hair was regulation, his eyes colored with vengeance. The likelihood of the need of a boarding party for combat was slim, but if they had an opportunity to board *Red Hammer*, North was going to make sure they regretted leaving Arara. After being beclowned by Chasm's point defense system at the Battle of *Marquette*, North was anxious to put his javelin to the test in hand-to-hand combat.

Sparks wore a lighter, tighter polycarbonic armor, jet black. She had followed North's lead and trimmed her strawberry blonde hair to regulation length as well. As perhaps the most skilled pilot on *Magnus*, Sparks sat at the navigator's station and fiddled with her half-mask. "That Caddo guy is as good as dead. He knows that right?"

"They are all good as dead if we are too late," North gritted.

Rhodes, who had just received and relayed the full sitrep from Hawkins on *American Spirit*, pushed back her bangs. "Pretty noble, trying to buy time until we get there."

"I can't believe Dek went AWOL," Sparks said, looking at North. "*I* should have gone AWOL to fight on *Magellan*. Decapitating a few of the Chairman's best would have been a thrill. That friend of yours better make good use of my – well – Ryder's katana."

"Skip will be all right," North said in ignorance.

"Stay focused people," the captain said, sweat starting to bead on his dark brow. "The window to save *American Spirit* will close quickly."

"Two minutes till firing range," Condi announced.

With his left hand, Caddo triggered the small firing thrusters to push his escape pod toward the *Red Hammer*. Like the other vessels in the Dark Armada, the warship's huge double-hull dwarfed every man-made object except a waypoint. In his right hand, *Magnus'* security chief had a simple button-actuated detonator, linked to the thousand or so liters of explosives sharing his ride.

Caddo smirked at the irony of a *life* pod ushering him to his imminent *death*. But this act of selflessness would be his ultimate proof, mostly to himself, that he was not a traitor; that he was right to shoot *American Spirit's* Security Chief Shreya West when he did, to save Dek. Dek was then able to save the *American Spirit* from the Chasm saboteurs. Caddo had replayed the scenario in his mind endlessly since that day. He felt lucky the courts had vindicated him, but an unrelenting guilt made him wonder if maybe he was just a murderer after all.

Resolution was coming. He navigated his pod toward the *Red Hammer's* main docking hangar. With any luck, he would get inside and then detonate, where he could create the most damage. Peace washed over him. No matter what happened now, Caddo felt his sacrifice would pay for his sins.

"Captain Ai'la'ausd!" *Red Hammer's* Tactical Officer Renee shouted. "I've found *Magnus*! And it's close."

"Dirt!" First Officer Comisky said, followed by a string of more colorful profanities.

"On an intercept path?" Captain Ai'la'ausd asked.

"No sir," Renee responded. "Traveling too fast. She'll buzz by us in under three minutes!"

"Hit and run then," Ai'la'ausd mused. "Bring the point defense system online. All hands prepare for battle. Helm, put some distance between us and *American Spirit*. As soon as we are outside the blast radius, nuke it. We can't have our attention divided when engaging *Magnus*. Move!"

At first, Ai'la'ausd was upset Admiral Björk had sent him on this milk run. But now with the opportunity to defeat both *American Spirit* and *Magnus*, he felt gushing winds of glory on his face.

"What about Dek Tigona and the life pod?" Comisky asked.

"No way to get him on board?" Ai'la'ausd asked.

"Not safely, sir."

"Make sure he dies then," Ai'la'ausd said.

"Two minutes till *Magnus* flyby," Ensign Hawkins announced.

"The *Red Hammer* is starting to pull away," Akachi said, who had moments earlier returned from sending off Caddo.

"Stay with them. Don't give them space to nuke us," Boro commanded Jefferson.

"Confirmed, Captain," the artificial voice replied.

"Damn it," Akachi swore.

"They know *Magnus* is on its way," Boro said. "Two minutes too late. I'm sorry, everyone. Akachi, you may go to your family now."

Boro stood from his chair. "Hawkins, patch me into the ship-wide comms."

"You're on, sir."

"This is the captain. We are about to engage in fatal conflict with our enemy. Military personnel remain at battle stations. Otherwise, all hands prepare to abandon ship. Civilians have priority on life pods. With any luck, the *Magnus* will be able to swing by and pick you up. May God have mercy on us all. Boro out."

For a brief moment, the bridge was quiet. *Time to go down with the ship*, Boro thought.

"Jefferson," Boro spoke to the VI. "Remove all safeties and get us as close to the *Red Hammer* as possible."

The VI asked for Boro's authorization codes, and the captain provided them. Boro looked over at Hawkins. "Betsy, you are revealed from duty. I am kicking you out of the service and off the bridge."

"What!?"

"You are a civilian now. Get to an escape pod. You are too young to die. Fight for your life," Boro explained. "Hurry. I have too many sins to pay for." Boro remembered his early alliance with Chasm, and how he switched sides after seeing Chasm's murderous intentions.

"I will not leave my post," the ensign insisted.

"Jefferson and I can see this to the end. Go!"

"No, captain," Hawkins was defiant.

Boro replied only with a sad smile.

"*Red Hammer* is trying to evade us," Jefferson announced. "Passengers and crew should secure themselves as I anticipate higher-than-normal G-forces as I attempt to stay close."

"Have a seat then, ensign," Boro said as he reached for his seat harness.

"Captain, the *American Spirit* is matching our course," the tactical officer reported on the bridge of the *Red Hammer*. The declaration was almost unnecessary. On the port screen, the deep space ship was looming large.

"More power to the thrusters, Renee," Captain Ai'la'ausd barked. "We should be able to outpace that dinosaur. What is going on?"

"Too much power is being used to keep the point defense system hot," Engineer Lews explained.

"*Magnus* is on us in less than a minute," First Officer Comisky spoke, his voice filled with terror. "Shall I take the firing solution off the *American Spirit* and aim our weapons on *Magnus*?"

"Fire the nuke on *American Spirit* now, then target *Magnus*," Ai'la'ausd sounded as urgent has he ever had.

"But sir, we'll get caught in the blast. We could take damage —"

Ai'la'ausd pulled his sidearm from its holster and put a bullet in Comisky's head. The officer fell, lifeless, to the base of the command platform. Shock at the violent display silenced the bridge. "Quit questioning my orders. We can get the *American Spirit* now. If she gets away, well… fire the nuke, Lews!"

"Aye captain. Warhead away," the Chasm engineer winced.

"Calculate new solutions. Hurry! Target the *Magnus!*" Ai'la'ausd shouted.

"We're hundreds of kilometers short of being clear of the blast!" Renee punched up the ship-wide comms. "All hands, brace for impact."

"Incoming warhead," Jefferson announced to the semi-deserted bridge of the *American Spirit*. The deep space ship was not designed for battle. When she launched from Earth nearly 80 years ago, no one suspected it would ever take a direct hit from a nuclear missile.

"Jefferson, as long as you still have control of this ship, your orders are to initiate a collision with the *Red Hammer,* even if I am killed or incapacitated."

"I understand, captain," Jefferson replied.

"Get out of here, Ensign Hawkins," Boro commanded with extra power in his deep voice.

The ship suddenly shook violently, as waves of snapping cracks and shrieks of ripping metal sounded through the *American Spirit* from stern to bow. Life support pipes ruptured, spewing clouds of hot gasses into the bridge cavity. The vibrations from the blast caused several bulkheads to splinter into hot shrapnel, pelting the bridge and its remaining crew.

Lights flickered and Elizabeth Hawkins felt herself becoming weightless. She undid her safety belt and started to float. She felt a sharp pain in her left foot. She looked behind her and saw a cloud of blood – hers – also floating as spinning droplets.

"Jefferson, how bad is it?" Betsy shouted, covering her face to protect it from a stream of steam.

"Life support and artificial gravity are disabled. Nineteen decks have significant hull breaches. Engines are 20 percent responsive, and falling."

"Captain?" Betsy shouted, looking around the bridge. Her eyes fell on Boro, ripped from his chair, floating in his own blood. The captain was dead. Beyond him, his Marine security officer and Akachi were both disfigured from blunt force trauma, also dead.

"Acting Captain Hawkins, shall we continue on a collision course?" the VI asked the only living human on the bridge.

"Yes, Jefferson," Elizabeth said, tears floating off her face. "Let's finish this."

"I'm sorry about Captain Boro," Jefferson said. "May I recommend immediate evacuation? There is an available life pod 30 meters away. I have sent the path with the least obstruction to your infopad."

"Thanks, Jefferson," Hawking said, as she struggled to find something to push or pull on to propel her towards the door. Hawking glanced one once more at her dead shipmates, closed her eyes and crossed herself, and kicked off the wall with her uninjured foot.

"Goodbye, Betsy," the VI replied. "Be well."

Ai'la'ausd stared at the port wall screen as the warhead made impact with *American Spirit*. A brilliant flash made the whole wall briefly go white. Ai'la'ausd instinctively covered his eyes, though the flash was no more dangerous than watching a vid recording of a nuclear explosion.

Before the flash receded, however, real shockwaves hit *Red Hammer*.

The ship snap-listed to the starboard. A member of Ai'la'ausd's guard, who was not strapped into his seat, was thrown head first from the elevated command platform five meters down to the bridge floor. Objects that were not secured, including the body of former First Officer Comisky, flew randomly as the inertia dampeners and artificial gravity fought against each other to compensate for the shockwave.

Painfully loud alarms sounded.

"Damage report!" Ai'la'ausd shouted. "Do we have a firing solution on *Magnus*? Move people, or we are all dead."

"The *Magnus* is moving too fast and erratically to get a firing solution," the gunnery chief said. "Making my best guess. They are in range. Ready to fire on your command."

"Thrusters have been knocked offline; point defense system still at full power. It will take us some time to get those thrusters rebooted," Renee sputtered.

"Fire everything you can, dirt licker!" the captain swore. "Fire at will. Fire, dammit! Fire!"

Tinny reverberations rung through the *Red Hammer* as missile silos emptied. The sound was sweet comfort to Ai'la'ausd's ears. Then he looked back at the *American Spirit* and smiled at the carnage.

Nearly a fourth of the tube-shaped ship's mass had disintegrated, as if something had taken a large bite out of *American Spirit's* underbelly. The ship was hemorrhaging all sorts of atmospheric gasses. Ai'la'ausd could make out a small flotilla of escape pods surrounding the flotsam and jetsam littering the wake of the *American Spirit. No matter*, he thought, *once we've dealt with the Magnus, they will die in those pods.* He knew no one from *Magellan* would be able to respond. They were so far away already, and momentum was taking the pods in the wrong direction. *Besides, Magellan is under Chasm control by now. Those life pods will become tombs.*

"Captain!" Renee shouted.

The large American flag painted on the ship was still intact, unmolested by the nuclear blast. And it was getting larger.

"Dammit! Dammit! They are going to ram us! Evasive! Helm, what is going on?"

"Thrusters and backup propulsion are still offline. *American Spirit* is speeding up. I'm unable to match their acceleration," said the short woman at the ship's navigation station.

"We need momentum! Vent something to get us out of the way!" Ai'la'ausd said. "Lews?"

"Maybe if we opened the port hangar without depressurizing the hangar first?" the engineer suggested.

"We'd lose a lot of ships," Renee said.

"We're about to lose the whole ship," Ai'la'ausd snapped. "Do it."

"I'll evacuate the hangar crew," Lews said, punching up his comm.

"No time, fool," Ai'la'ausd screamed. "Vent it now!"

From the viewport on her life pod, Elizabeth Hawkins could see the *Red Hammer,* slightly off kilter and emitting gasses from its rear engine thrusters, damaged by the radiation shockwaves of its own nuclear warhead. The enemy warship unleashed a bevy of missiles apparently targeting the *Magnus*, Hawkins' only hope of survival. She craned her neck at the window, straining to see the *Magnus.* She could not spot the friendly warship.

Suddenly her viewport filled with the *American Spirit,* no more than a kilometer away, as it slipped past her life pod. Jefferson was still online, executing the last orders of Boro, accelerating for collision.

Betsy's heart felt like it was being ripped from her chest as she saw exposed deck after deck. She knew those who weren't killed by the blast would have been sucked out into space. Then she saw the painted Old Glory, reflecting stellar light, unscathed. *Oh, say can you see*, Betsy, inspired by the great symbol, was moved to sing the anthem in her head. *Long may she wave.*

"Rotate 45 degrees. Let's minimize our profile." Captain Obadiah told his helm, then turned to the gunnery liaison Fuego

Boot. "Tell Suri to free the flak cannons. Let's not take any hit we can avoid. Condi, begin particle cannon intercept. See what you can take out."

North saw that the *Magnus'* erratic acceleration patterns he suggested had indeed confused at least some of the ordinance fired by *Red Hammer.* North allowed himself a smug smile. *I knew it would work,* he thought. But it wasn't time to celebrate yet

"We're in range; why aren't we returning fire?" Sparks asked nervously.

"Don't fire until you see the whites of their eyes," Obadiah muttered.

"That never made any sense to me," Operations Officer Alicia Blight echoed Sparks' nerves.

"Hold on," North said what everyone was already doing. "Here comes their volley. Fifty… maybe sixty have us targeted."

"Steady on return fire. Steady," the captain said.

All eyes were on the tactical screen which now delineated each enemy projectile as a moving red dot, closing in on the *Magnus.* Several of the red dots disappeared from the tactical, as Condi's computer controlled targeting successfully intercepted its targets.

"Way to go, Condi!" Rhodes yelled.

"Several of the missiles are equipped with point defense systems," the VI reported.

"That's what flack are cannons for," North said.

Half of the missiles reached the flack line, and it would only be seconds before some made it through to the ship. *But how many?* thought North.

The ship shook as the sounds of impact vibrated through the bulkheads.

"How bad?" Obadiah called out.

"Four impacts," Blight said, looking over her magnetic resonance screen. "Still running the diagnostics. Two hull breaches, but auto sealers are already in place. Power good. Life support is good. Engine two is offline, looks like some serious damage. One and three are fully operational."

"What about gunnery?"

"All weapon systems green."

"Minimum distance to *Red Hammer* in 15 seconds," Rhodes

reported. "Prepare for flyby."

"Gunnery command, fire everything we have. Let's show them our teeth. North, give me a casualty report."

"Chief Suri reports all silos emptied," Boot reported.

"Here's a little present for you, sons-of-bitches," Sparks pumped her fist in the air. "Sorry we were late to your welcome-to-*Magellan* party."

"My Lord," North pointed to the *Red Hammer* on the screen now in enhanced telescopic range. "The *American Spirit* is ramming *Red Hammer*!"

Sparks looked to the deep space ship which had been her home for three years. She felt a gut punch as she witnessed the *American Spirit's* violent end. The injured boat left a trail of sparking entrails as it plunged toward a clearly injured *Red Hammer*.

"Too late! Too... God, no," Obadiah cried, overcome with grief as he slumped in his chair, the restraining belts holding fast.

"It's not enough thrust!" Lews shouted across the bridge of *Red Hammer* as sweat poured off her round, bald head. "She's going to hit us!"

"Captain," Renee also shouted. "*Magnus* is hit, but not critically. They've launched a counter attack. Particle beams hitting us now, point defense holding. But the point defense might not stop so many projectiles."

"The point defense is meaningless if we can't evade the *American Spirit*," Ai'la'ausd words exploded with panic.

Ai'la'ausd did not think himself a coward, but his survival instinct kicked in. *If the American Spirit could be called off,* he thought, *our point defense could protect us from Magnus' onslaught.* "Signal our surrender! Surrender!"

Even if someone was on the bridge of *American Spirit* to receive the message, control was almost nonexistent as more and more of the ship crumbled into space. And Jefferson would not countermand Boro's final orders.

From her life pod, Elizabeth Hawkins had a ringside seat to the destructive spectacle. Her eyes were locked on her former ship as it plowed into the primary hull of the *Red Hammer*. The

American Spirit could take no more abuse; the remaining superstructure fractured into a dozen pieces, each digging into *Red Hammer* with so much force that the Utopia-class warship appeared to shred like cheap foil.

Seconds later, *Magnus'* barrage joined the chaos, as hundreds of missiles, undeterred by a non-functioning point defense system, found a target in the mass of intertwined hulls. The initial series of explosions were blindingly bright, and the shockwaves catapulted ship fragments and bodies and other items never meant for vacuum into space.

Elizabeth couldn't stop the sobs that shook her body.

The secondary hull of *Red Hammer*, mostly protected from *American Spirit's* kamikaze antics took multiple missile hits as the *Magnus* zoomed out of even telescopic visual range. The trauma ripped open the antimatter reactor, and whatever wasn't incinerated in the blast was flung away at incredible speeds.

CHAPTER EIGHT

January 1, 2607. Central Command, Waypoint Magellan, four days into the siege of Waypoint Magellan.

Amberly was right. I could not save her.

Dek Tigona was lost in his thoughts, sitting hopelessly on the floor in the corner of the *Magellan's* command center.

Moreno's sacrifice gambit, which tossed more than one hundred souls into the dark abyss of open space, did little to slow the Chasm advance. Chasm controlled nearly the entire waypoint now.

The *Utopia* herself was long gone, returning to Arara with the cruelest spoil of war, the only woman Dek ever loved, Amberly Macready. The Chairman promised to make Amberly suffer miserably, and Dek knew the Chasm leader would waste no time pouring her wrath out on Raven One's daughter.

Powerful, unresolved feelings of helplessness boiled over him again, and he opened his mouth to scream words of anguish for the 100th time, but no sound came out. His voice was stripped and hoarse. His lips were cracked and his eyes felt dry.

"Comms are still blocked. Damm. You'd think at some point the Chasm dirt lickers would turn off their dirty jammers. Is anyone left out there for a counter-push?" Acting Marine Commander Trish Moreton wondered aloud, looking desperately at *Magellan's* governor. "Did we do the right thing by locking down here instead of re-joining the fight?"

Rillio scanned the 20-some-odd *Magellan* soldiers and civilians who had trapped themselves in the barricaded *Magellan* cencomm. Thor took comfort in the fact that although Chasm controlled the rest of *Magellan*, it did not yet hold *Magellan's* heart.

Still, he didn't have an answer to Moreton's question.

Dek did. "There's no fight, Trish. We never stood a chance. We all made the mistake of underestimating the Chairman. We weren't ready. Time was not on our side. Now all we can do is wait."

The holdouts had successfully prevented Chasm from taking

cencomm for now. As long as loyalists controlled the command center, the Dark Armada would be delayed in completing its order to destroy the remaining waypoints and assault Earth. After retreating from the skirmish on the hangar, Trish used a drastic tactic she learned from the late Commander Rita Moreno: She decompressed all the chambers leading into the command center. Now in addition to trying to break into the most secure room in the waypoint, the enemy would have to make the attempt in a vacuum.

"Chasm engineers *must* be in vac suits by now," Mac Dillington said. "They'll be drilling through the doors soon."

"Maybe they are just waiting for us to die," Marcos DeLeon said. "They must know our rations and water are limited."

"What do you think, preacher man?" Mac looked at Ramos.

Still covered with dried blood from the previous battle, the tan man shrugged. "Doesn't matter what I think. I'm ready to go be with Jesus."

"I wish somehow we could get a message out," Thor said, "and let humanity know of the heroes that died for our freedom here on *Magellan*. Or maybe find out the fate of the *Magnus* and *American Spirit*."

"I hope Flora is okay," Mac thought of his sister.

"I would have liked to have one last ice-cold beer," Marcos said, licking his sore, dehydrated lips. "Even that piss that Kato served."

"Kato, that son of a dirt-licker," Thor swore. "At least he's rotting in hell now. Thank you, Dek."

Dek nodded, and felt a small wave of schadenfreude as he thought about that Hawk floating out in space with a bullet hole through his head.

"Let's count our blessings," Mac put on a brave face, "at least we still have air to breath."

"Yes, thank God this place had its own backup life support system," Ramos echoed words of gratitude.

Dek dismissed the optimism. "Let's not pretend otherwise," Dek coughed, his blue-grey eyes sullen, "this is the end. There are no options. None."

"Dammit, Dek! Rita gave her life so we could have a fighting chance," Trish scolded, irritated, wishing Moreno was still among the living. "Don't be pathetic. Don't give up. Think. There must be an option."

"We've spent four days thinking," Thor looked at Trish with sadness. "If we haven't figured out something by now, maybe it's best we accept our fates. Moreno didn't die in vain. Every hour we hold out is an hour we are buying for the other waypoints. That's all that matters now. Rita would have understood that."

Dek felt lower than he had ever been — worse than when he discovered Amberly's profession of love was a lie. Even then, hope lingered. Now, there was none. The Chairman had Amberly, and Dek knew he going to die.

After cheating death for so long, Dek tasted his impending mortality. "There is nothing to be done," Dek grimly croaked. "They've already killed the rest of *Magellan's* adults. They will train *Magellan's* children to be their drones, no doubt conditioning them to be shock troops when they assault the other waypoints. If they manage to get through that door before we die, we should be ready to kill ourselves. I've seen Chasm's protocols for prisoners."

Ramos raised his eyebrows as an idea struck him. "There *is* the Samson option," Ramos said. "But I am not sure if it is what God would want."

"What's the Samson option?" Thor asked what everyone was thinking.

"The Good Book tells a story of a judge of ancient Israel named Samson. He was captured by his enemies, all but defeated. In his last act, he used the great strength God had given him to pull down the pillars holding up the building he was in."

"Suicide," Trish murmured disapprovingly. "God would not want that."

"No, sacrifice," Ramos explained. "When the building came down, his enemies were crushed with him."

"The Samson option," Dek smiled, suddenly feeling his strength returning. "Why not? Kimberly Macready was going to use *Magellan's* own antimatter reactors as a self-destruct bomb. Take the Dark Armada with us."

Pinging vibrations from the primary command center portal drew everyone's attention.

"They are not waiting for us to die," Thor said. "They are

coming through the vacuum. Let's go out in a blaze of glory, then."

"You want us to blow up *Waypoint Magellan* by sabotaging our own antimatter reactor?" Trish said. "No way! You heard Dek. They have our children."

"We must. There is nothing we can do for the children now," Thor said, standing up and suddenly projecting more energy than his tired soul had felt in years. "Think about it. If *Magnus* takes out the *Red Hammer*, and then we take *Xander's Mace* and *People's Harvest* with us when we go out, the Dark Armada is done. We will have saved every waypoint from here to Earth. How many children is that?"

"There must be another way," Mac agreed with Trish.

"Death is the merciful course," Dek said. "Your children will be tortured and brainwashed to serve the Chairman, as the expendable fodder."

"You don't have children, Dek," Trish cried. "You can't understand."

"Chasm will do everything in their power to make them forget they had parents, family," Dek promised. "Chasm will only give them a release from intense pain when they renounce their birth family. For Chasm, the only family is the state."

"How could you have been part of that?" Marcos asked Dek.

"I was born in a cohort, from an artificial incubator. I only had the state to teach me, and Chasm poured its truth into my hungry ears my entire childhood. What happens if you are raised to believe liberty is a lie, that even the concept of love is just a toxic tool to create inequity between the sexes? When you believe that equity is better than freedom, Chasm's promise of an eternally ordered paradise is appealing. Of course, one day you wake up and realize that you don't want to be a drone, and that people have value beyond being a cog in the communal machine. Amberly woke me up, and I'm forever grateful."

"Amberly," Mac thought about the kidnapped woman. "What will they do to her, Dek?"

A loud popping noise vibrated through the main door. The persistent red light on the door confirmed the atmospheric condition on the other side of the door was still a vacuum.

"We're all dead in five minutes, tops," Dek said. "They get the door open, we suffocate. Then Chasm troopers in vac suits come in and take over *Magellan*, and the Dark Armada moves on to destroy *Waypoint Gilbert, Cartier, Estevanico*. What about the children on those stations, Trish? We can still save them. Let's blow this place."

"No. No. No!" Trish said, as she pulled her sidearm and swung it around. "They have my son! *My son*. How can you ask a mother to kill her son?"

Thor slipped behind Trish, drew his stun weapon, and fired two bolts into the woman. Fear filled her eyes as she dropped to the floor, convulsing briefly, then becoming unconscious and still.

"What the hell! You can't stun the Acting Commander," said a Marine. Another reached for his sidearm.

"Don't take that tone with me. I am the duly elected governor of *Magellan*." Thor bellowed authority.

Dek understood. "We can't ask Moreton to kill her own son, but it has to be done. It's better this way," he explained to the excited Marine.

Suddenly, a loud sucking sound drew everyone's attention to the door. A drill bit had finally pierced the cencomm's reinforced door.

"Get over there and give them some pain! Buy us time! Let's save the rest of the waypoints!" Thor ordered. "We will die today, but for God's sake, let's take them with us!"

Marcos DeLeon pulled his small-caliber pistol and ran to the door. He aligned the short barrel with the drill-puncture hole and fired twice. His first bullet hit the door, ricocheted and nearly hit him, but the second threaded the orifice.

"I got one! I think I got one," Marcos said, over the sound of atmosphere pushing through the small hole.

Ramos pulled a polyurethane strip from the bridge's toolkit and threw it over the hole. He looked to Thor. "Governor, it's time to pull down the pillars! It won't take them long to take down this door."

"So, Ramos, I guess that means you think God would approve," Thor smiled as he walked to the commander's station in the center of the room.

"Let's ask him when we see him," Dek said. "Governor, just command *Magellan* to shut down the antimatter coolant system."

"That will take a half hour to go critical," Mac said. "Won't

Chasm just be able to override from outside?"

"No. All the other functions of the waypoint can be overridden from external locations. But the waypoint designers wanted to keep a crazy person from being able to override a system that had the potential to do what we are going to do: self-destruct. They figured if a crazy person had captured the cencomm, the most watched and guarded location on the waypoint, they had won already. But a terrorist with override access to antimatter reactor –" Thor said.

"So, this is the only place you can take out a whole waypoint just by whispering a command?" Mac interrupted.

"That's why Kimberly Macready needed access to the command center during the Battle of *Magellan*. That's why Moreno was hell-bent on keeping her out," Dek explained.

The door pinged again, with the unmistakable rat-tat-tat of bullets impacting the exterior.

The doors atmosphere indicator was now green. "They've figured out a way to pressurize the other side. Marcos, everyone, we have to hold them off."

Thor pressed his hand to the command access station. "Governor Thor Rillio. *Magellan* command, prepare to receive critical override command."

Magellan's generic VI spoke back. "Ready, Governor Thor. Speak the override code in response to challenge question delta four epsilon now."

"Gamma-Tango-Three-Epsilon-Zeta-Four-Montana-Amazon."

"Present exposed skin for DNA scanning," *Magellan* said, and the governor complied.

"Verification accepted. What is your override command, Governor Rillio?"

"Override safety protocols on the antimatter coolant systems A, B, C and D. Then hard seal all coolant lines."

"Warning, Governor. If you proceed, the waypoint could experience catastrophic damage. Are you sure you want to proceed?"

"That's the point," Thor said. He looked across the room at the souls under his command. The last week had been a harrowing experience of the worst sort. *We will soon be at peace,* he thought.

Thor looked at Trish, who had the mannerism of someone having a dark dream. Then he looked at Dek, and Dek nodded.

"Have the automatic warnings turned off too," Dek suggested.

"Disable all automatic warnings and alerts, and proceed with the shut down," Thor commanded.

"Commands confirmed," the VI announced.

"It's done," Ramos said. "God have mercy on our souls."

The pounding on the exterior intensified. "It's a good thing they can't unlock that portal with Macready's hacking box," Thor smiled and poked a thumb at the door. "Manual. The only one on the station."

"Let's get ready for their rush," Marcos shouted to his fellow Marines.

Captain Fantmis, master of the *People's Harvest*, was studying a projected map of *Magellan's* Science Quarter in the conference room adjacent to her spacious captain's quarters. Fantmis rubbed her crew cut yellow hair as she made mental notes. Sitting across the table was Arif, the man designated to be governor of *Magellan* once the Dark Armada departed. He sipped on a cup of hot Araran tea as the door rang.

"Come," the captain said.

A frazzled, short ensign stepped into the room. He was already quite pale, even for a Lewis Island native, but the captain thought the ensign looked especially ghost-white today.

"Ensign," she spouted. "What is it?"

"Ma'am. We've lost the *Red Hammer*. She reported engaging *Magnus*, then stopped transmitting position data to the relay outside the jamming zone. The corvette we sent to collect the relay data just returned."

"I see," the captain considered the news. "The *Magnus* probably caught *Red Hammer* off guard. Captain Ai'la'ausd has always been sloppy."

Soon-to-be-governor Arif snorted. "The *Red Hammer* gone? That's a hard loss. Ai'la'ausd. A fool of the highest order."

Fantmis looked up, lost in a calculation. After a brief moment, she looked at the ensign. "*Magnus* is at least two days out. By the time she returns – if she returns – we'll have our two ships' armaments and those of *Magellan* ready to destroy *Magnus* once and for all," the captain said. "Be at peace, ensign. Now then, do you have a report on the efforts to access the command center. Surely we have it now?"

"Last report, the engineers had re-pressurized the access points, but they still have to open the security door," the ensign said.

"Go, report to the admiral about the unfortunate fate of *Red Hammer*, and confirm we have the command center."

"Yes ma'am."

Thor looked at the timer he had set up on his infopad: about 10 minutes before the antimatter reactors went critical. It wouldn't be long before Chasm discovered the kamikaze play. The Marines had set up a firing line ready for whatever Chasm trooper happened to step through the door first. Thor could hear the heavy cutting machines now. The reinforced doors would not last much longer.

Ramos went one-by-one to each Marine and prayed with them while they waited for their final destiny.

Trish started to stir and rubbed her head. She forced herself to sit up as an image of her five-year-old son popped in her head. She knew her husband was already dead at the hands of Chasm, and their son was all she had left of her love.

She saw the barricade, looked at the counter on Thor's info pad.

"The blood is on my hands," Thor said firmly as he caught Trish's gaze, "not yours."

Anger burned in her eyes. "I won't let you kill my son." Trish grabbed for her gun, but Dek had already removed it.

"It is done. There is nothing you can do now," Dek explained.

Anguish took over the Marine's face as she was forced to accept Thor's conclusion. Trish collapsed in Dek's arms and wept. Trish never cried, and now, pent up grief took over. "I'm sorry Trish. There was no right thing to do. This was the best wrong thing."

"Here they come!" Marcos shouted as a large chunk of the thick carbon polymer hardened steel alloy door flew forward, creating a meter-high hole. Immediately, Marcos threw a short-fuse grenade through the orifice.

Panic-filled voices called out before the grenade exploded.

The blast further damaged the door, and as the smoke cleared, Chasm troops began advancing through the hole. The Marines opened fire, and at first, the lead trooper's personal point defense system absorbed the bullets. But it only took a second or two of sustained fire for the system to overload, and then another second for the trooper's armor to be compromised.

The trooper screamed in pain and fell forward, and the other troops retreated back outside the door.

"We don't have enough ammo to keep that up," Marcos reported. "It won't take long before they realize we can only stop two or three more of them."

Thor looked at his infopad. Six minutes remaining. "We don't need much longer."

Admiral Björk stood on the observation deck of the *Xander's Mace*. She was not pleased with the destruction of the *Red Hammer*. *Magnus* was out there. That ship was not to be underestimated. Maja worried if *Magnus* engaged the two remaining Dark Armada warships while they were tethered to *Magellan*, the enemy would have a significant tactical advantage.

Björk summoned her yeoman. "Please tell Captain Clarke to recall any essential crew from *Magellan* and to decouple from the waypoint immediately. I'll meet her on the bridge."

The Magnus is coming, the admiral thought.

"Out of ammo," Marcos shouted. "Time for the knives." Several Marines, including DeLeon, had built makeshift bayonets, a melee counter-measure against point defense system-powered armor. Chasm troopers had made it into the far end of cencomm, and the Marines charged them, toppling magnetic resonance screens and pushing back sliding chairs.

"Governor, get back to the upper deck where it will be safe," Mac said.

"Why?" Thor Rillio said, as he pulled a six-inch knife from a sheath under his cloak. "I will go down fighting for my waypoint."

The governor followed his Marines, shouting as they closed the five meters between them and nearly dozen Chasm troops.

The troopers stepped over the fallen bodies of their comrades.

In the lead, Marcos DeLeon, hero of the Battle of *Magellan* and the best shot on the waypoint, was the first target when the Chasm troopers found their footing and brought weapons to bear. Bullets and stun blasts enveloped his body, and he fell face first a meter from the Chasm line.

Just before the lines clashed, a second marine fell, shredded by Chasm bullets. During the charge, Mac was hit once in his abdomen, but still managed to shove his bayonet deep into the neck of a trooper.

"For the glory of Arara! For the common good!" the Chasm assault leader shouted. Though she knew her troops were not expecting close quarters, hand-to-hand combat, the leader smiled as more of her reinforcements entered cencomm. *It's just a matter of time before the remaining Earth loyalists are extinguished,* she thought.

Mac removed his bayonet, blood spurting, and began to parry with a Chasm trooper, who was using his rifle to block the lethal blade. Thor took a bullet in his shoulder as he lunged with his knife for a trooper firing from behind the cover of the monitoring station.

"Almost there, friends! Almost there," Thor shouted.

The secondary access passage that led to the conference room and the *Magellan's* hangar slid open, and a new front of Chasm forces marched in. Dek and Trish Moreton had positioned themselves on the station control balcony above the access point.

Dek leaped, colliding with and bringing two Chasm troopers to the ground. He had his knife at the ready, and silt the throat of the one trooper before springing up and pushing another trooper back into the entering group.

Trish took Moreno's javelin, jumped down after Dek, and pierced the stomach of the second trooper Dek had knocked down.

The admiral walked onto the bridge of *Xander's Mace* to find a furious captain.

"With all due respect, Maja," Captain Clarke said, "you may be the admiral, but you must consult with me before recalling my team. I must insist–"

"Silence fool," the Admiral, flanked by two members of her guard. "You are no longer captain. Take this idiot to the brig." Her guards complied.

"What! Maja, you power-hungry bitch, you can't do this. I will tell the Chairman, and when I do –" The guards drug the captain out the door.

Maja looked at the officer on the helm. "As soon as we are detached from *Magellan*, prepare for evasive maneuvers. *Magnus* is missing. *Red Hammer* is dead. How long till we are detached?"

The helmsman checked a reading on her screen. "Another 15 minutes."

"Don't wait for anyone," Maja said sternly. "I want us free to move. This station was once saved by a last-minute appearance of that Earth warship. It will not happen again."

"Yes, ma'am."

The comm officer stood. "Admiral, engineering reports that … *Magellan's* antimatter reactors are… heating up. Maybe critically!"

"Hell. They are going to blow us all into history," Maja said. She didn't expect a suicide play. She had to think quickly. *The governor was in cencomm,* she thought. *He must have triggered the self-sabotage. He could countermand it if forced to do so.*

Maja was barking orders in rapid fire. "Engineering, how long till the reactor goes critical? Strike Force commander, redeploy two squads to the *Magellan* reactor with a tech team to see if they can cool that thing down. Comm officer, get me the squad commander leading the assault on *Magellan* cencomm."

"I have the squad leader on comms," the portly communications specialists reported.

Pastor Ramos huddled quietly, praying in a darker corner of the command center, away from the chaos of the battle. He had seen too much pain, too much bloodshed, too much evil. He longed for eternal release.

A Chasm trooper had found Ramos in his hiding spot, and raised his weapon. "Where is your fantasy God now? If he was real, wouldn't he save you?" the trooper mocked.

"He already saved me. Thousands of years ago," Ramos said.

Be closed his eyes and prayed, "Lord forgive them," as the Chasm trooper pulled his trigger.

In the middle of the melee, Governor Thor struggled to stay upright, fighting the searing pain as he bled out of his left shoulder. He raised his right hand and plunged his knife at the torso armor of the squad leader. But the knife point could not penetrate the polycarbonate fiber, and the reactive force caused the weapon to fly out of the governor's hand.

Under her helmet the Chasm leader smirked as she backhanded the Thor, who fell to the ground. The leader raised her rifle at the pinned governor.

"Nooo!" Mac yelled, in a desperate attempt to save Thor. He disengaged from his hand-to-hand combat and charged the Chasm squad leader. Before he could reach his target, the trooper he was struggling with took aim and shot three bullets. Two were stopped by Mac's vest armor, but the third pierced his neck, severing his spinal cord. *At least my sister is safe*, Mac thought as he collapsed to the floor.

Mac Dillington died defending his waypoint, the way he had wanted it.

The Chasm leader was temporarily distracted by Mac, but turned her attention back to the governor. Thor closed his eyes. By his estimations, less than two minutes remained before a critical reactor failure would doom *Magellan* and the attached Chasm warships.

"Too late," the governor laughed. "You are too late."

"Too late for what?" the Chasm squad leader asked. Instead of waiting for an answer, she shot Thor Rillio, governor of *Magellan*, in the head. "Stupid old man."

The leader's helmet comms signaled.

"What is it? I am in the middle of a battle here!" The leader shouted.

"This is the admiral," Björk's voice boomed in her helmet.

"I'm sorry Admira–"

"Shut up and listen to me," Maja spit. "Do not kill the governor under any circumstances! Find him and I must speak to him now. Now!"

The squad leader looked at the blood-splattered lifeless face of Thor. She felt the blood drain from her own face.

"Sergeant. Do you copy!?"

"Admiral, the governor is dead."

The communication line was cut suddenly. *Dirt. I'm in big trouble,* the squad leader thought.

"Pull us away from *Magellan*! Pull us away now!" Björk shouted.

"But Admiral," the engineer's mate who had bridge duty interrupted, "we are still attached. That will rip a hole in our primary hull."

"Do it, helm. Do it now!"

"Admiral, with all due respect, are you out of your mind?" the *Xander's Mace's* First Officer spoke up. "Belay that order, helm master. Clearly the admiral is insane. If we pull back while still coupled, we'd be extremely crippled."

Björk pointed at one of her personal guards and then at the First Officer. The First Officer, realizing that the admiral had just silently ordered his death, pulled his gun and shot at the guard. The bullets dissolved in the guard's point defense system, and the First Officer quickly dropped his gun and put up his hands.

"Helm, pull us away now, or I will shoot you and do it myself!" the Admiral shouted.

"Pulling away now, thrusters firing at reverse vector, powered to 80-m newtons," the helm officer replied, wiping sweat from her brow.

The *Xander's Mace* was nose-in to *Magellan*. On the forward bridge wall screen, the image of the two clamping gangways being stretched startled the bridge crew. The left clamp was the first to give, at the connecting joint to the *Xander's Mace's* primary hull. When the second gangway was fully extended from the escaping *Xander's Mace*, it didn't give, and the ship jerked. The crew lurched. Caught by the whiplash, the bridge officer monitoring environment controls slammed head-first into a bulkhead. He fell to the floor, knocked out cold.

"Hull breach," an engineering mate shouted.

"More power!" Björk screamed. On the screen, the bridge officers saw numerous *Xander's Mace* crew members, who, on the order of recall, had just been returning through the left gangway. They were floating, instantly killed as the umbilical cord between station and ship was ripped apart.

"You murdered them, admiral!" the First Officer shouted, arms still raised. "I will make sure that the Chairman has your head for this gross incompetence and failure! Did you hear me?"

The Admiral ignored the FO and walked behind the helm station.

"We are leaking atmosphere and people," the helm master replied. "I respectfully—"

Maja took a mighty swing and pushed the helm master out of her station. "You idiots. We are all going to die!" The admiral sat down at the controls and increased thruster power. She looked up and could see the remaining gangway was straining, but still holding them.

We must be pulling Magellan, Maja thought, trying to figure the physics of the situation. She increased the power and saw gasses shoot out into space at the forced joint on the waypoint side of the gangway. *Almost there.*

The bridge of the *People's Harvest* was now in full panic mode.

"Captain on the bridge," the junior lieutenant stood as Captain Fantmis ascended the command platform in the center of the bridge.

"What the hell is going on?" the captain said.

"It's chaos on *Xander's Mace*," the lieutenant said. "The admiral relieved the captain from duty and apparently ordered the ship to withdraw from *Magellan* without decoupling! They are tearing off!"

"What is she thinking?" the captain asked.

The comm officer spoke as if narrating a dream. "Just got word from *Xander's Mace* engineering group. *Magellan's* antimatter reactor – is going – is going – critical. In – minutes."

Fantmis immediately realized the finality of their impending doom, but her crisis training kicked in. *Remain level*, she thought.

"Begin our detachment then," the captain said calmly. "With haste, if you please."

We're not going to survive this, but no sense in sharing that opinion with my crew, she thought, then said aloud, "Comms, turn off our jammer and broadcast our situation and contingency data to Arara. Also, order any Chasm forces on *Magellan* to abandon station on an open channel. If they get to an escape pod, there is a chance they might survive, and we can pick them up."

"Can't a reactor build-up be countermanded?" asked the lieutenant.

"It must be too late," the captain said. "That's the only reason why the admiral would risk ripping her ship apart to free *Xander's Mace* from her grasp on *Magellan*."

The lieutenant stood close to his captain, looked her directly in the eyes and spoke nearly inaudibly. "If that's true, we're not going to make it, are we?"

Captain Fantmis shook her head.

Trish Moreton's eyes grew wide and panicked. Dek leapt towards her, stepping over the third Chasm comrade whose life he had taken that day.

As Dek reached out for her, Trish's face grew sullen. "It's going to be okay, Dek," she said and then toppled over into his arms, dead. Behind her, Dek saw the man who had put several bullets in her back. He smirked at Dek. "Next!"

Dek, in one smooth motion, dropped Trish's lifeless body, and threw his knife at the asshole trooper in front of him, impaling the assailant on the hand. The trooper dropped his gun, and fell to his knees and tried to pull the knife out.

Dek drew a deep breath. He was surprised when Trish's murderer turned and limped out the secondary access door. Dek whirled around and saw four remaining Chasm troops on the far side of the command center flee through the main portal. *Someone must have told them about our little surprise*, the rogue guessed.

Dek Tigona was the last man standing.

Bodies were scattered across the cencomm floor. Pools of blood expanded around dead Marines and troopers. He saw the governor, Marcos, Mac and a dozen others he knew, all dead. *Where's Ramos?*

An instant later, he spotted the fallen pastor, lying on his side, still clutching his worn Bible, in a dark nook. Dek ran to him, and fell down on his knees beside Ramos. The old man was soaked in his own blood. "Oh no, Ramos."

Ramos muttered softly. "I'm not home yet, Dek. But soon, soon, we'll be together with the Lord."

"You saved me, Ramos," Dek cried. "I'm sorry I can't save you."

"You know what the Good Book says," Ramos said in a whisper now, as he recited some ancient scripture. "The Savior, he said, 'Don't let your hearts be troubled.' He said, 'My Father's house has many rooms; if that were not so, would I have told you that I am going there to prepare a place for you?'"

Dek finished the verse he memorized when he was in solitary confinement as an exile on *American Spirit*. "Jesus said, 'And if I go and prepare a place for you, I will come back and take you to be with me that you also may be where I am. You know the way to the place where I am going.'"

Ramos smiled, closed his eyes, and died.

"See you soon, old man," Dek said, wiping a tear as he stood up. He knew his time was up. The antimatter reactor would melt through its casing and create an explosion that would rip *Magellan* apart any moment now.

"What now?" he said aloud to no one.

He reached into a pouch pocket on his left thigh and pulled out a small infopad. "Show me a picture of Amberly Macready." The VI complied, and Dek fixed on the image as he slumped into the commander's chair in the middle of cencomm.

The picture was of Midas, Ramos, Amberly and Dek playing cards on Fuentes Station just over two years ago. Dek zoomed in on Amberly as he remembered that day, just a few weeks after Amberly's fiancé, Skylar, had been exposed as a Hawk and cast out into the embrace of space.

He wanted to reach into the picture and pull his fingers through her red locks. Her green eyes seemed to call to him. He imagined his parched, cracked lips pressing her soft ones.

The ship jerked suddenly. Dek dropped his infopad. At first, he thought that the antimatter reactor had exploded, but he was still alive moments later. He called up a tactical map on the commander's station. He could see that *Xander's Mace* was trying to pull away from *Magellan*. *Maybe they are stuck,* Dek wondered. Then a thought occurred to him.

He pulled up the basic comm access on the commander's

station. The Chasm signal jamming was down. *Maybe there is still time*, Dek thought.

"Send a message to XO North on the *Magnus*," Dek told the cencomm VI.

An indicator light blinked, and Dek smiled.

"Hey North," Dek said. "I'm running out of time. We're about to blow *Magellan*, and hopefully take this Dark Armada with us. The Chairman has Amberly on *Utopia* and is long gone. We tried to stop them. Almost everyone died trying to fight back. Heroes. Now it's just me.

"Please, save Amberly. Take the *Magnus* back to Arara, and save her. It's up to you. Tell Sparks to stay out of trouble. North, this is the last request of a condemned man: When you save Amberly, and I know you will, please give her this message.

"Amberly, by the time you get this, you will be all that is left of *Magellan*. You are the heart of this place, and we should have known it could never survive without you. I wanted you to know I have never stopped loving you, and I never will. You were right; I couldn't save you. But I can still pray for you. So, I will. And that might be enough. Goodbye, Amberly Macready."

Dek pushed his hand into the magnetic resonance screen, and the VI responded that the message had been sent.

Warning klaxons sounded now. Dek slowly stood up and walked toward the secondary entrance, into the hallway that led to both the *Magellan* hangar and a large meeting room that had a floor-to-ceiling exterior plexiglass wall. Every step Dek took was painful, his leg muscles torn by Chasm bullets two days ago. He stopped wondering if every step and every breath would be his last.

He walked into the empty meeting room, past the table and chairs, and leaned against the transparent wall, sliding down so that he was sitting on the floor, looking out into the vastness of space. As he peered into the trillions upon trillions of kilometers of emptiness broken only by the occasional star, he wondered if, somewhere out there, God really was preparing a place for him.

"Protect Amberly. May she be comforted by unending love," eyes wide open, deeply breathing, Dek prayed.

His prayer was interrupted by a screaming voice from the hall. "Dammit! Open up!"

Dek stood up and stumbled out the secondary access door towards the hangar and the voice.

The Chasm trooper, Illiad Payne, tried to manually force the main door to the *Midway*. Anchored to the deck, the corvette did not evacuate out into space during Moreno's suicide play. The doors had since been closed as Chasm took over more of *Magellan*. Payne had been barely able to release the ship from its moorings owing to the fact his right hand was severely lacerated by Dek's knife. His blood was all over the deck.

Dek entered the hanger and saw Payne.

"Where are *you* going, trooper?" Dek asked. "Need some help with that?"

"Yes! Yes! Hurry or we're both dead?" Payne belted.

"Truce, then?" Dek suggested.

"Of course," Payne said. "I'll be your prisoner. Just get me off *Magellan* before it's too late."

"It's probably too late," Dek smiled, but then he entered his access code and biometrics into the *Midway's* lock and it opened. "Do you know how to fly this thing?"

"Well enough," Payne said as he hoisted himself into the ship, wincing in pain from his injured hand. Payne thought about closing the door and not letting Dek in, but then remembered he did not have codes that would re-open the space doors. Payne sat down in the pilot's seat. "Come on! Hurry!"

Dek climbed in after him and slipped into the *Midway's* navigator's seat. "Fire up the engines. I'll override the space doors."

Dek entered in the command codes Thor had authenticated for him days earlier, ordering the space doors open. The vacuum seal dropped in the rear of the hanger and the vast cavern began to depressurize.

"Come on! Come on!" Payne growled.

A minute passed, but to Payne, it seemed like an eternity. Finally, the artificial gravity deactivated and a brilliant star field waited beyond the retracted doors. Because the cavity of the hangar was a complete vacuum, Payne and Dek could not hear the excruciating loud crack snap through the waypoint. The *Midway* accelerated thousands of kilometers per second into open space away from the eminent doom. A few seconds later, all who remained on *Magellan* were incinerated in the blast.

From the bridge of *Xander's Mace*, Maja watched in amazement as *Waypoint Magellan* rippled in violent waves. *Xander's Mace* had broken away from the station seconds earlier, limping away from the doomed waypoint, hemorrhaging vital substances and people through the two rips in the primary hull. The bow thrusters had been damaged in the decoupling, and the ship, still facing *Magellan*, was struggling to move into a position to use its main engines.

As fear gripped her desperate bridge crew, Björk fell to her knees, weeping. She had failed the Chairman, and she had failed Chasm. Guilt and sorrow consumed Maja, and she wished she were dead.

The grey waypoint exploded into tens of thousands of fragments, tube cars, school desks, life support tanks, planters, toys and bodies, thrust by a blinding white orange flame at incredible speeds away from the reactor's epicenter. Maja watched as the *People's Harvest*, still attached to the waypoint, was consumed by maelstrom and ripped into uncountable fragments.

Not able to escape the blast in its crippled state, *Xander's Mace* was swallowed by the expanding radius of destruction. Admiral Maja Björk, the last person to see *Waypoint Magellan*, received her death wish.

L.S. ROEBUCK

CHAPTER NINE

The U.S.S. Magnus, February 24, 2608, 14 months after the destruction of Magellan, en route to Arara

Kora Macready Wilder stood quietly on the garden observation deck of the *U.S.S. Magnus*, with five-year-old Alroy Wilder holding her hand. The ruddy boy was fidgety, but he knew from experience that his mother would only be a minute, and then they would go have lunch in the commons with Aunt Sparks. He might even get to play with his friend, Nora.

Kora ran her hands over his name: Trot Wilder, her lover, husband, protector. Thousands of names were similarly etched on several panels of plexiglass hung on the garden's bow-side wall – names of those who died defending *Magellan*. The *Magellan* Memorial was completed six months into *Magnus*' pursuit of *Utopia, en route* to Arara. She bowed her head, and thanked God for his mercy, as was her ritual every Sunday after she attended religious services. Sometimes she cried, sometimes she didn't. Today, she cried.

She saw other names she recognized: Skip of President's Quarter, Midas of Science Quarter.

"I'm sorry about daddy," Alroy said. Although the boy *was* unusually empathetic, saying "sorry" was an automated response anytime he saw his mother distressed, particularly when Alroy knew he was in trouble. Barely four when Trot gave his life to save his family, Alroy had only hazy memories of his father.

"He loved you more than life itself," Kora looked at her son through her long, black locks that had fallen in front of her face. She offered Alroy a tender smile, wiped at her tears, and pushed her hair out of her face. "Ready for lunch little man? We're eating with North today."

"Captain North!" Alroy lit up.

North stood at the head of the tactical table on the bridge of the *Magnus*. He held up his shot glass. "To Captain Obadiah. May God rest his soul."

"To the captain," the *Magnus* officers surrounding the table said in unison.

"I only knew the captain for a few months," said Caddo, who had been rescued from a life pod after the *American Spirit* collided with *Red Hammer*. "I was grateful he gave me a commission after you guys plucked me out of space. He was a good man with a consistent moral compass."

"He was a true patriot," Lt. Rhodes said flatly.

"Hell, I served under three captains – Skylar Triggs, Dek Tigona and Boro, who were all Chasm at one point or another. I mean I am glad Dek and Boro – God rest his soul – came around, but Captain Obadiah seemed like he knew himself and the score. Steady as a rock, unlike some of our own, not even thinking about the Chasm turncoats." As Caddo said the word 'turncoats,' his eyes unintentionally fell on Sparks. "Um, sorry, no offense intended."

Sparks laughed curtly. "Like I care what you think. Seriously, I don't even know who you are. But, I agree, Obadiah was the real deal. I was glad to call him captain for –" Sparks did some quick math in her head "four years."

"He was captain to me my whole life. I can't believe it's been a year since —" Rhodes said.

"Since the old man blew his own brains out?" Sparks completed the young woman's thoughts.

"A little respect for the dead," Operations Chief Blight said crossly.

Her husband, engineering Chief Petty Officer Bollard put his hand on Blight's shoulder, then gently caressed her dyed-red hair. "My lady, we all have to deal with Obadiah's actions in our own way. When a man takes his life outside the normal cycles of biology or the hands of fate, it is only human to question *why*." He then tipped his head back and polished the shot of hard, synthetic liquor. It had a foul aftertaste which made Bollard grimace. He shook his head, and his dreadlocks jiggled.

Blight cooled at her husband's prompting, and she poured her own shot down her throat. She didn't like the taste; she enjoyed the burn. "We know why he did it. The guilt of losing *Magellan* and *Cortez* and *American Spirit*. I feel like dirt knowing those waypoints burned, too. But we could have helped him. We didn't need to lose him, too."

"I just wish he would have left us a note or something," Rhodes said. "It would have been nice if we would have had a chance to say goodbye."

"He hid his dark intentions well," North remarked. "Maybe we should have known."

"Here's to the captain," Sparks said, as she adjusted her half-mask, and lifted her glass. "*Maybe* he's better off among the honored dead. *We're* going back into the fight. If Chasm captures us, we're all going to torture-topia. You don't want to experience the Chairman's hospitality. Die fighting, my friends. Don't let them catch you!" Sparks threw back a second shot.

"Go out in a blaze of glory, I guess," Rhodes considered.

"If you are my friends, you'll put lead in my head before you let Chasm take me alive," Sparks requested.

North's expression turned dark. "Thank you all for taking this time to remember the anniversary of the captain's passing. Back to work. We're already losing too much time on this *Cortez* ghost station diversion; I want to spend as little time as possible getting what we need, so let's be ready to move once we reach the debris field."

Rhodes looked down awkwardly. Bollard nodded his agreement with North's urgency. Blight was already reading messages on her infopad.

As the group broke away from the meeting, Sparks lingered.

North had the tactical table displaying the navigation path to Arara. The bright line showed the course, colored yellow for the distance *Magnus* had already traveled since leaving the remains of *Magellan*.

Instead of a straight line to Arara, the ship was on a sharp deviation of nearly 15 degrees. *Utopia* was too fast; the *Magnus* couldn't catch her before she arrived at Arara. So North thought it wise to resupply fully while they had the chance. The *Magnus* computers calculated that most of the remains of *Waypoint Cortez* had probably spread out over an area of about a half-million cubic kilometers. More than 10,000 perished when Chasm destroyed *Cortez*, and the only remaining survivor they knew of was five-year-old Nora.

North studied the map, and Sparks could tell he was frustrated by the delay.

"Hey, boss," Sparks placed her hand on his shoulder, and slowly ran it down his arm. Her voice was irreverent, but her touch compassionate. "I see the darkness. Don't go there like that idiot Obadiah did. You and I, we're not like him. We're survivors. We do our best and then move on."

"Don't worry about that," North said, clenching his hand. "I will give Chasm hell, or I will die trying. I will not do Chasm the favor of me ending my own life."

"That's the spirit," Sparks attempted some cheer. "We're going to come out of this. I always do. I am a survivor, too."

"No, *Dek* is the survivor," North offered. "He almost died to protect Amberly … died like Skip and Trot and the others. I should have died that day."

"If you would have died, who would have brought the *Magnus* around to fish Dek out of the void?" Sparks said, feeling that she was failing to put some star shine into the conversation. "We saved hundreds of people from the remains of *American Spirit* and *Magellan*. If you would have died, who would we have who'd be up to the challenge of leading us now? Blight? Heh."

Sparks knew any of her own future plans required North to remain strong. She hated to bring up her rival for North's affections, but she knew if he could focus on Amberly, he would always choose to live to fight another day. Even if somehow, they managed to defeat Chasm, the chances they would find Amberly alive and well after years of being the personal prisoner of the Chairman seemed to be below calculation. Sparks tried not to linger on that sick hope. Still, in whatever post-Chasm world rose out of the coming Chaos, Sparks assumed that North would end up in a position of power. She would benefit by being close to his side.

"If you had died, there would be no one to save Amberly now," Sparks looked at North's pained eyes. She couldn't figure out if he was her friend or her mark. *Why not both?*

Are you sleeping any better?" Kora asked North as she took his arm and they strolled on the *Magnus'* running track. Virtual scenery panels lined the course, and currently it displayed a floor to ceiling rendering of a beach. Bondi blue waters crashed into white sands as pine trees swayed in a breeze. The beach wasn't a real place; just something a nine-year-old student had created in art class. North, who had been to the beaches on the Araran continent of Ingram, was impressed with the youth's realistic renderings, although he was unfamiliar with pine trees, which only existed on Earth.

"Not really," North admitted as he stepped aside for a jogging Marine in the middle of his workout.

"Amberly?" Kora pressed gently.

"I should probably get some medication," North said. "Can't you sneak me something in the med center that will help me get my vitamin Z's."

"You're the captain," Kora smiled. "I'm sure the doctors will prescribe you anything you want."

"Well, maybe I don't want the med staff to know... you know," North hushed his voice. "They need to know I am stable and in command. Not that I am going days without sleep."

"You can't sleep because you worry about Amberly," Kora pressed more firmly. She wanted to talk with North about her sister.

"Seems like everyone wants to bring up Amberly today. Yes, I'm worried for Amberly, but that doe—"

"Well, I feel the same way," Kora interrupted. "Losing Trot has torn me apart. I still turn over in bed and expect to find him sleeping next to me. I console myself knowing my husband is at peace and died a hero. But for Amberly, the unknown. I love my sister as much as anything, and the wondering where she is now, and how we are ever going to find her, and what she might be going through—"

"Don't say it," North stopped walking, his fists clenching, lowering his voice further. "I know I have my oath to Earth and to the people on *Magnus*, but I will use any resource, abuse any power I have as captain, to save her."

"I'm sorry, I shouldn't have – I mean..." Kora now regretted that she pushed about Amberly, though she desperately needed someone to share her lament for her sister. "Amberly would not want you to lose yourself in order to save her."

"She doesn't really have a say in the matter," North drew in a deep breath. "I'm okay, Kora."

Kora noticed the chronometer in the corner of the beach

rendering. "Shoot. I'm late for my shift. Can I tell them I was delayed by the captain on official business?"

"Ha. Sure," North said. "Anything for my friend."

Kora smiled as he said friend. She'd lost so many friends; she cherished the ones still with her. "Thanks for lunch and the walk. Little Alroy loves eating in the Captain's Mess. I'm so thankful Lydia was kind enough to watch Alroy and Nora while we walked."

"Lydia's a peach," North said. "You know, I never knew what she saw in Skip, but it was nice he had her in the end. Skip died the best sort of man. Sacrificing himself for what he loved."

"Skip. Midas. Rita. Trot...," Kora's voice quivered as she spoke her late husband's name. "If they hadn't destroyed those warships, it would be over for all of us." The tears started to flow down her cheeks now. "They died so we could go on fighting, right?"

Kora tried to swallow a sob to no avail. "Ugh! When will the crying stop!?" She wiped at her face in frustration. "I hate this ... horrible.... sad... I mean..." North pulled Kora into a hug.

"I know. All too well." He soothed and held her for a moment. "For what it's worth, you still got me. And Dek. That dirt licker can't die no matter what he does. How he survived the destruction of *Magellan* is ... almost irritating."

"Ooooh. Watch your mouth, North," Kora laughed and pulled away to wipe the remaining tears off her face. "I'm grateful for the two of you."

"Dek Tigona," North pondered the name of his one-time rival. "We both tried to kill each other. And we've both saved each other. Friend or arch-enemy? Who knows? Have you visited that neo-monk recently?"

"Dek? Not in a few weeks. Have you not seen him?"

"Dek has been pretty focused on trying to be a pastor to our Chasm POWs, filling Ramos' shoes," North mused. "I don't really want to see him, but I wish him well. He did everything he could to save Amberly. He's the better man."

"Maybe, maybe not," Kora said as she turned to head to the nursing station at *Magnus*' civilian med center. "Your story isn't done yet. You will lead *Magnus* to saving Amberly and Arara, and then sending the rest of Chasm to hell... um... with the love of

Jesus."

"What does that even mean?" North smiled.

"I don't know... that we should pray more? Gotta go."

"Bye, Kora," North smiled as he followed her with his eyes until she left the track. He felt encouraged. The path to Arara was long, and he had many preparations to complete before the inevitable conflict. North started for the bridge and suddenly stopped. He bowed his head to offer a quick, silent prayer.

Help me save Amberly. I am ready to pay any price.

***

April 21, 2609, Onboard Chasm's Utopia warship, 28 months years after the destruction of Magellan, six months out from Arara

Amberly tried to move. Her arms and legs were not restrained, but she could not will her limbs to move. Her breathing was shallow, but sounded loud in her head. She tried to turn her head to the right and left, but it too disobeyed her will.

She opened her eyes, but all she could see was foggy darkness above. She became aware she was laying down, face up. She felt a painful cold where her shoulders and buttocks pressed against what she assumed was some sort of metal gurney. She had no idea how long it had been since... anything. She tried to remember what was going on, and now a sense of panic started to overcome her. All she could remember for what seemed to be days or months or years was darkness.

Dek. She remembered Dek Tigona, shot down. Not dead. She watched him in her mind's eye take aim at her. Pull the trigger. Kato was dead now. Everything hurt. *Must fight to move*, Amberly thought.

"Dirty hell, she's coming around," a disembodied female voice said. "She is fighting it real hard now. Give her some more juice."

"Should we try the new stuff?" a male voice asked.

"Most of the other subjects survived, and they were in much worse shape than Amberly," the woman said. "But maybe we should ask the Chairman?"

Amberly tried to struggle, to scream, to do anything. She

found she could control her blinking, but couldn't focus her eyes. She blinked rapidly.

"Always afraid to take the risks," the male voice said.

"Go ahead, it's your funeral," the woman said.

"Fine," the man said. "Watch her brain waves light up when this hits her system."

Amberly screamed. She saw medical staff looking over her smiling in her periphery vision, laughing at her. Then suddenly, their heads exploded, brains and blood scattering all over her body. She found herself floating through space, toward the broken garden dome on Magellan, where Sparks had smashed it. She felt her space suit filling with water as she plunged toward the surface of the Magellan gardens. Stop this! *Amberly thought.* I want ... home. Please just let me go. *Then she blacked out.*

"What did you do!?" the Chairman demanded of her two pharmacological researchers as she burst into the dark room. "My infopad reported a spike in Amberly's brain activity."

The man and the woman stood, both steeped in fear. The male researcher, Dr. Stem Opio, nervously eyed the Chairman's heavily armed Honor Guard, two soldiers and their captain, Merwin One, whose bright face and friendly demeanor did not betray her lethal efficiency.

"Nothing to be concerned about, madam Chairman," Stem said nervously. "Macready is still completely sedated and vitals are stable."

"It was him," said the plump woman researcher, Dr. Michelle Leigh, pointing at her partner, "I told him–"

"Of course, it was *him*," the Chairman said. "But did you stop him? Or did you display weakness? Blah."

The Chairman reached out with one ashen hand and took Michelle's jaw between her pointer and thumb. With her other hand, the Chairman began to trace the edges of Michelle's dyed-blue bangs. The Chairman's iris-less eyes made Dr. Leigh even more frightened.

"I'm sorry, I–"

The Chairman thrust her hand to the side, sliding it off the woman's jaw and causing Michelle to wince in pain.

Like the researchers, the Chairman wore the white coat which had been associated with medical sciences for more than 500 years. Under the coat, she wore a grey, sleeveless jumpsuit, which showed off her petite and hard arms. Her perfectly pedicured feet were bare and exposed under the bell cut of the jumpsuit's legs. The Chasm leader's hair was brilliant silver-white, shoulder length, pulled into a perfect Dutch braid.

Staring at the woman, the Chairman spoke to the captain of her guard. Merwin was magnetic, with an angular beauty that was both intimidating and alluring. More fearsome was her unquestioning loyalty to the Chairman. "Merwin, please place Dr. Leigh in solitary confinement for 10 days. Water only. No food or light."

"As you wish, madam," Merwin bowed and grabbed the female researcher, powerfully and gracefully forcing her out through the medbay portal. The pair of soldiers followed their commander.

The Chairman stood silently next to Dr. Opio, looking down at the comatose Amberly Macready. Dr. Opio had an attractive, healthy, look about him, properly massed, tall and dark. In contrast, the Chairman noticed that Amberly had further emaciated since her last visit three months ago. The 25-year-old looked as if she were twice her age. *So much the better*, the Chairman thought. *Still, let's be careful not to push you into the abyss.*

Alone in the medbay, the two stood over Amberly's sickly, hairless body in silence. After a few moments, Stem decided he should say something.

"We've been tweaking the cocktail and have had great success with our last batch," he said. "Based on the brain waves, twice the pain. Even better, 90 percent survival rate, ma'am."

"That's very good," the Chairman turned to Stem and gently put her hand to his cheek, coaxing his head close to hers. She reduced her voice so it was barely a whisper. "But this is Amberly Macready here, not one of your poor waypoint refugees. Even with my gracious instruction, you lack ... the imagination to understand .... the worth." As the Chairman spoke, she interrupted her own sentence by moistly kissing the stubble on Dr. Opio's upper neck. "To expose her ... to even 10 percent risk...

is ... not advisable."

The Chairman opened her mouth wide and bit hard on Stem's neck, just above the Adam's apple, ripping off a large chunk of flesh, chewing it a few times, and then spitting it out. Stem tried to cry out in pain, but the Chairman had bitten through his trachea, and he just wheezed as his own blood ran down his windpipe.

The researcher put his hand to his neck instinctively, and looked around frantically for some tube and congealing agent he could use to help stop the bleeding and clear his air path before he suffocated.

The Chairman placed an axe kick masterfully on Dr. Opio's knee pit, and he fell to the ground face down, desperately gurgling grunts that the Chairman only assumed were pleas for help. She bent down, flipped him over, and grabbed an injector from the drug buffet next to Amberly's gurney.

"Is this the 'new stuff?'," the Chairman asked as she stabbed his arm with the concentrated psychosomatic pain serum injector.

Stem's eyes went wild and teary, and he flailed uncontrollably and forcefully. After a few minutes the intensity of his spasms slowed, and soon after stopped completely.

"Such a waste," the Chairman said. She noted her thumb was covered with a splattering of Stem's blood. She sucked it clean and wiped her salvia off on her white coat, turned and faced Amberly's resting body again. "Amberly, can you hear me?"

Amberly sat up and was in the corvette Claire De Lune, *with North in the pilot's seat. She was in searing pain, worse than she had ever felt before. She was wearing her sleeveless green dress. She looked down and saw thousands of needles protruding from her ashen white skin. Every square centimeter was populated with rust-covered needles, impaling her. She had no idea how deep they were, but the pain was so intense, she felt like she would lose consciousness. But as she approached the blackness, suddenly she was snapped back to full awareness of the excruciating pain. She wanted to move her arms to pull the needles out, but found that they were zip-cuffed to the chair.*

"North," Amberly cried. "Help me!"

North turned to Amberly. He was absolutely beautiful. The

scar on his chin perfectly complemented his Marine dress uniform. He offered his brilliant, charming smile as Amberly tried to lose herself in his deep brown eyes. If I can just focus on North, Amberly thought, and not this pain.

"North," Amberly asked weakly, "are you still praying for me? Do your prayers still travel faster than the speed of light?"

"Amberly can you hear me?" North opened his mouth to speak, but it wasn't his voice. It was that same voice she had been hearing, that everyone had been using for she didn't know how long. The voice was smooth and cold. And though it was soft and feminine, she felt as though hearing the sound of this voice would make her ears bleed.

"Yes! Yes," Amberly replied. "I'm trapped. It hurts. Save me! Help! What is wrong with your voice."

"That doesn't matter Amberly," the wrong voice said from North's mouth. "Why did you kill Kimberly Macready? Why did you murder your mother?"

"She was going to kill us all," Amberly screamed in pain. "I had to save you... save Dek ... save Kora."

"Ah yes, Kora, the older sister," North-not-North said. "She escaped me in that corvette with the boy. A pity. No doubt they will die alone and cold in space with no waypoint to guide them."

"What ... are you talking ... about?" Amberly asked North, confusion coating the ever-present pain.

"You failed, Amberly," North said. "I destroyed Magellan. At quite a cost, I might add. It will take me some time to replace The Dark Armada."

"What? North. Stop this," Amberly begged. "Please. Take me home."

"There ... is... no... Magellan," North laughed. "How could we not retaliate for what you did to my Raven One. Although I confess, I would have rather saved Magellan, but still the outcome was acceptable."

"Auuuuggghhhhhh!" Amberly screamed. The pain had grown so intense that Amberly could not entertain cohesive thoughts anymore. She wanted to go to into an abyss, to slip away, but the pain would not let her. Instead of everything growing dark, everything was even brighter and more confusing.

Amberly could no longer think. She felt sloshing sorrow and

unrelentingly sharp agony. Madness is coming, *she thought. Then she saw her skin ripping in pain off her body, exposing her muscles and bone. Her flesh began to spontaneously combust, burning crisp before her eyes.* "I.... am... Ma... cready..." *Amberly closed her eyes and then felt nothing.*

"Subject Macready is in cardiac arrest," a medical VI announced as the Chairman instinctively stepped back. "Beginning auto defibrillation. Medical personnel have been summoned."

Two medical attendants rushed into the room, followed by Merwin. The attendants were initially stunned to see the dead researcher's body bleeding on the floor.

The primary nurse looked at the Chairman, unsure how to respond.

The Chairman read her uncertainty. "Keep her alive, idiot." The Chairman stepped back further, giving the medical professionals space to work.

"She is not responding," the nurse said.

"Hit her again."

"Nothing."

"Don't lose her," the attendant said, knowing if Amberly Macready died, he'd be soon to follow.

"Again!"

"Heart stabilized. Injecting detoxification agents."

The Chairman felt satisfied, reveling in Amberly's misery, but also relieved that the fool researchers hadn't destroyed her genetic prize. She had already lingered too long; there was too much engineering to be done, and every minute was needed. Arara and the Infinite Order were just six months away.

She had been gone from Arara for nearly six years. *Yes Amberly, soon we'll be home*, the Chairman thought. *Soon we'll be home, and then I will have my Raven One again. What's left of her anyway.*

The Chairman left the room with her honor guard, and everyone on the medical team breathed an audible sigh of relief.

"We better clean that up," the nurse indicated the dead researcher to his fellow medical attendant. "We'll want to save the tissue for the bioresearch department."

"He was the bioresearch department."

Amberly opened her eyes. She was lying in her childhood bed in the Macready apartment on Waypoint Magellan. *The pain that had seemed to torment her for years was gone, but the memory of the pain was almost as bad. She tried to move, but the familiar invisible forces kept her still. She frowned. Her eyes focused through the portal at the star field. One of those stars was Viapos. She remembered when she was 12 or 13 years old, and her mother would teach her all about the wonders of the cosmos. She learned about things so far beyond her boring, formal schooling. It was a good memory. The amazing feeling of understanding for the first time flooded her again, and she smiled.*

Then she noticed he *was sitting on the edge of the bed, his back facing her. He wore the utilitarian khaki outfit of a common worker, and she studied the patterns of the fabric as his breathing slowly expanded and contracted his torso.*

She longed to touch his messy brown hair, but she could not move. "It's so good to see you," she said, tears forming in the corner of her eyes. "Things have been... dark. Horrible. How long has it been? Years? Hey!"

He turned around and smiled, with a strong, gentle glow in his blue-grey eyes.

"May you be comforted by unending love," Dek said. Amberly was surprised because as long as she could remember, everyone had spoken to her with the wrong voice, with the woman's frigid voice. Dek was speaking with his own.

"Dek!" Amberly said. "Oh, Dek, what is going on? I am trying to remember. Kato was taking me, and you shot him... and I can't remember. But here you are. And it's really you. I just want to be home. But this isn't home, is it?" Amberly's eyes darted around the familiar but slightly-off surroundings.

"I don't know Amberly," Dek said. "I am just here to comfort you with unending love." He reached out and ran his fingers through her smooth red hair. Amberly opened her mind fully to the sensation of his touch, calming and exciting at the same time.

"What is going on? Where am I?" Amberly asked. "She said Magellan *was gone. Are we dead, Dek?"*

"I don't know," Dek shrugged, and he took Amberly's hand.

She tried to squeeze his hand back, but could not. "Just rest now. Sleep. I'll stay with you until then."

For the first time in what seemed like years, Amberly felt her thoughts making sense. The insanity that had been tearing at her mind was receding. She knew this wasn't real, knew she was really somewhere dangerous, dark, threatening. But this dream wasn't like the others; this Dek had a familiarity, something she recognized intuitively. She felt him somehow, and with him came a sense of calm Amberly had forgotten existed.

"Dek," Amberly asked, as she yawned. "What are you?"

"An answer to prayer," he smiled, as Amberly drifted into an oblivious peace.

Amberly awoke an indeterminable amount of time later. Her childhood room was gone, replaced by her laboratory on Magellan. "Dek!" Amberly tried to look around her office space, but she seemed to be petrified, sitting on her work stool. "Dek! Come back." She called out again, but there was no answer.

She felt the pain crawling back into her awareness. "No! I can't do this again. Please someone help me!" Amberly screamed, but no sound escaped her mouth.

Two shadowy figures appeared from thin air, and they started to walk towards her. They were dark, wispy and out of focus. Amberly felt her heart rate increase. The first figure fully materialized in Marine battle armor, and Amberly smiled.

"North!" Amberly called out. "Is it you? Please save me."

"I am ready to pay any price to save you," North said, in his own voice. Amberly felt even more joy. Since the pain was returning, Amberly expected the evil voice. She wanted to move into his line of sight, to make eye contact with her friend. He was looking away from her, and she could not move to meet his gaze.

"I am here. Come save me!"

"I will pay any price," North said again, then dissipated into a thin, black cloud.

Amberly felt panic constrict her chest. She had seen too much, been tormented so much. The figure walked until he was only a few dozen centimeters away from her perch. As he materialized, Amberly started to cry

"Dad, I miss you so," Amberly said.

The apparitional Alroy Macready said nothing, only took his daughter into his arms and held her. Her father's embrace was a balm for the pain, and it receded somewhat, though still present.

"I've needed you. Why did you let mom kill you?" Amberly cried tenderly. "Did you defend yourself? Did you know?"

The red-haired man said nothing. Amberly returned the silence. She was so lost, and she could not understand what was going on. But she could accept her father's love while it lasted. Even in the chaotic confusion, Amberly felt certain that this was real, that her father's love had transcended time and space, and that this moment somehow symbolized more than she could understand. But the more she tried to understand, the more the pain increased...

"I'm so sorry," Alroy said, though the voice wasn't her dad's. It was a new one.

She stopped thinking, and let her brain rest, and bathed in dad's affection. She instinctively knew more pain to fight was yet to come.

The female pharmacological researcher was shaking, traumatized to be back at her post. Dr. Leigh's ten days in darkness birthed a terrifying thought that maybe the greater good was a lie, that maybe the chairman and everything she stood for, was somehow wrong. Dr. Leigh felt compassion, empathy, things she had thought were only chemical reactions in the unperfected body — she wanted to help Amberly.

Michelle was grateful she wasn't outright murdered by the Chairman like her colleague, Dr. Opio. She looked at Amberly, lying peacefully on the gurney, eyes closed with a slight smile on her lips. Michelle's faith in Chasm had been challenged, and now she wanted to help Amberly. She felt powerless, however, for fear that should she help the sickly daughter of Raven One, she would end up under permanent chemical torture, too.

The researcher felt an extreme wave of nausea as she gave Amberly another shot of juice, per the Chairman's orders. Almost immediately, Amberly's eyes popped open, though they were glossy and unaware. Any smile Amberly had melted from her face.

The researcher took Amberly's hand and held it. "I'm so sorry."

CHAPTER TEN

November 10, 2609. The wilds of The Verde Plains, four kilometers from Infinity Point, on the North Island of Lewis Islands, on the colony planet Arara, 34 months after the destruction of Magellan.

Red slowly wired 20 kilos of explosives to the simple detonator.

"Careful … with that …. captain," whispered Corporal Alfonsi, an obese, 60-year-old Araran native, sweat sliding off his portly cheeks. "Bring down this tunnel on the Chasm punks, not us."

Alfonsi pointed the lamp on his helmet down the dark dirt tunnel, which at its smallest point was barely more than a meter and a half high and wide. The tunnel was one of many that led to the Lewis Island Irregulars forward operating base, buried nearly 20 meters underground.

"You go ahead and get moving, corporal," Red said calmly. "Miss Blaisé will be along shortly; I will make sure she gets back safely. No offense, but you're not exactly speedy in these tunnels."

"None taken, Captain," Alfonsi said as he stooped down and started toward the base. "Brave of Blaisé to offer herself as bait. I'd be sad to see someone as bright as her die. We've lost so many youngsters already in this damn war."

"Don't worry, I'll take care of her. Like she was my own daughter," the Captain said.

"Did you have a daughter? Wait. Don't answer that," Alfonsi said as he turned back to his commanding officer. "I know. You can't remember."

"As a matter of fact, *I can't remember,*" Red said, fingers rubbing his chin through this dirty red beard. "I feel like, yes, I did have a daughter. But who knows? Now, off with you. Let the CO know Blaisé and I will be along after we have sealed off this tunnel and buried a few Chasm scouts."

Alfonsi lumbered down the tunnel. When he had gotten just over 50 meters away, he turned a corner so Red could no longer see the ambient glow of the corporal's headlamp. Red shut his own lamp off and sat down against the dirt tunnel wall in complete darkness.

"Jules," he spoke softly to his infopad's VI, "please activate voice only mode. Keep your screen off and be ready to blow the package on my word."

"Yes, sir," the VI spoke in a smooth, tenor voice.

"Are you still tracking Blaisé?" Red quietly asked.

"She should be here in three minutes," Jules said.

Red looked down the darkness in the direction where Blaisé would be coming. The tunnel went for a hundred meters before it dead-ended. Above the tunnel terminus, a two-meter vertical shaft had been cut to access a connecting tunnel. That passage led at about a five-degree angle for another 100 meters toward the open night sky. Because of the tall wild grasses that covered the untamed prairies of the Lewis Islands, the mouth of the secret tunnel was nearly impossible to find.

The Chasm scouting parties knew that the Irregulars had to be underground and had been executing a search pattern on foot to discover just where the resistance might be hiding.

From orbit, *Waypoint Marquette*, retrofitted as a space-based strike platform and capital city for the Chairman, had been hunting Irregulars that dared to show themselves on the surface of Lewis Islands more than a year.

Chasm had moved *Marquette* from its anchorage a half-light year away to Araran orbit after the station had fended off the Earth warship, *Magnus*. Now *Marquette* orbited far above the Lewis Islands holdouts.

Operation Brimstone had been completed nearly three years ago, and it was the catalyst for Chasm victories on Ingram and the mainland. Unable to defend its cities against death from above, the Earth-loyal Araran government surrendered to Chasm, which immediately began the process of engineering the Chairman's perfect society.

Natural-born children were summarily taken from their parents and sent to join the same schools filled with cohorts of lab-born children, gestated in similar fashion as Dek Tigona and Sparks. Originally, the controversial reproduction tubes were justified because they were able to help build a population exponentially faster than natural reproduction, essential for colony survival. However, Chasm conspirators controlled the schools for these lab-born and through its own values education program brought up generations of cohorts whose greatest conviction was the fundamental truth of Chasm: Humanity could be perfected, but only if it would cut itself from the corruption of mother Earth.

Realizing the devastation of a long war would retard efforts to build her utopian society, the Chairman plotted to control the planet through fear of death from orbit. She would not waste any resource without need; human beings were a useful commodity and not to be thrown away before their value to the Infinite Order could be extracted. In addition to human life, open warfare tended to lay waste to valuable infrastructure. So the Chairman preferred particle beam technology, which enabled lethal strikes from the safety of the waypoint, but did minimum damage to the surface.

The Lewis Islanders had always been the most bohemian and maverick of the Ararans. With only a few seaport towns (and one space port) for exporting agricultural products, the 6,400 square kilometers that made up five land masses were covered mostly with prairie and scattered farms. Anti-Chasm clandestine agents, passing on information during *Marquette's* half-year relocation, had given the Islanders and their Irregulars a chance to build an islands-wide defensive network of underground tunnels and bases.

More importantly, the Irregulars had developed a piece of technology that detected the advanced radiation plumes generated by *Marquette's* orbital particle beam fire. These plumes traveled faster than the lethal particle beams themselves. The time difference between the advanced, non-lethal radiation and the deadlier particle beams generating them when fired from orbit was around 30 seconds. This was just long enough for a target take evasive action and make a run for it. Unfortunately, the warning system, which could be carried in a back pack and weighed about 20 kilos, was only 80 percent accurate. Ten percent of the time, the system gave false positives. And ten percent of the time, it failed to go off at all.

Red sighed as he considered the traps he had laid for the unsuspecting Chasm troops. In the darkness, he thought about how he had come to be sitting there, alone, in a dirt tunnel several meters underground, preparing to kill people with a bomb ambush.

Red had parted ways with the crew of the *Butch Cassidy* almost a decade ago, not long after the pirate ship arrived at Arara. He knew the miscreants and buccaneers of the crew that had found him amnesiac, lost in space, would be his undoing. Although he could not remember any of his personal history before being found, he still retained his skills as a pilot. Red also remembered a significant portion of the religious scriptures which, apparently, he had committed to memory. *He who walks with the wise will grow wise, but a companion of fools suffers harm,* he recalled. Although they had saved him, for which he was grateful, the crew of the *Butch Cassidy* were most certainly fools, running afoul of the law with little regard for anything besides getting rich.

Red had been given a sizable number of credits by Captain Paul as hush money so he would purposefully forget the illegal activities he witnessed. He used the proceeds to purchase a small cottage and farming plot a few kilometers outside of Williamstown on the North Island of the Lewis Islands. Williamstown was a community that had a population of nearly four hundred — before the bombardment forced the residents underground months ago.

Red, who lived alone, worked hard to become a competent farmer, spending his days tending his ligrains and potato crops. He wasted away the nights next to his prairie grass-fueled fireplace trying with no success to extract memories of his former life, to remember *who* he was. He felt like the real Red was trapped inside, like someone underwater, running out of breath, but unable to break the water's surface.

Besides going into Williamstown to barter his crops for essentials, the only time Red went into town was to attend church services. Even then he only attended the three or four times a year when the small congregation conducted its traditional communion ceremonies.

Where is she? Red interrupted his own memory, focusing on the lethal task at hand, and resisted the temptation to turn on his lamp to illuminate the tunnel. *If anything happens to Blaisé,* he thought, *...no, no, she'll be fine.*

Two years ago, after Red had sold his harvest of ligrains at the auction house at Williamstown spaceport, he found himself at White Sands Supply Store. The warehouse was made from a whitewashed, durable molded composite of fibrous reeds that grew in vast quantities near the ocean's edge and construction-grade polycarbons. Red had pulled up to the loading dock with his track-scooter, a cheap, common, exterior mounted, electric-powered all-terrain vehicle used for transporting people and hauling small trailers full of agricultural goods.

A young woman with short, bright blond hair and a freckled nose threw open the loading door and looked down at Red and his track-scooter.

"Mister... Red?" She asked, checking the order on her info pad, "Um... I've pulled your order. 50 kilos of soap, 100 kilos of dehydrated beef, and other sundries, right? If you'll just thumb here, I'll have the boys load you up."

The young woman was probably no more than 20 years old, a good three decades younger than Red, based on what his doctor estimated his age was.

A pack of boys began loading supplies onto the large, flatbed trailer attached to his track-scooter. Red reached into his pocket for some credit chits to give to the boys, none of them probably over twelve. The young ones, who worked for tips, were dirty and playful, blissfully unaware of the unrest on the continents. One of the boys started staring at Red and his unusually crimson beard. Red smiled and stared back, considering the deep brown eyes of the child. *I hope the war doesn't come here*, Red thought. *But it will, and even these innocents won't be spared.*

"Mister Red," the woman said, "will you put your thumb print here. You're not from town, but you seem familiar. Did I see you at church last month?"

"Well...yes," Red smiled at the woman and placed his thumb on the infopad. "You a church-goer?"

"Well, my parents make me go," the woman said. "I don't mind it so much. Not much else to do here on the island."

"Your parents?" Red snorted. "How old are you?"

"I just turned 17," the girl said, pointing at the building behind her. "My parents own the store. Jim and Maryanne. Do you know them?

"Can't say I do," Red said. "I'm not from the Islands. What about you?"

"I was born here," the girl said. "Not much of a place to be born, but hey, it's home."

"This place must be a bore for a youngster," Red relaxed his face. "But for an old guy, it's just my speed."

"I suppose it's not so bad here. Did you come from the big continent or the little one? I've traveled to Alexander City once, a few years ago with my dad."

"No, I came on a ship from the Waypoints," Red explained.

"Whoa," the girl pepped up. "Are you from *Marquette? Cortez? Magellan?*"

"Honestly, I can't remember," Red said, "Can you keep a secret… um…"

"Blaisé. My name is Blaisé. Pleased to meet you," the blonde girl extended her hand and Red shook it.

"Okay, Blaisé. A group of mean pirates found me in a runabout–"

"A what?"

"A runabout. A small ship. Well, they found me beaten up and I had … I have amnesia. I can't remember my life before that day."

Blaisé lifted her info pad and began to type in notes.

"What are you doing?"

"Oh, I'm an author," Blaisé said. "You may be the most interesting person I've ever met. I think I'll make you a character in one of my books."

"Most interesting? You obviously haven't met many people," Red quipped. "You write books? What a coincidence, I love to read." Red smiled.

Blaisé laughed. "Would you be willing to read what I have written? Give me feedback? Mom and dad aren't really into … well… my books are about adventurers in space, who live on the waypoints! You could help me with my realism."

"I'd be honored, Amberly," Red replied. A brief flash of mild pain snapped in the back of Red's head, wrapped in a fuzzy memory of a small hand in his. Red instinctively shook his head to clear it.

Blaisé stared at Red with eyes of confusion.

"Um... why are you staring at me like that?"

"You just called me ... Amberly," Blaisé said. "Who is that?"

Unfortunately, Red had no idea why he blurted out that name. "I did? I don't know where that came from. Sorry, Blaisé. I guess I am a doughnut short of a dozen sometimes." Red feigned ambivalence, but made a mental note to add *Amberly* to the collection of memory fragments he was trying to connect the dots on.

"What's a doughnut?"

"Something you eat, I think," Red said. "It's just a cliché."

"Eating! Of course. Do you have time to come over tonight?" Blaisé asked. "I know my parents would love to have you over for dinner. I'd love to hear the rest of your adventures coming to the Lewis Islands."

"Well, not tonight; I've got animals back at the farm," Red said. "But send me your drafts, and the next time I'm in town for church, I'm sure I'd love to join your family for lunch."

"So nice to meet you, Mister Red," Blaisé stuck out her hand again.

Red took her hand and shook it firmly. "Nice to meet a new friend."

Red rubbed some dirt off his hand in the darkness as he thought about his relationship with the young woman. He remembered his sadness when a year after their meeting, Blaisé's parents both died after a particularly deadly strain of the Araran Sweats swept the Islands. Blaise was old enough by then to take care of the store and live independently, but Red had always kept a father's watchful eye over the growing woman.

A year later, open war had begun on the mainland.

Already a volunteer with the Lewis Island Irregular Militia, like everyone else, Red abandoned his home when Chasm bombardments started in Williamstown. Two weeks ago, Irregular spies had spotted Chasm taking possession of the village, with reports of dozens of Chasm shock and scout-class troops making camp there.

"Blaisé is about to enter this segment of tunnel," Jules said, startling Red out of his deep thought.

"Help! Red! Help!" Blaisé shouted. Red could see her helmet light as she scrambled down the woven-reed ladder a hundred meters away. When she was a meter up, he saw her thud hard down to the dirt floor. Red drew his pistol and stood, strapping his infopad onto his armband.

As he sprinted towards her, Jules spoke. "Don't forget you are on the wrong side of the explosives now."

"No worries," Red said. He was just a dozen meters away, and could see now that Blaisé was injured severely. A hole in her right leg pant was pierced from the inside with a shard of cracked bone sticking out. Blaisé was pushing herself along the floor with her good leg, pulling with her arms. Her bright eyes were panicked, and her face filthy with tears and dirt.

Behind her, a Chasm trooper in head-to-toe camouflaged armor dropped to the floor.

"Finally," the trooper said to Blaisé, "I have –"

The trooper turned her headlight up from its focus on Blaisé, and noticed Red sprinting toward him. Red, a natural marksman, immediately unloaded a pair of bullets from his pistol, aiming for the trooper's head. The bullets seemed to disappear into a fine mist just centimeters away from the trooper.

"Well, that's dirty inconvenient," Red swore as he came to a halt several meters away from Blaisé and twice that distance from the trooper. This was clearly the point defense system the Irregulars had heard rumors about.

"I guess we have to do this the hard way," Red mumbled as he pulled his modded swagger stick from a loop on his pants. The tip of the stick had been capped with a heavy layer of osmium alloy. The dense osmium was rare on Earth, but common on Arara.

The trooper raised her assault rifle to mow Red down. "I only need one captive," the trooper gritted through her clenched teeth as she stepped over the fallen Blaisé to take her shot.

"Auuuuggghhhh!" Blaisé swung her good leg into the knee pit of the trooper. This caused the trooper to stumble and misfire, the light cast from her lamp spilling from the wall onto the floor. When she kicked the trooper, Blaisé rotated her injured leg as well. She screamed in pain.

Bullets flew in the darkness as the three lamps danced in the action.

Red focused on the light from the trooper, twirled his stick for momentum and whacked the light source. The trooper cried in pain as the dense stick cap fractured the light diodes. The trooper stood up and raised the rifle at Red for a second shot, but not before Red hit the weapon on his backswing. The swagger stick hit with so much force, it broke the rifle and the hand that held it.

"Backup! I need backup," the Chasm trooper said into her radio.

Red hit her again, forcefully, on her helmet, and the trooper fell to the ground. Red didn't know if he had injured her or just knocked her out, but the trooper lay still.

"You saved my life, Blaisé," Red said, as he opened his medpac to get a splint kit for his fallen comrade.

"Great, give me a hand and save mine," Blaisé replied. She waved away the kit. "No time. Her backup is close."

Red hoisted Blaisé to his side and began to drag her down the tunnel to where Corporal Alfonsi had disappeared earlier. He remembered Jules' warning: they were on the wrong side of the explosives.

After two minutes of struggling, they were coming up to the ambush point, when two troopers jumped into the tunnel.

"Trooper down!" one of them said as he leaned to check on her fallen comrade. "Need a medic, ASAP."

The second trooper turned his headlight down the tunnel. "Look, there she is! Someone is with her. I'm going to get them." The second trooper drew a stun blaster and started an impressive crouching sprint.

"Blow the charges, Jules!" Red shouted as he struggled to pull Blaisé clear. Blaisé tried to hobble along, but she shrieked in uncontrollable pain as Red pulled her in haste, without care for her broken leg.

"Captain, you are still not at a safe distance –"

"He's going to stun us," Red spoke over Blaisé's painful shrieks. "Blow this tunnel! Override. Now!"

A flash just a few meters behind the fleeing pair caught the sprinting trooper at point blank range, and the explosive force easily ripped the man into a hundred pieces. A hot shockwave hit Red and Blaisé in the backs, throwing both forward to the dirt floor of the tunnel. Red did not stop his retreat, and crawling, he continued to pull Blaisé forward with every bit of strength he could muster.

As Red had engineered, the structural integrity of the tunnel was compromised by the blast, and passage began to fill with soil and rocks. The explosion was designed to destroy the tunnel back to the drop-in point, so Red knew the Chasm troopers not killed by the blast would be buried alive.

As he frantically scrambled, Red felt clods of earth fall on top of him. He grabbed Blaisé by the waste and thrust her forward. His back immediately spasmed as he over extended himself. He was fully covered to his torso now, and could not move his legs. He took a deep breath instinctively, anticipating his full burial.

He felt dirt slide over the back of his neck.

And then it was quiet. The collapse of the tunnel had buried Red to his head. He forced himself to remain calm. The weight of the soil made it extremely difficult, though not impossible, to breath.

"Blaisé! Blaisé!" Red called out, choking through dirt particles floating in the air. His shouting had caused an unexpected sharp pain in his torso.

"I'm here," the woman called back.

Red strained to turn his head so he could see Blaisé, but the dirt made it impossible. His helmet lamp was still on, and he could see ambient light from hers. "Are you okay?"

"I am… okay … I am doing better than those Chasm troops you just buried. You okay?"

A wave of sadness washed over Red. The Chasm plan to reengineer society was perverse and must be countered, but he hated taking life. It was so final. There was no recompense. In the grand cosmos, life was so rare, with small clusters of life every half-light year or so on the intergalactic bread crumb trail back to Earth. To extinguish any life unless absolutely necessary was wrong; on this Red and the Chairman would find agreement. It was the necessity that haunted Red.

"I am buried to my neck, actually. Is your radio working?" Red asked.

Before she could answer, Red heard the voice Corporal Alfonsi then saw the glow of his headlight. "Captain! You survived! Thank God." The corporal looked to the two militia privates he had in tow. "Don't just stand there! Dig him out!"

CHAPTER ELEVEN

February 2, 2610. Irregular Headquarters deep underground on the North Island of Lewis Islands, on the colony planet Arara, just over three years after the destruction of Magellan.

The Irregular headquarters was essentially a collection of reinforced plastic boxes buried twenty meters beneath the surface of the largest Lewis island. The underground area was excavated and then the plastic strips, originally used to build some of the islands' oldest and largest grain storage warehouses, were brought in through tunnels and assembled to create walls, floors and ceilings.

"It's time," said Rea, a wiry, middle-aged farmer with flowing nutmeg hair. Her tactical mind helped her plan the optimal crop rotations made her a natural logistic officer when Bloom chose her command team when the Militia was organized nearly five years ago. "*Utopia* is back. The Chairman is back. The time for patience is over. Every day, our odds of success get worse."

"I agree. We can't let them hold onto Williamstown any longer," Alfonsi said, his thin, dark hair shaking to match the passion in his voice. "With this foothold, it's only going to be a matter of time before they methodically smoke us out. It's been half a year. We must risk open conflict."

"Do you realize what you are saying?" Irregular Commanding Officer Nur Bloom asked calmly, hiding the condescension she felt for the fat man. "Corporal, we're a fighting force at maximum strength of 200. We're a homegrown militia. They are professional soldiers literally bred for war. The cost of driving them off would be at least half of us. Dead."

"With all due respect, *Commander*," Alfonsi gritted his teeth at the two-meter-tall woman, "If we don't drive them off now, if we don't show them we're willing to bleed a little, we are already dead. We still outnumber them. It's only a matter of time before they bring in an overwhelming force."

Nur looked around at the gathered officers, trying to assess if they were with her. The dim flicker of the hydrogen cell-powered lights fell on the exhausted eyes of women and men who were tired of hiding from the sky, sleeping on dirt floors instead of farm-feathered beds. None of them had ever seen war; only a few had witnessed lethal violence. Before Chasm forced the Islanders underground, Nur had been the chief of the Lewis Islands police force. In her 20-year career, she had only tasted a pair of firefights, the most recent nearly a decade in the past. Some pirates had come to the Islands to escape mainland law enforcement. She lost six men in that failed midnight spaceport raid; the pirates made off for *Marquette* and freedom.

Nur did not want another slaughter on her hands. Her troops were just farmers and tradesmen and homesteaders.

She frowned and looked to her ruddy ranking officer. In the chaos living in hiding, Red represented an attractive consistency. He was silent and strong. She also fancied his colorful hair. Though mysterious, Red was a no-nonsense farmer, and now she hoped he would talk sense into his fellow officers.

"Captain Red," Commander Bloom stuck a pleading hand out to him across the planning map table the officers had gathered around. "You have been keeping your counsel to yourself. Do you favor a strike?"

"Look around you. Look at your friends-in-arms," Red replied as he made eye contact with every person gathered as he said each name. "There are twelve officers. Me, I'm the oldest. Bloom, our lovely and capable commander. Charro. Ilam. Fiat. Musgrave. Alfonsi. Meganson. Rea. Shift. Piker. And Blaisé, the youngest. Jules has run the simulator. He predicts half of us won't be back here even if we win. If you had to pick six we could do without, could you do it? We won't even get to pick."

Bloom's heart beat a little faster; Red never stopped surpassing her expectations.

Red paused for a moment and looked down. "But I know what you are thinking."

The officers exchanged glances at each other, many of them wondering if the old redhead *really* knew.

Red continued. "You're thinking maybe we'll get lucky, 'cause Jules is full of dirt and the simulation is wrong and more of us walk away. Maybe we do. But maybe we get unlucky, and we all die. Me? I'm ready to roll the dice. But I've got nothing to lose. I don't know where I came from. But I know who I am today. I am a Lewis Islander. This clod of grass in the middle of the Monet Sea is my home. You are my family. And I'd rather die fighting for our freedom from the so-called perfection Chasm would impose on us then surrender by default. Our sovereign soil has been violated by those who would not just take away our autonomy, should they win, but they would take away our souls. These islands are the last free lands on Arara. Will we go quietly into the night, and let Chasm write over us in their history books? I will not. But as I said… I have nothing to lose. Many of you have family to look after and think about."

That was not the speech Nur had hoped for, but even she had been moved. She knew he was right: This could be the end, regardless of whether they chose to fight or hide.

"If I may," a teary Blaisé, standing with a metal exoskeleton supporting and protecting her healing leg, raised her hand, "I'd like to suggest an idea that could minimize the risk?"

Slowly crawling through the tall grass in the darkness of night, centimeter by centimeter, was painstaking. Captain Red had volunteered to lead the strike force, with officers Fiat and Blaisé and about 30 of the most agile and fit Irregulars. They had to position themselves, undetected, just a mere 100 meters away from the spaceport's launching ground so they could be ready when the diversion happened.

The spaceport was equipped with a ground radar system that would detect movement a kilometer out. Of course, that movement had to be above the grass line of the fields that surrounded the spaceport, and the system had to be on. The Irregulars had no way of knowing if Chasm had activated the ground-level security system, but for Blaisé's plan to work, Red's strike team had to get close to the spaceport undetected. So, they crawled.

The reedy ground was soggy and cold. It was nearly the 27th hour of the Arara's 28-hour day, and Blaisé was tired from carrying the 30 kilos of explosives on her back. Her healing leg was the least of her concerns. The exoskeleton automatically dosed her with mild, topical painkillers. The rest of her muscles burned, and her soaked underclothes chaffed. She had volunteered to carry the ordinance, so she didn't carry the heavy rifles the others were packing.

"Whose stupid idea was this anyway?" Blaisé complained in a self-depreciating fashion.

"Yours," Red answered the rhetorical question. "And it just might work."

Fiat, the tactical officer on the field, signaled the others. "We're in position. Now keep it quiet. If we get caught now..."

Fiat, the tall, dark and charming 26-year-old who was the youngest officer after Blaisé, didn't have to finish his sentence. If they couldn't remain hidden in essentially plain sight, woven in the tall Island grasses under Arara's moonless night sky, they would all be dead.

They all waited anxiously, prone in the swampy acres between the north end of the spaceport and the ocean, waiting for Commander Bloom's diversionary signal. The wait was short.

BOOOOOOOOOM!

An explosion from the Irregulars' "home brew" artillery rocked the paved road leading to the south entrance to the space port, and Red, Blaisé and the others could hear the occupying Chasm troops scrambling, voices alarmed.

"And there is the signal," Fiat smiled. "Commander Bloom's big boom! Ha ha!"

As Blaisé had predicted, the spaceport cleared out as the small contingent of Chasm troops went out to meet Bloom's forces. Bloom, of course, had no intention to fight Chasm head on. Instead, her company fell back in a strategic retreat to draw the enemy away from their three *Marquette*-based runabout ships in the spaceport.

Getting up from the muck proved a bit more challenging than Blaisé had expected. She blamed her bum leg the first time she face-planted back into the mud. Even in the dim light, Red gave a chortle. Again, she stood, not used to the heavy pack of explosives on her back, she tried to stand and went back into the mud.

Red walked up to the closest thing he had to family, smiled, extended his hand and hoisted the young woman to her feet.

"Let's go make these Chasm troops regret they ever set foot on the Island," Red said, absentmindedly using the back of his hand to wipe mud off of Blaisé's freckled-face. As they began to double-time march through the marshy terrain, Red put his hand on Blaisé's shoulder. She turned to him.

"What's the matter old man," she said, nearly giddy with an adrenal rush like she had never experienced before. "Worried you can't keep up?"

"I'll do my best, brat," Red teased, then his voice turned solemn. "Blaisé, stay close to me. You're the only family I have."

"Don't worry, I'll be careful," Blaisé said as she turned back toward the spaceport. "And you'd survive just fine without me."

"I could survive," Red called out after stepping into a trot to follow her, "but I'd have nothing left to survive for."

After about ten minutes, Red's troops had carefully moved into positions to secure the apparently abandoned spaceport. Many of them former dock hands once employed at the port, the Irregulars knew exactly where to secure a perimeter to ambush Chasm troops returning to their base from Bloom's feint.

Red knew once they turned the Valkyrie-class runabouts into fireworks, the Chasm troops would come running back, out of fear and terror, with their way off the Island in peril. Blaisé convinced Bloom and Red that the Chasm troops, though they had the equipment advantage, would be more likely to surrender if they had no fall back and faced the superior Irregular numbers out front and at their flank.

Red, Blaisé and two Irregular fighters made their way toward the heart of the multi-structured spaceport, where the Valkyries were stored in a large hanger to protect them from the occasionally super-violent weather cells that were known to quickly form over the oceans north of the Islands. Flood lights bathed the storage silos, lift tractors and other assorted obstacles scattered across the spaceport where millions of metric tons of grains had gone into space to support the waypoints. The spaceport was nearly four-square kilometers. Worried Bloom could not keep up the distraction for long, Red and his detachment had broken into a full sprint. Even with her exoskeleton-protected leg and heavy pack, Blaisé had pulled ahead of the others. Red stopped to catch his breath. *Must be nice to be young*, he thought as he spied a track-scooter. One of the Irregulars stopped with Red.

"Sir?"

"Go ahead, stay with Blaisé and the explosives," he pointed at the blonde who was already a hundred meters away. "Keep her safe and get those explosives planted. I'm getting a ride." Red jumped on the track scooter and pulled out his infopad.

"Jules, see if you can hack this thing and get it started."

Blaisé took only a few minutes to plant the explosive ordinance on three runabouts neatly aligned inside the hangar. The large main door, nearly 50 meters high and twice as wide, was open, allowing in the chilly night air. In the distance, Blaisé could see the flashing lights from the skirmish on the south side of the spaceport.

"Great, charges set. Let's get out of here and blow these things. Move, you don't want to be close by when they go," Blaisé shouted. "Where's the old man?"

"Ha! He was tuckered out from all the running and tried to commandeer a track-scooter," replied an Irregular.

"Step away from the ships!" a smoky female voice projected from the direction of the hangar door. Blaisé held the detonator tightly and glanced toward the voice and saw them – six Chasm troopers in full assault armor. Immediately, an Irregular brought his automatic rifle to bear on the closest Chasm troop, firing a stream of bullets.

The point defense system did its work, and the bullets seemed to dissolve into a growing mist. The Irregulars had expected the point defense. They had hoped that the point defense systems could be overloaded by the combined assault of two automatic rifles, and they trained based on that theory.

A second after the second stream of bullets hit the target, the trooper's armor was ripped up and bloody spray mixed with the atomic residue of disintegrated bullets floating in the air.

The militiamen were glad to have carried the heavy guns and extra ammo now.

The remaining five Chasm troops were momentarily shocked; but in seconds their training kicked in, and they returned fire.

Cover between the two camps was absent; it was a shootout. The Irregulars managed to rip apart a second Chasm trooper, but breaking down the point defense system took too long. The four remaining Chasm troops, expert marksmen, only needed a few bullets to take out Blaisé's escort. Two headshots with exploding ammo turned the skulls of the Irregulars inside out.

"Put your guns down or I blow us all to hell!" a shocked Blaisé yelled powerfully and desperately. "Now!"

"Hey, little girl," the female-voiced trooper said through her armored helmet. "We're not afraid to die for the greater good. Our lives don't matter. ... But no one else needs to die. Put down the detonator, and we'll let you live."

Blaisé was trying to consider what the best option was at this point. *There is no way out*, she thought, as her hand holding the detonator began to feel clammy. She felt the simple button with her thumb, and eyed a Chasm troop lifting her rifle to shoot. Blaise was afraid she couldn't do what she had to. *So, this is it* —

Her thought was interrupted as a charging track-scooter ran down the Chasm trooper before she got her shot off.

"Blaisé!" Red shouted, as he jumped off the scooter swinging his swagger stick at a trooper's rifle.

Red felt several bullets pierce both his legs, and he fell to the ground.

"That's the captain," the Chasm squad leader frantically shouted. "He'll have valuable tactical info on the Irregulars. Get him out of here before the crazy blonde kills us all."

"Red!" Blaisé shouted.

"Run!" Red screamed back through the pain. "Run!"

With urgent exertion, a Chasm trooper grabbed Red by one arm and started dragging him away from the hangar, leaving a trail of his blood along the pavement.

Blaisé made a sprint towards the side door.

"No, you don't," the Chasm leader said, taking two shots hitting the young woman in the shoulder and in the torso. Blaisé hit the ground hard, and she struggled to hold on to the detonator.

A dozen meters outside the hanger, Red thrashed as he was dragged across the gritty tarmac. The Chasm trooper, wanting to get clear of any blast, focused on pulling the man as fast as he could. Red managed to grab onto the swagger stick with his free arm, and with a swing from its tail, he hit the trooper in the knee-pit. The swing produced enough momentum to knock the trooper off balance, forcing him to drop Red at his feet.

Red released the swagger stick and swiftly pulled his knife from his sheath, driving the weapon into the foot of the trooper. Red could feel an expanding wooziness in his head, probably from blood loss, and he knew his time was short. Mustering the last few ounces of his strength and ignoring the searing pain, he pushed himself to stand while retrieving the knife, using the swagger stick as a makeshift cane. The trooper swung at him with a clumsy punch. Red fell back, but was able to keep standing, and then fell forward, on top of the trooper, plunging his knife through his opposite's helmet. The trooper fell over, dead.

Through punishing pain, Red twisted his head toward the hanger. He saw Blaisé on the ground, the remaining two troopers advancing on her, rifles drawn.

She made eye contact with him and smiled. *To die is gain. I'll see you on the other side, old man*, she thought. *I hope my parents are proud.*

Click.

The troopers saw her press the detonator and opened fire.

Too late.

The force of the explosion sent a blast of heat and light that could be seen kilometers away. Instantly caught up in the blast, Red was thrown for several meters. An equally powerful wave of gut-tearing sorrow hit him; and as he lost consciousness, his mind exploded with self-focused anger. He failed Blaisé.

Several hours later, the two dozen Chasm troopers who surrendered were huddled in a circle in an open area of the spaceport tarmac, disarmed, stripped of helmets and armor. Bright flood lights forced many of the prisoners to squint in the otherwise dark night. Commander Bloom noticed that under the faceless masks, the Chasm troops were diverse in ethnicity, gender and age.

"Who has a comm unit that can call back to your leader, your … Chairman?" Bloom shouted at the defeated soldiers. "I want to negotiate with the Chairman for your lives."

"Negotiations will get us nothing," Rea, standing next to Bloom, mumbled under her breath, so only Bloom could hear.

"Maybe," Bloom said. "But it's the best hand we've been dealt so far. We're going to see how it plays out."

"Come now, we just want to be left alone, and you just want to go home," Bloom pled her case.

The prisoners of war were silent for a while, and then one spoke up.

"The Chairman will not negotiate," said an older man with dark brown skin and brilliant white hair. "If we die by your hand, so be it. It is for the greater good. History will remember our sacrifice. Think of the perfect world the Chairman is building for our progeny."

Alfonsi stood with about two dozen Irregulars, rifles raised, the words of the Chasm officer having no meaning. He'd heard them all before.

Were these people really willing to die? Alfonsi thought. *I think not. Otherwise, why surrender?* The Irregulars had captured the spaceport, but Alfonsi was still skittish that they would lose their new bargaining chip: Several squads of prisoners of war. The eyes of a young Chasm fighter with dark bangs hanging over her forehead caught Alfonsi's attention. *She's afraid*, he thought. *She should be. We're desperate and desperate people are the most dangerous.* He felt a bit sorry for the woman, wondering how much she really believed in Chasm's new order. But his compassion did not compel him to ease his trigger finger.

"Where are they!" Captain Red came barreling through the line of Irregulars holding sights on the prisoners. He had been patched up, but was still covered with his own blood. The Irregular escort with Red was out of breath. He had no idea how the wounded officer could limp along so quickly.

"Commander Bloom!" the escort huffed. "Captain Red has a few bullet holes. I patched him, but—"

"Whoa, Red," Nur said, as she ran to her top officer, placing a calming hand on his face and looking in his eyes. "Hey, you look like hell … You look like you need to be in a medcenter. Charro get a medic over here! What happened?"

"We lost Blaisé," Red said softly. He briefly took solace in Bloom's sympathy, but quickly refocused on the prisoners. His eyes locked on the white-haired Chasm officer, "She's gone, you son-of-bitches!"

As Red swore, he raised his modded swagger stick and charged the officer, whacking him hard in the chest. The man cried out in pain and fell to the ground. The other Chasm troopers were thinking about intervening, but the rifles pointed at them dissuaded their action.

Red pounded the fallen man on the ground again and again. The man threw up his arms to defend his head and curled into a fetal position. In his delirium, Red closed his eyes tight.

The woman was hitting him with his own swagger stick. Red was inside a runabout, flailing his arms to defend himself. The woman, with raven-dark hair, was absolutely beautiful. Who is she? Red thought. Then he saw the young teenage girl. But her hair wasn't blonde. It was red. It didn't matter. He knew she was gone. They had killed her. The hallucination faded.

After the third or fourth whack, a clearly audible sound of cracking indicated the breaking of bones.

"She was so young. She's dead. Amberly's dead!" Red shouted as he lifted for another swing, reality and memory mixing in his snapped mind.

He didn't have a chance to bring it down before he was knocked to the ground by a running tackle from the portly Alfonsi. "Captain! No! Stop, stop!"

Red sat up and dropped his stick to the ground.

"I killed her. I didn't protect her. It's me. Give me your gun. I don't deserve... I don't... Blaisé. She's gone. No. Blaisé. No. Amberly. Why God? Why her. Why not me! Dirty hell, corporal, give me your damn side arm!"

"I'm sorry, Captain," Alfonsi said, stepping back from Red to prevent him from snatching his holstered gun. The mention of Amberly, a name he was unfamiliar with, caught Alfonsi's attention.

"Who is Amberly?" Alfonsi asked while focusing on keeping his captain from hurting himself out of severe guilt.

Rea shrugged. "He's gone cracked, that one has," she looked at Red with pity.

At Bloom's command, three of the Irregulars had picked up Red and started forcing the man away.

"It should have been me," Red shouted. "I'm so sorry Blaisé! I'm so sorry."

Insane anger boiled Red's mind. Chasm took away Blaisé, and she was his family. He felt like they had done it all before. The feeling was maddening, and Red started pounding the pavement rapidly with his fist, tearing up his knuckles.

"Give him a sedative and keep him under watch," Bloom ordered. Her heart was breaking for the man who was her unknown strength. The soldiers did as instructed, gently forcing Red to lie down onto a long crate and injecting him. He immediately relaxed, now fighting off sleep.

An Irregular medic began to attend to the beaten Chasm officer, still lying on the floor.

Bloom waited until she was sure Red was under control, then turned back to the prisoners. "There is only mercy if you open a channel with the Chairman. Now."

Bloom waited impatiently for only a few seconds as the captured Chasm warriors remained silent.

"Fine," she said, pulling her sidearm from its holster and holding it up to the head of a young Chasm solider with dark bangs. "Use your comm unit to signal the Chairman or I will put a bullet in your head."

"My death does not matter," the young woman said, in a rehearsed monotone. She forced herself to continue, and struggled not to cry. "I am willing to die to perfect humanity. What are you willing to die for, Commander?"

"Don't pretend you're not afraid to die," Bloom pushed the gun so it made physical contact with the woman's forehead. The woman winced reflexively.

"I didn't say I wasn't afraid," the Chasm trooper said, no longer holding back her tears. "I don't want to end. I don't want to go into oblivion. Who does? I want to see the perfect future the Chairman is building for all of us. But if I die now, I die knowing my life meant something, in service to humanity's greater good. What if you die? Look at you, selfishly trying to hold onto this island as if it is your personal property. Everything belongs to the greater good. Your individualism is *poison*."

"Spare me your sermons," Bloom said evenly and cleared the safety on her gun.

"No! Wait!" the white-haired officer shouted, "I'll make the comm link to the Chairman for you. Just don't kill Layla. I'll do

199

what you want."

"No!" Layla said as Bloom pulled the gun away from her head. "Why would you do this? Don't give into them."

"I'm sorry. Someday, maybe you'll understand," the officer said. "Everything I've sacrificed for Chasm, for the greater good, means nothing for me if you don't live to enjoy paradise."

"That is so wrong," Layla said, her heart about to burst with conflicting emotions. "If you favor me over the other daughters of the Infinite Order, the new order is already corrupt."

"Maybe, but that corruption will die with me. You will live on, pure in perfection. I'm willing to die with that sin on my hands."

"This is your dad?" Bloom asked, indicating the injured officer with her gun. Layla looked straight ahead and said nothing. "Don't bother. Clearly he is."

Layla wiped at the tears running down her face.

"All right, *dad*," Bloom said looking at the white-haired man. "What could be the harm in letting us talk to the Chairman? Fire up your infopad."

"No," Layla said. "I'll do it."

"But the Chairman–" Layla's father protested. "She'll… you could be…"

"You should have thought about that before you showed weakness," Layla said to her father as she turned to Bloom's gun pointed at her forehead. "I said I'll do it."

Layla slowly walked to the pile of Chasm armor her team was earlier relieved of when captured, found hers, and pulled out her infopad.

"Emergency Chasm operation channel for the Chairman," Layla spoke into her device. "Code Epsilon Beta."

"Confirmed, Epsilon Beta," the info pad spoke in an androgynous voice. "Challenge response, Theta, Gamma, Sigma."

"Confirmed, response sequence Dog Rife Cake Case Fire."

"Response correct. Priority signal out."

A nondescript quasi male image was projected from the infopad held by Layla. "Chasm operator three-four-three. Confirm priority connect to the Chairman, Agent Layla? She's not in a good mood."

"Yes, connect me," Layla said, resigned.

"Agent Layla," the Chairman's taught, aged face took the place of the operator's. "To what do I owe the honor? I already know of your failure on the Islands."

"Honored Chairman," Layla said, "these blights on humanity have captured us and are using me as leverage to control my father."

"Ah... I see, my dear Layla. This is why we must purge ourselves of the weakness of family. Family is tribal, and corrupts our purpose, giving people something to love before the state, subjugating the common good. When you are back on *Marquette*, remind me to tell you the story of how, because of the corruption of family, one of our best allowed *Magellan* to slip out of Chasm's grasp. A situation that has been resolved, though at considerable cost–"

Nur swiped the info pad out of Layla's hands. "Enough of your touching chat. I think you've seen our resolve. We will kill these prisoners of war one-by-one unless you meet our demands –"

"You think you have shown me resolve?" the Chairman replied with her own interruption, her voice controlled but raised. Her iris-less eyes offered an oppressive gaze that seemed to reach out to crush Bloom through the magnetic resonance image projected by Layla's infopad. "You have no idea what resolve I have. How long I have planned. How long I have waited."

"You must agree to never return to the Lewis Islands," Bloom ignored the Chairman.

"Insect, you have no leverage over me," the Chairman shouted with a righteous anger. She took a breath and said matter-of-factly. "Please stand by."

Suddenly, an alarm in Fiat's backpack started going off. It was the 30-second advance plume warning that detected the coming fire.

"Particle beams! We're caught on the surface," shouted Alfonsi, and immediately the Irregulars started to scatter, sprinting in various directions. The Chasm troops were confused as their captors went sprinting for cover, but quickly surmised that the Chairman was targeting their captors with *Marquette's* space-to-surface particle beams.

"Death from above," Bloom confirmed. "Run! Run!"

The Irregulars scattered like roaches exposed to sudden light, scampering to hide under any object that might offer some protection. Bloom herself had slid in the small gap between the rear tracks of a nearby utility vehicle.

For about twenty seconds, the Chasm troops were elated at seeing the Irregulars finally punished for their resistance. The snap-snap-snap sound of particle beams hitting targets echoed throughout the base, as dust stirred up by the impact made a small, dense cloud.

"You have nowhere to run," the Chairman said, still broadcasting from Layla's info pad held tightly in the hands of Commander Bloom. "But you mistake my intention. I don't want to kill you, yet. Those who I trusted, but who failed me, on the other hand, well…"

When the clouds settled, every Chasm trooper except Layla was dead, bodies shredded by particle beams. Peeking out of hiding places, examining the scene of the massacre, Bloom and the other Irregulars were shocked. Bloom, half foolish, half brave, walked up to the still bound Layla.

"They had no more use to Chasm," Layla, tears running down her face, explained. "They were a liability."

"Excellent, Layla, you understand," the Chairman said, still broadcasting from Layla's info pad held tightly in the hands of Commander Bloom.

"You killed your own people?" Bloom asked the obvious, also struggling to absorb the mass murder she just witnessed.

"I hate to waste good resources, and humans are the most valuable resource," the Chairman said. "But I hate failure more. Failure makes me question a person's value."

Bloom looked at her gathered Irregulars, trying to figure out what the next move was. The particle beam generators had a short recharge cycle. Run? Hide? Was there a next move?

"Commander Bloom, killing you and all the people on the Lewis Island would be a waste. Surrender to Layla. Add yourselves to our common good. You have so much to contribute. With the Lewis Islanders cooperating, we can bring perfection all the faster. You all could live to see it!"

"I… don't … understand," Bloom said. Her instinct was still to flee, but in her mind, she knew that the Chairman would have killed her by now if that is what she wanted.

"I still believe the Lewis Island can be a force for good," the Chairman pleaded. "I have faith that every human, with the proper... *instruction*... can be perfected. Even those with rebellious hearts."

"You can't be considering her offer," Alfonsi said through gritted teeth to Bloom.

"One of Chasm's most important resources was born on the Lewis Islands," the Chairman continued. "I first knew my Raven One there, and I dispatched her to the stars. When she finished her mission at *Magellan*, I was going to let her return, to govern the production of your islands, as a reward for her good service. But she was corrupted by her family. In the end, her daughter, the cursed Amberly, killed my Raven One."

Amberly. That name again, thought Alfonsi.

"What did you say?" the fat corporal said, jumping into view of the infopad. "Who is Amberly? Red said you killed her."

Red stood up from his crate, foggy from the sedative, and slowly walked toward the projection of the Chairman. "Yes, that name. Amberly. I keep saying that name, but I don't know why. An old memory?"

"Who said that?" the Chairman asked as Red stepped into view of the info pad's optics.

"By the heart of Viapos," the Chairman gasped. "Is that you, Alroy Macready?"

"Who?" Red replied.

"Raven One thought you dead. But... it *must* be you."

"I don't know any Alroy," Red replied, trying to remember, but only feeling frustrating, painful blocks in his head.

"I've seen your picture. I've heard recordings of your voice. But most importantly, she wrote to me about you. Kimberly didn't believe it, but I could smell your corruption on her every word. I haven't been exposed to that pungent scent in the six years since Amberly killed her mother in cold blood."

"I don't know what you are talking about," Red said, but there was something in her words that felt painfully true. *Amberly must be the key*, Red thought. *But who is Amberly?* "I can't... remember," Red thought aloud.

"No need to hide, anymore. I have found you, Alroy

Macready. You corrupted Kimberly, my Raven One, and you sired her daughter, the traitor who denied Raven One her destiny at my side."

"I have a daughter?" Alroy asked, confused and intensely curious. He focused on the name Amberly in his mind, but his mental fog did not lift.

"Listen to me Commander Bloom," the Chairman said. "The stakes have just become higher. And your value to the common good now hinges on the fact you now do have something I want: Alroy Macready, alive. If you turn him over to me, I will let you serve the Infinite Order. If not, I will kill all of you in the most painful way possible after you have suffered for years in the most violent and unrelenting ways science can conceive. Give me Macready!"

"Storytime is over," Bloom said as she tossed Layla's info pad in the air, drew her pistol and shot the device. The Chairman's image flickered away. "Fiat, take a few men and blow this spaceport sky high. Use the fuel reserves. Let's not make it easy for them to land again. The rest of you, underground, now."

"I don't remember anything. No Amberly. No Raven One," Alroy said. "Maybe you should give me to the Chairman. I won't be the cause of more suffering."

"Maybe the Chairman should go to hell. Now everyone double time it to the underground rendezvous. It takes what 15 minutes for those particle beams to recharge?"

"More like 10," Alfonsi said, sweat dripping from his head.

Bloom turned to Alroy. "You would give everything for us. We'll do the same for you if we have to. We're family. Fiat, grab the prisoner and let's go."

Fiat yanked Layla and pulled her toward the grassy fields. Layla let herself be led along, but kept looking behind her, not able to take her eyes off her dead father.

CHAPTER TWELVE

February 16, 2610. Aboard the Magnus, 735,000 kilometers from Arara, in a parallel orbit with the planet around the star Viapos.

"Engineering, confirm antimatter reactor emissions remain below 15 percent," Alecia Blight, executive officer and operations director for the *Magnus*, said as she stood at the captain's tactical table, in command of the second watch. Blight had been busy working with Lt. Cho, who also stood at the table, calibrating heat sinks to make *Magnus* invisible to long-range scanners.

"Do you think Chasm can really detect reactors running so low?" Caddo, now serving as *Magnus* bridge gunnery liaison, asked.

Blight rolled her eyes at the ignorance of the officer they recovered from the wreckage of the *American Spirit*. She had no quarter in her heart for Caddo – she believed he did not deserve forgiveness for shooting a fellow bridge officer, no matter the circumstances. Obadiah's commissioning of Caddo on *Magnus* was prompted by the old man's guilt, not because the runt had any talent, Blight thought. "No, they would need to be at least running 25 percent hot to be detected by the best radiological scanners," Blight replied flatly.

"We'll burn through our batteries pretty quickly with the generators running at one quarter capacity," Caddo stated the obvious.

"We need to run silent," Blight said. "As soon as Chasm sees us, they'll send *Utopia* to give chase. Captain North will need to figure out what the situation is on the ground, if there is any change for armed resistance from the citizens, and then, and only then, we make a coordinated attack on our terms, with the element of surprise on our side. It's a basic tactic, Caddo. If you have to give up playing your simulation games to save our battery power, I think you'll survive."

Disdain from Blight dripped off each word, and Caddo felt each acidic drop. He was glad to be going with North on the recon party to Arara. As XO, Blight would be master of the *Magnus* in

North's absence, and Caddo honestly worried for his livelihood under her command. Cho caught Caddo's eye and gave him a sympathetic look.

"Hawkins, report on positional data," Blight called from the tactical table over to the navigation station. Alternatively, Hawkins, another rescue from *American Spirit,* was favored by Blight. Hawkins was smart, sharp and respectful — and hadn't shot another officer, justified or not.

The blonde looked down at her magnetic resonance scanner. "Holding at 735,000 kilometers relative to Arara," Betsy reported. "Our Viapos orbit is showing negligible decay."

The *Magnus* had put itself in a parallel orbit with Arara around the star Viapos. All non-essential systems that could attract the attention of Chasm scanners were minimized or shut down. The *Magnus* crew figured Chasm was looking for them, but by minimizing its radiation profile and keeping a safe distance, the ship was virtually undetectable against the blackness of space.

North sat alone in Magnus' garden observatory. The lights were dim. He held a too hot cup of bitter brown sadness water that allegedly approximated coffee.

He was tired.

Most nights for more than three years, North barely slept. Amberly's abduction by the Chairman haunted his dreams when he did sleep. He used chemicals to stay awake. He used chemicals to go to sleep. Only Kora knew of North's inner turmoil, this overwhelming guilt for what surely was the suffering of the woman he loved.

He kept a brave front. He knew how important his crew saw his strength. Lydia, Alecia, Sparks, Caddo, Janna, Kora and the rest — they were counting on him. He pictured faces of the dead. Ramos, Midas, Moreno, Skip needed to be avenged.

The comforts afforded a captain of a deep space ship were like ashes in his mouth. The joys of regular life were tasteless.

He looked down at his cup, and flung it into a planter.

"God, where are you?" He folded his hands tightly, until his knuckles turned white. "Jesus, are you real anymore?"

He quietly wept.

Then he sensed another presence had entered the room.

"Commander North," Dek Tigona announced his presence. "Kora said I might find you here."

North didn't look up, but ran his hands over his face and then back through his hair. "Dek. I was just collecting my thoughts before my shift on the bridge."

"Can I join you?" Dek asked.

North nodded, and Dek sat on the bench next to him. Both men looked ahead into the starfield beyond the panoramic observation window.

"What's on your mind?" North asked quietly.

"I was praying. God told me you were hurting. So, I came to find you."

"God told you?" North scoffed. "He should have told me you were coming."

"Don't you believe anymore?"

North made a sideways glance at Dek. "I'm not sure. Sure. Sure, I do."

"I see. Faith is hard then we are walking in the valleys. But that's when we need it most."

"Tell that to Amberly," North looked sideways at Dek.

"Amberly is going to be okay," Dek said. "You can't lose hope for her."

"Did God tell you that?"

"No, but hey, with North and Dek on the same team, how can we fail?" Dek smiled.

"I'm not going to answer that."

After a moment of silence, Dek spoke again.

"I never thanked you for plucking me from space, North."

"I know it's what Amberly would have wanted. That's thanks enough for me," North said. "And then we also got to airlock that Chasm bastard who killed Trish. That was a bonus."

"We should have given him grace," Dek lamented.

"Maybe. War's a bitch," North said. "Anyway, after we got your message, we thought you were gone with *Magellan*. I know Amberly is going to be glad to see you if we save her—"

"*When* we save her."

"When we save her, then," North conceded. "Do you want me to delete that message?"

"No, I still may die before this is over," Dek said. "Save it just in case."

"What happened to your optimism?"

Dek shrugged.

North's infopad offered a soft beep. "Hey, I need to get to the bridge," North stood up.

"North…" Dek stood up and the pair squared off.

"Yeah?"

"God is with you."

"I know," North said as he walked off the deck. "Thanks for the reminder."

The main portal slid open.

"Captain on the bridge," Hawkins announced, her gaze lingering on the chiseled form of her commanding officer.

North strode to the command table and addressed his second-in-command. "Dek and the eggheads in the lab have run the math again. Simulations predict the optimal time to send the recon team is in 12 hours."

"Have you decided on your final team?" Blight asked North.

"I want to move fast and travel light," North explained. "Sparks as muscle, Caddo on logistics, Lydia as science–"

"Sir, let me come," Rhodes interrupted loudly from the far side of the bridge. "I'm worthless here. We've been radio silent for years now."

"Silent? I didn't think you knew the meaning of that word," Caddo quipped.

"Har har," Rhodes responded.

"Doesn't matter. You're not coming," North dismissed Rhode's request.

The junior officer looked to XO Blight for help, but Alecia just shrugged. They'd both been under North's command for nearly three years, and Alecia knew that if North was to change his mind, challenging him here, in the open, on the bridge, was not the way to do it. She believed Rhodes was perfect for the job, and she knew Rhodes knew it too. Blight knew the rejection must sting Rhodes, and she felt sorry for the 23-year-old. The young woman, born on *Magnus* and who had spent most of her life within the confines of their great ship, needed to spread her wings to grow. Few people were cut out for a lifetime trapped on a deep space ship. Arara is what Rhodes needed, reasoned Blight, to mature into the great woman she was meant to be.

"Who *is* going to run comms for you?" Alecia asked under her breath.

"Fuego Boot? I don't know yet," North replied with a hint of frustration, but then flashed his brilliant smile. "But I have some time to figure it out. Would you ask Chief Bollard if he is finished with the pre-launch checks on the *Prime*?"

"You think my procrastinating husband is done with pre-checks already? I'm sure he's thinking, 'Why rush? I have 12 hours to get it done.'"

North was reclining on a red in-wall couch in the captain quarters, staring at his framed photo of the Earth city Vancouver, circa 2000. Something about the skyline of tall buildings, checkerboards of lit windows, the foggy darkness, called to North. His ancestors had hailed from that Canadian city, so he kept the poster to remind him of his Earth heritage. For someone who had grown up on Arara and the waypoints (and in the deep space between), the misty cityscape was truly alien to him. *I've never been to Earth, but now I am leading her greatest warship to fight for the mother planet*, North pondered.

In six hours, he would give temporary command of *Magnus* to XO Blight. If all went well, he would command *Magnus* again. But North knew the odds of everything going well were slim. He'd have to find a resistance force on Arara or muster one to create a base of operations planet side. And Chasm had already had years to cement its control over the populace. Even if North and his team could find allies on Arara, *Magnus* would still have to disable both *Utopia* and *Marquette*. No rebellion stood a chance if either ship or waypoint continued to orbit Arara. If North failed, or if they deemed the operation impossible, North's team would stay on Arara to foment trouble for Chasm's indoctrination efforts. The *Magnus* however, would begin the two-decade trip back to Earth, report what it had found, and possibly return 40 years later with an overwhelming force to subdue Arara, if anyone at Earth still cared enough to fight for the colony and those on it. *If we fail, this very well could be my last trip into space*, North thought. *Maybe that's not so bad.*

North sat up and decided that it would be best for him to try to get a few hours of sleep before departing *Magnus* with the infiltration team. He pulled off his shirt and tossed it next to his infopad on the nightstand. He plopped on the bed, leaned over and picked up the infopad. After checking the watch's log, he pulled up a photo of Amberly from his personal media. He studied her green eyes and soft facial features. Her red hair flowed down her back, which dated the photo. North knew Amberly hadn't kept her hair that long since she was 17, a decade ago. *Those were better days. I wish I could go back,* North thought.

Amberly would be 27 if she is still alive. North pushed thought away. *Of course, she is alive. She must be alive. I have to save her.*

Condi interrupted North's thoughts. "You have a visitor," the VI announced with its artificially feminine voice. "Rhodes."

North sighed. He was hoping to avoid this discussion.

"Let her in," North said as he stood up and threw on his night robe.

The door to the captain's quarter slid open, and Rhodes entered the room. North was surprised to see his bridge communication officer dolled up reminiscent of the deceased spymaster Ryder. He recognized the dress as being one of the dead Chasm traitor's more alluring outfits.

"Rhodes," North said matter-of-factly, "It's the middle of the night. What do you want, Rhodes? Why are you wearing that dress?"

"Sparks and I have been living it up at the cantina. Singing with the baaaand. Did you know Sparks has some nice pipes... voice.... singy thingy," Rhodes said, her speech was slurred.

"You're drunk?" North asked, but it wasn't a question. "I'm surprised."

"First time," Rhodes said. "I swear, I sweeear! Sparks said that the whiskey was good... and she was RIGHT. I only had three ... or was it five... no, three shots."

"Sparks? Of course. After all these years of trying to corrupt you, she finally—"

Rhodes pointed at a leatherette chair near a desk in the corner of the spacious captain's quarters. "Do you mind if I ... sit down before I fall down?"

"Be my guest."

Rhodes plopped down into the chair hard, her bob cut hair flipping once.

"Okay, what's going on?" North asked, as he pulled a stool from his minibar next to the brown chair Rhodes collapsed into.

"You big idiot," Rhodes sputtered out, then looked up at North, his muscular torso hardly covered by the night robe. "You big, handsome, gorgeous idiot. Don't you understand?"

North pulled his robe closed. "Understand what?"

"How long have we known each other? Six or seven years? Don't you know how much you mean to me? How much I ... I..."

"Lieutenant Commander. You're drunk," North reiterated.

Rhodes shook her head to clear it, and forced herself to focus. "No... Maybe. Listen. You are about to go away on the mission of a lifetime, and I am never going to see you again. Let me say this," Rhodes spoke softly. North noted that unlike most people who became loud when drunk, Rhodes actually became quieter. She was still loud, *but just not as loud as normal.* "How do you think it makes me feel?"

"You don't know that the mission will be a failure–"

"Meh, who knows the odds? Anything could happen. But there is as good of a chance as anything that you don't make it. And I know we... you and me... are not anything, I know we'll never be, and you know, Amberly and Sparks and Kora are all lined up for you."

"Kora's not–"

"Shhht! I've been drinking up the courage to say this so shut up. I've been crushing on you since you saved Nora on the *Iron Star.* Every year it gets lonelier, you know..." Rhodes said as she reached out her hand and placed it between the folds of North's robe on his bare upper chest. She looked up at him and snapped back her hand, suddenly embarrassed.

"Well! That's what I came to say," Rhodes was now talking loudly at the floor, eyes wide. "I was hoping, at least, to be on the recon team. Maybeee find a farmer who was a part of the rebellion and make a life somewhere off this ship. Maybe have the kids Sparks and I talk about." Rhodes' eyes grew distant for a moment, then she focused on North's brown ones. "I'm just going to... miss you, North. And I'd kick myself the rest of my life if I didn't tell you how I feel ... and now I'm going to go before I make a bigger fool of myself or throw up. Probably throw up…"

"Well," North smiled, "I am not going to miss you."

"Well, North, that's not … I mean you want me to cry or something. Wow. You really know how to make a girl feel like a million credits. I'm leaving—"

"Rhodes!" North caught her arm. "I'm not going to miss you because you are going to run our mission comms. Blight called me out. She said I was being overprotective because I cared about you. She was right. You're the best we've got."

"You are letting me go! YES! Wait. What? You *care* about me?" sniffed Rhodes.

"Of course. I've watched you grow up, work your way to being the best comms officer in space. I've watched you do braver things in one year than most people do in a lifetime. You saved the *Iron Star*. You volunteered for the *Marquette* mission. I'm so proud of you. But I can't…it's not like…I mean, I don't…"

Rhodes held up her hands. "I get it. Stop before you hurt yourself." Then, letting her hands fall to her sides, she said "And thanks…for saying that stuff."

"You've become a part of my family out here. I love you like you're my sister."

"Sister…cool." Rhodes snapped her fingers and attempted to point them at North as she lost her balance. He grabbed her shoulders to steady her.

"Thanks, broooother," Rhodes said loudly, then grabbed at her head. "Ouch. Son of a dirt-licking … how bad is a hangover? I think I'm going to have one and I report for duty in six hours."

"Sparks can give you some pointers," North laughed, and then he reached forward and pulled Rhodes into a hug. "Now go get some sleep, mission comms officer," North gave Rhodes a gentle push towards the door.

"Good night," Rhodes said and put up her fingers in air quotes, "'brother.' Ha!" She smiled and stumbled out the door.

"You can lose the heels!" North called after her. "You won't need them on Arara."

A group of several hundred well-wishers had assembled on the *Magnus*' hangar deck. The air seemed fresher and the lights brighter, as the mission crew assembled in front of the Valkyrie-class *M.S.S. Prime*. Some photos and vids were being taken, as people assembled knew that this team would have significance in the annals of human history. Either they would be the beginning of the end of Chasm, or they would be martyrs for the cause of freedom and self-determination.

Caddo, stood alone, his face tight. He purposefully didn't get to know many people on *Magnus* during his time on the warship. He *wanted* to be a martyr and developing connections would make it all the harder. He tried to sacrifice himself to destroy the *Red Hammer*, to pay penance for his sins. His glorious death was snatched from him after *Magnus* defeated the *Red Hammer*, which drove him all the more to desire a glorious end fighting Chasm on the planet.

Sparks stood next to Caddo, wearing her battle armor. Most thought the black, tight-fitting-but-tough outfit was just for show during the debarkation, but she really wore it for the helmet. The headpiece blocked out most of the light, which was advantageous, as Sparks had overdone it last night while partying with Rhodes. The helmet also covered enough of her face so she didn't need to wear her half-mask.

Sparks had a new sword fashioned for this mission, specifically designed to disrupt point defense systems. The metallic black weapon was strapped to her back and gleaned in the flood lights of the hangar. Sparks had one mission now – to get onto the runabout as soon as possible and hit the rack to sleep off her self-medication. She had no great affection for the *Magnus*. She *was* attached to North and was ready to die at his side.

Maybe they would save Amberly. If so, she would be glad to have her "adopted" sister back. But if not, then she'd have a clear path to North. Sparks saw Kora at the front of the crowd, with not-so-little Alroy and Nora, both nearly eight. She gave both the children hugs. She almost broke when she held the weeping Nora.

Sparks had come to love that little girl, and she didn't want to lose it. She pointed to Kora, "I have a mission for you, Nora. You must watch out for Kora. Take care of her. She's special. She's the daughter of Kimberly Macready." Sparks then gave Kora an awkward hug then stepped back into line.

Lydia followed up behind Sparks. She was serving as the science specialist for the mission, but she had also spent the last three years on *Magnus* training to become a professional soldier. She wasn't as elegant in melee combat as Sparks, but she was now well-versed in firearms, and at least based on the *Magnus* simulation room leaderboard, she was an excellent shot. Unlike Sparks, her war gear was already packed away and she wore a utilitarian khaki jumpsuit, comfortable and practical for the trip to Arara.

"We will find Amberly," Lydia said as she squeezed Kora's hand. "I promise. We'll bring her back to you."

"I'll never stop praying for you. You are the best kind of friend. *No greater love.*"

"*No greater love,*" Lydia replied, smiled and entered the *Prime* through the main hatch.

Rhodes stepped up and gave a big hug to Nora. "I'm going to miss you, sweetness. Keep eating your veggies."

"No way," Nora responded. The girl was smiling as tears rolled down her cheek. *Poor Nora*, Rhodes thought, *so young to know the bitter taste of goodbyes.*

"What are you wearing?" Nora asked, pointing at the dark goggles covering Rhodes' eyes.

"Nothing. Just in case I need eye protection on the mission," Rhodes sighed, rubbing at her aching head. "I'll be back soon. You'll see. Love you."

"Love you too!" Nora said as Rhodes slipped onto the *Prime*. *I'm going to regret it if I can't keep my promise to Nora*, Rhodes thought as she found her way to the *Prime's* small bridge.

North saluted Bright. Seven years ago, the pair were like oil and water. Now they could finish each other's thoughts. She'd been an excellent second-in-command, and she would serve the *Magnus* well should he not return.

"Congratulations. You're in command now, acting captain Bright."

Alecia returned the salute sharply. "Thank you, sir. I won't let you down. Godspeed!"

"No worries, we'll all have some shore leave drinking our choice of poison on some beach of the Lewis Islands soon enough. Indeed, Godspeed to us al—"

North noticed some commotion from the back of the crowd, and recognized Dek pushing through. "I'm coming with you," the sandy-haired man said, hauling a duffle of his personal affects. Though he had come to respect Dek, North wasn't pleased to see him and had worked to avoid him. He couldn't imagine what Dek could say to convince North to allow him to tag along at this point.

"As what? Our spiritual advisor? Thanks, but I already know how to pray."

"No. As your spy," Dek smiled. "I have a plan to save Amberly."

CHAPTER THIRTEEN

February 17, 2610. The untamed grasslands south of the Farm Prairies of the Ingram continent, Arara.

North was getting worried. His headlamp glittered against the water's surface on the lake in front of him. An erratic wind whipped the reeds that grew at the lake's edge, and North strained to hear disturbances in the water.

"Where are they?" North grumbled. Dek put his hand on North's shoulder and leaned over the water's edge.

"Relax, Sparks is formidable," Dek said, as he strained his eyes to see in the dark night.

"Yes, I am aware," North said, turning to Dek, annoyed.

"She was trained in the same cohort as I was," Dek continued. "Don't underestimate her."

"I won't... I don't," North turned to Lydia. "Didn't they comm they were coming up now?"

"It's only been two minutes," Lydia said. The tall woman had a smile a kilometer wide. "This is amazing! I feel so free!"

"And Rhodes seems quite capable, also," Dek remarked. "She trained in the aquatank."

"There they are," Caddo pointed at two bodies in vac suits emerging a few meters from the shore. A second later, a white plastic crate bobbed to the surface.

North and Dek both waded into the lake, reaching to help pull Sparks and Rhodes to the shore. The women were attached by cable to the box, which the men also towed into the surface.

Sparks scrambled onto the shore and yanked off her mask, and thrust her arms into the air. "Woooooooooo! Woooooooooo! What a rush!" She ran a few paces into the meter-tall grasses surrounding the lake and kissed the ground, smelling the dirt. "So good to be home! I'm never going into to space again." She felt the wind whip her strawberry-blonde hair and the sensation was trilling. "So dirty good!"

North helped Rhodes to stand, and she slowly removed her vacsuit helmet. "Whoa. Whoa," Rhodes yelled, as she grabbed for and successfully clutched North. She slowly turned her head to look all around her, and then instinctively clung harder to North. "There are… no walls. I mean I knew that there would be no walls… but it goes on forever. Forever." Rhodes reached out into the night air tentatively, as if expecting to find a solid wall behind a magnetic resonance screen.

North smiled and nudged her to stand on her own. "Welcome to Arara. Go on. Take it in."

Rhodes stepped into the tall-grass fields that surrounded the lake. "Wow. This is better than I ever imagined!" Rhodes remembered when she was five and her parents took her onto a waypoint — *Balboa* — for the first time. The open space on *Waypoint Balboa's* relatively huge topside garden was scary and thrilling to her child self. But now, being on a planet for the first time ever, she couldn't even describe what she was feeling.

Rhodes sprinted a few meters and then doubled back. Her face was flush with adrenaline and joy, although her companions couldn't see her expression in the darkness. She ran up and threw her arms around Lydia.

"Can you believe this?!" Rhodes said.

"Ah!" Lydia laughed. "You're wet!" Rhodes held on to Lydia's arms and jumped in a circle around her, forcing the blonde to turn with her. Lydia gave into Rhodes giggles, and the two women let the wind and euphoria flow over them.

Dek and Caddo pulled the box ashore and began to unpack and distribute its contents into backpacks. Food, medicine, weapons, communications gear – everything needed to survive as they scoped out the Chasm-controlled cities from the wilderness.

"Do you think Chasm spotted us coming down?" Dek asked.

"Maybe," North said. "Hopefully not. But that's why we need to move quickly. My family homestead is 13 kilometers north from here."

"With any luck, they won't find the *Prime*," Caddo remarked. "We can't exactly walk back to *Magnus* without it."

"You doubt the genius of my idea, loser? I thought converting the airlock into a … water-lock was brilliant," Sparks bragged. "That lake is thirty meters deep, and there is a cave at the bottom. We tucked the Valkyrie in there."

"I'm just glad you dropped us off on the shore before you took the ship into the drink. I can't swim," Caddo said. "You don't think the water will damage the ship?"

"It would take months," Dek said. "The ship is pressurized for space and extreme atmosphere."

"Go find a dark spot and get changed," North tossed thick jumpsuits from the box at Sparks and Rhodes. Sparks caught the bundle, but Rhodes, still getting her planet-legs, fumbled the dry clothes. "The rest of you, go sink the box so Chasm doesn't find it. And be careful to not leave any footprints in the mud. Grab your gear!"

For the first several kilometers, even with the natural high from being free of the years of confinement in space, the squad found moving through the tall, thick reedy-red grasses difficult. Unlike the lighter, leafier grass on the Lewis Islands, the grass on the undeveloped, wild lands of the Ingram continent required significant exertion to push through.

"Auuugh!" Rhodes screamed and jumped. "Something buzzed by my ear! What is that!"

"Ha! Probably an Ingram wingding," North said. "You know, our genetically engineered bugs. They don't bite or sting, but they do pollinate!"

"You've got to admit, the bio-engineers who seeded Arara did a great job creating a perfect biome. They actually have to actively exterminate insects as nuisances back on Earth," Dek said. "The success in creating the perfect, balanced, human-engineered 'nature' really is what made the elders of Chasm believe they could perfect not just nature, but humans themselves."

"Plowing through this crap is not perfect," Sparks said, as she drew her sword and decapitated a tuft of tall, flowering grass.

"Let's keep it down," North said, taking for the group. "I know we're still several kilometers out, but Chasm may have the homestead occupied."

"Roger," Rhodes said in a loud whisper.

The group continued pressing through the grassy low hills in silence for another hour.

"Well, here we are," North said as he stepped out of the grass into the edge of plowed farmland. The clouds had broken and starlight flooded the Araran surface. "Home sweet home. It's been more than 20 years …"

Rhodes looked up into the starry sky and a sensation of vertigo overcame here. She grabbed Lydia's hand. Rhodes forced herself to believe that she would not fall out into the starry heavens.

"This is where you grow food?" Caddo asked. "How much food can you produce? This must be 10 times the size of the *Magellan* garden."

"This field? More like 100 times. And we have 24 fields the same size that my dad used to farm. Once Viapos rises, you'll be able to see it more clearly," North explained. He reached down and scooped up a handful of dirt and considered it. "But this field looks like it has been left fallow for at least a season. Maybe the farm is abandoned?"

"With any luck, it will be," Dek said. "It would be nice to have a base of operations to set up in and get our bearings."

"I hope not," Sparks said, slapping North on the buttocks. "I really wanted to meet your old man."

"Easy there, Sparks. The fresh air is going to your head," North rolled his eyes.

"Clouds are really *weird*. ... and the stars are so dim," Lydia frowned.

"The atmosphere diffuses the light," Dek explained.

"Okay everyone," North gathered his team. "There's only farm fields between us and the homestead. It's about four kilometers over that ridge. Let's double-time it. I want to scope it out in the cover of darkness in case the place is occupied. Don't know if my dad will be there or not. We only have... um..."

"Two hours remain until Viapos-rise," Condi spoke from the infopad strapped to North's arm.

Most of the members of the insertion team were winded by the time they were at the top of the hill that overlooked the five buildings in North's farm complex. North spied a light on through a window of the main farm house. He threw up his hand in a fist, and immediately everyone came to a standstill and crouched to the ground, as they had trained.

"Looks like someone's home," North whispered. "Could be a farm hand... could be dad..."

"Or it could be a Chasm squad detachment, waiting for us," Dek suggested.

"Yes, but I don't see any ships or transports of any kind," Sparks said. "Or maybe the place was abandoned a long time ago and someone just left the light on.

Rhodes looked in the opposite direction of the farmhouses, the transfixed on something in the distance. "Oh wow. It's more magical than I imagined!"

"Hey... quiet." North turned around to see what Rhodes was looking at.

Dawn had come. The fiery ball of Viapos peeked over the horizon. "Stay focused, lieutenant. Haven't you seen a vid of a sunrise before?"

"This is nothing like a video," she smiled. "I can feel the warm beams on my face. I've never felt so *real* before."

"Focus. And keep it down. We'll have time for tourism later," North said, turning his attention back to the complex. "Okay, we go in, quiet-like. Stay light, gear down everyone. Dek and Lydia, keep an eye on the perimeter. Take up positions in that grove of trees and stay out of sight. Caddo and Rhodes, stay here, guard the gear. Sparks and I will enter the main farmhouse. There is a front and a back door, I'll take the front, and Sparks the rear. They converge in a great room in the middle of the house. Hit your panic button if anything goes south."

"Godspeed," Dek nodded to North.

North looked at Sparks, decked again in her battle armor, pointed at the main house, drew his rifle and began to descend the hill. As they moved closer to the house, he noticed the farm animals, cattle and pigs, were gone. Holding pens were empty, and the strong manure smell he remembered and expected was faint and stale. The whole farm was quietly eerie, with just the whistling wind making noise.

North made his way to the north side of the house, while Sparks moved to the south. She drew her sword as she approached the rear door. The main home was like all the buildings in the farm complex, dirty-white walls crafted from a plaster-type material reinforced with treated reed-mesh. The cities on Arara had sprawling buildings three or four stories high built from concrete, steel and glass. But most of the rural buildings were single-floor constructed with locally-fabricated materials.

North stepped softly onto the front porch and approached the windowless front door. He looked at the access pad on the door and presented his hand for biometrics. To his surprise, the door was still programmed to recognize his signatures, so it slid open. With his access, he unlocked the back door as well, so Sparks wouldn't need to hack it.

He raised his gun and stepped over the threshold into the foyer. The house smelled musty. The first room off the front door was a sitting room with his father's library – a collection of printed Earth books, quite rare on Arara, many of them multiple centuries old. If the place was abandoned, North was surprised looters didn't steal these books. But then again, maybe there was no market for that sort of antiquity in the Infinite Order.

Through the next door was the kitchen and a portal to the great room. This was not a sliding door, but a hinged one, with a door knob. North smiled as he pulled the door open. *I haven't opened one of these in years*, the thought.

North heard the sound of humming from the kitchen.

He whipped around, his finger caressing the rifle's trigger. The room was dim, with only a skylight providing luminance. He saw a woman, maybe 40 or 50 years old, sitting at the plain white wooden table in the center of the kitchen. The woman wore a white, ill-fitting sleeveless dress. She looked up at North with her deep brown eyes and offered a smile that matched North's in brilliance. She had an open bottle of liquor, with four or five shot glasses filled to various levels on the table.

"Well you're something to look at, aren't you?" the apparently intoxicated woman said. "Won't you join me for a drink, soldier?"

North pointed his rifle down and returned the smile. He noted that she didn't seem surprised by his presence at all. "Sorry, ma'am. It's a little too early for me. Who are you?"

"Me? I'm nobody. My name is Isabel. Dr. Isabel Deanza. I used to be a doctor. Now I… well… you sure you don't want a drink? I hate to drink *alone*."

"You don't even know who I am. Aren't you worried that I might be Chasm? Or a pirate or something?" North asked.

"You aren't Chasm," Deanza laughed. "You're North. From

Magellan."

North raised his gun again. "How do you know that?" he demanded.

"Your picture is above the mantle," Deanza sighed. "Ogdin, your dad… he used to live here. I mean, this is the home you grew up in, correct? And you are *not* a pirate. I know pirates. I *was* a pirate."

North felt the unmistakable sensation of the barrel of a gun being pressed against his back.

A male voice spoke. "She *is* a pirate, and I am too. Gun on the floor, arms up, or Isabel is going to be cleaning your blood off the floor."

North slowly set his rifle down, frowning at Isabel, who seemed to have shaken off the effects of intoxication quickly. "Yeah, it's too early for me, too," she smirked. "I'd keep real still, North. Klungy has a nervous twitch ever since the Infinite Order drove us into hiding. And it would be a shame if he had to put down the nicest looking thing around here."

"Infinite Order. Chasm's government?" North said.

"That's the fancy name for the Chasm-installed taskmasters," Isabel smiled. "Chasm by any other name is still foul."

"Never mind them. How many people are here with you?" Klungy asked.

"Just me," North lied. "I just wanted to come and find where my mom is buried. I have no quarrel with you."

"Maybe," Klungy said. "But will need to keep you secure until we're sure you don't have a bunch of friends — yeeeech!"

Klungy froze as he felt a cold steel blade slide across his throat. It broke the skin, barely.

"You have two seconds to drop your gun before I cut your head off," Sparks said, filling each word with crazy.

Klungy dropped the gun to the kitchen floor. North immediately swooped down and picked up his rife and Klungy's firearm. He swung around and aimed a weapon at both Deanza and Klungy.

"Crap," Isabel said. "How could you let someone sneak up on you like that, Klungy?"

"I think *I* will have a drink," Sparks said, unwrapping her sword arm from Klungy's neck and returning the weapon to its sheath. "Not too early for me, prudes."

Sparks sat down in the chair next to Deanza and pulled off her helmet. Both Klungy and Deanza reacted to the scarring covering half of Spark's face. She noted this by rolling her eyes, blowing into an empty shot glass, and grabbing the whiskey bottle.

"Call the rest of the team down here," North told Sparks.

Sparks pounded back a shot and then pulled an infopad off its mount on her shoulder. "Oh, that's rich." She tapped the device and set it on the table. She considered the bottle of whiskey, gave it 'why not?' eyes, and poured herself a second shot.

Family photos practically wallpapered the greatroom.

"Oh, how old are you in this one?" Rhodes asked. "You were a cute kid."

North ignored his communication officer and continued his interrogation of Klungy and Deanza. "So, you have no idea where Ogdin is?"

"No. The place was abandoned when we found it," Deanza explained. "The Infinite Order has been trying to consolidate all the population on the main continent."

"Why is that?" Caddo asked.

"Efficiency. They want to make sure to maximize the utilization of the land," Isabella said.

"Also, it's easier to control the population by keeping them all together," Dek suggested.

"What do you know about it?" Klungy, who sat on a worn leather couch next to Isabella, said.

"I used to be a Chasm leader," Dek said.

"Used to be?" Klungy exhaled suspicion. "I didn't know you could get out of that cult."

"Let's just say love is a powerful thing," Dek muttered.

"So, what happens if Chasm captures pirates here?" Caddo pressed.

"People who do not comply with the regulation to immigrate to the big continent are subject to immediate execution," Isabella said, shifting her weight to sit away from Klungy. "There was an amnesty period, but that expired a long time ago."

"Why didn't you go?" Caddo asked.

"Are you kidding? I paid nearly half my fortune to get

smuggled *out* of that hell hole to Ingram," Isabella said. "There is no common good in the other land – only common misery. Oh, sure, our children and children's children, if you can even call them that, will enjoy the finished product of paradise. Until then, the rest of us suckers will have to sacrifice for something greater than ourselves."

"How big is your fortune?" Sparks wondered out loud.

"Well, piracy is very lucrative," Klungy said. "I have two crates of encrypted credit chits left. Self-authenticating. Maybe 2.3 billion worth? Help yourself to some when you *head out*." Klungy was hopeful North's party would be gone soon.

"Who said we are heading out?" North pushed.

"Well, you didn't come out here with a strike team to pick up your secondary school memorabilia," Isabel countered.

"It doesn't matter. As long as the Infinite Order can keep the black market smothered, those credits are worth nothing," Klungy sighed. "Honestly, we're just biding our time until we can find a way off this planet. See how far we can make it back to Earth. If we're lucky, I might get back before I'm 70-ish."

"If Chasm keeps its grip on Arara," North said, "there is no going back to Earth."

"Oh, I think if we could get a freighter or something, we could make it to *Cortez*. Then we could wait for the next ship to *Magellan*—" Klungy looked as if was running numbers in his pale head.

"Surely someone out there will sell us a deep space ship – or at least give us a ride to *Cortez*." Deanza interrupted.

"You don't understand. *Cortez* is gone. *Magellan* is gone," Lydia said, rage filling her head with the thought of what she had lost at the hands of Chasm.

"So it's true. *Damn*," Isabella said, the blood draining from her face. "I thought the whispers of waypoints being destroyed was just Chasm propaganda. Chasm accomplished their... well, chasm."

"If we only had the *Butch Cassidy*. I wonder whatever became of her. She wasn't much to look at, but for more than a decade, she was home. I sure wouldn't be complaining now if we were riding her Earthward."

"I'm sure the captain had to scrap her," Isabelle mused.

"Evidence. And it may have taken all our fortunes to get the old lady space worthy and back into orbit."

"*Magnus* is the only ship that could make it as far as the closest waypoint now. That's *Gilbert*," Rhodes said.

"Great! Let's go!" Klungy clapped his hands together. "I'll pay you 500 million credits for passage? No? How about a cool billion?"

"If we wanted to save our skins, we'd already be halfway to *Waypoint Estavncio* by now," North spoke sternly. "And I wouldn't take your dirty money, anyway."

"Sorry," Klungy stammered. "I didn't mean to offend–"

Sparks, who had removed her battle armor, and now wore a more comfortable black jumpsuit and her half-mask, stood and sat on the arm of the couch and leaned into Klungy. She spoke into his ear, "I've seen Captain North here cut off his crew members' fingers for lesser offenses. Watch yourself." Klungy's nervous eyes darted between Sparks and North.

"Sparks!" North palmed his forehead.

"Sorry," she slid off the couch. "Just having a little fun."

Klungy's eyes darted between Sparks and North. He didn't know what to think.

"Listen," Isabella stood up. Caddo reached for his sidearm, but North waved him down. "If you really are intent on trying to overthrow Chasm, and you want to find a resistance, there's nothing here on Ingram for you. Everything is deserted and going to waste. The only people here are outlaws like Klungy and me, hiding out, and the occasional Chasm patrols we see every month or so. And I promise you, you wouldn't last a minute on the big continent. You'd never make it past the electronic surveillance. Not without someone on the inside you can bribe. But money won't work. Chasm has outlawed credits. There is nothing of value to bribe with anymore."

Isabella glanced suggestively at Sparks and Rhodes, both attractive women to her thought. "Well, almost nothing. Some things about human nature even Chasm hasn't been able to undo yet."

"That's not an option," North said flatly.

"Where you need to go is the Lewis Islands," the doctor said.

"The Lewis Islands? That backwater place?" Dek said,

incredulously.

"When the clouds of civil war started gathering on the big continent, the island locals started forming some militia. Something underground," Isabell explained. "It's so remote and sparsely populated, Chasm didn't waste time subduing it early on."

"How do you know this?" Caddo was incredulous.

"One of our former shipmates – we called him Red," Klungy explained, "sent us an encrypted communication to warn us. We hadn't heard from him in years, so I was surprised to hear from him at all, and his news seemed so fantastic. He seemed genuinely concerned for our safety and told us to come join him. We should have left the continent that night."

"Another pirate?" Lydia groused. "How can we trust a pack of thieves and maybe even murders."

"Hey! I never killed anyone," Isabel protested.

"What about your comrades?" Dek countered.

Deanza pushed her lips closed and looked down.

"Well, now that I think of it, Red wasn't a pirate by choice," Klungy said. "We found him nearly dead, drifting in space. Now what was the name of that ship… we scrubbed it, and it was … I can't remember, it's been too long."

"Now your story is even less believable," Rhodes said. "I found someone drifting in space once. It doesn't happen very often."

"Maybe you know Red?" Klungy said. "I believe he was from *Magellan*. You're from *Magellan*, aren't you Captain North?"

"I don't know any pirates by the name of Red. The only person I knew who went by that name, well, it was my nickname for *her*, never mind it doesn't matter. Caddo, keep an eye on these pirates," North said. He stood up and walked into the kitchen, and motioned Dek and Sparks to come with him.

"What do you think?" he asked the pair once they were out of earshot.

"If we could get a foothold with some native support on Lewis Island, we could land some troops and defenses from *Magnus*. There is a spaceport on the north side of the islands," Sparks said. "I did some pilot training there when I was much younger. Quaint little port village."

"No!" Dek said. "That's the wrong way. We have to save Amberly. Don't forget my plan. That means we have to get closer to the Chasm stronghold, not further away."

"I want to save Amberly as much as you. But we don't even know where she is," North said. "Which city? On *Waypoint Marquette*? Still on *Utopia*? We should marshal some strength from where we can safely run recon."

"That could take months, years? Are you sure Amberly has that much time? We have to have faith now, move with confidence," Dek argued. "We are going to have to chance it. Waiting to figure out which path to take is the greater risk for Amberly."

"There is more here at stake than Amberly," North argued. "If we save her, then what? Hope we can make it back to *Magnus* and back to Earth?"

"Yes!"

"Dammit, Dek," North slammed his fist on the table. "I knew I should have left you back on the *Magnus*. This is about more than you and me, and more than her. She would tell you that if she were here."

"Let's keep our cool boys," Sparks said, as she adjusted her half-mask. She felt a huge wave of envy. She believed these men would never fight over her.

"Fine," Dek said. "You're in command North, but I am still going to tell you what I think. I have quite a bit of my own command experience. You should listen. I actually saved the *American Spirit*. Twice."

As soon as the words left Dek's mouth, he knew it was the wrong play. He felt childish.

"Listen, asshole," North responded, instinctively clenching his fist. "You–"

"Hey! Whoa…" Dek said, putting up his hands, open and palms forward. "Sorry. Let's just stop, take a breather and pray about this. Don't you think that–"

"Don't play the 'I-found-God-in-jail' card on me," North raised his voice. "You don't deserve the grace you received."

"Isn't that the point? The grace thing? I don't know much about your guys' whole 'religion' but —?" Sparks asked.

"What are you talking about, Sparks?" North snapped.

"That whole undeserved grace thing. Isn't that the crux of your whole belief system?" She pointed back and forth between the two of them.

North's growled an inaudible response, his fist still tight. Dek's face looked conflicted, halfway between fight and flight.

Sparks leaned her deceptively slender arms on the table. "Tsk, tsk, boys. So much testosterone. The Chairman wouldn't approve. But me? Mmmmm mmmm mmmm."

Dek rolled his eyes and stifled a snicker. North opened his hand.

"I'm sorry, Dek. I might be out of line," North mustered. "But you are going to have to trust me, or you are going to have to freelance. We'll get Amberly back."

Dek was silent for a moment, then nodded.

"Good. We leave four hours before dawn to recover the *Prime*. Then we attempt to travel under radar to Williamstown. Until then, let's get some R and R. Who knows when we'll have another chance to rest."

"Great, to the Lewis Islands then," Sparks smiled. "I've been wanting a beach vacation."

North sat alone on a woven-reed chair on the back porch of his childhood home, staring into Arara's moonless night. The gusty wind didn't quite drown out the noise of the poker game floating from the kitchen. He didn't mention it to the others, but he was heartbroken he didn't find his father at their farm — his farm now, or maybe the "common good's" farm, depending on who came out on top. In his heart, he knew that Ogdin was dead. *When Chasm reared its ugly head, dad would have been the first to fight,* North thought. *He would have been the first to die for what he believed in. I know it's true, because it's what I would do. Probably all that's left of dad this side of eternity is whatever of him is in me.*

The rear house door, also hinged, burst open, and Sparks stumbled out.

"I thought you were going to play poker with the others," North looked up at his friend. "Isabella had some swell hooch for the tourney prize."

"Meh, I'm already out," Sparks said. "I went all in with trips.

Stupid Caddo drew an inside straight."

"That's why they call it gambling," North said and turned his face back to the dark night.

Sparks pulled up a chair and slid it next to North's. She sat down and sighed heavily.

"You remember when we would sit together on the *Magnus* garden deck, when I was getting better?" Sparks said. "And you convinced me that someday I'd learn to love peace and quiet, that I would kick my adrenaline addiction. We talked about finding peace, together, retiring here or on the Lewis Islands."

"That was a long time ago," North closed his eyes.

"When I was broken, that dream was all I had, North," Sparks said. "To be with you."

"Good thing you got better. Your appetite for adventure was rekindled. You lost your taste for a peaceful end."

"But I didn't lose my taste for you," Sparks looked at the shadows on North's face. She reached over and laid her hand on his.

North didn't say anything.

"And then suddenly, unexpectedly, Amberly was back in the picture," Sparks continued, gently removing her hand from his. "Look at you and Dek. You're both practically willing to trade the whole of Arara to save your redheaded idol."

"Envy is not becoming," North muttered. "You're jealous."

"Damn right I am," Sparks admitted. "Sometimes, when my heart is dark, I hope that we don't save Amberly. That she is already dead. And you and I take our revenge on the Chairman together. But I hate that selfish part of myself."

"Don't be hard on yourself, Sparks," North turned to the beautiful woman seated next to him. "Your feelings are natural."

"Yes, selfishness is natural," Sparks said. "That's why we have to fight it. You know I've been sneaking off and listening to those bullshit sermons Dek's been giving to the gullible believers on *Magnus*. Eternal life, the ultimate hoax. It's what the Chairman promises, too."

"Not the same thing," North said, a little taken aback. Maybe North had "fallen off the wagon" in his faith journey, but he still believed in the bullshit, as Sparks so delicately put it.

"Yes, I agree, not the same thing. There is one thing that Dek talks about, this idea of *selflessness*, that somehow, we can tap into some supernatural power that can make us the better human, to fight that natural selfishness. I don't believe it, but I like it more than the Chairman's version."

"What do you mean?" North asked, legitimately intrigued.

"Dek says this Jesus," Sparks said, "will make us as if we were perfect before the God who created the whole universe. The Chairman wants to make people perfect, too. The Chairman wants to save the world like Jesus, but for some reason, her way seems to hurt lots of people. I can't believe I used to believe her lies. Raven One sold them well, I guess. Now, I much prefer the *myth* of your selfless Jesus to the *real* Chairman."

"Jesus was a real, historical figure," North offered.

"You are missing the point, jarhead. What I am trying to say," Sparks blustered, "is that the *selfish* me wants Amberly dead, but the *selfless* me wants her alive. And I guess *I want to be the selfless me*. But it's hard."

"Sparks … that's really noble," North said, surprised at her transparency.

"Not really. I love Amberly like a sister," Sparks said, leaning her head against North's broad shoulder.

"You hardly knew Amberly," North recalled. "I mean, you've spent like, what, less than two weeks with her?"

"It's not about quantity of time," Sparks said. "Think quality time."

"Sure."

"Besides, I knew where she came from — Raven One. Sure, our parents influence us with their genetics. But for those of you who were lucky enough to know your genetic donors, not like us cohort saps, your parents' personal nurturing – or abusive – influence was a greater shaper than pieces of hand-me-down DNA."

"Okay, what do you mean?"

"I knew Kimberly Macready," Sparks said. "I knew her good, her bad. She was my mentor. She was my idol. I aspired to be her. Amberly also aspired to be her mother. So much of Kimberly Macready is in Amberly, but so much of Kimberly Macready is in me, too."

"Kimberly was always an enigma to me," North recalled. "I

understood Alroy much better. He was a great pilot and navigator, like you. Of course, I never knew the real Kimberly until the very end."

"Some of the non-DNA stuff Kimberly gave Amberly, she gave me. She taught us to think critically, how to stand up for ourselves, how to reach for excellence, to believe in our potential," Sparks said. "That has to be worth something. Kimberly was so special. So unique. She's gone. But anything that is left of her lives on in Amberly. And Kimberly's love lives on in me. Ergo, sisters."

"You've been selling that theory for years," North sounded indifferent. "I still don't buy it."

"Thanks for your enlightened position, killjoy. You know what, it would be *awesome* if we save Amberly, and then because she is entirely more sensible and intelligent than both you and Dek, she doesn't *end up with either of you*. I know she tolerates your Christian cult, but, come on…" Sparks, stopped speaking, smiled and squeezed North's arm. "Hell, who am I kidding. For you, North, I'd convert."

"There may not be much of a future for either of us," North said. "We could get captured and executed, killed in combat, or even catch a fatal case of the Araran Sweats."

Sparks said nothing in reply for a few minutes, and the friends sat, looking up at the night sky.

A thought hit Sparks. "You're wrong about what you said – I didn't rediscover my appetite for adventure. I just found a new lust for revenge. For this," Sparks touched her mask. "And for all the pain the Chairman has caused everyone else."

North was pissed. Half his team was hungover from a card match that devolved into a drinking game. Only two hours remained until Viapos-rise, and they still had not set out to reclaim the *Prime* and make a break for the Lewis Islands.

"Caddo, hurry up and get those packs loaded," North said. Into his own pack, he placed a photo of his mother and father he rescued from a bedroom wall, along with the copy of *My Antonia*, his father's favorite novel, from the collection in the study.

"What are we going to do with them?" Sparks asked, pointing to Klungy and Deanza.

"Let us come with you," Isabel said. "I'd rather be on the run than stuck in one of their education centers or be conscripted to serve in one of their medical facilities. They are not practicing medicine. They are only doing human engineering. It's immoral. I will die before I'll help those inhumane bastards. Surely you could use a physician, even a pirate one?"

"Meh, I have no desire to go and die in some battle at the Lewis Islands," Klungy groaned. "I'll take my chances on Ingram. This is where we part ways, Isabel."

"Don't leave him, North" Dek thumbed toward Klungy. "Even if he doesn't voluntarily betray us, if Chasm catches him, they'll torture him, and he'll give us up."

"I wouldn't break," Klungy asserted.

"Please. Chasm would break him less than a minute," Sparks said to North, as she pulled her serrated knife. "I'm a trained Chasm interrogator. You want me to demonstrate?"

"Never mind. I'll come," Klungy said.

CHAPTER FOURTEEN

February 19, 2610. The Lewis Islands, the remains of the Williamstown Spaceport.

Lewis Island Irregulars Commander Bloom carefully poked her camera over the cover of the grass that she was lying in. "Fiat's scouting report was correct. A Valkyrie-class runabout landed at Williamstown spaceport."

"Just one?" Corporal Alfonsi squatted next to his commanding officer, out of breath. "That doesn't make any sense. "I figured the Chairman would come back in force to wipe us out. Why would she just send a single runabout. At most it could carry, what, ten troops?"

"Maybe it's not Chasm," Captain Red, Bloom's second-in-command, suggested. "Chasm has all the time in the world. You heard the Chairman; she thinks we're something special, and for some reason she'd rather be patient and wait to see if we'll voluntarily join her before she'd kill us."

"Maybe that ship belongs to a strike team to kidnap you?" Alfonsi suggested. "The Chairman seemed to want you bad enough."

"God knows why," Red said.

"Well, let's remind the Chairman what we do when she lands ships. Let's blow it to hell," Alfonsi said.

"Whoever flew that in is a decent pilot," Red remarked. "Finding a spot big enough for touchdown in this mess is near impossible. Fiat must have destroyed 90 percent of the tarmac when he took out the hangars last time we were out here."

"And since they don't have a hangar to hide their ship in now, it will be all the easier to take out," Alfonsi tapped the grenade launcher strapped to his gear.

"Calm down," Bloom commanded. "Taking out this ship in broad daylight… risky, not knowing where the crew is. We could reveal our position, assuming they are not onboard."

"Fiat should have never taken their eyes off that runabout once it landed," Alfonsi grumbled.

"We all make mistakes," Bloom said. "I don't think it was

unreasonable for him to not risk signaling and bring back his report in person."

"We could wait it out," Red outlined their options. "But I'd still feel better knowing for sure that we were taking out the enemy. Bloom, you have your sniper optics?"

"I do," Bloom confirmed, "but I don't like where this is going." She dug into her back and produced a digital scope.

"Great. I'm going over there for a little peek. You guys stay under the grass line and keep me covered. Commander, if this is the enemy, and I am captured, please use that sniper rifle of yours and take me out. I don't want to be fodder for the Chairman, whatever she wants from me."

"No," Bloom replied. The thought of losing Red terrified her. "The Chairman is after you. I should go."

"Nope. The Irregulars need their commander. I'm expendable."

"Expendable, my tight ass." Bloom was about to argue with Red, but she knew better. The redhead would win her over in the end. He always did. She took his hand and squeezed it knowingly. "I don't like this. But you can go."

"I'll be careful," Red said, as he shed his backpack, removing his side arm from the bag and holstering it. "This shouldn't take long."

Red elevated his body into a high crouch and stepped toward the ruined spaceport.

You're not expendable, Bloom thought as her eyes followed Red, *not expendable to me.*

Alfonsi stuck a tracer camera on a tall reed, and he reclined back under the grass line. He pulled out his info pad and watched the video feed from the tracer. "Careful, Red. Careful. You should have just let me take that out with a rocket, boss."

"Hush," Bloom said as she studied Red's progress on Alfonsi's infopad.

Five minutes later, Red was at the edge of the grass, and now stood mostly erect, climbing over the exploded remains of the starport's facilities, decimated by the handiwork of the Irregulars trying to destroy a potential Chasm foothold a few weeks earlier. He was careful not to lacerate himself as he stepped over jagged pieces of metal frames and jutting shards of dense polycarbonate. Red was trying to keep low, but now he was likely in view of anyone watching the approach to the Valkyrie.

"So far, so good," Alfonsi whispered. Red was far enough away from Alfonsi's camera now that image detail was beginning to deteriorate, but the corporal could still make out Red.

Then he saw someone else.

"Bloom! Look," Alfonsi said. "Someone is approaching from the east."

"Is it Chasm? Does she see Red?" Bloom said as she picked up her infopad and began to message a warning to Red.

"I don't think she sees him. She's pretty big – probably a he. Not wearing Chasm armor. Too far away to be sure. I'm gonna blow that ship while we have the chance," Alfonsi said. He dropped his infopad and pulled the launcher pieces from his sack. He connected the two barrel segments, loaded a grenade, stood up above the grass and took aim.

"Wait! Wait! That's an order," Bloom hissed.

Red was close enough to make out the registry on the runabout. *M.S.S. Prime. M.S.S.?* Red thought. *Marquette Space Ship, maybe?* He wished he had taken time to study the ship inventory on *Waypoint Marquette*, then he might know for sure the origin of the latest intruder. *Couldn't be from Magellan. Too far. No other M's. Must be Marquette. Which means probably Chasm-conscripted.*

Jules spoked urgently to Red. "Message from Bloom: Incoming hostile, 200 degrees south southwest."

Red pulled his side arm and whirled in the direction his VI indicated. He saw a tall, formidable man, still a dozen yards off climbing around the remains of an exploded fuel tank. Red moved quickly, gun drawn, to intercept the man before he spotted Red. *Surely, this guy came on that ship.*

"Red's moving away from that ship, toward the man," Alfonsi reported, looking through the grenade launcher's viewfinder. "Let me take it out now."

"Wait. Let's see if this new player is hostile or not. If he attacks Red, take it out," Bloom said. She poked her head above the grass line and scanned all around them. Chances were this intruder was not alone, and she didn't know if his comrades were in the ship or out scouting. Alfonsi could compromise their position. If he launched a grenade, almost certainly they would be outed – if anyone was looking for them.

"Hands up, sweetheart!" Bloom felt what she thought was some sort of blade painfully poking, but not puncturing, her back. One thrust would change that, so Bloom slowly lifted her hands. Chasm had her, but didn't notice Alfonsi, yet, Bloom thought. She considered ordering Alfonsi to fire, but knew once she did, the Chasm agent would react by impaling her. Bloom thought in an instant, *I suppose I always knew I'd go down fighting. There was really never any chance of us winning. And Red is right; anything but capture by Chasm. Who knows what horrors the Chairman has invented for us?*

Red was just three meters from the man, crouching behind a pile of upended asphalt. For the umpteenth time, Red double-checked to see his weapon was loaded and the safety was off. He sprung up, pointed his weapon at where he thought the man would be standing but there was ... no one.

"Looking for me?" A baritone voice behind Red asked.

Red whirled, ready to fire, but saw that the man, wearing a strangely familiar military uniform, had an automatic rifle pointed at him. The man was brawny, with short brown hair and a scar on his chin. Red considered whether he could get a shot off, and also wondered if Bloom was ready to snipe him.

"Drop it — whoa... you look like —"

"Are you Chasm?" Red asked, still holding his gun out. "If not, lower your weapon or I am dead. Sniper with a kill order!"

The word sniper made the man a little jumpy, and he glanced around. "I'm not Chasm. I'm North from *Magellan*. But I don't understand... you are. No. Can't be."

"Lower your gun with me," Red said and he started to move his gun down. "I'm Red, a captain with the Lewis Irregulars.

North followed Red's lead. "Red... Isabella sent us to you. But you look like... I mean it's been ten years, but you are a spitting image of... it's impossible."

"A spitting image of who?" Red pushed as he holstered his

gun. "Tell me who!?!"

"Impossible. He's dead."

"Who? Alroy Macready?"

North dropped his gun. "Yes, but he's dead. Kimberly killed him ...it's been ten years...Alroy??

"Apparently, yes," Alroy shrugged.

"Alroy!? It's me, *North*! Dear God, man! We thought you were dead! How did you...? I don't understand...Oh my god!" North barreled forward to throw his arms around Alroy.

Alroy stepped back, instinctively. "I'm sorry, North...you're familiar, but only...I mean, I can't rememb —"

Booooooooom!

Both North and Alroy dove for cover as the *Prime* was rocked by an explosion.

"What the hell? Who's attacking the ship!?" North shouted.

Scraped and bleeding from his fall impact on the jagged asphalt, Alroy clawed for his infopad. "Friendly! Friendly! Do not fire! Jules, tell them to hold their fire."

"You dirt-licker," Sparks groused as she brought the hilt of her sword hard on the back of Blooms head, knocking the Irregular commander out. *I'll deal with you later*, Sparks thought as she took off toward the Prime's assailant. The missile's plume led her to see Alfonsi standing several meters away through some thick grass, a smoking grenade launcher hoisted on his shoulders. She pushed her sword ahead of her, closing the distance forcefully, pulling one of her pistols from her thigh-holder.

"Surrender, bitch," Sparks shouted. "Quit shooting up my ride!"

Alfonsi was surprised to hear someone besides Bloom, and in his startled state, he dropped his launcher.

"Call your man off Red!" Alfonsi fumbled for his gun, but could not retrieve it before he was staring down a sword, wielded by a very attractive woman with a half-mask.

"Stop the attack. This is a friendly ship." Alfonsi's info pad, still on the ground, spit out Jules' voice.

"Friendly?" Sparks said. "I hope you know how to repair runabouts."

An alarm went off in Alfonsi's pack. Sparks looked at him

menacingly, and thrust her sword closer to his neck.

"It's the early warning system. Chasm must have spotted the missile explosion. *Marquette's* about to rain death from above. We've got to move. Now! What did you do to Bloom?"

"The woman? Double dirt-licking fool," Sparks said. "I'll grab her. Which way do we go?"

"*Any* way! Move or you're dead! Maybe 15 seconds!"

Sparks reversed her sprint, scooped up the unconscious Bloom, and threw the woman over her shoulder. Alfonsi was impressed with the strength of this mysterious, sword-wielding warrior.

"Head south. There is a tunnel about two kilometers from here. From there, we'll be safe."

Moments later, the retreating pair heard the unmistakable *zip* then *poof* sound of particle beams hitting the surface where they had been standing just a few meters behind them.

"Here it is!" Alroy called back to North through the tall grass. "Stay low! I didn't know they were watching. They must have adjusted their orbit."

North quickly glanced up into the bright green-blue Arara sky in the general direction of where *Marquette* might be orbiting the planet, even though he knew that seeing the waypoint with the naked eye during daylight was impossible.

"Come on," Alroy pulled a camouflaged board, covered with stalks of grass and reeds, off a dirty hole in the ground. "Down the tunnel. Go!"

"What do you mean, you didn't know they were watching?" North asked. He looked at the dark orifice suspiciously and glanced back at Alroy. "Are you sure this is safe?"

"Fine," Alroy slid down the tube, leaving North behind. "Replace the lid on your way in!"

North secured his weapon, pulled the board over his head as he lowered himself down. Alroy had activated his helmet lamp, and North saw he was already ten meters down the dirt-walled tunnel. North pulled out a glow stick from his pack, lit it, and hurried to catch Alroy.

"How far?" North asked, hunched over in the tight tunnel.

"To headquarters, pretty far," Alroy said. "We built this

network as large as we could, with lots of false paths and dead ends, to confuse the Infinite Order should they make it down here." Alroy waved his hand around at what his confederates had created. Then he pointed down the tunnel.

"Be careful. There's a four meter drop not too far from here. Let's go down one at a time — I'm not sure the rope ladder will hold both our weights. After the drop, there is an alcove maybe a half-kilometer past, we can stop, reset and report in."

Within minutes, then men were carefully defending the ladder fabricated from reedy grass. As they moved on past the drop, the pair walked in silence. Unexpectedly, Alroy's infopad spoke up. "Captain Red, you missed the door by two meters."

"Hmmm. Thanks. Jules," Alroy turned back toward North, tapping on the dirt wall, until his rapping hit a metallic surface and made a hollow ring. "Here we are. We can rest here for a while."

The door slid open, and Alroy stepped through. North followed. The room had a higher clearance than the tunnel, and North was able to stand fully upright. There were a few benches dug into the walls, and North took his pack and sat down on one of them. Alroy pulled a battery unit out of his pack and placed it in a box-shaped cabinet at the end of the small room. The air scrubber inside the cabinet immediately powered up, as did overhead lighting.

Alroy sat down opposite North and studied his face, and then shook his head. He was trying so hard to remember, his head started to hurt. "I don't know you, Commander. You are not in my head."

"Oh, sir, I know you well. We've flown together. I've eaten at your table. You have *no idea* how miraculous it is to see you again, Alroy," North said. "What happened? How did you get here? You were lost in space let's see, in 2596."

"Thirteen years."

"Then Kimberly shows back up at *Magellan* in 2602. Only not the friendly Kimberly we all knew, but the secret leader of Chasm on *Magellan*. We assumed she killed you because you left together, and only she came back. Do you remember anything?"

"I don't have any memories before the pirates on *Butch Cassidy* picked me up somewhere near the Spencer Belt. My ship was out of control, and I had a severe head injury. I'm pretty sure it was caused by this," Alroy said, tapping the swagger stick on his belt. "Maybe Kimberly... my wife... did me in. I don't know. Klungy and the others never mentioned another passenger on my runabout."

"What was the name of the runabout that the *Butch Cassidy* found you on? Was it the *M.S.S. Normandy*?"

"Sorry. Another blank. Paul scrubbed the ship of all identifiers. I knew they did it and hid it from me, but I was trying to get my bearings and survive. I'm sorry. The captain and crew were good to me, because I'm a good pilot. I was useful to them. They kept me around, and I kept my head down. I knew their thievery was wrong, and I knew they lied to me about what they knew about my past. So as soon as I could do so without making enemies, I parted ways with the *Butch Cassidy* crew."

"You settled here on the Lewis Islands to start a new life for yourself?" North said. His eyes were moist. "Wait until Amberly and Kora find out."

"So, I *do* have a daughter," Alroy was crying. "Oh. I always felt like I did, but I couldn't explain it... a daughter."

"Two. You have two beautiful daughters. And a grandson – named Alroy!"

"Wow. The Chairman said this Amberly killed her mother – Kimberly," Alroy remembered. He stood up, as if to pace, but just looked over the room. "The Chairman said Kimberly thought I was dead. What I don't understand is how I was married to someone who was so important to the Chairman. I'm just a humble farmer."

"Hold on. Wait. You *talked* with the Chairman?" North said. "When? How?"

"Yes, when we drove off the first Chasm wave from the Williamstown spaceport. We captured a Chasm company and were attempting to negotiate with our hostages and they established a commlink for us. The Chairman recognized me. She said *I was Alroy Macready.*"

"Where was the Chairman when you spoke to her?"

"I assume she was on *Marquette*, because she executed her own people using the fire from above while we were on comms with her. She's made that waypoint into her floating capital city, where she rules on high."

"Do you remember Kimberly?"

"No."

"But you do remember Amberly? Kora?"

"No, not really," Alroy explained. "I had a friend, Blaisé. A kind young woman — an aspiring novelist — who joined the Irregulars to fight Chasm. For some reason, several times when I meant to refer to Blaisé, I used the name Amberly. I wasn't sure why, but maybe, subconsciously, she reminded me of this Amberly. Blaisé is dead now. She was … a daughter to me. She died to save me."

"I'm sorry. The losses we've all faced have been horrific. … Alroy, listen, there's something you should know," North said, standing and gripping Alroy's hand in his. "The Chairman has her. The Chairman has Amberly. Probably on *Marquette*. She kidnapped your daughter from *Magellan* before we were forced to blow it up."

Even in the dimly lit room, North could see blood drain from Alroy's face. Alroy looked to the ground, shook his head slightly and mumbled a few inaudible words. Then he looked up to North and spoke clearly. "This is terrible. Why would the Chairman do that?"

"Alroy, your daughter Amberly, she's a real hero. She saved *Magellan*. Amberly saved us all. She's beautiful. She's a brilliant leader. You should be so proud of her."

Alroy said nothing as he thoughtfully considered North's description. He thought about his life, as far back as he could remember: a pilot, a pirate, a farmer, a soldier. *But what was I before?* he thought. *Good? Evil? Selfless? Selfish?* He desperately needed to know.

Alroy sat down, leaned forward and grasped North's hand firmly. "Tell me North, what sort of father was I? I mean, what sort of man am I?"

"The best sort of man."

North gave Alroy a reassuring smile. Alroy put his free hand on his chest and took in a deep breath. Alroy smiled back.

After a few moments, North offered, "Amberly and Kora both love you dearly."

"Well, that makes things difficult," Alroy said, his smile

melting away as he released North's hand. "It means the Chairman has leverage over me, if she has my daughter, even one I can't remember. A few hours ago, I didn't even know Amberly and Kora existed. As sure as I sit before you now, I tell you *I would do anything for them.*"

"So would I, sir. So would I," North said. "We have a plan to save Amberly. It's very risky. The cost could be high. But that's status quo since Chasm revealed themselves. Your daughter means the waypoints to me. Her capture ... it's really my fault. It's been my burden for three years now. I've been commander of deep space ship, and Amberly has been suffering who knows what as a prisoner of the Chairman"

"Let's go then," Alroy said, flipping on his headlamp and removing the battery from the console.

"Huh. We just got here? No rest for the weary?"

"I just found out I have two daughters who love me, and one of them is captive by a maniacal tyrant," Alroy said. "Do you think I can rest now?"

"Of course not. You might not remember who you were, but you haven't changed. You are the Alroy Macready I remember," North conceded and grabbed his own pack and pulled out his light stick. Alroy slid the metal door to the subterranean room open, and the men stepped into the tunnel and made for the HQ.

"Why does the Chairman care so much about my family? I don't understand."

"Kimberly was her protégé, as far as I could tell, a savant who was destined to lead in the Chairman's new order. She was on a deep undercover assignment when she married you. When the time came for Kimberly to capture *Magellan* for Chasm, Amberly stopped her. I wasn't there when it happened, but you'll meet someone who was once we rendezvous with the rest of my team at your HQ."

"My daughter thwarted my wife from destroying our home?"

"Yes. And as far as I can tell, the Chairman's interest is revenge, although Dek has other theories," North explained.

"Dek? Who is that?" Alroy said.

"That is another long story, but we have a long walk," North said. "It really started on Ship Day when *American Spirit* docked in 2602."

"Tell me everything."

"Why has it been so long?" Dek demanded, sitting across a table from Bloom in the large underground commons in the center of the Lewis Island Irregulars' headquarters. "I want to speak to this Red right away. I want to know that North is okay." The dim, hydrogen-cell powered illumination flickered.

"Easy there, turbo. Don't get your khakis twisted in a wad," Sparks stood behind Dek, patting her cohort brother on the head, and reached over him to grab a protein bar from a pile in the middle of the table. "We're all on the same side here. I think these Irregulars have been pretty nice to us, considering I almost impaled their commander. Sorry about that."

"Sorry we destroyed your ship," Bloom smiled weakly at Sparks, then turned to Isabella. "You were on the big continent? What is the situation out there? We get almost no news, now that Chasm has tightened its grip."

"The Chairman has wasted no time on her engineering efforts," Deanza answered grimly. "All families have been separated, and people have been assigned to their new tasks to help the common good. Most of the effort has gone into getting some new genetic engineering labs up and running. Anyone with any medical or research skill sets has been assigned to that effort. A lot of children have been brought to the labs for who-knows-what sort of experiments. I couldn't be a part of what they were doing and live with myself, so when Klungy and I had the chance, we bribed some people to help us escape. That was months ago."

"What hope do we have then?" Fiat asked.

"You have *no* hope," Klungy offered, "but I promise, you'd rather die fighting than surrender to what the Chairman and her social engineers have in store for us. I was hoping to hide out on Ingram and then maybe off myself if it looked like I was going to be captured. I have no taste for war. But North ... compelled me to come along."

"Wow. It's dark down here in more ways than one! Everyone, *we have hope*," Rhodes said with a passion that conveyed in her volume. "The *Magnus* is out there. She's powerful. She took out one of the Dark Armada flagships, and if we neutralize *Utopia*, we might be able to retake *Marquette*, then we're dealing with a whole new deck. *Magnus* was built for this. I was literally born for this. We won't let you down now. Trust Captain North. He is quite an amazing leader. Dek here is pretty capable as well."

"Speaking of North, can't we just signal him?" Lydia pushed. "I don't like not knowing he is on his way. What if he is hurt or something? Or if this Red hurt him?"

"No signals! Are you crazy?" Fiat said. "Even encrypted, Chasm could triangulate where we are located and then just drop a few nukes on the surface above us to cave everything in."

"The Chairman won't nuke the Islands," Bloom said. "She doesn't want this place to be an inhospitable glowing wasteland. The ecological consequences for all of Arara are too great. As for North—"

"Your North is with Captain Red. He'll bring him back here," Alfonsi said. "The captain always follows protocol. I saw them retreat together. They'll come back here."

A private walked over from a group of Irregulars at monitoring stations set up on the far side of the commons. "Excuse me, Commander," she said, "Captain Red's transponder has triggered the approach sensor. There's someone else with him who did not have a security transponder."

"That'll be North," Caddo smiled.

"Shall we send out a squad to bring him in under guard in case he is hostile?" The private suggested.

"No," Bloom glanced over at Sparks as she replied. "We're all on the same team, right? But do put the security chief on alert for me now that we have a new … guest coming in."

"Yes, ma'am."

When North finally came through the portal into the commons, Lydia felt a huge relief. She was made of stern stuff, but the foundation she planted herself into was growing thin. She lost her family, her home. North and the Macready sisters were about all she had left. North was beaming his gigawatt smile in a way that she hadn't seen in a long time.

Sparks smiled at North, though she wasn't really worried about him. After all these years, he was still nice to look at. He winked at her and announced, "You won't believe who I found."

"What in the—," Lydia started to freak out. "Alroy? Alroy!

But you were dead!?" Lydia moved toward Alroy and gave him an awkward hug, tears streaming down her face.

Alroy loosely patted Lydia on the back and looked to North. "Um, Commander, who is this?"

"This is Lydia. Amberly's childhood best friend."

"Alroy Macready," Lydia said, stepping back, seeing kindness but unfamiliarity in the man's eyes. "Don't you know me? I don't understand…"

North put a hand on Lydia's shoulder. "He survived what every Kimberly did to him, but he has some sort of amnesia." Red offered a what-can-you-do shrug. "I'm sorry, miss," Alroy tapped his head. "Brain damage. But I am glad you are happy to see me, even though I cannot —"

"Red!" Isabella stepped up and embraced her former comrade. "It's so good to see you alive and well."

"Bless me, it's Doctor Isabella Deanza. What are you doing here? How is the um… import-export business?" Alroy smiled at Isabella, then looked over at his other former *Butch Cassidy* crew mate. "Klungy!"

The Nordic pirate grunted a reply. And after a brief pause, extended his hand. Alroy took it and shook it.

"How's the captain?"

"Paul disappeared when the Araran government surrendered to Chasm. Don't know if he escaped or if he was captured and killed. Who am I kidding? Most likely he's dead."

"Dek, Sparks," North gestured a hand toward Alroy. "You knew Kimberly Macready. It's my privilege to introduce you to her better half, Alroy. Apparently around here, they just call him Red."

"Wow, I can see the family connection," Sparks said. "And not just in the color of your hair."

"My pleasure," Alroy said. "I've been very interested in meeting you both. I understand you have a plan to save my daughter."

CHAPTER FIFTEEN

February 17, 2610. Waypoint Marquette, in orbit around Arara, 38 months after the destruction of Magellan.

The Chairman sat in a crimson chair in front of a spartan white desk, the only two pieces of furniture in the expansive office which was nearly 20 meters in length and half that distance wide. The floors, walls and ceiling were polished white tile, all emitting balanced ambient light so no shadow manifested. The Chairman felt truly alone in her private office in the capital of the Infinite Order, the orbiting city of *Marquette*. She relished feeling alone. Being alone made sense. None were her equal – not any of her easily-manipulated puppets on the Infinite Order Counsel of Comrades. Nor were any of the Infinite Order's best scientists an intellectual match for her. Only one was better than her, one engineered to be superior. But that woman, Kimberly Macready, was dead.

Merwin One entered through an all-but-invisible door bounding with energy. She closed the distance between the door and the Chairman's desk seemingly instantaneously. The Chairman looked up at Merwin's brown-hazel eyes. The Chairman's own iris-less eyes were dark and bloodshot, her face painfully pale.

"I still haven't figured it out yet," the Chairman told her confidant and security chief. "I don't know if anyone can."

"Madam Chairman, you must get some rest," Merwin said, her demeanor oozing compassion for her liege. Merwin pushed her curly blonde hair from her face. "You must eat."

"Your concern is unfounded, child," the Chairman stood, trembling. "No one expects the old woman to be lethal until it's too late. Now you, you they see gushing with vitality. You *wear* your strength on your sleeve. Your presence drives away the weak and challenges the prideful. As it should, my chaperone."

"I *know* your secrets," Merwin said. "Please excuse my impudence, but your appearance is worse than usual—"

Like a whip, the Chairman's arm flung forward and slapped Merwin across the face. The smarting pain caused Merwin's automated systems to flood her body with adrenaline, but her reservoir of discipline empowered her to show no reaction. "Your impudence is not excused, Merwin One... to find such vanity in your heart to lead you to offer *me* counsel — *repulsive*."

Merwin remained silent, and the Chairman correctly interpreted the silence as an abject apology. Merwin felt a drop of moisture on her cheek and realized the Chairman broke her skin with the sudden strike. Merwin instinctively moved her hand to wipe at her face, but the Chairman caught and held her wrist.

With surprising strength, the Chairman forced Merwin's hands to her side. The Chairman took her own backhand and gently rubbed it over the small trickle of blood on Merwin's cheek. Blood had become irresistible for the Chairman. She licked her hand.

The Chairman pulled the Chinese sticks holding her bright-white hair in a bun. Her hair fell out past her shoulder blades. She turned her back on Merwin and appeared to study the vacant surface of the desk.

Merwin knew better than to think the Chairman was looking at a clean, blank surface. The Chairman had developed the ability to visualize complex formulas of her own conception and record them on a drawing pad that existed only in her mind's eye. If she imagined herself writing something down, she would remember it with photographic accuracy. There were thousands of pages of imagined documents – notes, formulas, favorite poems, plans – that she stored only in her head. No amount of encryption would ever crack those files, inaccessible to the world. The current file she had visualized on her desk was a 180-page gene sequencing protocol that she had developed nearly 50 years ago to improve her own genome.

"There may be one person who can help you figure it out," Merwin whispered tentatively, desperately wanting to be helpful to her idol and charge, but also instinctively fearing the striking hand. "It may be, Madam, she has capabilities of which we are not aware."

After a few seconds of silence from the Chairman, Merwin dared to continue. "The mating of Alroy Macready and Raven One may have produced some positive side effects."

"I have hoped for that for years, Merwin," the Chairman

smiled. Then she turned to face Merwin. "And my research suggests you are correct."

Merwin relaxed, relieved that she did not draw the ire of the Chairman for a second time in a single day. Merwin knew she was valuable, but she was not subject to delusions of grandeur. She knew, to the Chairman, even she was expendable.

"Is it time for Amberly to begin her journey," the Chairman asked rhetorically, "...time to start reeducating Raven One's daughter?"

"If she won't be reeducated?"

"I've had my fill of vengeance," the Chairman said. "Amberly has suffered three years for what she did to my Raven One. Her sins are paid. However, if she is unwilling to contribute to the greater good and submit to the Infinite Order, we will be forced to innovate new methods of motivation."

Amberly Macready focused on her blurry reflection in the steel basin of the sink in her cell. She felt as nebulous as the redhead looking back at her. The reflection was all she had to look at. No bunk or bed, chair or other furnishings were present. Amberly had roughly one square meter of floor that was her table, chair and bed.

A small ten-centimeter cubed box holding basic toiletries was set next to a waste vacuum tube that connected to the wall. The walls, floor and ceiling were all made from the same grey polycarbonate. The room was constantly cooled to 12 degrees Celsius and always dimly lit.

Weeks or months or years – Amberly had long since lost all sense of time – had passed since she was moved from the medical unit where she was perpetually drugged into this lonely cell.

Amberly had vague memories of faces and voices during her years' long drug induced coma. She did remember her painful hallucinations during that time, but had enough sanity left to be able to realize those memories were not real. When Amberly came out of her haze, she found herself here, in this small box of a prison, where it was always light, and it was always cold. Dressed too plainly for the cold, Amberly seemed to perpetually shiver.

"Hi, me," Amberly smiled at her sink. "I know I said I wouldn't talk to you because that was a sure sign of madness, but

I don't really have anyone else. I know they are probably listening to me. But I was wondering if you could help me? Do you know where I am? What the date is?"

The reflection smiled back, but said nothing.

"Yeah, that's what I thought," Amberly frowned, disappointed in herself. Her stomach rumbled. *Must be close to feeding time.*

Food did not come, so Amberly slept. Sometime later, maybe five minutes, maybe five hours, Amberly could not tell, she woke when her daily food ration arrived. She was grateful for the hot, bland paste, which came with an edible fibrous spoon. Amberly suspected the sustenance was a basic mixture of synthesized proteins and other vital nutrients. The paste was thick and smooth.

As usual, a small slot opened at the base of the wall next to the sink, and the small, rectangular pan containing her meal slid through. Amberly assumed that when she slept, somehow her captors removed her empty tray, because they were always gone when she woke. Occasionally, she would find fresh clothes and toiletries when she woke as well. She tried many times to pretend to sleep to catch whoever was removing her tray, leaving her clean clothes or taking her old ones, but no one ever came when she was just pretending to sleep. Amberly figured they were able to monitor her brain waves. Or maybe they drugged her. She couldn't be sure.

Amberly had figured that she could use the tray to scrape a hash mark on the wall, in an attempt to track time. However, every time she woke after marking the wall, the mark was gone. She had stopped trying the marking long ago.

Amberly liked to stand when she was eating, pretending she was eating a meal served up at the bar at Rick's on *Magellan*. She bent over and picked up the tray.

"Why thank you North, I'd love to have dinner with you. Rice and beef jerky? My favorite," Amberly fantasized aloud. "You wouldn't happen to have any tea?"

She rolled back the foil covering on the tray and suddenly dropped the tray in shock, which landed flatly, bottom down.

She looked around instinctively, knowing she was always monitored, and then down at the tray and picked it up again. "I'm such a klutz, North. I'm sure you have that effect on all the girls."

Amberly's eyes darted back down at the tray. Carved into the mush, were words: SHHHH! YOU ARE ON MARQUETTE. IT'S 2610.

Three years lost, Amberly thought. She started wolfing down the pasty meal. "Sorry to be rude. I'm so hungry, North."

A few hours later, Amberly slept and more time passed, though Amberly wasn't sure how long. When her stomach growled again, she walked over to her sink, and looked again at her unclear reflection.

"Hello, me," Amberly said again. "I was wondering, do you think I will ever get out of here?"

Sometime later, her food arrived. Amberly slowly picked the tray up. "Oh, dinner time, Dek," Amberly continued the charade. "Won't you join me?"

She cautiously pulled back the foil and again saw words carved into the paste: ESCAPE UNLIKELY. I'M SORRY.

Even this minimal connecting to another human after so long made Amberly want to explode with joy. But she was worried visible displays of emotion could betray her, so didn't allow herself tears.

Again, Amberly slept and woke. When she felt that she was getting hungry again, she walked up to the sink, and again focused on the blurry representation of her face on the surface of the sink.

"Hello, me, it's me again," Amberly said, slowly and clearly. "I was wondering, why would anyone care about us? I mean, who would even care about us out here."

Amberly could hardly wait for the next tray to come. She did extra exercises to cover her nervousness. Soon, the tray was pushed through the slot, and this time, she was dining with an imaginary Rita Moreno. But when she pulled the foil back, she found nothing inscribed in her meal. Her heart dipped, and she even wondered if she had imagined the last two episodes of the secret messages in the vitapaste. She wanted to cry, she was so lonely – but she knew she was being watched, and this time defiant pride prevented it. Maybe this was a new form of torture? Was someone playing cruel mind games with her. She couldn't be sure.

The next cycle she made no pretense of talking with her reflection on the sink. She was silent and depressed.

Her food slid through the portal again, and she did not stand to eat, instead leaning against the wall as she unwrapped her food. Her heart leaped when she saw a new message: I AM DR. LEIGH. I AM A BAD PERSON. I AM SORRY. THEY MAY KILL ME FOR THIS. BUT I DIDN'T WANT YOU TO BE ALONE.

Amberly quickly hid the message by eating it.

The next cycle, Amberly walked to her sink, and looked at her reflection. "Hello, me," Amberly smiled wide. "It's always nice to chat with a familiar face. Get it? A familiar face. No? Not funny. Never mind. Hey self, remember North? Captain of the *Magnus*? Whatever happened to him? And Dek, that guy who was the captain of the *American Spirit*? Is he dead? You don't know? Well, that's to be expected, I guess. It's hard to get news in here."

Amberly laid down on the floor to wait for her next feeding.

When the tray slid through, she looked around the room. "Lydia, it's been a long time. Let me share my lunch with you. I've missed you so."

Amberly carefully pulled the foil back, exposing the hot paste. The paste had been carved up with almost too many words, and Amberly had to study them for a while to make out what they said.

MAGNUS MISSING. AS DESTROYED. MAGELLAN GONE. SORRY. SORRY. SORRY. WARNING! SHE WILL CALL YOU SOON. BE STRONG. YOU ARE THE STRONGEST PERSON I KNOW. WILL HELP IF CAN. FORGIVE ME.

Shocked, Amberly dropped the tray to the floor, grey paste splattering over the small cell.

"No!" Amberly screamed. "No. No. No!"

The psychoanalyst monitoring Amberly's cell video feed wasn't paying attention when Amberly dropped the tray, but the splattering caught her attention. She assumed that Amberly was upset over losing her food on the floor and made a note for Dr. Leigh to bring someone in to clean the cell next time Amberly slept.

Amberly fell to the floor into a kneeling position, letting her long red hair fall over her face. A solar flare of grief enveloped her. *Magellan gone? Were there any survivors? Kora? Little Alroy? Lydia? Skip? Commander Moreno? Midas? Ramos?* Her thoughts were frenetic. She last saw Dek, shot, back on the *Magellan* hangar trying to save her from the traitor Kato. All dead? The *American*

Spirit, gone? So many of her friends had taken sanctuary on that deep space ship in hopes of returning to the mother planet. Dead?

North? Amberly thought. *Where are you?* She knew she was on *Waypoint Marquette,* just one light year away, so she thought, from *Waypoint Magellan.* Where else would the *Magnus* be besides looking for her? She pushed her hair out of her face. She was so full of fury, and she wanted to run and scream and break free. But there was nothing but claustrophobic walls, holding her in. *Don't be foolish, Amberly. Don't be arrogant, like your mother. You are not that important. The Magnus isn't coming.*

Amberly curled up into a ball and cried herself to sleep.

Several hours later, Amberly awoke to a foot kicking her shoulder. Amberly's eyes popped open, and she immediately sprang up, filled with adrenaline.

The last person she remembered seeing when she was fully conscious was Dek, just before a chasm trooper stunned her. Dek had just been shot in the hangar of *Magellan.* That memory was three years old.

The woman who woke Amberly, Dr. Michelle Leigh, had spent ten days in a nearly identical solitary confinement unit, and that almost made her insane. Being here with Amberly now brought uncomfortable echoes in her head.

After her punishment, the Chairman noted that Dr. Leigh had become a disciplined woman, both physically and mentally. She had lost unneeded weight and her job performance soared. The Chairman didn't know if what motivated Michelle was her fear of additional punishment or wanting to avoid the fate of her dead colleague, but it didn't matter. The Chairman liked what she saw, and rewarded Michelle with full medical responsibility and the general welfare of the subject.

Dr. Leigh spoke with pure stoicism, burying her true feelings as deep as she could within herself.

Amberly strenuously studied Dr. Leigh. Carrying a dress and screen strip. *Female. Middle-aged. Healthy build. Polished nails. Contact lenses.* She noticed the woman's breathing, as her chest rose and fell. She counted her blinks. She oddly found herself calculating the ratio of blinks to breaths.

"Miss Amberly. Please make yourself presentable. Put on this. You have an audience with my supervisor in 30 minutes. I will be back in ten minutes. Be ready."

Dr. Leigh set the screen strip – a device that displayed the time with simple glowing red Arabic numerals on a magnetic resonance screen – on top of the room's small cabinet. "Please observe the time and see to it that you are ready when I return."

Time. Order. Meaning. Amberly stared at the clock, which was a sanity balm for Amberly's troubled mind. *This is it. I have an opportunity. I can figure a path out. I just need to start building a matrix of the variables so I can start analyzing potential actions. It's simple, really.* Amberly remembered what Dek had told her about how her mother could consider any situation, then would withdraw into deep analytical thought until she reemerged with a precise course promising the likely path to success. Dek had explained what Kimberly had taught him of the technique, cataloging the variables, then visualizing each variation and combination, until the situation was unlocked. Dek said that Kimberly claimed even in complex situations with hundreds of knowable variables, she would process thousands of outcomes in her head in minutes. A key technique, Kimberly told Dek, was the mental purging of a combination once it deemed to not produce a favorable outcome.

Michelle handed Amberly the neatly folded blue dress. In the process of handing the dress to Amberly, Dr. Leigh grabbed *Amberly's* hand under the fabric and squeezed it reassuringly, simultaneously looking hard into Amberly's green eyes. Dr. Leigh contrasted them with the large pupils of the Chairman in her own mind's eye.

Physical contact with another person for one as starved as Amberly opened a wellspring of humanity. *I am something.* Amberly's countenance fell immediately when Dr. Leigh withdrew her hand, leaving Amberly with the dress.

"You can address me as Dr. Leigh if you have any questions, though I am not authorized to answer much."

New variable. This is my clandestine benefactor. Amberly thought. *Must be careful not to compromise her.*

Michelle tapped a code on her info pad and presented herself for a biometrics scan, and a portal to the cell slid open to the right of the sink. Logic suggested there must be some sort of door in her room, but it was so well camouflaged Amberly could only guess at its location. Now she knew where it was hidden. Another variable for her matrix.

CHAPTER SIXTEEN

Amberly felt intoxicatingly light. For the last three years, she was either in a foggy nightmare of perpetual pain or trapped in a windowless cage, deprived of human contact. Now she was out, walking on her own power. This simple freedom was a torrent of water flooding her arid soul.

Dr. Leigh was her only escort; and if she was armed, Amberly couldn't tell. *Chasm must have this waypoint in some state of military occupation,* Amberly surmised. If she fled from Dr. Leigh, she did not have enough data to know if she could survive or hide from her enemies.

The capillary corridors of *Waypoint Marquette* were similar enough to those she knew on *Magellan*. The halls were not busy, but they were not deserted either. Everyone wore a similar jumpsuit, with minor variations in color. As they passed through commons, Amberly could feel the eyes of people falling upon her. Unintelligible whispers and awkward glances focused on Amberly. She wasn't sure if she smelled pity or fear, or a mixture of both, but if the occupants of *Marquette* once held any joy, it was gone now.

She observed the people. No children. No elderly. She started mapping the distances between corridor access points in her mind's eye. After so long with so little to look at in her bland cell, she found her mind was a sponge, absorbing every detail with crystal clarity.

After about a kilometer-long walk and a three-minute ride on a tube car, Dr. Leigh stopped a few meters short of a tall set of unmarked glass doors at the edge of a large, sparsely populated commons. The normal tables and chairs had been removed, so that only a dark obelisk, more than two meters high, interrupted the empty space. Just a few bureaucratic workers – wearing gray jumpsuits – were making beelines around the common's periphery.

Amberly noted, for the first time, armed guards, wearing gleaming blue armor, the color of the Infinite Order. They were stationed on either side of the doors.

"We wait here until you are summoned."

Amberly stepped in behind her escort. "Where are we?"

The doctor said nothing, but pointed to the obelisk. Amberly walked the ten meters to the center of the commons, and started to circulate around the stone monument. She reached out and touched the chiseled work, running her hand along the cold, irregular surface. Her hand stopped when she noticed, on the side facing away from the glass doors, engraved in the rock was a familiar face – her mother's. She read the inscription aloud, "In Memory of the First Daughter of the Infinite Order. Raven One." In smaller type, beneath the name, she read: "Killed during the Battle of *Magellan* in Pursuit of the Common Good by Amberly Macready."

"It's quite an honor, really," a snappy, pleasant mezzo voice sounded behind Amberly. She twirled around to see a woman wearing a white kimono, with piecing brown-hazel eyes and flowing curly blonde hair. Her facial features were sharp and symmetrical and without flaw, except for what appeared to be a recent cut on her cheek. Strapped to her back, Amberly noticed the woman wore a sheathed sword, similar to the one she remembered Sparks had worn. *The Chairman*? Amberly thought, but dismissed the thought. *Too young.*

"Excuse me?" Amberly asked.

"Yes, in the Infinite Order, we remember our fallen in the digital archive of human history. But to have a physical memoriam, well, that is *rare*."

"She was my mother," Amberly said, looking back at the obelisk and for a moment, remembering the first 13 years of her life and the sweet memories of Kimberly Macready.

"Yes, of course," the woman said. "The infamy for you, Amberly Macready, etched in stone will last for 100,000 years. Still, you have my *respect*. You defeated Raven One, and she truly was the best of us."

"Better than the Chairman?"

Merwin ignored the question and stepped closer to Amberly. "I am Merwin One of Ingram, and I have the honor of serving as prime chaperone for the Chairman." She offered her hand to Amberly, and Amberly shook it. Merwin held her hand briefly, but tightly. Amberly noted the intentional demonstration of Merwin's strength. *She is not to be underestimated*, Amberly thought.

"Chaperone?"

"Yes. We don't want the same fate that befell your mother to end the Chairman," Merwin smiled her brilliant white smile as she issued her clear warning. "That's why I am here. Shall we go and see her now?" Merwin motioned toward the door with her arm. Dr. Leigh semi-bowed to Merwin and took off walking back down the hall where she and Amberly had entered the commons.

Amberly turned to Merwin as they entered an antechamber. "Why does the Chairman want to see me?"

"Mine is not to reason why," Merwin replied melodiously with an ancient couplet. "Mine is to do and die."

As soon as the pair walked through the doors, the glass panes tinted automatically until the room was nearly pitch black. Then a door slid open in front of Amberly and Merwin One and bright white light poured out. Amberly covered her eyes until they adjusted, and she entered into the Chairman's private office.

At the far side of the room, two luxurious place settings were evenly spaced on either side of the Chairman's desk. The plates were piled with meats that Amberly didn't recognize.

The woman at the far side of the room stood and seemed to float, though Amberly was sure her bare feet were touching the ground. She glided toward Amberly, wearing a common sleeveless jumpsuit, only this one was jet black; and the bell bottoms seemed to sway in synchronization as she walked.

The Chairman, Amberly thought. A mixture of fear, anger and awe made the hair on the back of Amberly's neck rise.

When she was less than a pace away from Amberly, the Chairman stopped and extended her hand toward the heroine of *Magellan*. Amberly took her cold, dry hand.

"Amberly Macready. It's pleasing to see you so robust."

That voice. It's her. Amberly recognized the voice of torment that spoke to her through years of endless hallucinations. Waves of revulsion hit her as she steeled herself.

Determined to show strength, Amberly curtly withdrew her hand from the shake, resisted the temptation to wipe it on her blue dress, and stared unflinchingly into the Chairman's iris-less eyes.

"Come. Dine with me, child. You honor my table with your presence. As Merwin must have told you, I am the Chairman, tasked with the burden of stewardship of the Infinite Order."

"Why am I here?"

"Come. Sit. Eat," the Chairman ignored her question and indicated the desk with her open hand. "Relax. You have suffered enough – by my hand no less. But I swear, your suffering has come to an end."

"I said, why am I here?" Amberly insisted.

"Your friend North was full of questions when he visited me on this very station," the Chairman said. "Now there was a specimen worth studying. He left without saying goodbye."

"He mentioned your chat," Amberly said, considering whether she would sit or not. The Chairman did sit and lifted a utensil, plunging it into the perfectly stacked pile of raw beef on her plate.

"He told you my intentions and *still* my people were able to capture you," the Chairman said as she considered the cut of animal flesh on her fork. "How very disappointing. Please, *sit down*."

Amberly remained silent and unmoving.

"Oh, I see. You didn't want to abandon your home — your family — to save your own skin," the Chairman read Amberly.

"You wouldn't understand."

"I understand family more than you know," the Chairman said, and looked up at Merwin, who was standing at attention a few meters back from the table. "Merwin, that will be all. I will summon you when we are done."

"Forgive me. Madam Chairman, I am concerned for your safety. Amberly Macready is a murde—"

"That will be all," the Chairman said again, forcefully. Merwin bowed and left, but not before giving Amberly an I-will-kill-you-if-anything-happens look through her otherwise kind smile.

"Please. Sit."

Amberly looked at the empty chair and again at the Chairman's eerie eyes. She sat down.

Amberly considered the Chairman's face as the elderly woman worked through a particularly chewy portion of raw bovine flesh. The Chairman's face was more roundish than oval, and her nose was small and button-like. North had told Amberly about the lack of an iris, and Amberly briefly tried to figure out how her eyes worked, biologically, without an optimal diaphragm. Clearly bright light did not bother the Chairman.

Amberly was distracted by the smell of the bloody meat. The amount the Chairman ate would have made most anyone sick, but she ate it as easily as cotton candy.

"Why am I here?" Amberly ignored the well-cooked meat on her own plate.

"That blue dress was your mother's favorite. I bought it for her, for a graduation party celebrating her completed her studies at North Platte."

"I know you knew my mother. I'm not interested in your games. Tell me why I am here, or take me back to my cell," Amberly demanded.

"Don't be hasty, Amberly," the Chairman said. "Your suffering is about to pay dividends. Look at my face, tell me what you see. Don't be bashful. Examine my face. Your brain is capable of so much more than you realize. Study, please." The Chairman waved her now empty fork in front of her face in a loop pattern.

At first, Amberly thought the Chairman was either über vain, crazy, or both. She was about to look away in defiance, but then she saw something she didn't expect. *The Chairman looks … familiar,* Amberly thought. *Why?*

"You see it, don't you Amberly. The resemblance. Something familiar," the Chairman spoke with a hint of excitement hanging on her words. "Familiar. The same root as the word *family*, I suspect. Perhaps I look familiar because I am familiar, in the biological sense."

"I don't understand," Amberly said, a twisted revulsion growing in the pit of her stomach.

"Yes, you do," the Chairman smiled. "You are a woman of science. Why deny the truth that is right before your very eyes?"

"No," Amberly grimaced. "Your soul is too evil."

"Soul? *Soul?* There is no soul and *you know that,*" the Chairman weighed her words. "You've spent too long with North and the traditionalists on *Magellan.* You've been corrupted by your cancerous father, coward that he is. Maybe you have more of him in you than I know."

Blood flushed Amberly's face, revealing rage proportional to the Chairman's insults of her late father. Amberly stood, grabbed the plate in front of her and flung it at the Chairman, meat and sides flying everywhere. The plate was on course to hit the Chairman when it poofed into a cloud of fine ceramic dust inches from her face.

The point defense system North warned us about, Amberly thought. She immediately chastised herself for losing her cool and brought up her matrix of variables and started adding data to it. Amberly thought if she was going to win, it would not be through rage.

"My father was the kindest, most gentle man I ever knew," Amberly gritted her teeth. "If I have easily triggered anger, it is from my mother."

"No, my child," the Chairman stood up and opened her arms. "It is from *me.*"

The facts add up. Could it be? Amberly thought. She knew. The Chairman was right, the truth was right before her eyes.

"Grandmother."

The word came out of Amberly's mouth sounding more like an accusation than a revelation.

"Genetically, I suppose that is the best description," the Chairman said as she took a step toward Amberly.

"A clone. Kimberly Macready is *a clone* of you," Amberly opened her eyes wide at the realization.

"Clever girl," the Chairman smiled. "Yes, like all children should be for their parent, Raven One was the very best of me. She was my only begotten daughter, my one and only child. Her birth was astronomically improbable – a once-in-a-universe event. And you, Amberly Macready, you killed the miracle. You shot her while she was giving you a mother's embrace."

"We were *all* going to die! She had us on a kamikaze run into *Magellan.* I had to stop her."

"You really think the great Raven One did not have an escape plan. That she would not make her way back to Fuentes Station where I would send someone to collect her? Don't be so naive. *You* killed her."

"Don't blame me for my mother's death. Your stupid statue out there is wrong. An angry mob threw my mother out an airlock."

"AND THAT MOB WOULD HAVE BEEN DEAD IF NOT FOR YOU!" The Chairman shouted in a painful, shrieking voice. She pulled back her hand to strike Amberly, and the redhead threw up her arms to protect herself. The Chairman took a deep breath and dropped her striking hand. Amberly put her arms down and saw tears streaming out of the Chairman's eyes. "You allowed the mob to live. So they could kill my dear Raven One."

"Save your tears. Believe what lies you want," Amberly countered, confident and trying to take the upper hand in the conversation. "I was there when my mother ordered the escape pods ejected to keep the Chasm officers on the *American Spirit* from a mutiny to save their own lives. She wanted to die for your worthless 'greater good.' It might as well have been you that killed her. She was dead when you gave the Scorched Earth order."

The Chairman was silent. She seemed to be searching a decade's worth of communiques in her mind. *I ordered Tigona to save Raven One,* the Chairman thought. *My command to preserve Kimberly was clear. I am not responsible for her death.* "No, with the Scorched Earth order, I sent Dek Tigona the command to retrieve Raven One at all costs," the Chairman mumbled with uncharacteristic inaudibility.

"And he did retrieve her. I was there. Your knowledge is... *incomplete.*"

For a moment the Chairman seemed off-balance. *Did I fail in trusting Dek? I overestimated him, clearly.* The Chairman thought. Then she exhaled, and smiled again. *No, this insolent woman will not lay her mother's death on me.* "I know what I know, child. I commend you on trying to get under my skin. An excellent tactic. By all accounts, you should be dead, too. And yet here you are."

"I was there at the Battle of *Magellan.* You were—"

The Chairman interrupted Amberly, her voice raised slightly. "Your experience doesn't give you understanding. Raven One was the apex of humanity. You destroyed her, and all that is left of her is your DNA, tainted with material from Alroy Macready."

"So Dek was right. That is why you want me. For your DNA experiments. I'll never submit to them. I'll kill myself first. Go make another dirt-licking clone of yourself." Amberly turned to walk out the door with confidence and defiance, as if somehow, she could just waltz out of the Chairman's grasp, commandeer a ship and head home.

"Wait, child. *Wait, please*. It's not that simple."

Amberly faced the Chairman and glared at her. Any fear she had was melted from the heat of her rage. But Amberly reminded herself again she must maintain control. She needed to understand the Chairman's intentions to chart her next steps. Amberly inclined her head to indicate she was listening.

"Your mother was not an *exact* clone of me. Think of your mother as version 1.1 of me. With all my strengths, but also with... improvements. Weaknesses and imperfections excised. I spent decades developing the process.

"But imprinting genetic improvements is maddeningly difficult," the Chairman continued. "In order to survive, modifications must be made to a critical mass of stem cells after the zygote phase but during prenatal gestation. The sequencing is horribly complex. Any idea how many times I failed before I finally succeeded? Three thousand and twenty-six failures. And on the three thousand and twenty seventh try, I created a truly new life."

"Those don't sound like bad odds," Amberly said. "Surely in time you would have accomplished the task again."

"No, randomness just made me lucky. I could do the process a million times over, and still not have another positive imprinting. Succeeding in creating Kimberly was like being asked to pick a random number between one and one trillion and then guessing it correctly within the first thousand guesses," the Chairman explained. "It's like rolling 1,000 dice independently, and to have a successful modification take, you have to roll a six every time. But you can only roll one die a time, and you can't read the dice until you roll them all. So, you could roll a three or a five the first time, meaning failure, no reason to continue. But not knowing, you would continue to roll the other 999 anyway."

The Chairman appeared to be lost in her memories of monotony. After a brief pause, she spoke again. "The technology is analogous to the dice rolling mechanism itself. Like rolling a dice, one can't control the exact outcome – but can *limit* the outcomes, one through six. Rolling a seven is impossible, but the odds are against you every single time – sixteen percent – to get the six. The ability to limit the outcomes is my greatest scientific accomplishment. I got us to 16 percent."

"You were lucky," Amberly scoffed. "You just created a more murderous version of yourself. Did my mother even know she was a clone?"

"No. Your mother never knew how special she was. Your mother was a better me. Smarter. More resilient. I was going to tell her everything upon her triumphant return from *Magellan*. But she never came back. So now I am telling you."

Although Amberly's disdain for the Chairman remained strong, her empirical mind had wrapped itself around the Chairman's impressive scientific accomplishment. She forced herself not to lose perspective and be blinded by the Chairman's brilliance. "Why did you spend so much of your life trying to do something you were never going to, mathematically, accomplish?"

"The answer to that, child, is why *I* am truly special. If anyone was going to uplift humanity, I knew it would be me – or it wouldn't happen at all. I always knew the odds predicted that I would die before I succeeded in creating your mother. When I did succeed, I knew the possibility of duplicating the feat again was beyond astronomic. Not that we haven't been trying. I've devoted the best minds of Chasm for decades to try to replicate my success for decades with the imprinting protocol."

"Okay, Mom was unique. Her genetically-engineered brain cracked the uncrackable *Magellan* encryption codes," Amberly said, sitting back down in the chair. "But *why*?"

"Ah, you believe the fiction I've built for Chasm. You think Chasm is about creating the perfect society for the common good, and so do the adherents to the Infinite Order. And truly I tell you: The society we are making is better than the barbarian status quo on Earth. Those fundamentalists on Earth would hang us all for the so-called *immoral* genetic engineering I've been doing. But people are flawed. Even me. I'm no idiot. I have my … weaknesses." The Chairman wiped the corner of her mouth with three of her fingers, a Pavlovian response to her thoughts of blood.

"No one is perfect," Amberly sauced. Her stomach growled slightly, and she now wished she had not been so stubborn and eaten the rare entree she tossed at the Chairman.

"Not yet. But we live in the present. The humanist who

believes humans today are inherently perfect and only corrupted by their environment — well that fool clearly has no comprehension of history. *That* fool is a useful idiot to me. Humanity is populated with useful idiots."

Amberly was surprised at this admission from the Chairman. She almost sounded like North and Moreno, who argued that mankind was inherently depraved. For North, religious faith was how humanity must fight its propensity for evil. Amberly's rage grew again. "If you secretly believe the cause is hopeless, then why must you make so many suffer? Why did you destroy my entire waypoint, my home!?" Amberly's blood pulsed heavy again.

The Chairman did not reciprocate Amberly's elevated tone. She replied calmly, "Don't you see? The true purpose of the Infinite Order is to create the perfect version of me. Kimberly was the first iteration. I am a genius incarnate, but she was far ahead of me. The things she could comprehend. She was just the beginning. With all the resources of Arara at my beck and call, we — mother and daughter — could accelerate the process. Chasm was necessary to marshal those resources. Separation from Earth was necessary too, obviously, lest they slip a noose around my abominable neck. I am the Alpha. That is my destiny. But I am not the Omega. If I hadn't co-opted the Chasm movement, well, humanity would be irrevocably retarded."

"Why not let evolution take its natural course?"

"Amberly, adherents to science worship evolution as if it were a deity, that somehow through the random so-called natural selection of genetic mutation, humans would mutate into a higher plane of being. The theistic evolutionists even posited that a god used random selection to evolve humanity. I ask you, what sort of god would use *random chance* to usher in perfection? Idiots and more idiots. To make the improvements that I have made would take trillions and trillions of years of random chance. Do you really believe fragile humanity will survive that long? That we won't kill ourselves through war? Or be wiped out by disease? Or natural disaster? Think about it."

"You believe betting on evolution to lift humanity higher before we are destroyed is a fool's bet," Amberly continued the Chairman's logic.

"Yes. Exactly. Who knows how future enhanced versions of

me will be able to improve our DNA? It's a geometric progression. Every generation is that much more intelligent and that much more able to accelerate human ascension. I needed Kimberly to advance my protocol. The computations and methods to take the next step are beyond me. Which means they are beyond anyone... except—"

"How can you not see your profound arrogance?" Amberly interrupted. "Why do you think *you* should be the genetic foundation of future humanity?"

"I am arrogant, but not without cause. If I succeed, my greatness is self-proving. Should I fail, then I guess I was wrong. Come now. To get humanity this far takes more than nurture. Raw ability coded in my DNA, distilled by evolution, cannot be denied. Your mother's existence proved this. And now that I've lost Raven One, I must work harder. Fortunately, I have you."

"Me? You mean my genetic code? But my genetic code is tainted with my dad's DNA, don't you remember?" Amberly tossed the comment sarcastically.

"No, I mean *you*. Even though you are an adulterated version of your mother, your base genome is still superior to mine. I have spent the last three years studying your genetic material; and I am confident, you are superior to me."

"Me? Superior?" Amberly asked. Although Amberly was intellectually ambitious, she was not vain. Before today, she would have dismissed the Chairman's claim out of hand. But even now, she could feel a new level of complexity to her thoughts. It felt like her mind was expanding exponentially as she conversed with the Chairman. But to be on the level of her mother? "Doubtful. I will never come close to what my mother could accomplish."

"That is true," the Chairman started pacing the room. "I did not say you were superior to Kimberly. She was not diluted. However, Amberly, you do have more potential than *me*. I need you to carry on what I have started. In time, you will catch, then surpass, my intellect, and then you must use what you have learned to create an improved clone of yourself. You would have to study and train for years to achieve this end, but I see you've already begun to discipline your mind."

Amberly immediately, emotionally rejected the Chairman's entreaty. "I won't help you," Amberly turned away.

"When you were 13, didn't you tell your mom you would become the smartest scientist among all the waypoints? Kimberly Macready believed you would. When your mom was your age, she put herself in solitary confinement for a year to hone her mental agility. Your time in confinement here has sharpened your mind, hasn't it? No need to answer, we've been monitoring your brain wave activity. Quite impressive."

"Stop it. You need my mind to move forward. I have something you want that can't be extracted in a lab. You have no leverage over me."

The Chairman did not seem phased by Amberly's posturing; instead she articulated internal musings aloud. "When she killed Alroy, I thought Kimberly was in the clear… her love for you is what I didn't calculate. It was her undoing."

In Amberly's mind's eye, the data in her matrix was aligning. She didn't have a solution figured out yet, but now she realized more aggressive outcomes than merely her own survival were possible. There could be other assets to be leveraged she previously hadn't included in the equation. Amberly saw an opening. "Kimberly Macready is gone. I am here. Let's negotiate."

The Chairman sat down again, leaning back in her chair and looking to the ceiling. "Your position is not as strong as you believe, but I'll humor you, child." She sat upright and focused on Amberly with a slight curl on her lips. "What do you want?"

Amberly remained standing and spoke firmly. "Where is the *Magnus*? Where is Commander North? Signal *Magnus* and end your claim on Arara, stand down your fleet, and I will stay here on *Marquette* with you. We can dedicate ourselves to creating the perfect person until we die." Amberly didn't know if she would really commit to such a thing, but she wanted to see how the Chairman would react to her probable bluff. Her matrix still had too many missing variables.

"I wish I knew where the *Magnus* was," the Chairman laughed. "But we are watching for her and waiting, I assure you. What you don't understand yet, but you will learn when you study my imprinting protocol, is that we cannot improve your DNA for the next generation without first being able to purge it of the imperfections introduced from your father."

"The part of Alroy Macready that lives in me is *not* an

imperfection," Amberly countered defensively.

"It doesn't matter. Work in a lab cannot uplift us unless we introduce it into the world. Your offer is unsatisfactory," the Chairman sighed. "What good would perfect people be without a planet to call home?"

"Why bring up my father at all? I'm sure you know my father is gone, lost in space, murdered by my mother."

"Your mother died believing that Alroy Macready had perished," the Chairman said as she waved her hand in a pattern that opened a nearly invisible door on the wall three meters behind her desk, exposing a small observation room. "Merwin!"

Amberly felt the magnetic presence of the athletic blonde behind her. Merwin seemed to appear as out of nowhere at the summons of her leader. "Amberly and I are retiring to my observation lounge for further discussion. See that we are not disturbed. And please bring me the latest intelligence reports on the Lewis Islands insurgents."

"Yes, Chairman," Merwin bowed while delivering each word with a contagious cheer. "It is my pleasure to serve." She exited into the antechamber where she and Amberly had first entered, on the opposite side of the ostentatious office from the desk.

"Amberly, walk with me," the Chairman pointed to what Amberly assumed was the observation lounge beyond the wall behind the desk. The pair walked through them.

The lounge was a small room outfitted with three luxurious leather benches facing a floor-to-ceiling plexiglass window into space. The view was filled not with the lonely star fields Amberly expected, but with a glorious blue-green orb: the planet Arara.

"Is that…Arara?" Amberly gasped as she moved into the room and pressed her hand on the panoramic window. "It's … beautiful. Breathtaking. But how?"

"We moved *Marquette* four years ago into Araran orbit," the Chairman revealed. "This station is now the glorious capital of the Infinite Order. Look there, at my planet. See those land masses. Do you know them?"

"The Lewis Islands."

"Very good, child," the Chairman said. "Here is my counter-offer. You help me to continue my work, I will teach you everything I know, and you will be first prince of Arara, second only to me. I did not selfishly use my immense talent to find a path to my own immortality. Eventually, I will perish – though I suppose in some way I will live on in you, Amberly – leaving you to rule Arara and the Infinite Order as *you* see fit. I trust that when you have the knowledge and understanding that I do, that you will continue the greatest quest in the history of humanity. The only condition is this: When I die, and only when I perish by natural causes, will you have the power to determine the fate of humanity."

Amberly could hardly fathom what the Chairman was offering her. Literally, a whole world to rule for the benefit of all. Could her ascension be a path to the peace that so many had sacrificed for? She did not have ambition to rule for its own sake, much preferring the solitude of the laboratory. But was it her burden to rule?

"How do you know I won't kill you the first chance I get?" Amberly asked, trying not to show how much her mind was reeling at what was being offered her.

"Merwin wouldn't allow it. Don't underestimate her," the Chairman said. "And I have hundreds of Hawks who would avenge me should they believe I came to an untimely demise. Oh, someday you might figure out a way to defeat my protections and defenders. However, by then, *you won't want to*. Once you are able to achieve such a feat, I know you will see reason."

Amberly's heart pushed her to argue with the Chairman, the woman she believed to be evil, but whose reasoning seemed sound. At the same time, the Chairman's revelations had made Amberly realize her mind was processing outcomes at a level she had never done before.

Her mind blossomed.

She became aware she had *multiple* simultaneous conscious thought streams, as if she had several brains she could assign to different mental tasks. Currently, she was evaluating the potential validity of the Chairman's offer. A trap? The truth? A delusion on the Chairman's part? All questions were being weighed at the same time. She was also processing the likelihood of *Magnus* being close to Arara and how she might feel about North if he reentered her life. Overlapping those thoughts, she was already reviewing what she knew about genetic sequencing to realize it was unlikely they could reverse engineer Alroy's DNA from hers, her mother's and the Chairman's DNA. To Amberly, as her multi-threaded mental processes multiplied, everything felt sharper, more in focus, and comfortably simple. But she needed more data for the numerous problem matrices she had active in her mind.

"Trusting that I'll soldier on once I have control of everything seems like a big gamble to bet your life's ambition, *Madam Chairman*," Amberly suggested.

"In my years of wisdom, Amberly, I have found *faith*. In this case, faith in you. You are not Kimberly, but you are the better person in our company. And now you must have faith that the path that I have set us on is the right one. As you grow in your mental prowess, you will see. Then, you will follow, and finish what I have started. I know you will, because you are me."

Amberly felt the temptation. She also recalled her friends and family who inexplicably sacrificed themselves so she could live. *Magellan*, destroyed. The *American Spirit*, gone. But the *Magnus*? Did the Marine Jana Smith get away with her sister and her nephew? After what Dr. Leigh had written and the Chairman had readily confessed, Amberly had no reason to think the *Magnus* didn't survive its encounter with the Dark Armada, outside the fact the Infinite Order didn't know the warship's whereabouts. But that was no reason to think it was destroyed. That matrix of information returned a conclusion with high certainty — some of her loved ones could still be alive.

The Chairman spoke to address Amberly's concerns, almost as if she could read Amberly's thoughts. "Amberly, I'm sorry for the loss of *Magellan*. It was a terrible necessity, a worthwhile sacrifice, for the sake of a greater humanity. If you find anyone still alive, perhaps on the *Magnus*, who you think worthy of joining this cause, that invitation is in your hands. Consider this offer carefully. You can move humanity forward if you work with me, but if you oppose me, I will grieve the loss of your potential, but I will not let you subvert my destiny."

Amberly was silent as she looked at a planet with her own eyes. The world mesmerized her. And it could all be hers, in time. But did she even want it? Amberly was surprised to find herself considering the Chairman's offer. Was this the path she had been seeking all along? She could be the greatest mind to uplift humanity, as her mother had predicted so many years ago, and along the way *she would right the wrongs created by Chasm.* She could save North and those on the *Magnus.* It made sense. She could have the power to protect those she loved. She couldn't bring back those that she had lost, but she could bring peace to those who remained. Her mind started to fill with the faces of the people who she knew were gone – the Dinos, Anderson, Skylar, Eaton, her mother ... and her *dad.*

"Wait. We need my dad's DNA to have any real hope of moving forward," Amberly snapped out of her deep thinking. "That is lost. Your plan is defeated before you've begun."

The Chairman floated up to the viewport, and joined the younger woman in planet gazing. She reached out and gently slipped some of her icy fingers through Amberly's hair.

"Your red hair, a recessive gene. An imperfection I carry I suppose. I should have edited that out of your mother. North called you 'Red' on account of your hair color, I understand. Alroy Macready's hair color is as hot as yours. I suppose that's why they call him Red, too."

Amberly eyes widened. "What do you mean?"

"I found him," the Chairman said. "Amberly, your mother was wrong. Alroy Macready is alive."

CHAPTER SEVENTEEN

February 19, 2610. The Lewis Islands, the remains of the Williamstown Spaceport.

Bloom did not like Dek's plan. The risk was too great. She angrily summoned her second-in-command to her private briefing room to express her displeasure. Now that Alroy was here, flooding the underground chamber with his farmer's charm, she was disoriented. She was weary and had to resist the impulse to throw herself into Alroy's comforting arms.

"Red. Alroy. Roy... I don't know what to call you now," the frustrated commander of the Irregulars fumbled over her words. Alroy looked at Commander Bloom and placed a calloused hand on her nutmeg check.

"I'm always just Red to you," Alroy studied Bloom's clear, dark brown eyes. "Nur, we've been through hell together. My honor has been to follow you into the fire time after time. You are more than commander to me. You are more than a friend. But I am a *father*, and everything within me says I have to save my child if there is a chance," Alroy said as he placed his other hand on the other side of Bloom's face, and she leaned her forehead into his. "We may just save Arara in the process."

"I don't want to lose you," Bloom whispered, catching Red's masculine scent from his closeness. "I can't lead them without you."

"You can, and you will. You've always done what you must. Your strength will not fail you," Alroy gently ran two fingertips over Bloom's cheek. "I will come back, Nur. I want to find out what this is." Bloom's head started to spin.

Alroy could not remember the last time he had kissed a woman. As he gave into his impulse, he wondered if he could make this a new habit.

After North had outlined the basics, Corporal Alfonsi was of a similar disposition to Bloom – he thought Dek's plan was too risky, and he wasn't bashful about sharing his feelings.

"You cannot trick the Chairman," the rotund islander said

definitively. "She is not going to take the bait. And then she'll have all of you and Red, too."

"Corporal, I understand your concern," North said. "Leave the convincing of the Chairman to Sparks and Dek. They know the Chasm playbook."

"How are you even going to get up to that dirty waypoint?" Alfonsi pressed. North ignored Alfonsi, reviewing the pre-mission checklist on his infopad.

"Roy... Red... said he had a way," Dek walked into the room, and tossed a fresh ammo pack to North, who stowed it into his pack. North checked ammo off his packing list.

"And you two are good with that? Not knowing such a significant detail, a day before your mission," Alfonsi was starting to annoy North.

"Are you saying that Alroy Macready is not a trustworthy man?" North replied. "I've known Alroy for more than a decade. He has *never* let me down."

"No." Alfonsi hung his head and repeated himself. "No, I'm not saying *that*. It's just–"

"We didn't come here to play it safe," Dek said. "If we can pull this off, we'll not only save Alroy's daughter, but we'll also cripple the Infinite Order."

"But the simulations have given you terrible odds!" Alfonsi said. "We've run it 134 times now, and —"

"Simulations don't know how to quantify the power of raging vendettas," North winked at Alfonsi and then put his hand on the man's shoulder. "Friend, we're doing this, no matter the odds. The *Magnus* was made for this, and frankly, so were we." North nodded toward Dek.

"Don't worry. It'll make more sense at the mission briefing."

Alfonsi snorted and left Dek and North alone in the men's bunk room. Dek started fishing in his pack to find his body armor.

"He's right you know," Dek said. "Chances are we're both dead by the end of this."

"You don't have faith in the plan?" North frowned. "It's *your* plan!"

"Well, my plan gives us a *small* chance of success," Dek inspected his armor for fractures. "The other plans gave us *no* chance."

"Doesn't matter," North said. "If we don't try now, it will be too late for Amberly – if it's not too late already."

"North, when we save Amberly...," Dek pressed his finger against the blade of his knife, testing the sharpness, "... what are your intentions?"

North didn't want to have this conversation. Not now. Certainly not with Dek. Still, North felt the rogue had earned a straight answer. Dek was about to put everything on the line for Amberly, again.

"To help find waypoint or world where she can live in peace again. To make her happy, no matter what – or who – she chooses," North looked at Dek, a little nervous with him wielding the unsheathed knife. Dek put it away, and North continued. "Before Sparks knew your contingency plan, she said she hoped Amberly passed on both of us, that Amberly was way out of our league anyway."

"She is. We both want Amberly to have some peace. After all she's been through, she deserves that. I fear her trials are not over. Promise me if fate puts her in your hands, that you'd sacrifice everything for her."

"In as much as my duty allows," North sealed his pack, stood, and threw it over his shoulder. "Amberly means the waypoints to me, but there are things bigger than you, me and her."

"But if the plan works..." Dek trailed off.

"Dek, I used to hate your guts. We wouldn't be in this mess if it weren't for you. But you've proven yourself, and Amberly has faith in you. If the plan works, you have my word as a Marine, should her fate fall to me, I would lose everything to protect her. But let's not give up before we start."

"I'm not giving up. But I have this...feeling. You know ... a premonition"

"A premonition? Like God is telling you something?" North eyes filled with skepticism.

"I've always believed I was a survivor – somehow fate had chosen me above others to walk right up to death's line, dance around a bit, but always come back. I never feared death, because I never really believed I could die. I was always clever enough to survive, to carry on, so I thought. My wit and resolve would always pull my ass out of the fire. You changed that for me."

"Me?" North was incredulous. "How?"

"When you had me dead to rights during the Battle of *Magellan*. That was when I first thought, 'This is it. This is the end.'"

North unconsciously rubbed his arm where Dek had stabbed him during that skirmish seven years ago. The scars remained. "Amberly saved you."

"Yes. I would have died by your hand that day, if not for her intervention. After that day, I feared coming out on the losing end of every life-or-death situation, but somehow I still survived."

"Life and death?" North asked.

"During the coup on *American Spirit* – I should have died. Captain Eaton, dead. Engineer Grace, too. Totum – Skylar shot the poor bastard. *But I endured.* I almost tasted vacuum when Eli Wong was tricked by Triggs to shoot me out the airlock. Ramos intervened. When Governor Rillio self-destructed *Magellan* to destroy the Dark Armada, I was sure I would go with the waypoint. I even composed that good-bye note. I escaped in the absolute last moment, and *you*, of all people, picked me up from deep space."

"Well, if we had known it was you on that corvette, maybe…" North attempted a light joke.

"I feel as if every time the author of my fate is about to kill me, someone comes to him and says, 'Let Dek live a little longer. You might still have use for him yet.'"

"So, you're a lucky man," North said, sitting down on a bare bunk. "You know what I think. The man upstairs has a plan for you."

"I think so, too," Dek's eyes lit up. "But this time it's different, North. It's like God is telling me this is it. I am not coming back."

"Now don't get ahead of yourself," North chided Dek. "I know you appointed yourself the fall guy should things go south or the Chairman raises the stakes; but if you go in with that attitude, you're going to get iced! This is not a suicide mission. This is a rescue mission. It's the biggest rescue mission, ever. We're rescuing Amberly and we're rescuing Arara."

"I hear you. I just can't shake the feeling that this is my end."

"Dek, come on–"

"North, listen," Dek put his hands up. "I don't want to die, but I am *ready* to go. I've made my peace with everyone who is still alive. With Sparks. With Amberly. But not with you."

"This isn't necessary," North said, trying to stay business-like and standing to walk toward the door.

"Maybe not for you. But it is for me. It's an odd coincidence that we love the same girl. I admit I schemed to make her mine. I still love her, but I know now that I am not what's best for her. The greatest way to show my love is to die for her."

"Your life has meaning without Amberly, Dek."

"Of course. But my love has no meaning if I am not willing to die for her."

"No one is going kamikaze. We're going to pull this off," North was becoming impatient.

Dek retreated as advised. "I understand. But let me square up with you now. In case I die. Or in case you die."

North crossed his arms and leaned against the bunk rail. "Dek, I forgave you long ago. You were fighting for your cause. I was fighting for mine. War between honorable soldiers should never be personal. Amberly was just an innocent bystander in our war," North exhaled then continued. "I can't believe I am saying this, but don't sell yourself short, Dek. You're a good man. You cared for Amberly when I was gone, and for that, I am grateful. You mean a great deal to her."

Dek glanced to the ground. "Do you love her?"

"I always have," North replied. "But it doesn't matter. The question is, will Amberly ever let anyone love her?"

Dek nodded in agreement, stood up, and clasped North's hand firmly. "Let's do what we have to do to make sure she has that chance."

Commander North, captain of the *Magnus*, and Commander Bloom, leader of the Lewis Island Irregulars, stood across from each other on either side of the tactical table in the operations center of the Irregular HQ. Dek Tigona stood at the end of the table.

"We have to be correct so many times in our guess of enemy response… I don't know," Bloom sighed. She looked up from the table display at the dimly lit North. "I'm just a country cop who became a commander by accident. You're the real deal,

Commander. Trained in tactics. If you want to green light Mr. Tigona's plan…"

"Sparks and I have a read on the Chairman," Dek explained. "We might not be able to predict her every move, but we're making very *educated* guesses."

"Honestly, we aren't in a great position," North admitted, "but as time goes on, our hand gets weaker, and the Chairman's gets stronger. If they find the *Magnus* before we make our play, our chances get substantially worse."

"Let's start the briefing then," Bloom said. "I'll assemble everyone in the commons."

Air circulators made constant dull drones through the HQ commons. Various Irregulars and members of the *Magnus* advance team were engaged in murmuring conversations. Lydia sat alone at the edge of the space, quietly taking a moment to grieve her loss of friends and home. As opposed to the wide-open spaces on the surface of Arara, the tunnels of the underground HQ of the Lewis Island Irregulars reminded her of *Magellan*. In many ways, the technology and best practices that helped humans live indefinitely on a waypoint were similar to what was needed for long-term subterranean survival.

The commanders and Dek walked in the room, and the murmuring died. North scanned the room and took comfort in the gathered allies and friends. Rhodes, Sparks, Lydia, and Caddo were as capable as they were loyal, he thought. Alroy Macready had been a supremely competent man when North knew him a decade ago. Now he was battle hardened, even more capable. The Irregulars and the remnants of the *Butch Cassidy* crew were solid backups that North felt he could trust. Especially Bloom. Well, maybe not so much Klungy, but that bean counter was not being put in any position where he could compromise anything significant.

In total, a force of nearly 100 strong had gathered for the briefing. Bloom took a deep breath and began to speak. "Okay, team. We've been waiting more than a year now for the opportunity to take our shot," Bloom focused on her people. "This is the best one we are going to get, so I told Commander North of the *Magellan Marines* here that we'd support the plan.

Commander, the floor is yours."

"Fire up the screen, Condi," North spoke to his VI, and the info pad threw up a three-dimensional magnetic resonance screen. The screen displayed the basic tactical points of the plan. "We have two mission objectives. The primary mission is to capture, if possible, or destroy, if necessary, *Waypoint Marquette*."

North expected the commotion from the teams at the idea that *Marquette* may be destroyed. A captured *Marquette* could be returned to its waypoint anchorage in deep space a half-light year away, undoing part of the damage done to Arara's connection to Mother Earth. *Cortes* and *Magellan's* destruction already created a nearly insurmountable gap.

"We can't destroy another waypoint," an Irregular shouted from the back of the room.

"Destroying *Marquette* is a last resort," North explained. "The waypoint cannot remain under Chasm control, even if that means the unthinkable."

Bloom nodded her support of North.

"What's the second objective?" Fiat asked.

"The secondary objective is to rescue Amberly Macready. The Chairman personally went to great lengths to capture her. We believe the Chairman has a critical role for Amberly to play in Chasm's plans and recovering her could set back those plans irrevocably," North said. "Our best intel places Amberly on *Marquette*, near the Chairman."

"Forget about the girl," Fiat spoke up. "If we capture *Marquette*, it's game over for the Chairman. We can turn the reign of death on the forces of Chasm and make the Infinite Order the shortest infinity ever."

"I agree," Klungy stood from the bench he was sitting on as he spoke up. "This Amberly is a distraction. And a bad one. We won't have another shot at getting rid of our orbiting overlord. Let's be honest here. The only reason we are even talking about this woman is because she may be Red's daughter, and those two —" Klungy thumbed at both North and Dek "— are sweet on her. We all have to make sacrifices to win this thing, and maybe Red and those two jokers need to sacrifice the girl to make sure we reach the primary objective."

North wanted to gut Klungy right then and there. But North

kept his cool, in full command mode now, and only those who knew him best could see any indication of his fury. Alroy also kept quiet.

North was about to reply when Dek spoke. "So what? This plan doesn't work unless I am willing to put myself on the line. I'm willing to do that, but making Amberly a secondary objective is part of the price. Without my absolute commitment to this mission, the primary objective is almost impossible."

"Once a turncoat, always a turncoat," Klungy said. "I don't trust you, Dek Tigona."

"Once a pirate, always a pirate," Sparks quipped.

"That will be enough, Mr. Klungy, Ms. Sparks," Bloom stepped in to cut off the debate. It only served to divide factions that needed to be unified. "Klungy, if you don't like the plan, you are welcome to leave the protection of the Irregulars. Of course, we'll have to detain you in our brig until the operation is complete. The risk of Chasm capturing and interrogating you is too great."

Klungy huffed and crossed his arms, but he said nothing.

North focused back on the map. "Now the *Magnus* has a highly trained fighting force with the strength of more than 300. Most have trained for decades on the specific skill sets needed to capture a waypoint. Our challenge is to get that force onto *Marquette* with minimal losses, so we can take the station. Once the strike force is on the station, I am confident we'll be able to overcome whatever Chasm throws at us."

"That's not a challenge!" Alfonsi sputtered. "That's impossible! They'll see the *Magnus* coming from 50,000 kilometers away and summon *Utopia*. *Magnus* is neutralized."

"We're counting on that," Dek explained. "We know they are looking for *Magnus,* because it is the only real threat to the Infinite Order now. We've hidden the battleship well, but we'll turn on the lights here–" Dek pointed at orbit coordinates on the map roughly above the capital city on the large continent – "and with any luck, they'll believe we are trying to stage an attack on the capital or on their highly guarded medical research community."

North indicated a location not far from the coordinates Dek pointed out. "This is also near the shipyards where they built the Dark Armada. We know they are trying to replace the ships they lost, so that is another potential faux target. They'll summon

Utopia to counter *Magnus*. And this time, *Magnus* will be ready for a fair fight. Once *Utopia* is revealed and far away from *Marquette's* orbit, we move into phase two — landing our troops on *Marquette*. Caddo?"

The *Magnus* bridge officer took over the briefing. "The full complement of Valkyries on *Magnus* is six, minus the *Prime*."

"Which is currently out of commission because of this loser," Sparks thumbed Alfonsi. "Thanks, mister-shoot-first-ask-questions later."

"Hey, I was just following orders," Alfonsi frowned. "We'll get her fixed … eventually."

Caddo ignored the interruption and continued. "Those runabouts will have been offloaded from *Magnus* at the hiding point, packed with our strike force. When we've confirmed *Magnus* has engaged *Utopia* on the other side of Arara, the *Magnus* Valkyrie flotilla will make for *Marquette*. To arrive at *Marquette* will take about six hours."

"Where are you hiding your big bird?" one of the Irregulars asked from the back of the room.

"That's need-to-know information," North said. "Right now, that information in the wrong hands could eliminate any chance we have for success."

"But how are you going to get inside?" Alfonsi asked. "Even without *Utopia*, that waypoint is well-defended."

"Hopefully, we'll land them in the hangar bay," North answered. "But if we cannot, our Valkyrie can cut a soft seal through many locations in the waypoint's exterior hull. That's not optimal, and we'll definitely have more casualties."

"How in the waypoint will you land them in an enemy hangar bay?" Fiat stood and gave North a you-are-deep-space-crazy look.

"That's where we come in," Bloom spoke unexpectedly. "We are going to *Marquette*, and we are going to hold the bay through force long enough for them to land their strike force. Red has it all worked out, and he'll be leading our detachment to that end."

Alroy Macready stood up and cleared his throat. "Yeah. Thanks Commander. Uh, there are two things you should know. The first is that Captain Paul gave me the runabout I was found in. The *Sundance Kid* is well hidden back on my farmstead. I understand in another life that runabout was known as the

Normandy. The second is that I learned a thing or two about smuggling during my years on the *Butch Cassidy*."

"That's the truth," snorted Isabella. "He's a hell of a smuggler."

Alroy continued. "Back when I was …er… pirating, we outfitted the *Sundance Kid* with smuggling compartments that blocked all sorts of scanning. Those outfits are going to come in handy now. We should be able to hide a contingent of Irregulars that could hold the hangar for long enough. While that is happening, Commander North will be leading his team to locate and recover Amberly Macready. I'll need twenty volunteers for this mission, preferably people who have already been in space. I won't call it a suicide mission; but if we fail, there is no path of retreat."

The room grew still. Some Irregulars glanced around to see who would volunteer, while others stared at the floor, wondering in their own guts if they had the courage for such a task

Alfonsi cleared his throat and pushed his chair back to stand. "Well, I'm volunteering, captain." He smiled at Alroy. "But let me get this straight… *Magnus* distracts *Utopia* so the *Magnus* strike force can land on *Marquette*. But before that happens, an Irregular force is going to travel up to *Marquette* on a secret runabout from your farm and hold the hangar long enough so the strike force can land?"

"Um… That's the long and short of it, I suppose," Alroy said. "North?"

"So far, so good," Alfonsi continued. "What I don't understand is how we are going to get *Marquette* to allow us to land your runabout?"

"Because, I am going to betray you," Sparks laughed and winked at Klungy. "Once a turncoat, always a turncoat."

Elizabeth "Betsy" Hawkins sat alone as the officer of the watch on the bridge of the *Magnus*. A single Marine was posted as security just outside the bridge. Betsy looked relaxed. Acting Captain Alecia Blight was lax on the dress code, so Hawkins wore a cool, loose fitting t-shirt and flexible pants designed for exercise regimen. She was re-reading one of her favorite detective novels, a noir caper set on *Waypoint Columbia* while it was still being built in Moon orbit. The novel was somewhat obscure, partially owing to the fact it was nearly 200 years old. Between chapters, Hawkins would check navigation to make sure the *Magnus'* drift was still within standard tolerance, look for any approaching objects, and see if they had received any tightbeam communiques from North's team.

The powerful warship had been floating for nearly four days now, careful to minimize its radiation output, hiding against the darkness of space. Captain Blight had the *Magnus* down to a skeleton operation, partially to conserve power, partially to allow the crew and Marines to have a time of rest before what she anticipated would be a final, costly push.

Betsy finished a chapter and checked the navigation indicators. No drift. She looked at the tactical chart and saw only a green triangle indicating the *Magnus* itself. She pulled up the exterior cameras and did a visual scan. She stopped when Arara came into view. The blue green planet seemed to call to her, and she wondered about the adventures her colleagues Rhodes and Caddo were having on the surface.

I hope they haven't run into trouble, Hawkins thought the worst as she grabbed her infopad and went back to her novel. *Maybe they are dead. No, I should put that thought away before it gets out of hand.*

Ensign Hawkins had read a few pages when she realized she forgot to check the comms. She punched up the communication logs and leapt out of her chair when she saw a new message had been received over the tightbeam. The decryption was almost complete.

She called the acting captain in her quarters, and Blight's husband answered the page.

"Hawkins, what is it?" Chief Petty Officer Bollard asked. "We're trying to … sleep."

"Hush. Does she have a report?" Hawkins heard Blight say. "Ensign, you have a report?"

The message decryption completed as soon as Blight had gotten on the line.

"It's North!" Hawkins said. "We're on."

"Well, let's hope we can tease *Utopia* out of hiding," Blight said. "Very good. Prepare to sound general quarters. Have Cho gather the Marine squad commanders in the conference room in one hour. We'll dump them off and be on our way. I'm on my way up to the bridge. I'll bring the Engineer, too."

"Confirmed. See you soon."

Before Hawkins closed the connection, she heard Bollard complain, "What was that you said about teasing, love?"

CHAPTER EIGHTEEN

February 20, 2610. Aboard the Sundance Kid, on final approach to Waypoint Marquette.

Wearing her jet-black, form-fitting pilot's jump suit and sporting ultra-short, freshly cropped strawberry blonde hair, Sparks looked the part of a Chasm officer. By all external appearances, Sparks and her cohort sibling, Dek, were the only two lives aboard the runabout. She entered the bridge and made her way to the pilot's station.

Trained as a space pilot, Sparks relished being at the helm of the *Sundance Kid.*

"Alroy says it's cramped, but everyone in the locker is making do. Those Irregulars will be itching for a fight after being packed like ligrains in the smuggle pods," Sparks reported to Dek. He had been secured with restraining ties to complete the fiction.

Sparks went through a mental checklist. "Secret squad ready for action. Check. Encrypted message to *Magnus*. Check. Dek tied up by Sparks. Check. Hmmm. Lucky you."

"I think I just threw up a little," Dek rolled his eyes.

"I'm ready," Sparks looked over from the pilot's chair to the bound Dek, seated in the navigation station. "Let's do this."

"If you don't sell this, the twenty-four people we have in the freezer are dead," Dek spoke nervously.

"Worried about me spinning a great lie? Deception is my best skill," Sparks sassed Dek. "If they catch us, it will be because you didn't fake the flight logs well enough."

"No. The ship's records are good," Dek said, trying to force a smile. His premonition of eminent death had grown intense. "Are you sure you can go all the way on this?"

The pilot ran her left hand over her half-mask. She spoke in a suddenly somber tone. "I know what you want, Dek, and I am willing. Amberly saved you. My sister saved me, too, in more ways than one. We're paying her back. And if I get revenge on the Chairman along the way, all the better."

"We've had a crazy journey, haven't we?" Dek said, instinctively struggling against the zip ties pressing into his wrists.

"Dek and Sparks. Quite a pair. Traitors to our birthright, but not to our friends."

"I wondered if I switched to the right side, after I signed on to the *Magnus* with North," Sparks admitted. "But I remembered I was still on the same side Dek Tigona, and somehow, I felt absolved for my treachery."

"I know you think I'm full of shit," Dek smiled, "but God is on *our* side."

"You are correct, of course."

"What, that I am full of shit or God is on our side?"

"Yes," Sparks smirked, and she tapped her comm control screen. She punched in a code through the magnetic resonance interface. "We'll be in *Marquette* weapons range in about three minutes. Shut up and say your prayers. Here goes."

Sparks set a timer to see how long it would take for the waypoint to acknowledge her. Dek and Sparks waited in silence.

Just over two minutes had passed when the bridge comm unit lit up. "*Sundance Kid*, this is *Marquette* control duty officer. We've received your Chasm authorization code. Your code is registered to a known enemy of the state. So, either you have a forged code, or you are actually an enemy of the state. Either way, I've sent for permission to destroy your runabout."

"*Marquette* control, this is the infamous Sparks. If you haven't heard of me, maybe you've heard of my mentor: Raven One. Don't be so hasty to shoot up the best thing that happened to you all day. Let the Chairman know that I intend to defect to the Infinite Order."

Sparks could hear laughing through the channel.

"Wait. Are you actually laughing at *me?*" Sparks mused. "I guess my reputation does not proceed me. I'll have to cut some tongues out later."

"Um… you don't defect *back*, traitor. You signed your death sentence when you joined the enemies of the Infinite Order. Permission to destroy your ship has been granted."

That was fast, Dek thought.

"Fine. I have the information that you want – the location of the *Magnus*. How do you think I got here? I also have a prisoner as a token of my good faith, Dek Tigona."

They could hear some stressed chatter, and then they heard

the voice of the officer on duty again. "Please hold your relative position, *Sundance Kid*."

A few more minutes passed, and then the duty officer spoke again. "*Sundance Kid*, please prepare to answer questions from the Chairman's envoy. Know that if your responses displease her, you will be destroyed without prejudice. Please hold."

About ten minutes of silence transpired. Sparks noted that Dek's head was bowed. She assumed he was deep in some sort of prayer meditation. She had seen him practice it numerous times since the *Magnus* picked up his corvette from the ruins of *Magellan*. She decided to let him be.

A familiar voice spoke over the open channel. "Sparks, is that really you? After all these years. Amazing."

"Is that … Merwin? Merwin!" Sparks asked the disembodied voice. She smiled.

Dek's head popped up from its bowed position. He made eye contact with Sparks, confirming that it sounded like the voice he remembered as well. They both had been good friends with Merwin, who was two batches behind the laboratory spawning cycle that gestated Dek and Sparks in pre-Chasm Arara.

"I'm touched you remembered my voice, Sparks," Merwin said sincerely. "When I saw your authorization codes come through vetting, I couldn't believe it was you after all these years."

"What are you doing on *Marquette*?" Sparks asked. "I figured you would have some leadership role on the big continent!"

"We'll get to that, I'm sure, old friend. I wish this greeting was on better terms Sparks. Apparently, you have become *persona non grata*. You betrayed Raven One. I understand you tried to assassinate the Chairman."

"News travels fast," Sparks quipped. "To be fair, I was just sort of surprised to run into the Chairman so I unloaded my pistol in shock."

"Of course. Of course. But this puts us in an awkward situation. I am special assistant to the Chairman now," Merwin said. "My job is actually to terminate risks to the Chairman. Which you pose."

"I see. Bodyguard?"

"*Chaperone*. The duty officer said you wanted to defect back.

You know that isn't possible–"

Sparks interrupted. "I understand you may have to kill me. No hard feelings. But I believe the Chairman might make an exception since I brought a worthy gift. Actually, I have three gifts, but I'll need help opening one."

"I'm listening."

"The first one is I have apprehended our brother Dek, who continued to aid and abet the enemy. I am prepared to turn him over to you so you may render judgment. He is on the *Sundance Kid* now. Would you like to speak to him?"

Dek was conflicted. Before he left Arara, Dek had been close with Merwin. He focused on pushing those old emotions down. His mind needed to be clear and fully engaged in the present, not distracted by puppy love nostalgia.

"This will be welcome news to the Chairman. I'm sure I'll visit with him in due time," Merwin replied over the comm, "Your gift of bringing the turncoat home is appreciated, friend, but would not buy you clemency."

"A little short? Let me up the ante, then, and give you cause to not incinerate us and the *Sundance Kid*. I was not trusted – apparently with good cause – with Marine secrets. But Dek was. He knows where in close space the *Magnus* is hiding. The ship is in a synchronous orbit with Arara around Viapos, I'm sure you know. But Dek knows the navigational coordinates. I have been unable to extract them from him."

"Unable?" Merwin asked. "Or unwilling? You were never so squeamish before."

"Let's not split hairs. If I had the coordinates in my own brain, then perhaps you would intend for me the suffering that will befall Dek."

"So, we bring Dek on board," Merwin suggested. "Then we toss you out an airlock? I can't imagine the Chairman would accept any less. She may want you to suffer first. Are you sure you wouldn't rather me order your ship shot down? I would do that, for our friendship's sake."

Okay, now we're getting somewhere, Sparks thought. *Getting the* Sundance Kid *on* Marquette *is an important first step. Now, let's see if I can keep my life, too.*

"No, I've got lots of good mileage on me before I'm ready to check out," Sparks said. "Surely, the Chairman would see that I am a valuable asset for Chasm."

"My dear Sparks," Merwin spoke in a way that seemed hopeful, and even encouraging, even though the meaning of her words were anything but. "Once the *Magnus* is dealt with, Chasm will truly become obsolete. The Infinite Order's grasp will be complete, and the pathway to social nirvana will be fixed. Warriors, spies, muscle – people like you and me – we will no longer be needed. We've done our part for the common good. We've been programmed for war. The war is over. We need to fade away now, our purpose fulfilled. So, no, I don't think the Chairman would find use for you."

"I was afraid just being awesome would not put me over the top, so I have my third gift," Sparks said. "It's not much, but it might serve as an insurance policy. Be ready to have your mind blown: Alroy Macready is alive." Sparks was paying close attention to Merwin's response. Sparks knew the Chairman already knew that Alroy had survived, but the Chairman didn't know that Sparks knew what Chasm knew.

"I wouldn't waste the Chairman's time with that so-called gift. Unfortunately, information on Alroy Macready is cheap," Merwin said. "We've known of his survival for some time."

"You have?!?" Sparks acted surprised. After a brief pause she continued, "I see. Well, then perhaps the Chairman is more interested in knowing that I can bring him to you with little to no mess."

Merwin sighed. "I see that he is not on your ship now – unless he is dead. I'm reading two heat signatures now. Dek is the other one I assume."

"Oh, Mr. Raven One is no stiff. He's still burning oxygen on the Lewis Islands," Sparks offered.

"Very well. How will you get him for us?"

"Ha! Tea time with the Chairman," Sparks said, "is my price. Don't take this hard, but I won't be handing over what seems like the only chip I have to the Chairman's lackey. Now, if we don't have a deal, maybe give me a heads up so I can get a running start and a slight chance to escape?"

"Still the same old Sparks. Still laughing at death. And why not? Beats the alternative," Merwin said. "Very well, I'll make sure you get your audience with the Chairman."

"*Wow*. You can do that without even consulting with her? I'm impressed!" Sparks said. "Thanks."

Sparks could hear the smile in Merwin's voice. "I only have power because I have no ambition. Nothing to be impressed with. It's why the Chairman trusts me. If you survive this, maybe you could adopt this principle."

"I don't have ambition," Sparks said. "I'm just a simple girl looking for her next rush."

"Well, you've brought the excitement this time. I don't see how you don't end up dead, but it will be good to see you friend. Welcome back to the cause," Merwin said, and then adopted a formal tone. "Commander *Sundance Kid*, you are ordered to surrender your vessel. Release control of your vessel to hangar control and prepare to be boarded. Your illegal vessel is now property of the Infinite Order, and all crew and passengers are to be detained pending judicial review. *Marquette* out."

Through the front and starboard portals, in clear view was the seven-kilometer diameter spinning mass of grey polycarbonate speckled with lit portals. The last time Sparks had seen *Marquette* was during a harrowing escape five years ago. The *Magnus* survived, and so did Sparks, but both had permanent scars to remind them of the pain inflicted.

Sparks looked at Dek, who smiled broadly. "So far, so good. I can't believe it. Running into Merwin all these years later," Dek said. "Do you think she can be persuaded to help us?"

"No," Sparks frowned. "She already suspects I am faking. The minute she knows that I am a fraud, she'll do me in."

"Are you sure? If she didn't believe you, why is she letting us on the waypoint."

"She is overconfident. She figures she can handle me if I am full of it."

"Can she?"

"Can anybody handle me? Well, maybe I'd let North handle me."

"What is it with you?"

"Never mind. I think Alroy Macready is more valuable than we realize. Speaking of the old man, why don't you go back to the freezer and let them know we are in?"

Dek shrugged and indicated his bound hands.

"Right, I'll go do it, then," mumbled Sparks. "I have to do everything around here."

Twenty minutes later, the main portal of the *Sundance Kid* opened, safely tucked away in a secondary hangar bay of *Marquette*. Unlike *Magellan*, with single large bay, *Marquette* had a primary hangar originally intended for public, civilian traffic, and a smaller hangar for military and government use. Once the Chairman had established *Marquette* as her capital, the secondary bay was exclusively used for her business.

Sparks slid down the ladder, then turned and helped Dek. With his hands secured in front of his body, Dek had only a little trouble coming out the primary hatch.

They were greeted by a platoon of blue-green armored troops of the Infinite Order, with Merwin One standing a few meters out in front, wearing a light, white dress to make her enemies feel less threatened than they should have been. Sparks, on the other hand, wore her flattering but powerful black battle armor. She did not have on her dual thigh gun holsters, but did have her untested, newly fashioned anti-PDS sword strapped in the sheath on her back. On either side of Merwin were warriors from the Chairman's Honor Guard.

"Welcome home, Sparks," Merwin stepped forward and embraced her old friend. "I hope you find mercy in the generous spirit of the Chairman, friend."

"Merwin!" Sparks said. "Thank you for getting me a chat with the boss lady."

"Technically, it's Merwin One now," Merwin clarified. The Chairman affixed the word "one" as an honorific to bestow prominence and reward her most loyal comrades. Only a few of the chairman's most trusted researchers and advisers knew that the first number signified the Chairman's intentional preservation of that individual's genetic makeup. Genetic children of the One would be so indicated by Two and so on.

"Your highness," Sparks did a mock bow. Merwin smiled at Sparks' jest.

Merwin pointed at Dek, and the Honor Guards immediately removed the zip ties from his hands in front of his body, only to re-tie them behind his back.

"Hey, that hurts!" Dek yelped.

One of the guards, an unusually tall and bulky male, went to remove Sparks' sword. Sparks jerked back. "Hands off my hardware, asshole!"

"Let her keep it," Merwin ordered the burley guard.

"But ma'am," the guard objected, "we can't let this potential threat remain armed in the sphere of the glorious Chairman."

"The Chairman wishes it," Merwin said in pleasant tones. "That is a good enough reason for *you*. But this one is no threat."

"See? I'm no threat!" Sparks huffed at the guard, then took a moment to survey the deck, and noted three other ships in port. A large ship — in a class with which she was not familiar — dominated the hangar. Sized somewhere between a Valkyrie and a frigate, Sparks assumed the vessel was the personal yacht of the Chairman. Next to the yacht were two corvettes, likely permanently assigned escorts.

"Look at the guns on that ship," Dek said, whistling at the Chairman's yacht. "Nice. Hey, Merwin. When I escape, it's going to be on that beauty."

"Dek Tigona," Merwin One said flatly. "I'm pleased to see you didn't perish when the terrorists destroyed *Magellan*. Now you will face justice for your misdeeds and betrayal of Chasm. I am sorry for you only for the sake of the memory of what we once were. Farewell, Dek. Take him to the holding block and report back to me when he is secured." The guards threw a dark hood over Dek's head and pulled him toward a door on the far side of the bay.

"So, long Tigona!" Sparks projected sarcasm, but in her heart, she worried for her cohort brother. "I'm going to miss you. Thanks for being my meal ticket."

"Screw you, Sparks!" Dek called back. "I'll see you in hell, you lying, treacherous bitch."

The burly guard punched Dek in the gut as they exited. "Shut up." Dek grunted and complied.

Merwin One turned to the platoon leader. "Lieutenant, please have your team conduct a level two search of Sparks' ship. Double check for explosives, biohazards or other potential dangers to the *Marquette*. Report back to me when you have completed your investigation. And be quick about it."

The lieutenant turned to her platoon. "You heard the lady. Chief, get your scanners out. Move it."

Merwin took Sparks by her arm. "Walk with me? Would you like to dine?"

"When will I get to see the Chairman?"

"Soon, but hopefully not too soon," Merwin said as she led Sparks out of the hangar. She pointed at one of the Chasm troopers and indicated for him to follow. "I don't see how the Chairman doesn't conclude that you should die. But I suppose she has agreed to see you, so you have a chance."

"Thanks for that, by the way."

"What are friends for," Merwin said. "Although I should be cross with you. And you should know I don't really trust you. Not after what you did to Ryder."

"Ryder? I put her out of her misery," Sparks protested. "I protected her identity for more than a year and helped her get access to *Magnus'* secrets. She could have let me know that the Chairman was on *Marquette* the last time I was here. I was to be tortured and killed along with a *Marquette* doctor. Can you blame me for defending myself?"

"I suppose not," Merwin admitted. "But Ryder was a loyal comrade. I mourn her."

"As do I."

As they walked from a capillary corridor into a larger corridor, Sparks noticed that the entire place had been redecorated in the colors of the Infinite Order. The commercial advertising that dominated waypoints, and that used to dominate *Marquette,* had been removed. In their place were flattering abstract renderings of the Chairman or the symbol of the Infinite Order – a minimalist representation that could be interpreted as two hands clasping or a "lazy eight" infinity symbol. A pleasant, hopeful orchestral fanfare, heavy on the brass, was playing at background volume over the ship wide comms.

"When you were here last … is that when *that* happened?" Merwin pointed at Sparks' half-mask.

"Yes. Sort of," Sparks said. "Commander North and I were sort of caught in a nuclear blast. A welcome to the neighborhood gift from *Utopia* to *Magnus.*"

"I heard the warhead was deployed," Merwin One said, as she pointed toward the tube station down the hall passed the commons. Sparks saw that most everyone was wearing similar jumpsuits. The pattern and functionality were the same, but the colors were different. There was a little chatter, Sparks noticed, when the two women, one wearing white, the other black, walked by. People seemed to know to give Merwin One a wide clearance. "It might be blasphemy to say so, but to build a ship that can take a nuclear blast and walk away – those are people we should not underestimate."

"Meh," Sparks shrugged. "The Earth loyalists at *Magellan* knew you were coming for years, and they had the technology from *Magnus*. They still lost everything. That's when I knew I was fooling myself that the future was anything other than the Infinite Order, and I began planning my return."

"You're quite the mercenary, Sparks," Merwin said. "It doesn't suit you. The loss of *Magellan* was existential for the loyalists, to be sure; but they inflicted a painful price on us. Not only were we denied using the waypoint as an early warning platform, but they also canceled out half of the Dark Armada. Clearly their governor believed that suicide was the best outcome. Impressive resolve."

"I suppose. But it wasn't enough," Sparks said.

The line for a tube car, nearly 50 people deep, melted away as Merwin One approached. Merwin, Sparks and the conscripted escort boarded the egg-shaped public transport.

"So, you've done well for yourself," Sparks tried to change the subject. "I thought once you dusted Ingram off of your shoes, you'd maybe make it on the Council of Comrades or maybe as a district governor."

"I promise you, this is so much better. The governors have their administrative purposes, but they are mostly cogs in the system. The Comrades only help those of the dying generation who cannot shake the need to have some sort of personal representation in their government. As if the masses could somehow design the future. Democracy outlived its usefulness centuries ago. Mob rule has retarded human progress for so long. I'm surprised the Chairman hasn't dissolved the Council yet."

"Wow. Dissolve the Council?" Sparks said. "She's that

powerful?"

"That was the beauty of the Dark Armada. The temptation for glory attracted most of the Chairman's rivals. The power of those ships drew the ambitious like wingdings to the sweet spring ligrain blooms," Merwin reflected. "It was a happy coincidence, then, that most of her rivals perished at *Magellan*, although most would not have returned anyway."

"The Chairman pulled an inside straight," Sparks said, as she adjusted the sword from grinding into her lower back as she sat back in the chair. "Maybe I should have figured it out, but politics was never my strong suit. Mine not to reason why…"

"Ours but to do, and die," Merwin completed the refrain. "So how did you convince Dek to surrender to you? By force?"

"Oh, it was super easy. Barely an inconvenience," Sparks said almost with too much jocularity. "Dek is obsessed with Amberly Macready. We were on an espionage team on Ingram, attempting to find any sort of resistance we could ally with. We did get a lead from some pirates, but I convinced Dek to help me steal a runabout so we could find and maybe rescue Amberly on *Marquette*. Once we were alone, I overpowered him while he was sleeping. He wasn't really even angry at me. It's almost like he expected it."

"Well, if anyone knows you, it's Dek Tigona," Merwin said.

"No, Dek is not the same man you knew, Merwin. He's changed. He's weird religious. Gone off the deep end. The years he spent with the Macready girl in the Spencer Belt warped him. He has a martyr complex. I don't even know if Amberly is even on this station. But Dek was convinced she must be. He's going to so disappointed if she's not. If he lives long enough to find out one way or another."

"Fascinating. This is our stop," Merwin said as the door to the tubecar hissed open. With a hand signal, she indicated that the escort should not follow. The station area was completely deserted, and after the pair walked down a short corridor, they came into an open area with an obelisk in the middle and tall glass double doors on the far side. "Through there is the Chairman's personal office. Your audience with her will not be until after dinner, and then we'll find out what the final fate of Sparks, Chasm revolutionary leader, will be. Until then, through that door over there is the Chairman's cafeteria. Almost every type of food imaginable, grown or raised on Arara — not from synthesizers, is available to Sparks, my dear friend."

"Wow. Thanks! I suppose that is the advantage of being on a waypoint that is only a few hours from the surface of the closest planet."

"We'll be dining with Dr. Michelle Leigh, the physician personally responsible for the well-being of Amberly Macready."

So far so good, Sparks thought. *We've managed to land our team. And Amberly is here. We could pull this off yet. The greatest rescue, ever.* Sparks focused to hide her nervousness for Dek and the others. If they did discover Alroy, North and their teams on the *Sundance Kid*, Sparks assumed Merwin and her ilk wouldn't confront her about it. They would just kill her.

"So, the daughter of Raven One is here," Sparks smiled. "You know Dek and Commander North always hated something I always believed – that Amberly and I are sisters."

"Sisters? I don't understand," Merwin furrowed her eyebrows in confusion.

"Well, maybe spending all the time with the natural-borns has made me wishful I had traditional parents. Of course, we've gotten some impressive genes from our DNA donors. But I've come to observe that the nurture of parents is almost as significant as the random pairing of genes from dear old mom and dad, whoever they were. So, the closest thing I had to a nurturing mother was Raven One. She made me so much of who I am. The short time I had with her was deeply impactful. In our lightyears-apart correspondence, the wisdom of Kimberly Macready shaped me."

"I understand," Merwin smiled her attractive smile. "Raven One was like a mother to you; and she genetically was Amberly's mother. Ergo, sisters."

"See! You get it! Everyone else seems to think I'm so weird when I call her sister," Sparks said as the pair walked into the cafeteria. The sensations that hit Sparks almost overwhelmed her. She had never seen or even imagined anything like what she saw and smelled: A smorgasbord of the savoriest hot and cold prepared foods she had ever seen. Fruits chopped up into salads, raw meats, baked goods, cheeses and soups spread out in cabinets designed to display the culinary masterpieces as if they were art. "Holy cow! Where's the line?"

"No, sit down. The wait staff will bring you what you want," Merwin pointed at one of about a dozen round tables in the cafeteria, all of them vacant. "Relax. Enjoy the meal. Let's celebrate the return of the prodigal daughter."

I should enjoy it because it could be my last, you mean, Sparks thought but didn't say.

As soon as they sat down, a woman with blue hair appeared.

"Oh, finally," Sparks joked and looked at the white-coated woman. "I think I'll have … oh, just bring me a sample of everything. It all looks great."

The woman looked anxiously at Merwin One, wondering if she should comply with Sparks' request, and laughed nervously.

"Sparks, meet Dr. Michelle Leigh," Merwin said. "Dr. Leigh, thanks for joining us on such short notice. I know your work is very important." Michelle wanted to blurt out, "Like I had a choice." But she put that power fantasy away.

"Pleased to meet you, Sparks," Michelle said as she sat at the table. A young man came up to the table.

"What is your pleasure, ma'am?" the waiter said.

"I'll have my usual, Franklin," Merwin said, "but hold the raw beef. No need to impress the Chairman today."

"And madam," the server looked at Dr. Leigh.

"Please bring me an avocado salad, with no onions."

"And for the new lady," the server winked at Sparks.

"Don't get fresh with me," Sparks smirked. "I have no idea what I want. Let's start with hooch. I bet you have top shelf stuff here. Whiskey?"

The waiter looked to Merwin, who nodded.

"What is your whiskey preference?" the waiter asked.

"Surprise me. Bring me a flight. Begone, and don't come back without my booze!" Sparks sung. When the waiter had left bewildered, Sparks continued. "I think I am going to like it here." Secretly, she hoped alcohol would ease her nerves. But she would have to be careful. If she became inebriated, Sparks could blow the operation.

"Sparks, if I may, a little business over dinner," Dr. Leigh said softly. "During Amberly's time with us, she has spoken at length about Dek Tigona and Commander North. I understand you know them both personally. It would help in my research to understand, … um…, what is their relationship with Amberly? From an objective perspective, I mean."

"Well… ha. That's a billion-credit question," Sparks said.

CHAPTER NINETEEN

After being confined in what was essentially a torpedo-shaped casket for more than eight hours, Alroy Macready was going a bit stir crazy. He was a patient, calm man, so he was worried what his younger, less disciplined squad mates were feeling right now, particularly those who were used to the wide-open spaces on the Lewis Islands. Many of them were sharing slightly larger hiding spaces, but Alroy had volunteered for the smallest solo space. "Status report, Jules?"

Alroy's VI had been pragmatically altered to look like a generic runabout VI when probed with electronic forensic evaluation. The spy VI instead was monitoring the situation outside the smuggler's "freezer" for Chasm presences. "Request acknowledged. The main chambers are unoccupied. Two Chasm guards have been posted on the exteriors, one near the stern and the other near the bow."

Alroy clutched his swagger stick. "Okay, warn the others, pop the boxes and tell everyone to quietly meet me in the hold."

Within a few moments, North and Alroy, along with their teams, were huddled in the slightly less cramped cargo hold, donning their armor and checking their weapons.

"Hey, keep it quiet until we get confirmation from Dek on *Utopia's* location," Alroy hushed his forces. "God knows what we'll have to do if they decide to come back in before then. Timing is everything. If we reveal ourselves too early, we won't be able to hold out until the cavalry arrives."

"Let's hope *Utopia* takes the bait," North said, looking through his infopad at the external camera from Jules on the *Sundance Kid*. He had Condi linked into Jules' video feeds.

"Let's hope *Magnus* can dispatch *Utopia*," Fiat said.

"*Magnus* is up to the task," North sounded defensive. "Now, when Sparks signals us that she found Amberly, how do we get past those guards."

North had Condi project what he was seeing and indicated to his team to take a look.

"Maybe some sort of distraction? Could we have the *Kid*

project something?" Lydia suggested.

Caddo studied the video view of the guards. They didn't look the sort that would just be derelict in their duty. "No, we can't draw additional attention to the ship. We need to save the theatrics for when it is time to get the Irregulars in place. I am assuming that Dek and Sparks will find Amberly before the *Magnus* Marines arrive."

"You could try my plan," Rhodes unsuccessfully whispered. "The one I devised for this very scenario."

"Shhhh! Keep it down loudmouth," Caddo said. "That's the loudest whisper between here and Earth."

"We're not doing your plan, Rhodes" North sternly added. "I've already been through this with you. Too risky."

"Fine. But you don't have a better idea," Rhodes sulked.

"Of course, I have a better plan," North said. After a silent moment, he added again. "I have a plan. I do."

"A good one?" Rhodes pushed.

"What was *your* plan that we are not doing?" Lydia asked Rhodes.

"Someone... me... I pretend to be a stowaway," Rhodes explained. "Draw their attention to the front door while the rest of you exit out the rear. Make a lot of commotion. They'll have to take me to the brig of course, and it could cause a little chaos to help out Sparks and Dek."

"That is too dangerous," North said. "Even if they don't kill you on the spot, they could torture you."

"Yes, but I'll be okay when the Marines take control of *Marquette* and you come and get me," Rhodes said.

"But there is a big chance that will fail," North said. "We all know that. The fact that the assault could fail is the main reason why we are going to try to extract Amberly."

"Hey, look at this," Caddo pointed to the exterior monitor. A blue-haired woman in a lab coat walked up to the ship and signaled for the guards to join her. North watched as the woman flashed some sort of identification chit.

"Condi, can you lip read this conversation?"

"Only with 12 percent accuracy. The angle is blocked."

"Twelve percent? Go ahead and make a transcript just in case, but I don't need to hear it in real time."

Rhodes looked over at North to get his read on what they were watching. After a brief conversation, the guards shrugged and walked away. The woman walked around the ship, looking very nervous. She looked at the control deck. And then paced a circle around the *Sundance Kid* a second time.

"What the hell is she doing?" Caddo asked. "She keeps eyeing the hatch, like she is going to come in."

"I could take her, no problem!" Lydia suggested.

"That idea is worse than Rhodes," North rolled his eyes. "We wait for a signal from Dek or Sparks that Amberly is in the clear, or that *Utopia* has taken the bait. Until then, we wait."

Sparks focused on calming herself. The last time she encountered the Chairman, out of justified fear, she shot at the Chasm leader until her both pistols were empty — but the personal implementation of point defense technology neutralized the barrage. Afterward, Sparks barely escaped before facing the worst sorts of chemical torture. Now, she was walking right back into the fire.

Merwin One walked two paces in front of Sparks through the large glass doors. *Everything feels wrong*, Sparks thought. *Have we already been compromised?* She had hoped Dek was all right. As she stepped into the foyer, she was immediately flanked by four blue-clad, armed-to-the-teeth members of the Chairman's Honor Guard. She instinctively wanted to unsheathe her sword, but fought the temptation. With all that firepower guarding her, Sparks saw Merwin didn't deem her melee weapon any real threat.

Sparks covered her eyes briefly as they adjusted to the light as she entered the consistently bright Chairman's office. *Stall the Chairman. Throw her off Alroy's scent. Intercede for Dek, if possible. Find out where Amberly is,* Sparks went over the plan in her mind. *Stay alive. Don't forget that one.*

As her eyes adjusted, across the room she saw the Chairman's table. It was bare, and surrounded by three chairs. One was facing her and was occupied by a woman Sparks instantly recognized as the Chairman, with her pulled back white hair and pale face. She was still too far away to see those freaky eyes. The chair on her left was empty.

In the chair on the right was Amberly Macready.

Found her! That was easy. Sparks suddenly had a horrific thought. *Oh no! What if—*

"Sparks, please come and join us," the Chairman stood up and pointed to the empty chair. "I believe you know Raven Two."

"Madam Chairman," Sparks said, feeling more intimidated than ever before and struggling to bury the feeling, "Thank you for your grace. I am humbled by, and grateful for, the opportunity to prove myself to Chasm again. Good to see you alive and well, sister. I believe the last time we met, we were having drinks at Rick's on *Magellan*." Sparks felt inauthentic — using tones and vocabulary that was unnatural for her flippant style.

Amberly stood up and politely hugged and kissed the cheek of the Chasm turncoat. Then she stood at arm's length from her, smiling. "Hello, Sparks. It's good to see you." Inside Amberly was trying to control a burning rage at a sister-in-arms who would betray a brother. *Maybe Sparks didn't really betray Dek*, Amberly thought. *Maybe they have some other plan. Does the Chairman suspect Sparks like I do? Of course. That must be why I am here now.* Amberly focused three thought threads from her newly developed mental skills on trying to figure out the true intentions of Sparks, including how to ascertain those intentions without the Chairman knowing. After a long time drowning in loneliness, Amberly was also thrilled to see anyone connected to her old life and friends. *I must remain calm*, Amberly controlled her emotions as she processed dozens of questions. *I need to figure out what the best path forward is. Should I try to manipulate the Chairman? To what end? Does she really have the upper hand and is she just manipulating me? The presence of Sparks adds new variables to the problem matrix. What is her true intention? Does it matter?*

Sparks was trying to keep everything lined up as well, although she did not have the mental acuity Amberly had. *Dirt. Amberly being here is going to make things even more difficult, and the Chairman knows it. It's going to be harder for me to keep my story straight. What if Amberly believes I really did betray Dek?*

"Amberly," Sparks tried to slip on her attitude. "You should have seen Dek and North fret after the Chairman… acquired you on *Magellan*. I knew you would overcome any threat. You are like me, we were both trained by Raven One, nurtured for success.

Except… you have her name now?" Sparks looked inquisitively at the Chairman, as if expecting an explanation. She saw the iris-less eyes and resisted the temptation to react.

"Please, let's all sit down," the Chairman said. "All will be explained. I am sure we all have lots of things to discuss amongst ourselves. We are in no hurry." The two women sat. As they did, the Honor Guard assumed posts a meter from each corner of the table, and Merwin seemed to melt into the wall.

"Go ahead, Raven Two," the Chairman encouraged Amberly, "explain your new name to Sparks. If we end up not trusting her, she won't be able to tell anyone in the vacuum of space. But I am optimistic that Sparks will pass her test. She is forged in real fire, and if she *is* loyal to you like a sister, would be a worthy chaperone."

Test? Motherless dirt licker! What test? thought Sparks.

"Raven One, my birth mother and your mentor, is a modified clone of the Chairman," Amberly said. She was smiling with her mouth, but not with her eyes, Sparks perceived. Or was Sparks just seeing what she wanted to believe? *What if the Chairman has broken Amberly*? In their years of planning for this rescue, no one – not Dek, North, or anyone – ever once even considered that the Chairman might have turned Amberly to her side. Sparks realized now that may be a fatal oversight. *Wait. What? A clone?*

"I am the second generation – Raven Two, one step closer to perfection, apparently," Amberly said with the levity of someone offering a childhood secret. "That makes the Chairman my *grandmother.*"

Holy dirt. This is getting even more complicated, Sparks thought, but just said, "Wow."

"I was a lot closer to perfection with Kimberly Macready," the Chairman scowled, darkening the mood of the conversation. "And then she was taken from me. At the same time your strength failed, Sparks. Do you know the suffering you caused me? DO YOU! WHY ARE YOU NOT FLOATING OUT IN SPACE INSTEAD OF HER!"

Sparks and Amberly were both jolted by the sudden shouting of the Chairman. Amberly noted Sparks' negative reaction and began to reason if that could expose Sparks' true intentions. After a brief flash of fear, Sparks resolved she would not be bullied.

No you don't, old lady, Sparks thought.

Sparks slowly removed her half-mask to reveal the grotesque scarring. "We've all suffered in our quest to shape human history. In our revolution to change everything, suffering has been the only constant. Did you think you would be protected from it?"

The Chairman seemed delighted by Sparks' answer, and any hint of anger in her demeanor was gone. "Well said. But don't think you have any sympathy from me for your disfigurement. You tried to assassinate me," the Chairman said matter-of-factly.

"Only because Ryder betrayed me first," Sparks said as she replaced her mask. "I would have betrayed her in time, but she beat me to the punch. I skewered her for it, though. They say the last laugh is the sweetest laugh. They are right."

"So, Sparks, thank you for your 'three gifts' as Merwin One called them," the Chairman said, changing the subject. "But they did not buy you my graces or this audience."

The Chairman's declaration spooked Sparks, and again she had to fight the temptation to draw her sword and die fighting.

"Gifts?" Amberly asked.

"We'll get to that. First things first. Sparks, you are only alive because I surmised that it is what Raven Two wishes. Under normal circumstances, I would have been content to spread your molecules in Arara orbit with a missile or two," the Chairman said as she turned to Amberly. "Please forgive me for taking liberties in anticipating your desires. Did I anticipate them correctly?"

"Of course," Amberly could clearly see the Chairman's machinations now.

"Of course, I did," the Chairman said to herself. "Sparks, I will not live forever. Even now, the balance of my life is spent. I intend for Raven Two to succeed me in the place of her mother. It will take decades for her to become competent enough to replace me, but during that time, she will need a chaperone."

"A chaperone? Like Merwin?" Sparks asked. *Did the Chairman really just say that she was going to make Amberly ruler of Chasm? Is Amberly okay with that?*

"Merwin is my chaperone. My protector. A person who is fully responsible for my well-being. My security. My health."

"A Hawk then?"

"No. No. You don't understand. Hawks are my sword. The

chaperone is my shield. Hawks are instruments of my will, taking risks. Executing missions. Even sacrificing themselves. A chaperone must survive so their charge will survive. She is a supremely competent person always at my side. Her mission is never changing. Her purpose is singular. Protect the Chairman at all costs."

Sparks looked to Amberly to get a read, but Amberly's eyes were distant, almost as if she were looking past Sparks, studying something inside her mind.

The Chairman continued. "If she accepts my offer to become a prince of the Infinite Order, Amberly will become a target to our enemies, internal and external. She needs a chaperone. Someone who is competent, lethal and someone she can trust to be absolutely loyal to her. I don't believe you are loyal to much, but you are loyal to her, your … adoptive sister."

"I hate to question a proverbial free shot of hooch," Sparks asked tentatively, "but why wouldn't you choose someone who, you know, has never… failed *you*?"

"Amberly must trust her chaperone fully and completely, and it goes without saying that she is no idiot. A chaperone that is not fully loyal to their charge, but to another interest, will not be an effective one."

"So, you are going to make Amberly queen bee on Arara, and you want me to be her personal bodyguard?" Sparks asked. "Amberly?"

Amberly wanted to say, "If I reject her, she is just going to kill me and you," but instead said, "Of course, I could think of no one better to be my chaperone than you." *I must find a way to have an unmonitored conversation with Sparks to find out where her heart lies,* Amberly thought. *I must be ready for that opportunity.*

"Should Raven Two chose you to be her chaperone, your conscription begins immediately. Should she reject you, your execution will commence once we have determined you have no information on the whereabouts of *Magnus*."

"If Amberly rejects me, save us all the drama and shoot me into space," Sparks sounded more annoyed than fearful at this point. "I didn't learn the coordinates of *Magnus* on purpose. That's why I brought you Dek Tigona. You haven't broken him yet?" Sparks spoke like she hoped the answer was yes, but she would be horrified if they had started an interrogation process so quickly.

Amberly's heart was breaking for Dek, if the Chairman did have him. If Sparks was capable of betraying Dek, Amberly figured, then she was also capable of working with the Chairman to create this lie to test Amberly. Chasm may not have Dek, or he could be dead. Amberly didn't have enough information to be sure. If they did have him, Amberly was terrified of what they would do to him. She knew first-hand the pain the Chairman could inflict. Amberly couldn't also help but hope that Sparks and Dek had created some elaborate ruse to save her from her captivity. For now, she thought submitting to the Chairman's may be the only path forward.

In truth, Dek did not know the actual location of the *Magnus,* because by this point the ship was in motion. Sparks knew it was only a matter of hours or even minutes before *Magnus* was revealed, all according to plan. It wasn't a simple plan, but it was straightforward, thought Sparks. *Magnus* revealed, *Utopia* distracted, North's team rescues Amberly, Alroy's team secures the hangar bay, and Sparks rescues Dek if needed. If *Magnus'* Marines took *Marquette*, then it was an endgame. If not, reserve runabouts would be ready to rendezvous with *Magnus* or ditch on the Lewis Islands. Alroy's team would also try to steal getaway ships from *Marquette's* hangar. *What could go wrong*? Sparks silently laughed at her own internal joke.

"I'm not sure if threatening Sparks with death if she doesn't agree is a way to ascertain if she is willing to be a good chaperone," Amberly said, hoping to increase the number of outcomes that didn't involve people dying. "Madam Chairman, couldn't we offer her another role, another alternative so she would have a legitimate choice. I don't want her to agree just because she knows it is the only way to live. Perhaps I could have a private conference with Sparks in the observation room."

"The facilitation of such a discussion would be premature. You make a good point, but when followed through to its logical conclusion, you will find it is not valid," the Chairman said. "I've studied Sparks psychological profile and all her extensive Chasm records. If she believes being your shield provides her the prerequisite … adventure, she will join you. If she doesn't, she'd rather die fighting us. She'll make us kill her before we even reach an airlock, no doubt."

"No need to wonder," Sparks jumped in. "I'm your girl. If Amberly is going to be Raven Two, where do I sign up? Sounds like a blast." *The Chairman knows you well enough*, Sparks reminded herself. *So just be who you are.*

"Good. We'll get to that in a moment," the Chairman said. "I do have one concern I'd like the two of you to address. Assuming this North is brought to heel, although he seems more like the type to fight to his needless end, I'm worried that he may create some jealousy between you two. This situation would have to be resolved to my satisfaction before I would consent to Sparks assuming a chaperone role."

"I intend to put North in my entourage. I would task him to develop my own Hawk program. As for any romantic entanglements," Amberly tried to say what she thought the Chairman would want to hear, "I wouldn't have any problem *sharing* the Commander with a loyal chaperone. It might create a closer bond."

"Unlikely," hmphed the Chairman, "but I'll consider your case."

"There would be no problem," Sparks agreed. "First of all, I've already given North the chance to blow my mind…" — Amberly heart started to race a bit. Back on *Magellan*, she had wondered how intimate North and Sparks had been — "…and he rejected me. He won't get a second chance. Second, and more importantly, if I am to be Amberly's right hand, I would never get in the way of anything she wanted. I want what she wants. … wait, that didn't sound right. What I meant to say —"

"Never mind Commander North now, as I said, I'll think on it," the Chairman interrupted. "Let's discuss something else. My chaperone told me of a third gift – that you could *deliver Alroy Macready to me.*"

The Chairman found her wedge, Sparks thought. *If Amberly is just playing along, the prospect of her father suffering at the hands of the Chairman would unnerve her. But if she really is planning to be the next Chairman…* Sparks studied Amberly's face to see her reaction, but Amberly gave Sparks nothing.

Merwin One seemed to appear out of nowhere and whispered

into the Chairman's ear. The Chairman replied to her trusted adviser in a normal voice, "So she's come out of hiding? Very well, have Mr. Tigona brought here immediately then. He has only one more use to us."

Sparks shot a private "oh, crap" look at Amberly. Amberly saw the glance and wondered if it was a warning or just a reaction to an unexpected happening.

"Well, comrades," the Chairman said. "It looks like *Magnus* has shown herself."

North and Caddo, hidden inside the *Sundance Kid*, kept a vigilant watch on North's info pad screen, which displayed the ship's exterior cameras.

"Just that woman in the white coat is guarding now," Caddo said the obvious. "She doesn't seem so tough. She looks nervous, like she wants to come in here and find something... she keeps eyeing the hatch."

Alroy Macready sat quietly across the cargo bay next to his squad. He scratched at his red beard, and then toyed with his swagger stick. Though he knew the odds were against his team, he wasn't nervous. He was ready to die. Still, he wanted to meet his daughter, if possible, before he did. He looked over at the leader of the Marines that had come to save him, the Lewis Islanders, Amberly and everyone from the Chasm tyranny.

"Thank you North, for caring for my daughter," Alroy said. "We're both lucky to count you as friend."

"Until God takes me home..." North pledged.

Standing next to North, Rhodes held a small hacking box, loosely based on the device developed by Kimberly Macready. Attached to the box were two simple receivers designed to detect transmissions on a single frequency. A light on top of the box would activate when Dek confirmed that Chasm had seen the *Magnus* bait. The second, sent by Sparks, would signal that it was a good time to try to recover Amberly.

Dek's signal lit green. "It's Dek!" Rhodes said a little too loudly.

Heads shot up from around the interior chamber.

"Okay," Alroy took command. "Remember the plan. We're going to activate the smoke. Move quickly to take your defensive positions across the bay. Make sure your vac suits are sealed and you have an extra tank of O2. Kill any Chasm troops on sight, quietly if possible. Save your grenades in case they come in force. If we lose today, a dark shadow will be cast on our beautiful island for thousands of years. But if we win today, every human from Arara to Earth wins something today – liberty. I say, liberty or death! With me?"

"Liberty or death!" several of the Irregulars chanted in response.

North looked at his strike team. "Stay together. Keep your heads. Let's find a quiet place to hide until we get Sparks' signal. Acquire the target quickly so we can help the Irregulars get a foothold for our Marines."

"North, Alroy!" Caddo called from the other side of the room. "There is no guard out there now. The doctor guarding us seems to have left also."

"A trap?" Alroy asked North.

"Maybe. Let's spring it. Ready?" North took Alroy's hand, and Alroy nodded his head. "Lydia, activate the smoke bombs."

Out of each corner of the Sundance Kid, high pressured chemical smoke plumes suddenly erupted, filling the whole bay with a white cloud in a few seconds.

"Hatch is open," an Irregular soldier shouted. "Go! Go! Go!"

Amberly gasped when a half-dozen Honor Guards marched Dek Tigona into the Chairman's private office. Since the Chasm insurrection had begun, Amberly had witnessed and been subjected to a myriad of horrific acts, but she was not sufficiently calloused for what she saw. Shirtless and shoeless, Dek's torso was covered with red, lacerations inflamed with chemical burns. His face was swollen and bruised. Many of his teeth were absent. Dek looked as if he had been beaten to within a centimeter of his life. Amberly wanted to burst into tears, but found strength in a righteous fury brewing in her heart. Any small chance that she could truly work with the Chairman to some agreeable end evaporated.

Sparks was shocked at what wasn't there: Dek's right arm. *Cleanly amputated and cauterized! They found the transmitter!* Sparks thought. *Is the mission a bust?* Sparks once again resisted the supremely strong urge to draw her sword and start slaying her enemies.

The Chairman saw Dek's bloodied body and absentmindedly licked her lips.

"Amberly," Dek smiled weakly. "I am so sorry for *Magellan*. Sorry I could not protect you then—"

"Mr. Tigona, silence, please. You are not permitted to speak here," Merwin One commanded, her voice odd harmony of malice and grace.

"What else can you do to me?" Dek mumbled to Merwin, and then spoke clearly to his muse. "Amberly, you are as beautiful as when I first saw you on Ship Day, through the observation deck window of the *American Spirit*."

"I remember… Dek, I …" Amberly struggled for words.

"Madam Chairman. Tigona sent a signal. He had this transceiver implanted in his right arm. We *removed* it," Merwin said. "The situation is moving rapidly, and I fear for your safety."

"Just tell me what happened," the Chairman projected impatience.

"About 15 minutes ago, the Command Center Duty Officer reported that *Magnus* had been detected, with all appearances of heading for a geosynchronous orbit over the main continent. I was notified and came to tell you," Merwin reported. As she spoke, Chairman seemed to go into a thoughtful trance, not unlike the one Sparks had seen Kimberly Macready perform when gathering new, critical information.

"In the meantime," Merwin continued, "the intelligence officer was notified and asked the interrogator to confront Tigona about *Magnus'* intentions, to see what he knew. I did not authorize this disclosure. When he did, Tigona somehow activated a weak, encoded transmission, by pounding his arm on a hard surface. The Duty Officer suspected a transmitter implanted in his arm, ordered the transmitter removed and then contacted me again. At this point, I was already *en route* to retrieve Tigona for you."

This isn't a tube wreck yet, Sparks thought. *We may pull this off.* The Chairman's black eyes suddenly focused on Sparks. *Shit.*

"Dek, what the dirty hell. Did you lie…?" Sparks shook her head at Dek. Sparks felt sick for throwing Dek out the proverbial airlock, but it was part of the plan. "You lied to get a free ride to

Marquette, you bastard. I thought this was about Amberly!"

"What do you know about this?" the Chairman spat at Sparks.

"Nothing, Madam chairman," Sparks glared at Dek, but her heart was bursting. "Dek made it clear he intended to save Amberly. I know the *Magnus* is ill equipped to handle *Marquette*. What is your plan, Dek?"

Dek had made Sparks promise if it came to it, she would sacrifice him if it would save Amberly. Sparks also thought about the transmitter in her own arm. She was tempted to activate it, to call North's strike team to her position, but Sparks knew that would be condemning them to death. North was good, but he wasn't going to take down the entire Honor Guard. The plan was to wait and signal with Amberly once the chaos of the Marine attack had started. *I have to stay on top of this situation*, Sparks thought. *I have to manipulate Amberly into a less secure setting, then I can come back and save Dek.*

Sparks continued, reinforcing her deception. "What the hell are you playing at, Dek? Suicide by Chasm? Really? You want to be a martyr for the redhead?"

Amberly was trying to figure out a way to help Dek. There wasn't enough time to calculate a successful path. She felt desperate and blurted out, "Madam Chairman, I will accept your terms if I have Dek Tigona for my team. He was an excellent second in command in command for me after Skylar-"

"No! We can't trust Dek or Sparks," Merwin interrupted, and drew her sidearm, pointing it in the general direction of Sparks. "This must be a set-up. We should not have brought that ship on board. Let me kill them both now. This threat is too great."

"Now wait just a dirty second," Sparks said, slowly drawing her sword and taking a step back. "Let's all keep our heads on."

"An interesting idea, *chaperone elect* of Raven Two," the Chairman smiled at Sparks, all anger and tension seeming to drain from her face. She then turned to Merwin. "Everything is fine. Relax." Merwin grudgingly pointed her gun toward the floor, and the Honor Guard under her command followed suit, but she kept a finger on the rifle's trigger.

Sparks was still in an athletic stance, sword held vertically with two hands in front of her. "What idea?"

"Merwin doesn't think you are loyal. I do. But perhaps a loyalty *test* is in order. Prove me right. Separate Mr. Tigona's head from his body."

"What!?" Sparks jaw dropped. "He's my … I mean…"

"No!" Amberly stood up. "You can't."

"Can't she?" The Chairman sounded suddenly excited, then spoke more slowly. "Can't she? Merwin, if Sparks hasn't proven her loyalty to Chasm in 60 seconds, kill both her and Dek Tigona."

"Absolutely!" Merwin's voice was laced with positive overtones. "A task to my liking."

"Now, Sparks," the Chairman said. "*Magnus* has revealed itself. Dek has no value to Chasm anymore. Eliminate him for me. It's a just and merciful sentence for a traitor to his planet and his cohort siblings."

"I won't permit it!" Amberly ran to Dek's side.

The Chairman frowned and took on the tone of a primary school teacher. "See, Merwin One, Dek has contributed even more to the common good than we had hoped. We've learned so much in this short moment about our new prince. Never be afraid to apply pressure to help distill the truth of the situation. Observe that we now know that Amberly's potential profession of faith in Chasm has little resolve. If you have to kill Sparks and Dek, please be mindful that you do not harm Raven Two. Her wavering is understandable and can be remediated. Few have been through the gauntlet like she has."

There is no way out, Sparks reasoned. *Either I take Dek out now, and maybe I can save Amberly; or Dek and I both die, and we lose everything. Dammit. Dek knew this would happen. Why did he have to be right?*

She thought again about signaling North and stalling, but with the Chairman and Amberly both in the Chairman's stronghold, Sparks knew the outcome would be failure. *So be it. Time to put on my big girl pants.*

Sparks looked to the Honor Guards escorting Dek. "Force the traitor to kneel." The guards on either side of Dek pushed down on his shoulders. He fell to his knees and winced from the pain.

"Sparks, what are you doing? Dek is your brother! He's your family," Amberly's mental matrix had just exploded, data fragments randomly flying into the dark corner of her mind. She had hoped that Sparks was just playing along, but now…

"In the Infinite Order, the only family is our glorious State, and my brothers and sisters are those who belong to the Order. Not this … zero-honor backstabber," Sparks replied flatly.

Amberly moved to stand between Sparks and Dek. The Chairman chortled in delight at the drama unfolding. Merwin was visibly nervous and calculated how quickly Sparks could turn that sword on Merwin's mistress. *Not before I could fill Sparks with bullets,* she figured. Merwin relaxed slightly.

"Sparks, *chaperone*, I order you to stand down!" Amberly tried to play the Chairman's game.

"She's not your chaperone. Not yet," the Chairman nearly shouted through a dismissing laugh, as she sat down in an empty chair next to her table and crossed her legs. "And Sparks will never be if she doesn't execute the traitor. Step aside, Amberly. Dek Tigona was dead the moment he landed on *Marquette*. Grieve him if you must. But he has forfeited his place in the Infinite Order."

"For a place much better," Dek managed to choke out, along with some blood.

Sparks looked hard into Amberly's green eyes, and shook her head ever so slightly side to side. Amberly locked into the gaze, one of Sparks' eyes in the open, and one peering through her half-mask. *I recognize the pain. What are you doing, Sparks?* she thought.

"I'm sorry, Amberly. You keep losing. Looks like the Chairman is not done making you suffer. Please, step aside," Sparks no longer held back her tears, which matched Amberly's.

"Never underestimate how powerful emotions can be, Merwin One. Rational or not, they motivate strong, decisive behavior," the Chairman instructed her chaperone, then called to Sparks. "This has become tiresome. End it, Sparks, and be fully welcomed back into the Infinite Order."

"No!" Amberly cried and threw herself on the floor next to Dek, putting her arms around his broken, bound body. She kissed him on his bloodied forehead. "Dek, please don't go now."

Dek smiled and leaned into Amberly, nuzzling his face into her hair. The closeness created a euphoria that deadened his pain and confirmed his resolve. Then he whispered into her ear so softly Amberly could barely make out what he was saying. "Trust Sparks. North is coming. I want to die for the one I love."

"Please no," Amberly sobbed. "Not yet."

Amberly turned and looked over her shoulder hard at Sparks. Sparks shook her head again, and sheathed her sword.

Dek made brief eye contact with Sparks. *Don't lose your nerve, sister,* Dek thought. *God be with you now.*

Amberly was briefly confused until Sparks reached down and yanked Amberly off of Dek. She pushed Amberly a few meters back onto the floor and stood in front of her kneeling brother.

"No!" Amberly screamed, and she tried to lunge back toward Dek. Merwin stepped forward, caught Amberly and forcefully restrained her.

"Forgive me," Sparks said, although it was not clear if she was speaking to Amberly or Dek.

Merwin looked to Dek. "Sorry for you to go, old friend. See you in hell," she spoke with an anachronistic joy.

"No," Dek smiled. "I won't be there."

In one swift motion, Sparks drew her blade, swung it high over her shoulders, then cleanly took off Dek's head.

CHAPTER TWENTY

Laden with an impressive armament, North's strike team moved out of the cover of the smoke-filled bay and into a capillary corridor. North was on point, with his anti-PDS javelin weapon at the ready. Behind him, Caddo had his explosive ammo rifle at the ready. Rhodes had no weapons out, but held the hacking box to help them through locked portals. She anxiously waited for the signal from Sparks. "Come on, roomie. Don't fail me now."

Lydia, formidable as ever, brought up the rear.

"Quickly, the storage bay is up here," North pointed to a hatch on a low ceiling 10 meters ahead. "This place will be filled with Chasm troops any second."

"Another storeroom?" Caddo sighed. "Couldn't we find a less boring place to hide?"

"Shhhh!" Rhodes turned the tables.

The team looked at Rhodes. "Rhodes? Shushing us. You of all—"

"Shut it, Caddo," North said, then he turned to Rhodes. "Come on, open this door." Rhodes moved to the front of the line, reached up and with a few taps, activated the box.

"Let's hope this thing still works," Rhodes said.

"Worked great the last time I was here," North said.

The hatch hissed open. "Everyone up the chute," the Marine commander ordered.

Caddo pulled himself up and through.

"Give me a boost," Rhodes told North.

North made a step out of his hands and lifted his communications officer through the hole. Then he followed her. Lydia came up the chute last.

Once she was through, North manually pulled the hatch shut. He surveyed the dimly lit room, mostly filled with spare parts for corvettes and runabouts. He looked over at Caddo who was chewing on a protein ball. North rolled his eyes.

"Hey, man's gotta eat."

"Any word from Sparks?" North asked.

"Think I would be just sitting on this box if I heard from Sparks?" Rhodes replied.

"Lydia, did anyone see us come in?" North asked the woman who had been bringing up the rear.

"Nope," Lydia replied.

Three knocks were heard on the floor hatch.

"I didn't see anyone," Lydia mouthed.

"Let's just be quiet and see if they'll go away?" Rhodes said under her breath.

North put a finger over his mouth, grabbed the javelin from the strap on his back, and gripped it firmly.

Again, knocking, and then a muffled voice. "Commander North. I need to talk to you."

North considered the others' expressions. "I'm gonna open it."

"No, you'll blow our cover," Caddo whispered.

"If they know that North is in here, our cover is blown already," Lydia straightened up and said in a normal voice. "See what she wants."

North pointed to the far corner of the storage unit, and the rest of the squad moved to hide back in that direction. He tapped on the hatch three times and said, "I'm coming down." He double-checked the pressure indicator as a force of habit, and when he noted the light was green, he swung the manual wheel on the hatch. He peered through the hatch and saw no one. "Hello?"

North grabbed onto his javelin with one hand, and assisted with his free arm, he sprung himself down onto the floor of the corridor.

"Drop the weapon," a female voice said from behind him. "I mean you no harm."

North did not comply with the command. Instead, he whirled around to face not two meters away the same woman who had dismissed the guards earlier from the *Sundance Kid*. She held what looked like a stun gun aimed squarely at North's brawny chest.

"How do you know who I am?" North asked, poised to strike.

Dr. Michelle Leigh lowered her weapon, resigned. *What does it matter anyway?* she thought. *If he doesn't kill me, the Chairman will.*

North looked up and down the hall and feeling exposed, grabbed Dr. Leigh and pulled her into a capillary nook less than a meter from the open hatch. "How do you know me?" North repeated his question, but didn't release the doctor.

"I saw you leading a team up into that storage room," Michelle said, taking the Marine in again with her eyes. "You look, well, just like she described you,"

"She?"

"Amberly Macready. I'm her doctor," Michelle explained. "She talked a lot about you. And Dek Tigona. Someone named Sparks turned him into the Chairman. Poor man. Doesn't matter. Are you here to free Amberly?"

"Do you know where she is?" North demanded. "Tell me."

"Of course. She is with the Chairman now. When she's done, I'll be summoned to escort her back to her room and do her daily health diagnostics. That is going to be your best chance to nab her."

"Where? How far?"

Lydia slid down the hatch and stepped into the nook. "Sorry. Eavesdropping. Why do you trust this woman? Let's bring her into the storage room and interrogate her properly!" Lydia made a menacing fist.

North looked at Dr. Leigh. "Why are you helping us? Isn't Amberly your prisoner?"

"I am trying to make up for ... the horrible things... I did," Michelle said.

"What horrible things?" Lydia demanded. She stepped closer to Michelle, towering over the doctor.

"For nearly two years..." Michelle hesitated. "I'm sorry... I was..."

"Spit it out," Lydia growled.

"I... I was part of a team of medical scientists who were responsible for ... torturing Amberly. It was her punishment for killing Raven One," Michelle confessed. "But all that is done now. She's okay, mostly. Amberly was in solitary confinement for the past year, but we brought her out within the last week. The Chairman is trying to recruit Amberly to help her cloning project."

"Cloning project?" Lydia asked and turned to North. "That must have been what Isabella was talking about."

"Take this info chit," the doctor produced an isolated data storage device from the pocket in her white coat. "It will show you the best place you can set up an ambush when I am escorting Amberly back. It also has the random-assigned patrol routes for today. It may be just me on the escort, but I won't help you – you'll have to take her from me by force. They'll be watching and I prefer *not* to be tortured and killed for helping you."

"That's reasonable, I suppose," Lydia deadpanned.

"I am assuming you have a way off this station, but don't tell me your plan," Michelle said. "I can't promise I'll keep it secret if they find me out."

"On behalf of Amberly, thanks for this," North said, taking the chit and placing it close to Condi, which wirelessly absorbed the data.

"Commander North, Amberly is the most remarkable person I have ever known. She has been so strong, so clever through the worst sorts of… well. Of course, she was engineered for greatness."

Dr. Leigh's use of the word engineered caught Lydia's attention. She wanted to ask the doctor to elaborate, but thought better of it.

"Listen. I used to believe in the Chairman, but she's insane. All I want is for Amberly to have a chance to live a normal life again. Look, they may already suspect me. I'm not brave. If they torture me, it won't take long before I'm blabbing about you. So take Amberly and get her out of here. I'm sorry."

With that, Dr. Leigh turned and walked around the corner and out of sight.

Sparks kneeled beside Amberly to comfort her, pushing down her own grief and self-loathing at what she had just done. *I am a survivor. I do what I must. I am an adopted daughter of the great Raven One,* Sparks thought. *I will overcome, and I can be strong for my sister. I'm sorry Dek, but you asked for it.*

Amberly hid her face under her long hair and wept. With Dek's final words, she reassembled her mental matrix and placed the data back in proper order. *North is coming. Sparks and Dek were working together on a bigger plan. Sparks is undercover. Dek gave his life to sell it,* Amberly processed. *I must not compromise Sparks.* She clutched at Sparks hand with the appearance of intense grieving, but carefully and clandestinely traced two words into her palm: I KNOW.

"Well done, Sparks," the Chairman beamed, though she was distracted by the smell of Dek's blood flowing onto the floor. Her dark eyes kept darting back to the sight, even though she was trying to resist. "You will be a most excellent chaperone for Raven Two!"

"That murderous slut will never be my chaperone, grandmother," Amberly growled, picking herself off of the floor.

"Oh, the emotionalism of youth," the Chairman said, "is good for recruiting useful idiots, but unbecoming for a prince of Arara. Don't be wasteful. Sparks is a great asset." The Chairman nodded, and a pair of orderlies stepped forward and began to slip Tigona's remains into a body bag. The macabre sight tore at Amberly and briefly captured the attention of those collected in the Chairman's office.

"With all due respect, madam Chairman," Merwin called attention back to herself, "may I place both Sparks and Amberly under guard for now? I've summoned Dr. Leigh to escort them to the holding center."

"Fine, fine. I must be getting to the Command Center anyway," the Chairman said. "*Utopia* and her flotilla will be engaging the *Magnus* soon, and I'd like to oversee the fall of Earth's mightiest warship."

"Thank you, madam Chairman. I will see to—" Merwin was suddenly silent as she listened to someone on her inner ear radio. The blood seemed to drain from her face. She spoke directly back to the caller. "Thank you, Captain. Take prisoners if you can. I'll inform the Chairman and will send down a detachment of the Honor Guard as soon as the Chairman is secured in the command center."

The pale Merwin turned to her boss. "Madam Chairman, your personal hangar bay has been infiltrated with hostile forces." Merwin waved her hand, and a screen materialized from nowhere, showing security footage from the hangar bay. A firefight had broken out between at least a dozen intruders, and then the Chairman, studying the screen, saw their leader and recognized him. "Alroy Macready. What? How! Oh, now I see. Sparks, what a clever girl. She almost put one over on the Chairman of the Infinite Order. Impressive," the Chairman said as she focused on the battle scene.

"Dad? Dad!" Even Amberly's impressive new brainpower was beginning to be overwhelmed by the fast turn of events. *Sparks must have killed Dek to protect something much larger,* Amberly thought.

"Merwin, make sure you do not let Alroy Macready off this station. Bring him to me alive. But first secure Amberly and Sparks. Merwin, where *is* Sparks?"

Merwin One surveyed the office. Near a side exit, an Honor Guard was slumped against the wall, motionless, his neck oddly angled and obviously broken. Sparks was nowhere to be seen. *I've underestimated Sparks,* Merwin thought.

The chaperone looked at her Chairman. "She can't be far. We will recover her shortly." Merwin's fear of the Chairman in this moment dimmed her bright demeanor. She turned to one of her guard captains. "Recover Sparks. Go!"

"Take Amberly and secure her, then meet me and the rest of my war council at the command center," the Chairman ordered Merwin.

"With all due respect, one of my Honor Guard can handle escort duty," Merwin pleaded. "The station is under some sort of attack. As your chaperone, I should personally be protecting you."

"The quality of your chaperone skills has recently come under question," the Chairman said. The words smacked Merwin harder than any backhand could. "Besides, Amberly is much more valuable than I am. Go and do as I say."

Merwin took Amberly by the arm.

Dr. Leigh walked into the office with her armed escort. She was visibly disturbed.

"We've had a productive meeting, Amberly," the Chairman smiled as Amberly was escorted out of the door. "We'll visit again soon; and when we do, your father will be with me."

North and his team had taken up positions in vacant offices along a large corridor about 200 meters around a bend from the Raven One Memorial Commons. The entire quadrant of *Marquette* was sparsely populated, dedicated to the Chairman's personal use. North's plan would be a simple ambush, then a fast break for the Chairman's hangar bay and while the *Magnus*

Marines take the waypoint.

Lydia heard footfalls. "Someone's running this way." The squad, two in offices on either side of the hall, crouched below the window line.

"Wait for it," North said under his breath, broadcast to the inner ear radios of his team.

The footsteps slowed then stopped, but based on the sounds, North figured the runner stopped about five meters from their ambush point.

"Keep it quiet, everyone," North whispered.

Suddenly the second light on Rhodes' hacking box lit up. "Sparks signaled us!"

Caddo slapped his hand over Rhodes' mouth. "Shhhh!"

"Come on North, get here soon," a familiar voice said in the direction of the runner.

"It's Sparks," Lydia said, and she and North popped out of cover.

"Sparks!" North called out.

Sparks saw North, and North saw that she had been crying. "What's going on?"

"That was faster than I thought," Sparks forced a smile through her tears. "No time to explain. Draw your weapons. Here come the bad guys." Sparks turned her back on North and faced the way she came. She drew her bloodied sword and took a defensive stance. North in turn drew his javelin, and Lydia readied her shoulder-mounted stun cannon.

Within a few seconds, four blue and green clad Honor Guards rounded the corner.

"There she is!" one shouted. "Wait, who are *they*?" The Guard pointed at the North and Lydia.

"Who cares? Mow 'em down and get Sparks!"

Lydia opened fire, and blasted down a Guard. The stun cannon had limited effect on the Guard, whose armor was designed to absorb stun energy. But he was unable to activate his own weapon. North had simultaneously flung his javelin, piercing the face of Lydia's target.

Sparks jumped and rolled to avoid taking fire, holding her sword with one hand and pulling out a pistol with her other. She discharged the weapon several times as she charged the Guard.

The bullets melted in the Guard's PDS, but they created enough chaos to keep her target off balance until she was in melee range.

Sparks dropped her gun, so both of her hands could grasp the hilt of her sword. The Guard she was attacking raised up her heavily armored arm, which took little damage as Sparks brought her blade down. The Guard pushed Sparks back and drew her own two-sided, 30-centimeter serrated short blade. The women squared off, and Sparks took a bold swing for the neck, missing, but driving her opponent back. The Chasm warrior sliced at Spark's exposed torso, but she was able to parry the blow by bringing her sword into an underhanded spin.

One Guard was dead from a javelin to the face, and the second was locked in a blade fight with Sparks, leaving two to deal with. North was moving behind cover fire from Lydia to retrieve his javelin when several bullets struck his chest armor. The armor held, but North was knocked down and the wind was knocked out of him. One of the two Guards fired a semi-automatic bullet rifle at Lydia, forcing her to duck through an office door to take cover. She threw off the stun cannon and grabbed a hand stun gun and poked around the cover, throwing random bolts to distract the Guards. The free Guard pulled North's javelin out of his dead comrade's face, twirled it and started closing the three-meter gap to North, who was struggling to catch his breath.

Sparks saw North was in trouble out of the corner of her eye. She feigned a swipe, then kicked her opponent in the shin, spun around and flung her sword at the javelin-wielding Guard attacking North. North saw the point of Spark's sword exit between the Guard's mouth and nose. The Guard's eyes went wide, and he collapsed at North's feet, dead. North grabbed the javelin from the dead man's hands and sprinted toward Sparks.

Sparks opponent leapt on Sparks from behind, her blade deflected by Sparks' armor, and they both fell to the ground. Sparks rolled over with enough time to grab the wrist of the arm that held the short blade. She was struggling to keep the Guard who had pinned her from lethally lacerating her throat.

A shot fired, blood splattered, and the Guard rolled off of Sparks, dead.

"Someone told me the PDS doesn't work at point blank range," North smiled wearily.

"That was me," Sparks said.

The remaining Guard dropped her weapon and raised her hands as Lydia and North and Sparks confronted her, weapons drawn. "I surrender."

Sparks retrieved her sword.

"Where is Amberly?" North asked the Guard.

"Who?" the Guard played dumb.

Sparks took a swinging leap and brought her blade around, cleaning decapitating a second person in one day.

"That was for Dek, bitch."

"I was trying to find out where Amberly is," North tried to control his anger. "Dek? Dead?"

"I had to off him," Sparks said distantly. "It's what the fool wanted."

"You had to *off* Dek? You mean kill him?" Lydia was trying to understand what happened. "Amberly will be crushed."

"She knows. She was there," Sparks said, trying to clean the blood from her blade before returning it to its sheath.

"I'm sorry, Sparks," North placed a hand on Sparks' shoulder. "He said he knew he was going —"

"We can all have a cry party about Tigona later. Amberly will be by here soon. Let's make sure we get her so Dek didn't die for nothing."

"We have Caddo and Rhodes for the ambush just a dozen or so yards away," Lydia informed Sparks.

"There are too many of them to take conventionally. They also have Merwin – the Chairman's *numero uno* bodyguard. She'll kick your ass, lickety-split."

"You have a plan, though," North suggested.

"You bet your skin-tight polyvinyl pants. Let's move these bodies. Hurry up, suckers."

Merwin led the escort. The apartment where Amberly had been under house arrest for the past several days wasn't far from the Chairman's Office. Amberly and Dr. Leigh walked in the middle of eight Honor Guards – two in front, two in back, and two on each side.

"Hold up!" Merwin shouted and drew her blade. She saw a large pool blood on the floor of the corridor with red streaks leading around the corner. *Sparks!* Merwin thought. *She must have taken out the squad I sent after her. I've underestimated her again. But where are the bodies?*

"Taki, Shehzad, stay with Raven Two," Merwin sternly ordered. "The rest of you, room-by-room, clear each of the offices along this corridor. Be wary of ambush."

Merwin and four of her guards rounded the corner, but before they could start their search, they found what they were looking for.

Merwin One saw a fine, brown-haired Marine with a scar on his chin. The Marine hoisted the head of a member of the Chairman's Honor guard on a javelin-like pike. Merwin was momentarily repulsed at the grotesque display, but kept her composure.

North was flanked by two armed females – one impressive looking one with a shoulder-mounted stun cannon, the other a dark-haired, with just a pistol pointed for action. She did note that along about four meters back, leaning next to the piled bodies of her missing squad, was an unimpressive looking man working a vape stick.

"Where's Sparks?" North demanded.

"Commander North, you are just as … impressive… as Amberly described you," Merwin smiled, stepping into a defensive stance. Her guards raised their weapons on the cue. "Why are you looking for Sparks?"

"And, you must be the invincible Merwin One," North said. "I must say, you are even … better looking than Dek described you. He was an old boyfriend?"

"Sorry, I do have one traditionalist custom," Merwin bantered. "No kissing and telling."

"I'm not in the mood anyway. Give us Sparks. She betrayed our brother Dek," North said.

"I don't understand," Merwin was confused. "Sparks isn't with you? Bah. By orders of the Chairman, surrender now or prepare to die."

"It doesn't matter," North said, as he pounded the blunt end of his javelin weapon against the floor. The decapitated head dislodged and rolled across the floor.

"You Earth loyalists are sick," Merwin said, and turned to the

Guard immediately to her left. "Get backup."

"Do you think she's hiding a point-defense system under that pretty white dress?" Lydia smirked.

Merwin instinctively jumped into action, following her life of combat training. Sensing she was going to be Lydia's target, she dove toward North, swiping her blade. She was too far to strike, but forced him into a back step between her and Lydia's weapon.

Lydia ignored Merwin and instead blasted one of the Guards with her stun rifle. He fell, but another took shots at Lydia, forcing her to retreat through an office door. Rhodes similarly had picked her target, an androgynous Honor Guard escort. She hit the target in the head, or would have, if the PDS hadn't dissolved the bullets into molecular dust.

"That was not encouraging," Rhodes quipped as she turned tail and ran down the hall.

"Capture her!" Merwin said. "We need to know how many of them are on the waypoint and what their plans are." Two guards took off after Rhodes. The first sprinted by Caddo, who had his arms up to signify his surrender. When the second one passed, Caddo dropped his arms and tackled her from behind. She dropped her gun, and the pair struggled for it.

Merwin leapt for North, sword held high. North grabbed both ends of his javelin and used the staff's mid-section to block the blade. As the blade bounced off the javelin, Merwin swung her elbow hard into North's gut. The unexpectedly powerful blow knocked wind out of the Marine for a second time, but Merwin also recoiled in pain, as her bare elbow slammed into North's armored abdomen.

North sucked hard and swung his javelin around and squared off against Merwin again, who already had her blade in the *en garde* position. She feigned a strike for North's head, then thrusted for his left leg. North parried the strike and moved to round her, looking for an opening to use the javelin offensively.

"Well met," Merwin gave a quick nod of her head, smiling joyfully at North while stepping in a rounding pattern to keep closer to her adversary. She knew if he had too much space, he'd impale her with that pointed stick of his. She hadn't had this much fun in a long time.

North thought he might be able to slip his weapon by

Merwin's defenses and maybe peg her foot. He moved closer, stabbing for her right foot while keeping the javelin positioned between him and Merwin's sword.

Too easy, Merwin thought as she brought her left foot around kicking the javelin, directing it harmlessly away. North fumbled and almost lost his grasp on his weapon, and Merwin found her opportunity after an elegant twirl, slicing at North's left arm. North attempted to leap back out of the way, but he was too late. Her blade made contact and sliced through polycarbon into flesh. North grunted as he rolled backward, but he knew from experience the wound wasn't serious.

The escort Guard who had taken the brunt of Lydia's stun fire roused himself, looked for Lydia and didn't see her. He saw Caddo and his comrade struggling over a gun on the floor, and his commander, Merwin, and the lead Marine squaring off. *Merwin's got this*, he thought as he raised his rifle and paced over to struggling Caddo. He poked Caddo with his rifle. "Give up or eat lead."

"Okay, I give," Caddo said, relaxing his grip on the gun, and the guard he was wrestling seized it. With two guns now pointing at him, Caddo was more emphatic, and curled into a fetal position. "I surrender. I give up. You win."

"Stand down," the androgynous Honor Guard called out from down the hall. The guard had Rhodes zip cuffed and was flanked by at least a dozen additional Chasm troops.

"Sorry, boss," Rhodes said loudly. "I couldn't get away."

A scream came from back down the corridor, which was silenced suddenly, followed by a thud.

North winked at Merwin.

"Taki, Shehzad, report. What's going on?" Merwin spoke into her comm unit. "Taki, Shehzad!"

"Yeah, they're not in a talking mood anymore," Sparks said as she appeared from around the corner. She pushed Amberly in front of her, her arm wrapped around Amberly's upper torso with her sword drawn against the redhead's neck. "Merwin, you've lost three heads for Dek's. And the exchange rate is only going to go up."

"No one made you kill Dek," Merwin argued. "That blood is on your hands."

"Maybe," Sparks growled. "All the more reason I need to avenge him. But never mind Dek. I have the Chairman's prize. You want her to be the fifth head I take today? I'm a regular eff'n guillotine!"

"Let Amberly go, Sparks," Merwin commanded. "You've lost. Go with grace, old friend."

"Yeah, no," Sparks said. "You see I don't really care about the Chairman's science fair project. But I do know that the Chairman needs Amberly alive. From my side of the looking glass, the only thing keeping me alive now is Amberly. So, you and your group are going to stand down and give us safe passage back to the Chairman's hangar, or you are going to have to explain to the Chairman why Amberly Macready couldn't keep her head."

Amberly looked up, her face blotted with tears. Dek had told her to trust Sparks, but the next moment, Sparks killed Dek. Clearly, Dek sacrificed himself to buy Sparks time. *Dek sacrificed himself for me*, Amberly thought. *No greater love.* It was the only explanation that made sense. Which meant Sparks was bluffing … Amberly hoped. Amberly's not-dead father's presence on *Marquette* also indicated some plan was going on that was multiple levels deep. She would have to trust Sparks. As she felt the bloodied steel against her throat, she figured she didn't really have much of a choice. *Play along*, Amberly told herself. *Play along.* Amberly took a deep breath and lifted her head, and looked beyond Merwin down the hallway.

Her heart leapt.

North! Amberly wanted to call out, but she refrained. Seeing him, here now, as Dek had promised, steadied Amberly. After years of pain, including the searing wound of losing Dek, she willed herself to endure a little longer. When she was in isolation, she would fight insane loneliness by imagining North taking her into his strong arms and holding her tight against his chest. There he was, just meters away. *So close. Keep it together, Amberly,* she thought, though she could not stop what seemed like endless tears.

"You don't mean that. You wouldn't decapitate Raven Two," Merwin said, slowly sheathing her own sword and putting her hands forward to signal calm.

"I just took my brother's head off for the sake of this mission,"

Sparks laughed. "He was the closest thing to family I'll ever have. You don't think I'll slit the throat of my *adopted* sister?"

"Amberly's not the mission? If you didn't come here to recover Amberly, then why did you come? Why are you here?"

"Wouldn't you like to know?" Sparks asked. "It doesn't matter. If you don't make a path for North, me and our pals, Amberly Macready is dead. Sure, we all die, too, but somehow, I don't think the Chairman will really care about us at that point. Let us go, and Amberly lives so maybe you can recruit her to be your queen another day. Don't let us go, and well, the miracle is over." Sparks pulled her blade so it indented the pale skin on Amberly's exposed neck.

"Sparks is crazy, Merwin," Amberly squirmed in Sparks's grip.

"Help us on our way. Chop, chop, Merwin," Sparks said with a wry smile. "Pun intended."

"Sparks, don't do anything drastic," North said. "I'm sure Merwin here will see reason."

"North, Lydia, all of you," Sparks called across the standoff. "Come to me now. Hurry."

Sparks started pulling Amberly back toward the hall.

"Bah!" Merwin felt helpless. "Go, Sparks. You know she'll kill me."

"Come with us then," Sparks said. "We'll give you a better shake than the Chairman."

"No thanks," Merwin said. "The worst parts of hell are reserved for traitors. You and your allies are not going to come out on top of this. The Chairman will have Amberly, sooner or later. She is a patient woman."

North, Caddo, Lydia and Rhodes crossed past Merwin. The Chasm squad leader gave Merwin a look as if to ask if he should stop them, but Merwin responded by pushing her hands down, palms open. North pulled out his knife and cut Rhodes free.

Walking backwards, Sparks pulled Amberly around the corner.

"Nice to meet you," Caddo waved at Merwin. She fumed.

"If I see anyone tailing us, or you try to ambush us, I will kill Amberly cleanly," Sparks shouted.

CHAPTER TWENTY-ONE

Lewis Island Irregular Captain Red, *nee* Alroy Macready, was full of fight. Chasm had taken away everything from him, twice.

With him were a score of Lewis Island Irregulars, former farmers, shopkeepers and craftsmen, whose only care, live or die, was making Chasm bleed.

Disregard for survival made them especially dangerous.

Alroy himself was not as carefree. He had almost recovered what he had longed for – a family. He couldn't remember life with his daughters, but he felt a huge hole in his soul — and now he knew why. He tried to fill that hole with the lost Blaisé. Now, with the hope of making a family again with Amberly, Kora and grandson Alroy, Red was ready to kill.

They only had to hold the hangar for an hour or less now, until North's backup Marines could land and take *Waypoint Marquette* by force.

Armed with powerful shock sticks, melee weapons designed to bypass Chasm personal defenses, the Irregulars fanned out of the *Sundance Kid* and put down the handful of unsuspecting Chasm agents guarding Chairman's private hangar. The exchange took longer than Alroy had hoped, but the Chasm backup he had feared hadn't come… yet.

"Fiat, Alfonsi," Roy shouted. "Quick, get the goop!"

Alfonsi, whose hobby was chemistry, had mixed a quick expanding compound that formed an almost impassible, flame resistant and gelatinous blue foam wall. Packed into grenades for distribution, Fiat pulled one from his bandoleer.

"Goop grenade away," he smiled and chucked the grenade so it landed at the exit portal which led to the interior of the waypoint. A blob of sticky substance began to swell in and around the door, making the way was impassable. If a Chasm trooper did manage to push herself through the goop filling the doorway, she'd be vulnerable to enemy attack as she emerged.

Fiat bombed the secondary maintenance portal.

"Okay, alpha and beta squads take up positions around the doors. Anything comes through the goop, give them the stick," Alroy commanded. "Gamma squad, keep patrolling the parameter. Sooner or later, they are going to find another way in here, so let's not get caught with our britches down. Engineering team, see if you can bust into that yacht and hack it. May come in handy. And for God's sake, everyone, make sure you have your vacsuit helmets handy if we need to open the door in a hurry for North's jarheads."

Elizabeth Hawkins looked through *Magnus*' bridge viewport down onto the capital of Arara, thousands of miles below. She longed for the surface; to experience humanity on a planet before she died. It was so close. However, the planet might as well be a light year or twelve away if they were unable to neutralize *Utopia*. If that were the case, the *Magnus* itself was likely to be her space tomb.

It wasn't that she feared death. Rather, she was insatiably curious what sand on a beach felt like between her toes. Hawkins wanted to experience the wind on her face and the sun on her skin. The whole world right before her catalyzed desire.

After surviving the coup of Skylar Triggs and the destruction of the *American Spirit*, she no longer worried about things she could not control. For instance, the threatening approach of the *Utopia* along with nearly a dozen escort corvettes.

"Captain," Hawkins stoically reported, "here she comes."

"Great. They are taking the bait this time," XO and Acting Captain Alecia Blight stood up from the captain's chair and bounded over to the tactical table. "Helm, get us out of orbit. Full maneuvering thrusters. Everyone, it's just like we practiced. Start with more space between us and *Arara*."

Lt. Cho was already at the tactical table, examining the red triangle that represented *Utopia* as it rapidly closed in on the green circle in the center of the display. "Missile range in two minutes."

"Mr. Fuego, tell gunnery to stick to our training. Let them fire first. Remember our first salvo must take their escort. We need a clear field of battle," Alecia encouraged.

"Flak cannons standing by," the gunnery liaison Boot Fuego reported.

"I wish we hadn't left our fighter escorts in dark space," Cho groused. "If they can't inject our Marines onto *Marquette*—"

"North will get the job done," Alecia defended her rival-turned-ally. "Besides, they don't have *Marquette* to save them this time. It's a fair fight. Gunnery, open tubes 22 through 35. Prep the VI for targeting those corvettes."

"Prepare for inertia dampening," the helmsman announced. Cho gripped the table. "Here we go. Three, two, one."

The *Magnus* jumped away from Arara at thousands of kilometers per second. "*Utopia* and escort are adjusting course to pursue," Cho read the tactical screen. He forced himself to ignore the now familiar, weird feeling in his gut caused by the artificial gravity system compensating for what otherwise would be human-crushing inertia.

"They'll hit us first with a missile barrage, and then the corvettes will come in while we are reeling to finish the job," Alecia said. "But their escort fleet will be cautious. They don't know where our fighters are."

"Hopefully by the time they realize our corvettes and runabouts are assaulting *Marquette* it will be too late for *Marquette* to mount a defense," Elizabeth said.

"That's the idea," Alecia replied.

About seventy red dots departed from the red triangle. "Looks like they emptied *all* their silos," Cho said. "Radiological scans indicate several nuclear warheads."

Elizabeth gave Cho a dirt-is-about-to-hit-the-fan look. He nodded.

"All the silos. That's bold. If we survive, it will take them a while to rearm. We should be able to destroy the escort before then," Blight said. "Flack cannons free in 60 seconds. Damage control teams stand by. Release command of particle beams to the VI. Focus on those nukes.

Blight looked around the bridge at her officers. She was proud of them all.

"God have mercy on us. This is it. All hands, brace for impact."

The Chairman stood on *Marquette's* commander's platform in the middle of the waypoint's central command center. *Marquette's* cencomm was almost identical to *Magellan's*, with three balconies of duty stations situated in an oval around the command station. From that point, the Chairman could give orders to the officers and bureaucrats that ran the entire station.

Yeoman Carnell, perfectly made up in his Infinite Order officer's uniform, called to the Chairman from the nearby communications station. "Madam Chairman. Per your orders, *Utopia* reports it has launched a hard strike against *Magnus*. Five nuclear warheads are away."

The Chairman waved at the pretty young woman sitting at the primary tactical station. "Throw up a tactical for me."

The junior Chasm officer did as instructed, and a magnetic resonance screen materialized. The missiles would strike the *Magnus* any second now. That ship represented the last real threat to Chasm. The Chairman was anxious to see its demise.

The Honor Guard's second-in-command, Ka Top, walked up to the command platform to report. Ka was a hulking, swarthy man, graceless to a fault. What he lacked in class, he made up for in slavish devotion to the Chairman. His desire to please her above all else made his current task, delivering bad news, particularly undesirable.

"Madam Chairman," Ka Top bowed his clean-shaven head. "We've lost contact with the security team that engaged the intruders in your hangar. We presume they are incapacitated or dead."

"Of course," the Chairman smiled, but anger pulsated from her dark eyes. "Alroy Macready should not be underestimated. I assume you've deployed sufficient troop support to finish them."

"Well, ma'am," Ka Top nervously stuttered, "by the time backup arrived, the enemy sealed us off from the hanger by jamming the portals with some sort of sticky, semi-fluid matter. We can't get through presently. Our engineers are working on a solution."

"Let us end this distraction," the Chairman sighed. "Vent them out. Just open the space doors and let the vacuum do your work. Poetic, really. They did that *twice* to us, you remember."

"As you wish. I'll see to it immediately."

"Ka Tap. One point that is critically important. Please personally see to it that you recover all the bodies that go out into space, particularly Alroy Macready's. His is of the utmost importance to me. If you fail in this, your punishment would be

… severe."

"I would not fail you," Ka Top bowed again.

"Now, make haste." The Chairman turned back to her yeoman. "What's the status of those nukes?"

"Looks like four, no three nukes are going to make it into the flack field," Cho shouted.

"We can take that hit, right?" Hawkins asked. Her stoic resolve had melted, and her heart beat wildly.

"Direct hits from three? No way. The flack fields will hopefully tear those missiles up before they hit us. If we're lucky, they won't detonate. But better they detonate away from the ship than on our hull."

Blight wrung her hands as she watched red dots move into the flack field. The first dot disappeared.

"Yes!" Boot pumped his hand in the air.

The second dot disappeared, and in the same instant a loud clap rang through the *Magnus* and the viewports flashed a blinding white.

"Detonated in the flack field, two kilometers starboard," Boot reported.

"Hawkins, patch me with engineering," Blight said.

"Ouch," Bollard, the engineering chief, said over the comms. "That shook us up."

"How bad?" Blight asked her husband. "Damage report!"

"Still working on figuring it out."

Screeeeeeeacccccchhhh! A loud, high-pitched sound that made Alecia think of metal ripping filled the bridge, along with a second, more blinding flash.

"Hull breach!" Cho said.

A hundred automated warnings seemed to fire off at the same time, and the bridge buzzed with fresh frantic activity.

"It wasn't a direct hit, but it was close, less than a kilometer off the bow," the gunnery liaison reported.

Betsy let out a breath she'd been holding in. "We've cleared the board," Hawkins told the captain. "No more incoming."

"Where's that hull breach?" the captain demanded. "Let's get it contained." "E deck. Looks like it was just below observation!"

Bollard shouted through the comms. "Sending rapid response teams now to seal it off."

"Chief, how are the engines?"

"Everything is fully green," Bollard replied. "No damage to engines or the power plant."

"Helm, bring us around. Set a direct course for the *Utopia*. Let's play chicken. Gunnery, prepare to fire missiles. Target the escorts only, not the *Utopia*."

Hawkins instinctively gripped the armrest of her chair as the *Magnus* executed a 180-degree maneuver while traveling at thousands of kilometers per second. A small wave of nausea hit her, but she fought it from freeing whatever was in her stomach.

"You think these missiles will get past their point defense system?" she looked to Cho.

"Oh yeah. Ten hydra warheads in each missile. They couldn't touch the *Utopia*, but when they deploy, the sheer number and disbursement of projectiles should easily overload the PDS of the small ships," Cho explained, but Hawkins didn't hear him.

"No," Hawkins put her hand over her mouth as she read a report off her infopad. "Rapid response team reports dozens of fatalities on E deck. Some vented into space," Hawkins immediately wondered which of her friends had been killed.

"Damnit!" Cho swore, clenching his teeth.

"Don't lose heart!" Alecia said. "Focus. We can take the hit. On my mark, gunnery liaison."

"Yes ma'am."

The helmsman looked up from his control deck. "On course for *Utopia*. They are attempting evasion. Looks like they are buying that we're gunning for the big bird."

"Here come the little birds," Cho said. "They are vectoring for the lower bow, going at us where we are wounded."

"Son of a dirt-licker. Bollard, pull your response teams back!" Alecia commed the engineer. "Gunnery control, fire at your discretion."

"How long before the *Utopia* has reloaded its silos?" Hawkins asked.

"Maybe three, four minutes," Cho guessed.

A tinny woosh sound reverberated through the bulkheads.

"Missiles away," Fuego announced.

"That can't be right, check your equipment," Chasm agent Shambhav, the *Marquette* surveillance officer on duty, directed his lieutenant. "Runabouts can't just show up out of deep space. Where did they come from?"

The pair sat in a small monitoring room fixed on a tower that rose above the *Marquette* garden dome. The room was the 'highest' point on the waypoint. Through plexiglass viewports on the floor, the pair could see the vast gardens that help to feed the citizens of *Marquette* before it was moved to Arara orbit. The whole ceiling was plexiglass as well, and from that perspective, there was nothing to see but millions of stars.

"No way the scanner is wrong," Kanokwan, the junior officer, defended her work. "Look! What else could those be besides runabouts running silent?"

"I dunno, maybe those are meteors or something," Shambhav surmised.

"In *formation*?" Kanokwan challenged her boss.

"You are right. Meteors wouldn't run in formation. Probably a glitch. Get IT up here."

"What the hell?" Kanokwan raised both her hands to her head and pulled on her short black hair in frustration. "You've got to warn command!"

"Now wait a minute," Shambhav pushed back, his face flush with anger, offended for being shoved around by his subordinate. "We don't want to look like we are *paranoid*. Give it some time. Run the scan again in a few minutes and verify. Then, have the engineers check the scanners."

He paused, and then to make sure Kanokwan understood her place, he added, "That's an order, Kan."

Kanokwan turned around in her seat and humphed. She always suspected that Shambhav was an idiot, and now she knew she was right. *Well, if those ships are coming and it's bad news, I guess it's on his head,* she thought. *But what if those ships are really bad news? A rebellion against the Chairman? It wouldn't matter whose fault it was. Dirty idiot!*

She quietly pulled out her infopad and started manually entering a warning. She'd send a message to that cute member of the Chairman's staff she'd hooked up with last week. *Carnell will know what to do.*

"The calm before the storm, eh Captain?" Alfonsi asked Roy.

"I can't imagine they are going to be happy to just let us wait here in our own self-made prison. They are up to something, Corporal," Red said, as he rubbed his ruddy beard. "Have the snipes broken into the Chairman's Yacht, yet?"

"Nope."

"Did those yahoos even study engineering? Pull them off and have them get ready to hack the space doors so we can let the cavalry in. They should be here soon."

"Yes, sir. Shouldn't take long with that handy hacking box your ex-wife made," Alfonsi said, and he immediately wished he hadn't.

"Kimberly Macready isn't my *ex*-wife," Alroy sounded annoyed. Try as he may, he didn't remember her and was still surprised that he would be suckered into a fifteen-year long relationship with the enemy. "She's my *late* wife."

Alfonsi turned and started waving down the engineers tinkering on the exterior of the Chairman's private ship. "Hey, start to work on cracking the doors."

Alroy sighed and looked at the large space doors. The enemy was sealed out of the hangar for now. But they would figure out a way to dissolve the goop soon enough. *Or they might blast through with explosives. But we're sealed in too, trapped between our own mischief and the coldness of space,* Alroy thought. *Unless those doors open.* "Hey, everyone, double-check your vacsuit integrity."

"You think they would, you know?" Alfonsi tilted his head in the direction of the space doors.

"Yes. Now that you mention it. Everyone, put your vacuum helmets on, now," Roy shouted urgently.

Alfonsi snapped the helmet off of his gear pack and started to pull it over his large, sweaty head. Alroy looked toward the main door, where Alpha Squad had taken position, and saw his troops doing the same. Roy swung around to glance at the beta squad by the maintenance portal. They were closely watching the goop. He shouted at them, "Hey Beta Squad, get your helmets on. Piker! Charro! Hoods on!"

"Yea, yea," Charro shouted back, as his squad started to

unclasp their helmets from their packs and place them on their heads.

Alroy did the same, slipping his helmet on. He was immediately distracted by hearing the sound of his own breathing as the radio communicator powered up.

"I'm installed and online," Alroy's VI spoke in the helmet. "Encrypted communications established."

"Thanks Jules," Alroy smiled. "Make sure I'm not using my reserve air unless —"

An unwelcome klaxon alarm suddenly blared. "Warning! Safety measures have been disengaged," the generic *Marquette* VI voice spoke over loudspeakers in the hangar. "Space doors opening. Space doors opening."

"Everyone, find something to hold onto! Use your cable anchor," Alroy shouted through the encrypted radio. "Alfonsi, did you see Fiat and the rest of Gamma Squad?"

"No. They should be patrolling on the other side of the hangar," Alfonsi voice piped into Alroy's helmet.

"Fiat? Ilam?" Alroy spoke into his radio. "Where the hell are you guys?"

Alroy wrapped his arm around a steel cable anchoring the escort corvettes on the deck. The space doors started to pull apart in the middle, and immediately the atmosphere started to suck out into the cold deadly vacuum. Nothing gave Alroy the existential feeling that facing the infinity of space did.

Alroy scanned the hangar, his view partially restricted by his helmet. He saw the Alpha Squad had plunged themselves into the goop itself, using the sticky substance to hold them in during the air evacuation.

He swung around to see a flailing woman, no helmet being pulled out into space.

"Rea!" Alroy shouted. He wanted to jump after her to try to save her, but knew that even if he caught her, without her helmet on she'd be dead in seconds. Even with a helmet, they would likely not survive for more than a few minutes. He was helpless.

Yeoman Carnell was watching the tactical screen. None of the nuclear warheads made it to the surface of *Magnus*, but surely the ship must have been damaged from the proximity of detonation.

He heard the Chairman inquire for a status from the captain of the *Utopia*. Then, he noticed he had a message from Kanokwan. He smiled as he remembered their recent rendezvous, recalling her soft, creamy tan skin and her dark black hair.

His smile turned into a dropped jaw as he read the message. Carnell sprang up and shouted. "It's a trick! Madam Chairman! It's a trick. There's an incoming flotilla running silent. Must be from *Magnus*! They are almost on top of us!"

The Chairman closed her eyes for one second, but time stopped in her brain. Of course. *Magnus* was a distraction to smoke out the location of *Utopia,* which was not unable to render assistance, tied up in battle with the Earth ship. Sparks and Dek's appearance, along with Alroy Macready's appearance was no coincidence. They were here for Amberly. No doubt the majority of *Magnus*' Marines were on those ships. *An excellent plan,* the Chairman thought. She wasn't worried. She had more than 2,000 troops garrisoned on *Marquette.* Even with *Utopia* temporarily out of play, *Marquette* boasted dozens of military-equipped corvettes with point defense systems, the technology that finally gave Arara the advantage over Mother Earth. It appeared her enemies believed they had come to cut off the head of the Infinite Order, but as they had been for time immemorial, the hearts of men were prideful to a fault. *They've overestimated their strength and underestimated mine,* the Chairman thought. *It's a common mistake.*

Her eyes popped open, and the Chairman's straight mouth curved into a soft smile. "Scramble the corvettes. And close my hangar. Let's not make the enemy's landing path so easy. Recall the *Utopia* and its escort wing."

A commotion on the far side of the command center drew the Chairman's attention, and the master of the Infinite Order saw her Chaperone on approach. Merwin One was bloodied, but did not appear to be injured. The Chairman absentmindedly licked her lips, but quickly controlled her thoughts when she saw something she had never seen in Merwin's eyes before: Fear.

"Madam Chairman," Merwin bowed. "They have Amberly. We were ambushed by Commander North and a strike team, and Sparks took Amberly hostage with the threat to kill her. I did not want to risk her death, so I let them go. I took the liberty of locking down all the escape pods, so Sparks could not escape like she did last time. I apologize for my failure and submit myself to your judgment."

"This is not the time for theatrics and finger pointing, my chaperone," the Chairman said smoothly, but Merwin felt the subtext of condemnation. "You can redeem yourself. Please see the legion commander, and sequester whatever troops you need to recover Amberly and Alroy Macready. There is no escape for them off this waypoint. Our enemies have saved us the trouble of finding them, they have come to us. Eliminate them."

"But, I cannot leave you now," Merwin objected. "My oath is to protect you, not fight on the front lines. I am a chaperone, not a captain of war—"

The Chairman lashed out with her left hand, slapping Merwin hard enough to leave an immediate red welt on her face. "Say nothing more. Ka Top will be my chaperone until you return to me with the Macready's. Go, and do as I say."

"Yes, madam," Merwin said, backing away.

"Do not think I've lost faith in you," the Chairman said. "Amberly is the most important person to the Infinite Order. You are my most capable asset. Bring her back to me."

With the air evacuated, Alroy was able to walk around the hangar without fear of a wind current being blown out the door. He wanted to find the rest of Rea's team, which he could not get on the radio. *This hangar isn't so big, I should be able to find them quickly*, Alroy thought, as he scanned the room. Four ships and a dozen piles of cargo containers, blocked a clear view of the three walls. And Alroy could see the fourth wall, or lack thereof, as he gazed through the open space doors.

"Irregular Commander. *Magnus* away lead, Master Sergeant Jana Smith, here," Alroy heard the flotilla commander through the encrypted channel North provided. "Thanks for opening the door. Be careful, we're coming in hot, about a minute out. How many ships can we fit in there?"

"Away lead, looks like four or five," Alroy replied, "but we didn't open the door. They were trying to flush us out. Have they not seen you yet?"

"No resistance so far. We actually pulled off... Wait, I see corvettes launching from the other hangars. All corvettes, this is the Master Sergeant. Break escort formation and engage enemy fighters. The runabouts are almost inserted here."

Flashing strobes lit up on the space doors' interior edges.

"Do you see that," Alroy said over the radio. "They are closing the doors."

"Can you keep them open? We're almost there."

"Not sure."

"Okay, this is going to be tight."

Alroy started waving his hands to get the Irregulars' attention. "Clear the deck. Incoming. Our boys are landing hot. Move, move!"

The first Valkyrie passed through the closing space doors and engaged its reverse thrusters, barely avoiding a collision with the Chairman's Yacht before setting down. Two more Valkyries slipped into the hangar before bouncing off each other and coming to a crashing halt, slamming into the interior hangar wall. Alroy figured the passengers would be fine, but was unsure if those ships would not fly again.

A fourth runabout squeezed through, but not before the rear thruster was scraped off by the closing space door. The runabout rear's flashed, and the space vessel careened nose first toward the pile of goop blocking the maintenance door. Two of Beta Squad were still anchored in the goop, and the others were trying to pull them free.

At the last moment, the squad commander leapt clear, only able to free one of his troops. The other was crushed in the silence of the vacuum as the runabout jerked to a halt, stopped by the wall.

With the doors closed, the hangar started to re-pressurize. Alroy did some quick math. Four Valkyries meant about 200 Marines made it one, with another 100 trapped on two runabouts outside the hangar.

Alroy heard chatter on his radio between Jana and the remaining ships.

"Who didn't make it in?"

"This is the *Tinkerbell*. We're sitting out here with *Phoenix*. We're going to try to cut a soft seal through the hull to inject our Marines. Wait. Shoot. I see incoming corvettes; I'm not sure we can make a seal safely while under fire."

"Retreat or proceed at your discretion, captain," Master Sergeant Smith said on the radio. "But we only get this shot."

"Hold on, we're under fire. *Marquette* is launching ship-to-ship missiles at us. They definitely know we are here," the captain of the *Tinkerbell* said, and Alroy overheard her commanding her crew. "Evasive maneuvers. Swing us around. Put the waypoint between us and those missiles if you can. Hurry! Dirty hell, they got the *Phoenix*. Repeat, the *Phoenix* just bought it."

The hanger had re-pressurized, so Alroy pulled off his helmet and drew his swagger stick. He lamented losing dozens of lives already, but high risk meant casualties were certain. He was a little comforted as he saw hundreds of Marines flowing out of the four runabouts that made it inside. Armed and armored, the Marines looked impressive and ready to bring the fight to the Chairman. The charged feeling from the Marines as they assembled was contagious. After two decades, they were finally able to do their job. Alroy thought about his amateur soldiers as the Marines prepped in formation. *Finally, the professionals are here,* he thought. He started looking through the ranks for the strike force commander and waved down Alfonsi.

"Hey, start dissolving the goop, stat!" Alroy commanded, and Alfonsi pulled a canister with the breakdown formula from his belt. "Let's go kill the Chasm queen."

"Alroy Macready?" Jana walked up to Red. "I'm Master Sergeant Jana Smith. Thanks for securing the landing pad for us. You still good using your Irregulars to hold the hangar in case we need to escape?"

Alroy shook Jana's hand. "We're ready to do our part, Master Sergeant. But, I would like to accompany you and your command group. I'll leave Corporal Alfonsi here in command of the Irregulars.

"Fine with me," Jana said. "You know the risks."

"Dek tells me I have you to thank you for saving my daughter Kora and my grandson, Sergeant."

"Just Jana, please," she said. "Don't thank me. A lot of people give their lives to save your family. I'm sorry we didn't save Amberly back on *Magellan*. North will get her back."

"I'm sure he will," Alroy said. "He seems like a good man."

"North's the best. Okay, there are two circular routes to the command center from this hanger large enough to move our entire force. After much debate, we've decided against deploying in two smaller groups, so we're going to take the left path here. What's the status on resistance?"

Alroy rubbed his beard again. "They know we're here, of course. After we took out the initial guard and gooped them out, it's been pretty quiet. But we know they are up to something. Commander North is already on the inside with his strike team to recover Amberly."

"We'll see them soon enough, I'm sure. Thank you, Captain Macready. You are a true patriot. We better get moving before they block us off. Gear up and meet me at the head of the column," Smith saluted Alroy and started moving to give final orders to her squad commanders. When she was several meters away, she turned back and looked at the Irregular captain again. "You really are little Alroy's granddad, aren't you? That's something else."

When Elizabeth Hawkins saw the first missiles hit the *Utopia's* escort corvettes, she gave a celebratory cheer. Six of eight had been either completely annihilated or disabled. The remaining two were in full retreat, following *Utopia*, making its way back to *Marquette*. Cho and the others cheered as well, and after a moment, Hawkins' joy melted, as she thought about the dead Chasm pilots and crew, probably who were only following orders, caught in this interplanetary war against their own will. They all couldn't be evil like that Hawk Skylar. Some of them just had to be grunts.

"Helm, pursue the *Utopia*. Stay on top of her," Alecia said. "Don't worry about the remaining corvettes."

"Can we catch *Utopia*?" Cho asked.

"Gunnery liaison, open silos one through 22," Alecia said. "If we get into range, open fire. Once we get back to *Marquette*, we'll be outgunned again. I don't want a repeat of the last time we fought those two together. There's no *Magellan* to retreat to anymore. We're playing for keeps."

CHAPTER TWENTY-TWO

Decked in black armor and sporting melee weapons suited for close-quarters combat, hundreds of Marines poured out of the hangar into the main corridors. The handful of Chasm troops guarding the interior side of the goop laden door were quickly taken down, and Jana and Alroy both were surprised by the lack of any real resistance from Chasm. Surly there was some sort of formidable force on *Marquette*.

The goal for the two hundred-strong assault force was straightforward: Neutralize the Chasm troops and take the command center by force. The column took the left major corridor that ran parallel to the *Marquette's* cross-section tube system toward the command center, on the other side of the waypoint, near the primary hangar.

Jana was near the front of the advance squad, as her hundred Marines double-timed it toward their objective. Dynamic signage and audio alerts filled the air, warning *Marquette's* residents to lock down until the intruders had been dealt with. North had promoted Jana, a veteran of both the battles of *Magellan*, to Master Sergeant because of her heroism and her natural leadership abilities. She'd spent the last three years training with her team to complete this very strike.

After a kilometer of unimpeded advancing, they came into one of the dozen commons on *Marquette*. This large chamber, cubic in shape, was filled with a luxurious meeting plaza, including a fountain and large planters with tall palm trees. Twenty meters high, the plaza had several balconies that opened into offices, shuttered retail outlets, and other commercial spaces.

"Hold here," Jana said, and the Marine line behind her came to an efficient stop. Alroy, who had joined the rear squad, came up the line to consult with the Master Sargent.

"Perfect place for an ambush," Alroy murmured to Jana.

"My thoughts exactly," Jana said. "Recon Echo, clear the stairwell and the third balcony. If we're going through the kill box, at least let's take the high ground."

"Great, let's not stay in one place too long, or we could get flanked. The enemy could be transporting in tube cars or moving in force down the right circular path."

North pulled Amberly along as fast as she could run toward the Chairman's hangar. Amberly hadn't done any sustained running for years. Her lungs burned and her legs felt rubbery. She faltered.

"Hold up," North said. Sparks who had never been in better form, signaled with a closed fist she heard the order. Sparks was running point and had already dispatched a few low-level Chasm troops that had inadvertently gotten between her party and the secondary hangar.

"Are you okay?" North grabbed Amberly's other hand.

"I'm fine," Amberly smiled dimmly. "I'm just… out of shape."

"We can take a minute," North said, studying her. He had never seen Amberly this weak. *What did the Chairman do to her?* he wondered. "Let's duck in here." North pointed to an entrance to a micro factory where, judging by the crowned oval painted on the door, sporks were made.

"I'll scout ahead," Sparks said. "Take a holiday. Let Amberly catch her breath."

"She's something else," Amberly said to North as Sparks moved ahead to look for the enemy.

North turned to Caddo and Lydia, who were performing rear guard. "Caddo take up a position just a click behind. Signal us if there is trouble."

"Yes, sir," Caddo replied. He lifted his shock stick and made his way back.

"Rhodes, Lydia," North pointed to abandoned storefronts a few meters away. "Take up ambush positions."

Lydia took Amberly's hand and squeezed it. She gave Amberly a worried look.

"I just need to catch my breath," Amberly offered as she followed North into the spork factory. Lydia and Rhodes grabbed their gear and headed off to their hiding spots.

"All this for me?" Amberly slumped down on the cold steel floor.

"Everyone is worth saving," North said to Amberly. "When we stop believing that, we're no different than the Chairman.

Besides, the Chairman thinks you're something and wants you. That's reason enough to steal you back."

"But at what cost?"

North looked into Amberly's green eyes and swallowed hard. "No price would have been too high. Live or die, we fight to the end."

"North, I have to tell you what is going on — in me. I understand now, what my mother was. I am becoming her."

North immediately looked troubled. He knelt beside Amberly.

"No, not like that," Amberly read his eyes. "But my mind, the logical part of it, has been unlocked. Everything is a decision matrix. I see it as clearly as I see your face. Infinite detail. I can process complex multivariate problems like … a computer. I was genetically engineered that way. Well, my mother was. It was how she was able to break the *Magellan* master codes those ten years ago. Whatever she had, she gave it to me."

"What do you mean, she gave it to you?" North asked, desperately wanting to understand the woman he loved.

"My brain is *on*, North, in a way I've never experienced. I'm processing information faster than I knew was possible. But all this new power up here," Amberly tapped her head, "is doing nothing to help me process what's going on in here." She put her hand over her heart.

"What's going on in there?" North dared to ask.

"So much," Amberly took a deep sobbing breath. "I'm diving into painful lows and soaring to the highest highs. I'm totally disoriented," Amberly teared up again. "Like when I had to free jump from the *Firebird* to the *Magellan* Gardens, and it was just me in a suit facing the universe. I feel so small, just like then … scared of being lost in the infinity of space. But … more intense."

Amberly squeezed her eyes shut as a new wave of emotion swept over her. She half expected when she opened them to awake from this dream, back in her cell. After a moment, she opened her eyes, and saw North's welcome face looking back at her.

"North, she offered me everything!" Amberly said, tears streaming down her face. "The Chairman offered me the world, literally. And I wanted it, I felt like my suffering was about to transform into something meaningful."

"But...?"

"You came for me. All of you. Sparks. Lydia. And Dek," Amberly didn't even try to keep from crying. "So why? Dammit, North. I never asked for this. But you all loved me. I wouldn't trade that love for the world. I *didn't* trade that love for the world. But I don't know if I can bear it. How many people have died for me? Skip. Midas. Trot. Moreno. Dek..."

"We all knew the potential cost. And we all took the risk. And Dek ... he was the best of us."

"Dek. It was ... horrible. I was so thankful to be with him ... in the end," Amberly wept, placing her hand on North's shoulder. "But his death ... watching him die so dramatically. North, I was *so* tempted. The Chairman's offer seemed so good, so noble. I could end the pain and death. I started to see things her way. But when she made Sparks kill Dek — and I saw everything clearly and what the Chairman really was. Evil."

"Dek saved you," North wiped at his own moist eyes. "It's exactly as he wanted it."

"I prayed you both would come, but I was losing faith."

"Amberly, anyone else would have lost their way long ago," North sat and leaned against Amberly's shoulder. "You are so strong. You don't just have the marbles of Kimberly Macready. You have the *heart* of your dad."

"My dad. My God, North, *my dad is alive*," Amberly spoke excitedly. "And he's here. How can any person deal with all this emotional solar flare?"

"He has quite the story; I'll let him tell you himself. Um, Amberly," North hesitated, "He's lost a lot of his memory. ... He doesn't remember your time on *Magellan*. But as soon as he knew you existed, and that you were prisoner of the Chairman, he hasn't stopped trying to get you back. We're close. I honestly thought we'd fail before this."

"*Magellan*, oh sweet *Magellan*," Amberly said. "Were you there when...?"

"No, but I saw the aftermath. The only balm for the horror was finding the survivors. Kora's waiting for you on *Magnus*," North broke into a huge smile.

"My dear Kora. Wow, North, captain of the most powerful warship ever built," Amberly eked out a smile. "I remember when you were just a cocky junior officer. I bet you have some stories to tell."

"Oh, he does. But they can wait," Sparks, just returned, said. "Come on. The coast looks clear between us and the hangar. We're almost home free."

Amberly stood up and hugged Sparks. "Thank you, sister. Let's go home, wherever that is."

"We'll never catch them," Hawkins said. "*Utopia* is too fast since she was upgraded."

"If she were running away, you'd be right," Blight said. She stood with her engineer husband at the tactical table, reviewing damage reports. "But *Utopia* is making a beeline for *Marquette*. They are not going to just blow by the station. They are going to protect it from us. With the weaponized waypoint, they figure they'll have better odds. Two verses one all over again."

"You're smiling, captain, but I don't see how that makes the situation any better," Hawkins said.

Bollard also offered his brilliant smile and laughed. "That ship will have to slow down to match *Marquette's* orbit speed. If we're lucky, we'll get her then."

Blight kissed her husband's cheek. "I'm glad you upgraded the EMP shielding after the nuke hit us during the Battle of *Marquette*. If you hadn't, the multiple explosion we just took would have wiped out our electrical systems."

"Don't thank me," Bollard said, "It was Caddo's idea."

"Well, if we survive, I'll buy him a beer," Blight said, as she forced down her natural revulsion for Caddo. "Okay, everyone, focus. We'll be closing on *Marquette* in less than a half hour. With any luck, our Marines have already done the heavy lifting for us and have taken the control center."

"The heavy lifting? What do you call what we've been doing?" Bollard asked.

Pvt. Randall Belle, a small blonde Marine who was born on, and lived his entire life on, *Magnus* led his three-person recon squad, room by room on the top balcony overlooking the commons.

"So far so, good," he quietly whispered to his squad, as two of them slipped into the next door to clear it. Belle himself pushed ahead into the last adjacent room that needed to be checked before he could clear the whole balcony for the Sergeant Master and her forces to cross the commons safely.

He swung around in the dark room. "Lights."

The room's VI complied, and the space illuminated, revealing a kitchen facility, messy with hundreds of ration containers strewn everywhere. Belle softly walked over toward a meter-high counter with his shock stick in hand. He thrust over the counter top to only discover more trash. He was about to clear the room, when a rattle in a food storage box caught his attention. He took a deep breath, put his left hand on the box's door handle, and with his right hand clutching the shock stick, he swung the door open.

A young girl, maybe six or seven, screamed in surprise. Belle gave a startled holler in reply

"Shhhhh!" Both Belle and the girl shushed each other as soon as they had gotten over their mutual shock.

"You're not Chasm," the girl said. "Be quiet or they'll find you."

"It's okay, sweetheart," Belle said. "I'm Belle. We're going to protect you. What's your name?"

"That's a funny name. That's a girl's name," the young one said.

"Well, it's my last name. Do you have a name?"

"Afryea," the girl said. "But my parents just call me Frya. It's my nickname. Do you have a nickname? Do you know what Afryea means?"

"No," Belle was surprised at the question.

"It means 'born in good times.' That's what my mom told me."

"Where is your mom, Frya?"

"They took her," Afryea said.

Afryea's eyes went wide. She let out another scream and leaned back into the box, closing the door.

Belle whirled around and saw a beautiful woman with golden flowing hair. She wore a respirator mask, but it didn't hide her attractive face. He started to smile instinctively, but was suddenly shocked as she put a sword through his torso. Belle wondered how it was possible she could have the strength to push a sword through his armor as he died.

Merwin One pulled her sword out of the Marine, wiped the blade off on his uniform, and sheathed the weapon. She hoisted the body over her shoulder and walked out the room onto the balcony. Merwin threw the body over the balcony at the same time the other members of his squad were coming out of the rooms they were clearing.

"Where is Alroy Macready?" Merwin demanded flatly, drawing her sword again and closing on the pair.

The first Marine lit his shock stick and plunged it at Merwin. She parried the stick easily and rounded about to bring her blade across the Marine's neck. It wasn't a clean cut, so she pushed her foot into the quivering body to dislodge her sword. Merwin stepped forward and flung the half-dead Marine over the balcony, with a loud thud filling the commons as the body bounced off a palm tree and hit the floor.

Merwin pointed her sword at the remaining Marine on the terrace, a woman of similar stature as Merwin. The Marine had her stun gun trained on Merwin, but the gun was shaking in her hands.

"I'm Private Parks," the Marine said, her voice quivering. "You need to stand down."

"Don't," Merwin said, stepping without fear toward the woman. "Your head will come off much easier than the other fellow's. Tell me now, where is Alroy Macready?" Merwin tried to make a menacing face, but just ended up twisting her nose slightly under her respirator.

"I'm right here," Alroy called from the floor, where he was verifying the fallen bodies were dead.

In a flash, Merwin hacked at Park's hand which held the stun gun. Both the gun and several digits went flying in a spurt of blood. As the Marine clutched her hand, Merwin again sheathed her sword and jumped over across the corner of the room onto the second level balcony, first breaking her fall by grabbing a rail, and then landing in a low squat. She pulled out her sword, jumped over the rail and flipped down the final story to the ground level of the commons, rolling into a defensive stance.

Merwin surveyed Alroy, flanked by an impressive number of troops in the corridor opening and back down the hall. She stood about 10 meters away from her enemy.

"You don't have enough people to do this, Alroy Macready, unfortunate betrothed of Raven One," Merwin. "What do you have? A hundred? A hundred and fifty? We have thousands of troops here."

"I don't see them," Alroy said, as he pulled out his swagger stick. He offered bravado, but knew Merwin wasn't bluffing.

"You can end this bloodshed, Alroy," Merwin said, muffled by her respirator. "I've studied who you are. A man of peace. A man of faith. You and your daughter can live together in peace for the rest of your natural lives. No harm will come to you. Surrender to me now."

As she spoke, dozens of Chasm troops rushed out on every balcony with powerful automatic rifles.

Jana cursed under her breath. This open area was the worst place for a battle. In the melee battle of tight corridors, shock sticks that weren't neutralized by personal PDS were superior weapons. In the relative open, the distance gave the advantage to rifles. Her Marines wore bullet-resistant armor. But those systems could not defend against assault fire like the Chasm PDS. Chasm had the advantage. She would have to retreat and find another way.

"Think about it, Macready," Merwin called out again. "The Infinite Order has no desire for more bloodshed. You are the aggressors here, now. Submit yourself and enjoy the fruits of the coming paradise. If more of your Marines die needlessly, the blood is on your hands, not mine.

"All this blood is on the hands of the Chairman. Our freedom does not belong to her or your mis-named Infinite Order," Alroy called out. He considered Merwin, clearly an accomplished combatant, but not wearing a warrior's garb — just a loose-fitting white dress and … a military-grade respirator strapped onto her face. The same mask that every Chasm trooper was wearing.

"Jana, everyone, gas masks! Now!" Alroy shouted.

"Put them to sleep," Merwin said into a hidden radio. "Careful not to shoot Macready."

The Marines trained to put on their masks in seconds, but some of them were not as snappy as others pulling them off packs and locking them onto the standard-issue helmets. Hazy aerosol mists began to fill the corridor. Weapons fired. Jules spoke to Roy as he slipped on his mask, "My analysis is this gas is likely derivative of remifentanil."

Bullets started to fire into the dangerous cloud. Alroy dove to the ground.

"Careful idiots," Merwin shouted. "If Alroy dies, you all die too!"

Jana had her mask on and shouted over the chaos. "Fall back, fall back!" Jana looked at Alroy who scrambled back to his feet. They would have a better chance in the corridor.

Alroy retreated few meters back into the corridor out of the line of sight of the balconies. The mist was thick now. Alroy nearly tripped over a fallen Marine, incapacitated by the "knock-out" gas. He stopped and faced in the direction of his enemy, gripping his swagger stick. Master Sergeant Jana Smith and several other Marines came to his side, forming a line.

Merwin stood in the center of the commons as Chasm troops rushed past her into the mist, pursuing the Marines back into the large hallway. "Captain Delloway, bring in your garrison now. The Marines are retreating your way," she said into her radio. "We have them trapped. Wait them out. Don't kill Alroy. If you do, the Chairman will airlock us both."

The first trooper ran into the smoke, rifle at the ready, as he nearly smacked into Alroy Macready. Before he pulled the trigger, he noted the red hair and remembered Merwin's warning as the osmium alloy tip of Red's swagger stick cracked his head open. More troopers charged into the literal fog of war, and Jana's line disintegrated into asymmetrical melee combat.

Jana saw a wisp in the gas cloud and stabbed with her shock stick, and a Chasm trooper cried out. A gap in the cloud revealed another trooper moving for her. The trooper recognized Jana's female form, ergo not Alroy, and pulled the trigger on his rifle as a Marine bumped into him from behind. With no aim, the spray of bullets shot toward the ground, and one ricocheted into Jana's foot. She cried out and fell to her knees. Alroy swung his stick around and slammed it into the hand holding the rifle, cracking nearly every bone in the hand and fracturing the wrist as well.

"Thanks," Jana said.

"You okay?"

"Think so… just my foot." The pair heard more shots ring out, though the slow pace of gunfire made it clear the Chasm troops were placing their shots, making sure they had green targets.

Alroy saw three more Marines on the floor as the gas started to clear. He couldn't tell if they were shot or gassed.

"Master Sergeant, they're on our flank," a corporal shouted, running toward the front of the line where she presumed Jana was. "We're trapped."

"Then we fight to the last man!" Jana shouted back.

"As soon as this gas clears, they will be able to pick us off cleanly," Alroy said. He pulled two smoke grenades and a frag grenade off of a fallen Marine. He activated the smoke grenades and tossed them down on the floor where he stood. Visibility reduced to less than a meter. "Let's keep this smoke up and see if we can hide in the rooms along this stretch of the corridor. It may buy us some time, and maybe they'll get caught in their own crossfire."

"Corporal, break radio silence and report our status to the Irregulars and *Magnus*," Jana commanded. "No reason to keep quiet now they know where we are. Tell them we need help or we're all dead."

Alroy tossed a frag grenade into the main commons and it made a satisfying boom.

Sparks ran through the main door into the Chairman's hangar. Immediately a dozen rifles from the Lewis Irregulars pointed up at her.

"Easy boys," she said. "I didn't mean to give you a rise."

North, Amberly, Lydia, Caddo and Rhodes slipped in behind Sparks. North spotted Alfonsi and went straight to him.

"Where is Alroy?" North asked impatiently.

"Red? He went with the Master Sergeant on the assault of the command center. They are running radio silent."

North looked at Rhodes. "Get your comms running. Chasm has a pretty good idea of what's going on now. Listen for anything from Jana or the *Magnus*. Also, see if the *Tinkerbell* has reported in."

"The *Tinkerbell*? That ship made a soft seal just on the other side of that wall," Alfonsi pointed toward the maintenance portal. I was glad to see a few dozen more Marines for backup."

"That's good news," North said. "They are still on board?"

"Apparently waiting for orders, but we couldn't raise the Master Sergeant on account of the radio silence," Alfonsi said.

Rhodes pulled her powerful, portable radio unit from her pack and began to activate its advanced communication functions. North walked over to her temporary comm station and began to study the traffic with Rhodes.

Alfonsi looked at Amberly. "You are her? You're Red's little girl? You are as beautiful as everyone said."

"Um, thank you," Amberly said. "You know my dad?"

"Red, I mean Roy?" Alfonsi said. "Best man I've ever met. There's nothing I wouldn't do for him. That's why I am here."

"This is Amberly?" Fiat walked into the conversation. "No way. I thought maybe you were just a figment of his imagination."

"Wait, I thought he didn't remember me?" Amberly said.

"Well, he doesn't," Alfonsi explained. "From time to time, when he was talking to… well… pretty young women like yourself… he would say your name, Amberly, when he meant to say hers. It was the weirdest thing."

"Clearly, his love for you was greater than his loss of memory," Fiat added. "He is going to be so happy to see you."

North paced back from Rhodes' comm station.

"Alroy and Jana are pinned down here," North pulled out his infopad which displayed a waypoint map. "They must have been flanked by a second unit that came around through the tube or the counter-corridor. Everyone get your full helmets back on. They are using some sort of sleeping gas."

"Alroy's in trouble?" Alfonsi asked. "I have to go save him!"

"No. You Irregulars need to keep working on getting as many ships here operational. Crack into that yacht, too. Even if the ships won't fly, if we can get them out into space with life support, that is better than nothing. Get to it. I'll take the *Tinkerbell* Marines and go for Alroy. Rhodes, you're in charge. Alfonsi, you watch out for Amberly."

"North! I'm going with you!" Amberly said, distressed.

"No way. We're going into battle. You are neither equipped or trained. Stay here. Stay safe," North said. "Alfonsi, Rhodes, listen to me. If you are in trouble, take Amberly and get on the *Tinkerbell* if you can get there safely. Rendezvous with the *Magnus*. Don't wait for anyone. No one else matters. Do you understand?"

"But if Red—" Alfonsi objected.

"I promise you, whatever happens to Alroy, he would want Amberly to survive."

"Back into the fire," Sparks said, trying to sound put out, but then she smiled. "Hell, I was getting bored here anyway."

The Chairman was pleased to hear that Merwin One had contained the Marine threat with an excellent bit of battle stratagem. She was upset, of course, that Amberly Macready was not yet accounted for, but it was only a matter of time before her granddaughter was recovered and her work could continue in earnest. In containing the Marines, and even Alroy Macready, Merwin at least had cleaned up her own mess, and the Chairman almost felt bad for being so hard on her chaperone. *No one is perfect*, she thought, *yet*.

"Madam Chairman," Carnell interrupted her thoughts. "*Utopia* is on final approach; *Magnus* is trailing behind. We estimated minimal damage on the ships major systems – *Magnus* weapons and engines seem to be at nearly full capacity based on our recon scans."

The Chairman sat in her throne-like chair on her platform in the middle of the command center. "Tell the defensive systems captain to target *Magnus* as soon as she is in range. No need to wait for further orders. Fire at will."

The waypoint defensive systems liaison responded, "Wilco, Madam Chairman," as she picked up her mic and started relaying orders.

"Ka Top," the Chairman said softly.

The substitute chaperone appeared. "At your service."

"With all this violence, I am worried about my granddaughters' safety. With the life pods locked down, she may try to escape on a ship from my personal hangar. Put together a light and fast-moving strike squad purposed to recover her. She must be at my hangar. That is the only logical place."

"Immediately, madam."

"Ka," the Chairman stood up, just a half-dozen centimeters from the bodyguard. She scraped a finger down his clean-shaven cheek and onto his neck, where she scratched him and drew the slightest amount of blood. "If you succeed in securing Amberly, it may be time to find a replacement for Merwin One. Let me know when your team is assembled and the hangar antechamber is secure. I want to be there when you capture her."

"As you wish."

Ka Top turned and trotted off to his new mission. The Chairman followed him with her eyes, and she licked her fingernail.

"Almost there," the *Magnus* gunnery liaison Boot watched his tactical display closely.

"Helm," Acting Captain Blight cautioned, "easy does it. Let's make sure we don't accidentally run into *Marquette*. We'll catch *Utopia* soon enough."

"Visual on *Waypoint Marquette*," the Magnus VI announced and circled the small point of light in green on the forward viewscreen. The point was growing rapidly. So was another reflective point on the screen, tagged with red – the *Utopia*.

"Almost there," Boot again.

"Ughhh…" Hawkins felt nauseous. Ships like *Magnus* often accelerated and decelerated over days, not hours or minutes, requiring heavy use of the inertia dampeners. Hawkins, like most of the crew, was not used to these short bursts.

"We're in range!"

"Fire!"

The sound of smooth metal slipping from precision silos echoed as *Magnus* emptied the remaining ordnance from its missile bays.

"Get those silos reloaded. Start charging the particle cannons," Blight ordered.

"Slowing to full stop relative to *Marquette*; matching orbit," the helmsman reported.

The *Magnus* had arrived for its rematch.

CHAPTER TWENTY-THREE

After a year in confinement, this new wave of human contact overwhelmed Amberly. Rhodes seemed like a kindred spirit or a little sister, as she loudly jabbered. Fiat and Alfonsi were nice enough, and she was enjoying hearing about her dad, the lonely Lewis Island *farmer*.

But Amberly wasn't in the mood for small talk. She was worried for North and her father. Her heavy heart was coping with the traumatic death of her dear friend Dek. Amberly excused herself to wander a few meters and look out one of the three small windows in the corner of the Chairman's hangar.

She gazed into the open starry space and then down on the colorful blue-green Arara. The star Viapos was rising over the planet's horizon, bright and hopeful. The star was just as Amberly had dreamed when she was a young girl. She remembered how her mother would talk about playing in the sand while the warm rays of Viapos hit her face.

Amberly jumped as a shadow suddenly fell across her window. The dual-hull *Utopia* slid into a parallel orbit with the waypoint, blocking Viapos. She jumped a second time as the shadow was illuminated by hundreds of bright explosions cascading around *Utopia*.

Amberly had never seen space combat so close; few people had.

Amberly watched missiles disintegrate as if by magic as they encountered *Utopia's* point defense system, while others multiplied into dozens of independent warheads, gleaming with a blue green tint from Arara's reflected light.

The point defense system could not counter the hundreds of new contacts, and several dozen weapons hit their target, tearing into *Utopia*. Just a thousand meters or so away, Amberly could make out hull breaches and the dark consequences as Chasm lives were snuffed out by space.

"Rhodes, look!" Amberly called. Rhodes ran over to the second window just as *Magnus* came into view.

"Dirty hell," Rhodes said, "looks like *Magnus* just ripped into *Utopia*."

Utopia was venting atmosphere. The ship was attempting a defensive reposition — to put *Marquette* between *Magnus* and itself. It slipped out of the line of sight of the secondary hangar windows.

Suddenly, the whole hangar shook with "zing ting" sounds that were momentarily ear-piercing.

"Is *Marquette* under attack?" Fiat cried out.

"No, those must be ship-to-ship missiles launching," Alfonsi surmised. "*Marquette* is counter attacking the *Magnus.*"

Amberly craned her neck to see the *Magnus* through her window. The ship was now surrounded by what looked like a thick grey cloud.

"Flack," Rhodes answered the unasked question. "Come on baby, hold fast."

Almost faster than the eye could track, a barrage of missiles intersected with *Magnus*' flack field. Many of the missiles were disabled by the flack, but others survived long enough to detonate on the hull of the earth-loyal warship. The hull vented multiple gas streams, and the uneven impacts caused the mono-hulled ship to spin, apparently out of control.

"Dirt! Dirt! Dirt! That doesn't look good," Rhodes swore as she ran back to her makeshift comm operation to raise the *Magnus.*

Alroy estimated they had lost about half of their fighting force to gas or bullets, and they were being driven into a smaller section of the corridor, sandwiched between two groups of Chasm troopers. The only reason why they were still alive was because the corridors required close-quarters melee combat, and Chasm was unable to bring their superior numbers to bear. Also, Macready knew he hadn't personally perished yet because the Chairman wanted him taken alive.

Alroy fought like a madman. A wave of exhaustion hit him, but he ignored it. He had come this far to meet his daughter, he wasn't going to rest now. He expertly twirled his lethal swagger stick. Dozens of Chasm troopers had fallen by his hand, cracked skulls and fractured femurs courtesy of the density of osmium.

The air was clearing again, and Alory could find no more smoke grenades to give them additional cover. Seeing an opening and a target, Chasm troops tried again to break the mis-formed line, charging and firing. The Chasm troops had grown more confident, picking off a Marine standing to Alroy's right with an explosive headshot.

To his left, a limping Jana pulled from her belt a rare neo-napalm grenade she had been saving for a special occasion. She timed the toss so that it created a four meter-high, floor-to-ceiling wall of fire that not only enveloped the approaching Chasm squad, but it also triggered the fire suppressors. The neo-napalm was pre-oxygenated and continued to rage while the suppressors' pink retardant flooded the area.

"That may buy us a minute or two," Jana said over the screams of Chasm troops whose bodies had become additional carbon to fuel the fire.

The private on comms shouted for the Master Sergeant. "Sergeant Smith. I just received a comm from Lt. Rhodes. Amberly has been secured in the hangar."

"Thank God," Macready said. *North and Dek were successful,* he thought.

The private continued, distracted by the flames leaping through the pink foam. "The *Magnus* and the *Utopia* are engaged in combat in parallel orbit with *Marquette.* Both have taken critical damage."

"Thank you, private," Jana replied. "Confirm with the lieutenant we've received a message and report our status."

"What's our next move?" Alroy asked Jana.

"We can't move getting forward," Jana said. "We might be able to retreat and overtake the Chasm troops on our flank and find another way to the command center. Either way, I say you get back to the hangar and your daughter, put your piracy and piloting skills to good use. Get off the station while you still can."

"You would all die for Amberly?"

"For her, and all humanity. No time to discuss, Roy," Jana said, and then loudly continued, "everyone, rear assault. Let's muster everything while this fire's still hot. Double-time!"

As the Marines reoriented themselves, Alroy ran to the rear of the line, now the front, where the rear guard had been trying to hold off the Chasm force that outflanked them.

"Yeaaaach!" Alroy shouted as he ran to engage Chasm. His

whole body was hurting; his reserves were nearly spent. As he brought his weapon down on the Chasm officer at the front of the flanking force, he again felt his age had caught up with him. The athletic officer parried his stick and then quickly snatched it from Macready's hand.

The younger Marines began to engage the Chasm trooper in Alroy's vicinity, but the Irregular captain saw that even with their concentrated forces, the enemy numbers were too thick to break through. Out of his right-sided peripheral vision, Alroy observed a Chasm trooper fall after being impaled with a javelin.

Alroy put up his fists and took a failed swing at the robust officer, a man in his twenties with blue-green hair poking out from under his helmet. Macready thought about going for the knife in his boot, but didn't think he could pull it before he was subdued.

Alroy heard a sudden, loud burst of automatic fire from multiple guns. The Chasm officer heard it too, from behind his position, dropped the swagger stick, and turned to assess the threat. Alroy took the opportunity to give the Chasm officer a right-handed uppercut, catching his chin, and knocking the man off his feet and out cold. Wheezing from overexertion, Macready picked up his swagger stick.

Jana, slowed by her injured foot, had caught up with Alroy, and stepped next to the downed Chasm officer, and drove her shock stick through his left leg.

"How are you feeling, old man?" Jana smirked as she pulled her stick out of the officer's fleshy limb.

"Old. Definitely old." As Macready spoke, the whole Chasm flanking line had fallen into chaos. He peered down the hall and he saw why.

"North!" Jana shouted. North, Sparks and about thirty Marines and a dozen Irregulars had started to mow the Chasm backup a few dozen meters away. They advanced quickly over the fallen bodies. Some of the Chasm troopers had dropped their weapons in surrender, and Marines quickly zip cuffed them face down on the ground.

"Did you know that with enough bullets you can overwhelm the personal PDS?" North said, hoisting a machine gun in the air. "We flanked those flankers!"

Sparks also had a smoking machine gun in her hands. She tossed the large, heavy weapon on the floor with some measure of disgust. "Crude," Sparks offered her opinion of the weapon, and after a brief pause, reflected, "Takes away from the art of the kill. But whatever works —"

Alroy looked back up the hall toward the commons. The neo-napalm barrier had burnt out.

"Form the line!" Jana shouted to the Marines. "We're not in the clear yet."

"North, we can't get to the Chairman that way," Alroy said. "We'll have to get to the command center by another path."

"We've lost too many troops to take the command center anyway," North said. "But we have Amberly."

"So what? Retreat? Is everything lost?" Jana asked plainly.

"Blight has a plan," Sparks said. "It's so crazy, *I* like it."

"Jana, get everyone back to the hangar and off the waypoint," North commanded. "If possible, get back to the *Magnus*. If not, rendezvous in Williamston on the Lewis Islands. That's an order. And take Alroy with you. Make sure he gets back to Amberly. My squad will hold these guys off for as long as we can, then we'll follow."

"North, we can't abandon—"

"Go, that's an order, Sargent," North demanded. "Besides, Sparks brought some party orbs."

"Yes, Commander," Jana saluted. "Fall back!" she shouted. "Everyone, fall back. Back to the hangar."

North and five machine gunners from the *M.S.S. Tinkerbell* formed a line facing the commons. Through the hazy hallway, they saw an approaching formation. The hazard lights blinked red, tinting the approaching force and creating odd shadows.

Just behind the line, Sparks drew her sword and angled it in front of her, as she took an athletic stance. "Still hungry, sweetheart?" Sparks asked her weapon. "Me too. Who knew violent revenge was great therapy to cope with horrible deeds? Wait. I did!"

North held his javelin high.

Walking two meters ahead of the Chasm front, Merwin One stopped, eyed North and his companions, and stood firm. Sparks did some quick math and figured at least 100 troops were supporting Merwin.

"Surrender to me, and I will make your deaths swift and painless," Merwin said, an odd kindness in her voice. "If I have to capture you by force, should you survive, I will be compelled to turn you over to my Chairman, and she will savor every long moment of the torture you will suffer."

"Huh, that's funny, because we were thinking that you would surrender to *us* and we'd spare *your* lives," North rubbed his jaw for effect.

"You didn't tell me that North had a sense of humor to go with his dashing looks, Sparks," Merwin smiled and extended a hand in the direction of Sparks. "Sparks, join me now, cohort sister, when it matters the most. It's over for the Earth loyalists. All you've done is collect them for us."

"Whatever," Sparks clinched her sword a little tighter.

"Please, come home now," Merwin offered. "I'll make sure that the Chairman gives you North as a prize."

"Now... wait–" North started, but Merwin interrupted. "Besides, do you really think Amberly and the others will welcome you back after you killed Dek Tigona?"

Thinking about the horrific end of Dek's life made blood pound in Spark's head. Guilt transformed into rage, filling Sparks, and she was no longer able to hold herself back. She leaped toward Merwin, sword in her right hand, and with her left flung three small white orbs, concentrated explosives developed from advanced Earth technology – decades ahead of anything on Arara. The orbs, each only a centimeter in diameter, landed a few rows back into the phalanx of Chasm troops behind Merwin. The tiny bombs exploded with a generous amount of force, ripping off the limbs of some troopers, cleanly throwing others multiple meters into the air, and slamming others lethally into the corridor walls.

Merwin, knocked forward by the blast, immediately sprung to her feet. "Come, on form up, get through these enemies of the Chairman," Merwin commanded her disoriented forces, realizing the opportunity for negotiation had passed. "They are covering the escape of the Macready!" Dozens of troopers charged past Merwin.

North speared the first Chasm trooper he saw, while the

remaining Marines opened fire on the troops, careful not to catch Sparks or North in the crossfire. The first bullets were meaningless, poofing in the point defense system of so many troopers. But where it concentrated, the repeat fire shredded through the armor.

The first line of Chasm troops went down, but return fire came quick enough, and with no PDS of their own, the Marines had to take cover in the nooks and crannies that lined the corridor. Marine armor could take a bullet or two, but bullets that didn't penetrate armor still hit with tremendous force. The Marine armor had classic weak spots at the neck and armpits. Two Marines were taken down permanently by Chasm fire.

Sparks, in her dark, slender armor, blotted out the flashing emergency lights as she came down from her high leap on Merwin. The chaperone rolled back out of the Sparks' reach and then artfully swung her own blade up, her white dress, stained with a spattering of blood, twirling gracefully as Merwin found solid footings.

The swords clanked hard.

Sparks pushed Merwin's blade down and lunged for a torso cut. Merwin sprung back and knocked the sword off target. Merwin took the opening to swiftly pierce Sparks' shoulder. Her specialized alloy blade found its way through Spark's lightweight polycarbonate armor and into flesh. The armor retarded the swing's momentum as the blade circled out.

Sparks grimaced and lashed out with a sharp kick that cracked on Merwin's knee. The blonde fell back as she failed to connect a second hit on Spark's shoulder.

A Chasm sharpshooter took aim at the dueling duo. Before she could trigger her sniper rifle, North whacked her hard on the side of her head with the butt end of his javelin. The sniper lost consciousness, dropped her weapon, and fell to the ground.

North caught the falling rifle just as another trooper, less than a meter away, was lifting his stun cannon on North. The Marine Commander discharged the weapon at point blank range through his target's heart.

North's remaining three Marines were popping out of cover to take some pot shots, but not with enough consistency to overcome enemy PDS. The troopers were advancing more cautiously, as they stepped over the bloody carcasses of their fallen comrades.

"Sparks! We need to get out of here!" North called out, stepping back behind the covering fire from the diminished *Tinkerbell* squad.

"Go ahead! I'm not leaving 'till," Sparks sword caught Merwin's blade above her head as she kicked Merwin in the stomach "...this bitch's head is severed..." she spun and slashed at Merwin's feet. "...from her body for what she did to Dek!" Sparks emptied her rage, but Merwin deftly blocked her blows.

Merwin pushed forward, sliding her blade across Sparks' sword, sounding a spine-crawling grind. Bleeding out from the shoulder, Sparks stumbled back and quickly put her sword in the front defensive position again.

"Sparks, old friend," Merwin grunted as she took an aggressive swing that Sparks was only able to weakly parry. "I didn't kill Dek. *You* did."

"Don't play games. You forced it," Sparks said as she found another opportunity to kick at Merwin. Of the two, Merwin was the better swordsman. But Sparks had trained more extensively in mixed martial arts and other forms of physical battle, giving her melee arsenal more offensive options.

The kick was mostly ineffective, but Sparks followed with an elbow jab into Merwin's torso, knocking the white-clad woman down. Merwin's sword bounced out of her hand and slid several meters across the floor.

May Dek rest in peace, Sparks thought as she channeled her wrath to end the life of the chaperone. "So long, Merwin."

Sparks brought the killing swing down on her foe. Merwin scrambled, pushing with legs as she threw her arms up to protect herself. As her blade came down on Merwin, a Trooper's bullet hit Spark's torso. The impact didn't pierce her armor, but the force knocked Sparks off balance, and her blade created an epidural laceration across Merwin's pale, bare arms. Blood surfaced as Merwin instinctively clutched her arms. Using only her legs and shifting weight, she sprung up and looked for her weapon.

North ran to Sparks. "Come on!" He pulled her up, reaching into a hip pouch to pull out a small white orb. He pressed his fingernail in the trigger and tossed it toward a group of Troopers taking aim.

Sparks buckled and fell again as three more bullets entered her torso. North took a bullet in the chest, but his armor held. The hit was painful, but North was beyond acknowledging pain. He saw Sparks had fallen unconscious.

The orb exploded and mutilated several unfortunate Chasm troopers.

North pulled the last orb out of Sparks' pouch and immediately tossed it. This time the Troopers scattered and were mostly outside the blast radius when the orb exploded.

North hoisted Sparks over his shoulder, snatched his javelin and took off running down the corridor. The *Tinkebell* Marines started backing out of their cover, laying down a lot of intimidating, but ineffective, cover fire.

Several Troopers had their sniper rifles trained on North's as the Marine commander fled.

Suddenly, the corridor jolted with so much force that everyone was thrown to the floor.

"What the hell was that?" A Marine asked.

"That was the plan," North said, as he quickly scrambled up again, picking up the bleeding-out Sparks and with all the strength left in him, started sprinting down the corridor.

New klaxons sounded, and the corridor rumbled again, though not as intensely as the first time.

Merwin stood up to give chase, but quickly grew faint, likely from blood loss, she thought. She signaled a medic to treat her bleeding arms. As she saw the Commander North disappear around a far corner, she was both angry and happy. *A formidable foe, worthy of battle,* Merwin thought.

Fifteen minutes earlier, Acting Captain Alecia Blight was attempting to get control of her ship.

"What do we have working?" she said over comms to her husband, who was back at his engineering station.

"Short range thrusters and the power plant are still in good shape. I can keep you in orbit or we can get around Arara, but we won't be able to back into deep space or even escape Arara's gravity until we repair at least one of the main engines."

"Get your best people on it, then," Blight ordered.

"We've lost all atmosphere on G deck from the midship forward. There were hundreds…" Elizabeth's voice trailed off before she finished her sentence.

I can't grieve them now, Blight thought, as she wiped beads of sweat off her forehead. She looked at gunnery liaison Boot Fuego. "How long before the gunnery teams reload the silos? What's going on down there?"

Boot looked back at the captain, teary eyed and shaking his head. "I think we took a direct hit on weapons control. There was screaming for a second and then… silence."

"Look at me, Boot. Stay focused. I need you to find out for sure what's going on with our weapons," Blight tried to keep calm in the chaos.

"I'm okay," Boot nodded.

"Can we get a status on Amberly? Is it safe to transport her off *Marquette*?" Blight asked. They could bring Amberly back to the *Magnus*, but considering the status of the warship, it might not be a better choice than the waypoint. They could send her on a runabout down to the Lewis Island base, but with *Utopia* still lurking around, that was a dangerous proposition as well. *Amberly is safest where she is now,* Blight thought. *If we execute the contingency, Amberly will be able to get off the station safely under the cover of chaos.* "Cho, what's the status of *Utopia*?"

"Still hiding on the underside of the waypoint," Cho said. "We must have hit her pretty hard. If she had any fight left, she'd be on us by now."

"Sure looked that way," Elizabeth said.

"*Utopia* doesn't matter. We won't be able to survive another attack from *Marquette*. And with only thrusters to keep us in orbit, we're stuck here. It won't be long before *Marquette* reloads its silos." Cho said.

"Helmsman, we practiced for this," Blight said.

"We practiced for everything, a hundred times," the helmsman said. "What are your orders?"

"Point our nose on the *Marquette* garden dome. Give the thrusters fifty mega-newtons," Blight ordered, moving from the tactical table into her command chair, putting on the seat harness. "Once you make contact, increase to 100."

"Ah, yes," the helmsman said. "The Sparks Maneuver. Right

then."

"Hawkins, please signal for all bow chambers to be evacuated on the shipwides," Blight said, rubbing her bald head.

"Ramming them, captain?" Hawkins looked worried. "That's the Sparks Maneuver."

"Heavens no, we're not committing suicide," Blight smiled. "I just want to give them a little push. Radio Rhodes and give her the evacuation code. Get everyone off *Marquette*.

"Yes, ma'am. Rhodes reports that North is leading a rescue mission to save a continent of trapped Marines."

"Let's get ready to collect ships and pods, or everyone will need to find their own way to the rendezvous point on the Lewis Islands," Blight ordered. "Signal Commander Bloom down there. Tell her to muster any search and rescue resources she has. And relay to North that it's going to get bumpy."

Amberly kept looking out the bay window at the injured *Magnus*. The ship had stabilized after the assault from *Marquette*. "The *Magnus* is getting closer, Rhodes. She's getting really close."

"Good," Rhodes said. "I need to get you off of this station and on the *Magnus*. It's too risky with you on here. We're too exposed. If *Magnus* is close by, it means the ferry will be shorter."

"I've already gone over this with you, lieutenant. I am *not* leaving without my dad," Amberly insisted.

"That call is above my pay grade. Let me radio the XO and see what she says," Rhodes replied and moved to her portable comm station to signal *Magnus*.

Alfonsi walked over to Amberly and handed her a pistol. "You know how to use this?"

Amberly took the weapon and considered it. "Not really."

"It's a point and shoot. Thirty bullets in the magazine. Try not to put any holes in the hull or out goes the air. You may have to shoot someone to survive. You should try to steel yourself for that time. Don't choke. Remember, it's you or them. Have you ever shot someone?"

"Just my mother."

"You shot … Red's… You?" Alfonsi was mildly shocked.

"This is the safety?" Amberly asked, pointing to a knob on the gun.

"Um… yes."

Amberly checked the safety and slipped the gun into the left-side pocket on her dress.

"Hey guys," Rhodes shouted in her normal voice, looking up from the comm station. She held a receiver to one ear. "*Magnus* says it's going to get bumpy. Time to evacuate. They are going to try to … oh dirty son a dirty dirt licker … to push *Marquette* out of orbit."

"Crash her into the planet?" Fiat asked, horrified.

"Of course! Without death from above, the *Infinite Order* will lose its grip on the people," Alfonsi said. "This is it."

"We can't afford to lose another waypoint," Amberly objected. "We need the link to Earth–"

"Yes, darling, but this is for all the marbles," Alfonsi said. "It's worth it. It's brilliant. We'll rebuild."

"At least we're in the hangar and close to the escape ships. With any luck North and Alroy's teams will be back soon and we can load up and get out of here. We may actually win this," Rhodes said glancing between her Lewis Island friends and Amberly. "Guys, *we may actually win this*. And when we do, I'm going to take a long vacation on Arara. Amberly, have you ever been on the planet? It's so amazing! We went down there to look for you and it was so—"

An armor-piercing bullet hit Rhodes in the abdomen. She reached down, felt blood, and looked at her red hand. *This is a surreal experience*, Rhodes thought. Two more *thwacks*, and the *Magnus* officer fell to the ground.

Panicked, Alfonsi swung around and scanned the hangar to find where the enemy fire came from. He saw a contingent of Chairman's Honor Guard at the maintenance entrance. He pulled his rifle up, but didn't get a shot off before he was hit between the eyes. Alfonsi desperately wanted to say something to Amberly, but couldn't manage it before he died.

Fiat trained a pistol on the lead guard, the burly Ka Top, who was now charging the Irregular. He sent several bullets to disintegrate in Ka Top's PDS. Fiat frantically grabbed his shock stick and jabbed it at Ka Top when he was just steps away. Ka Top knocked the stick out of Fiat's hand with his forearm, and it nearly hit Amberly. Ka Top sprung a flip over the Irregular, grabbing

Fiat's head and snapping the neck as he landed behind the Lewis Islander.

Amberly stood alone.

"Amberly, I've lost my patience with you," the Chairman seemed to float from out of a tight circle of Honor Guards. "Either you don't really understand how valuable you are to humanity, or perhaps you are just too selfish to care. If you leave now, you are condemning humanity to eternal *depravity*. Be humanity's savior, Amberly. *You* are the key to perfection."

"I'm no savior," Amberly said. "And neither are you. I may be selfish, but it's not because I reject your vision. Saviors free people. I will not sit as master over an enslaved people to chase an unknowable perfection."

"Perfection *is* the only freedom, child. Freedom from slavery to our own folly," the Chairman frowned. "Ka Top, take her."

The big man approached Amberly. Amberly grabbed Fiat's shock stick and waved it at Ka Top. He moved closer, now only a meter. With her left hand, she pushed the stick forward.

"Careful, Ka Top," the Chairman called. Flexing his muscles and throwing his huge arms up to stretch his back, Ka Top wondered if she meant be careful not to hurt Amberly, or if he should be wary of Amberly for his own safety. *Clearly the former*, he thought.

Amberly steadied herself. Ka Top's chest armor bobbed as he laughed, now only an arms' length away from Amberly. She stepped back, then appeared to stumble onto her backside, dropping the shock stick.

Ka Top bent over and reached his arm around Amberly's torso, and began to hoist her into a standing position so he could then lift her over his shoulder. As he pulled her up, Amberly slid her right arm into the left pocket of her blue dress. Ka Top moved his other arm around Amberly's right shoulder and locked his hands in a quasi-embrace, ready to lift her over his shoulder, and present her to his mistress, the Chairman.

Standing face to face with Amberly, his prey pulled to him, he smiled with dominance. *My time for glory has come*, Ka Top thought. The powerful anger in Amberly's clear eyes blazed like fire, and Ka Top's smile became confused as he tightened his grip and prepared to hoist her.

"This is how I shot Kimberly Macready, asshole," Amberly growled, as she jabbed the pistol Alfonsi had given her into Ka Top's abdomen and pulled the trigger twice. Ka Top grimaced, while his eyes faded from shock to darkness. Amberly pushed the large body away, and Ka Top fell to the floor, dead.

The redhead glared at the Chairman as faint smoke rose from her gun.

Amberly stood defiant.

A sudden, severe jolt knocked everyone – the half-dozen Honor Guards, the Chairman, Amberly – to the floor. As several Honor Guards recovered their footing, they did not wait for the Chairman's command to move in on Raven Two.

The bridge of the *Magnus* jerked violently. "I'm glad I strapped in," Blight said to no one in particular. Following a second jerk, the whole ship groaned.

"Contact with *Waypoint Marquette*," Hawkins reported what everyone knew.

"Increasing thrusters to 100 mega-newtons," the helm announced.

"Careful, the structural integrity of our nose is certainly weakened from the missile attack," Cho cautioned.

The *Magnus* shuttered slightly, as the groan changed pitch.

"They're pushing back."

Blight signaled Bollard in engineering. "Honey, how much can the thrusters put out?"

"We can get to a thousand, but once the inertia gets going, we could get caught in the gravity of Arara without the mains," Bollard said over the comms.

"What's the latest estimate on getting the main engines back up?"

"I can't be everywhere at once," Bollard said, exasperated. "Eight or nine hours. Maybe sooner if we are lucky. But it could be days."

"A normal orbit decay would take us years to reach critical atmosphere. In that case, we should be able to fix it," Cho said. "But we're not talking about a normal decay. We're pushing this waypoint essentially straight toward the surface. We'll have to pull up into a better orbit. Not sure if we can do that."

"Go to 500, Helm," Blight commanded. "Cho, do you think we can land this thing on the Lewis Islands if we have too?"

Cho was about to answer, but paused while odd vibrations reverberated through the *Magnus*. Then the ship leapt forward.

"We're moving her!" Elizabeth shouted, looking at the tactical screen at her station.

"The emergency landing equipment is still green, so in theory, we could land," he answered the acting captain, "but we'd never be able to get into orbit again on our own power. We'd have to commandeer some booster rockets."

"North can worry about that later," Blight said. "Okay, let's push this thing all the way down as fast as possible. If we do, and we can survive, we win. Betsy, have our remaining corvettes and runabouts be on the lookout for escape pods and other evacuees from *Marquette*. If we can't keep *Magnus* afloat, it will be up to the little ships to make sure everyone makes it home. Bollard, how's the nose?"

"Holding up. Structural integrity is still good."

"Full thrusters, helm," Blight said. "The Chairman's reign of terror is about to end."

"Please get North off of there," Hawkins quietly prayed.

Cho looked out the starboard viewport. "Where's *Utopia?*"

From the exterior, the one-kilometer long cylindrical warship *Magnus* was pointed directly into the center of the saucer shaped, seven-kilometer diameter waypoint, having massively indented the garden dome in the process. The vector of force from the green-tinted *Magnus* was nearly straight toward the planet, as the pair of space objects' orbits began to decay.

Between *Marquette* and Arara – beneath *Marquette* relative to the planet – was the wounded *Utopia*, still spewing air and licking its wounds. The dark-colored ship, with flames spitting out from hull breaches to consume the escaping oxygen, had caught the full starshine of the rising Viapos, and the ship gleamed with a purple hue.

As the humongous *Marquette* was pushed closer to the *Utopia*, the disabled warship attempted to maneuver out of the waypoint's downward, crushing path. The primary hull cleared the rim of the descending station, but *Utopia's* secondary hull did not.

The accelerating edge of the waypoint, pushed by the full power of the *Magnus*, cut into the *Utopia*, exposing the antimatter-fueled power plant and its ten power generators. *Some* of the safeties triggered, boxing the reactors and shutting them down. But not all.

A large explosion created an energy fireball that consumed most of *Utopia*, and nearly a square kilometer of *Marquette*. A huge fissure opened up near the point of impact and started several fault lines along the surface of the waypoint.

The remains of *Utopia* – hundreds of thousands of shards of metal, random fragments of polycarbonate strips, charred people, snap-frozen ice chucks – began a more aggressive orbital decay, propelled in all directions from the reactor explosion.

The final ship of the Dark Armada had fallen.

CHAPTER TWENTY-FOUR

Jana led the survivors of the failed assault back into *Marquette's* secondary hangar. The Master Sergeant didn't have an exact count, but she knew she had fewer than 100 of the 250 Marines and Irregulars that had originally stormed the waypoint. Alroy came in behind Jana with the surviving Irregulars. The hangar seemed abandoned.

"Secure your ships. Get on board. Make sure you can power up. As soon as North gets back, we'll blow the space doors and get out of here." Marines started to comply, scrambling up the various hatches on the runabouts they had littered and crash-landed into the waypoint.

"Where's Amberly?" Alroy cried out.

Illam, an irregular officer, shouted with unmistakable agony. "Captain Red! The corporal! He was guarding Amberly."

Alroy sprinted over to the triple window. He saw the bodies of Alfonsi and Fiat on the floor. He didn't have to check to know they were dead. "God have mercy on their souls." Grief started to overwhelm him. *Where's Amberly?* Alroy started to frantically look around, when he spotted Rhodes on the floor a few meters away.

"Who did this? Chasm's been here!" Illam ansered his own question as he instinctively started to scan the large room.

A moment later, North stumbled in, carrying Sparks with the help of another Marine. Breathless, he gasped, "Medic! I need a medic! Now. Multiple bullet wounds. She's fading fast! Medic!"

Jana looked at Sparks and then pointed at two Marines. "Get her into the medbay on the *Solar Flare*," Jana referred to the runabout that brought her. The Marines grabbed Sparks' limp body and passed her up the hatch.

"North!" Alroy shouted. "Help! You have a casualty over here. It's Rhodes."

North and Alroy hoisted Rhodes up and carried the woman toward the *Solar Flare*.

Jana and another officer moved to take Rhodes. "She's in bad shape," Jana observed, then looked to North. "I hope we can save her."

North and Alroy handed over the comm officer. North took a breath, but Alroy did not relax.

"North, I can't find Amberly. Her guards are dead."

"What? No!" North scanned the hangar. *There were plenty of places on the hangar, behind one of the ships, or even in the ships, where Amberly could be*, he thought. *Behind or in the cargo containers, under a corvette.* North began to fear the worse.

"Amberly," Alroy called out. "Where are you?"

Several shots buzzed by Alroy's ears, bullets pinging on the metal wall behind them.

"A warning shot, Alroy Macready," the Chairman said, revealing herself by seemingly floating on top of her yacht, looking down on the hangar. "Those snipers have your head in scope. Have your Marines stand down."

Illam saw the Chairman, aimed his rifle, and let loose a volley. His bullets turned into mist. Suddenly, Illam collapsed on the floor as master shots from unseen places took him out.

"Stop it!" North said, dropping his javelin on the floor. "What do you want? Where's Amberly?"

"Commander North," the Chairman smiled. "I'm so glad to see you again. Amberly is where she belongs. With her community. With *me*. See for yourself. And then for the common good, surrender. No more deaths."

A pair of Chasm Honor Guards, along with Dr. Michelle Leigh, pulled Amberly through the top hatch. Amberly and Michelle stood alongside the Chairman on the roof of the Yacht. Amberly's hands were zip cuffed, and she looked rough, as if she had been in a prolonged physical struggle.

Then, for the first time in over a decade, Amberly saw her dad.

"Dad!" Amberly shouted. But she did not see recognition in his eyes, so she added, "It's me. I'm grown up now."

Alroy's eyes lit up. *It's her.* Fragments floated at the edges of his brain. *Amberly.* All the details weren't there, but the feeling he knew her and she was important to him were powerfully strong. "Amberly," Alroy noted her red hair. "Of course, you are."

He cried large tears.

It was no flood, but his memory had started to trickle back.

Here she was, his daughter. *His* family. Not the Chairman's.

"I'm sorry for not being there to protect you."

"I love you," Amberly wept severely.

"Give us Amberly, and we'll go in peace," North demanded of the Chairman.

"Commander North, I've only shown you Amberly is well as a token of my goodwill. You are severely presumptuous. Alroy Macready, I've hated you for a long time," the Chairman announced. "Ever since Kimberly first wrote to me about you during her mission on *Magellan*. With every word she used to describe you, I knew it would not end well for my daughter."

"Kimberly," Alroy felt a hazy sense of his dead mate return. "My beautiful wife."

"Yes, she thought you dead Alroy," the Chairman looked sad. "She was so magnificent. She was the most perfect human ever. But not fully perfect, and the evidence is here." The Chairman tipped her head toward Amberly.

"Your perfection is an illusion," Alroy declared. "Flaws make us great."

"We should not quarrel, Alroy. I believe Raven One *would be* happy to know you survived," the Chairman said. "Of course, she's *not* happy. She's not *anything*. She was taken —"

"Mom gave us the message, Dad," Amberly interrupted, shouting as she squirmed against her restraints. "You wanted Kora and I to know you loved us. Mom gave me the message."

"Love. Hate. Hmmm… My hate has expired, and now I offer you, Alroy, the chance for reconciliation. Come join our family. Be with Amberly. Help us perfect humanity. Or die. Your choice. I only need your DNA which could be harvested off your dead body. But I know our dear Raven Two – Amberly – would be much happier if you were with her as she ascends to her destined glory."

Yeoman Carnell, looking ghostly nervous because of all the weapons being bandied about, emerged from the yacht's topside hatch, approached the Chairman and whispered in her ear. The Chairman closed her eyes for a half-second to run a hundred calculations about orbital decay in her head. Her iris-less eyes popped open.

"Of course. You can order the life pods unlocked. Start an evacuation," the Chairman said to her aide, who retreated back into the docked yacht. The Chairman turned back to the North and Alroy. "Looks like your allies are doing our Chasm work for us. You destroyed *Magellan* for me, and now you are dooming this waypoint as well. Thanks to the *Magnus*, I'm out of time, Alroy Macready. What do you say? Join us, or will *Marquette* be your tomb?"

"Madam Chairman!" Merwin One appeared in the main door, her sword drawn, her dress torn and bloodied, her hair wild, and her arms bandaged. "We're going to hit *Uto—*"

A painfully loud clap shook the hangar, and the waypoint's hull seemed to groan in pain so loudly that several Marines and Troopers covered their ears. Waves of cracking sounds made freaky vibrations and nearly everyone on the deck believed their death was imminent.

A bright light flashed through the bridge, as the *Magnus* was rocked from the antimatter blast.

"Dirty hell," Cho shouted, as the bridge of the *Magnus* erupted once again into chaos. He stood and ran to the starboard viewport, leaning up against the window and pressing his hands against the scene of Armageddon. "God help us! *Marquette* is breaking up!" Cho's eyes widened as he saw cracks snake across the surface of the waypoint in bursts hundreds of meters at a time.

"Helm!" Alecia called urgently. "Helm! Cut the forward thrusters. Reverse, reverse! Pull us off!"

Engineering hailed the bridge. "Alecia, what's going on? We're not sinking the *Marquette* anymore?"

"There's not going to be a *Marquette* to push," the acting captain replied.

Hawkins gritted her teeth to avoid passing out as the *Magnus* decelerated, fighting both its own momentum and the growing gravitational pull from Arara. The G-forces were building as the inertia dampeners were struggling to cope with the sudden maneuvering.

"I'm going to be sick," she announced.

A gap between *Magnus* and *Marquette* opened up and became exponentially larger as *Magnus'* retro-thrusters powered up.

"Helm, find me an orbit! Find me an orbit! Keep us from

going down," Blight insisted.

"Yes, captain!"

"Hawkins, put me on the shipwides."

"You're on, captain," Hawkins looked green.

"This is the captain. *Marquette* is suffering from catastrophic fragmentation. We're ending our assault. With our main engines off line, we'll attempt a low-Arara orbit with our thrusters. Until now, war has been our mission. Now every one of you has a new mission. Our new priority is to rescue as many people as we can. Do your jobs. We've been trained to take lives, now it's time to save them. Calibrate the scanners. Get the lifeboats ready for when we come around the orbit. Blight out."

In the pandemonium of the waypoint-quake, North ran towards the Chairman's Yacht determined to rescue Amberly. Suddenly, his steps were meaningless as he began to float.

Marquette's artificial gravity had failed.

Dr. Leigh pulled Amberly to herself as she floated, producing a knife and cutting Amberly's cuffs, freeing her patient. "Forgive me, Amberly." The Chairman squinted her eyes, focusing on Michelle. She powerfully kicked off the top of the Yacht and floated towards the doctor, and as she passed she grabbed Dr. Leigh by her hair.

Michelle swung her knife toward the Chairman, but the leader of the Infinite Order harmlessly knocked it out of her hand.

The pair floated toward the hangar's ceiling as the Chairman grabbed the doctor by the throat, crushing her trachea. The doctor flailed her arms and legs in an attempt to escape the Chairman's grip, but by the time they hit the top, Dr. Michelle Leigh was dead.

A huge fissure ripped open on the hangar deck, exposing lower floors where the hull had already been compromised, sucking air, creating a current pulling everyone down. Another crack opened up above the main doorway into the interior of the waypoint, and the higher pressure pushed air into the hangar, creating a wind tunnel as atmosphere uncontrollably rushed in one tear and out the other. The wind caught Amberly and pulled her toward the fissure in the floor.

Amberly frantically scraped at the floor to slow her movement as the wind pulled her out. She scanned the room, her brain instantly analyzing dozens of objects, rejecting all of them except one — an anchor cable, connected to the deck on one side, but not to any ship on the other. As she slid by, she reached for an anchor cable, her fingers desperately digging into the wiry braid. She estimated her grip strength and the friction coefficient of the metal fibers that made up the cable and calculated she did not have the manual dexterity to keep her grip with her one hand. Pushing against massive wind shear, she got her second arm around the cable and held fast, stopping her movement toward the lower fissure. Amberly looped the 10-meter cable around her arm as it whipped Amberly through waves of rushing air.

"Amberly!" North called, grasping for the tops of the anchored ships he was floating over, unable to reach anything. "Hold on. I'm coming. Don't get sucked down!"

A sudden air blast flung the floating North into the hardened space door. The concussive hit knocked him out and cracked several of his ribs.

Alroy and Jana were holding onto the end of an escort corvette, trying to figure out their next move.

"Jana, go for North, get him on the *Solar Flare*, and get out of here," Alroy said. "I'm going for Amberly. Don't wait for us if you have the chance to escape. If those doors open, and we're not back, we're probably dead anyway."

Jana started to protest, but then nodded her agreement. Now was the time for action, not sentimentality. Jana pulled on her helmet, popped in an oxygen canister to her armor's limited life support system, and produced a small grappling line with a robotic suction head from her pack. *Always be prepared*, she thought. She shot the line to the space door, and then anchored it on the enemy corvette. *I wish I had the key codes to this bird*. It was going to be tricky getting North all the way over to the *Solar Flare*.

The Chairman kicked off the ceiling and floated back down to her yacht, expertly navigating the airstreams as if she had done it a million times. She saw Amberly struggling, and for the first time in a long time, experienced worry.

One of *Magnus'* runabouts, overloaded with many surviving *Marines*, had partially fired up its damaged thrusters. Inside, the pilot was hoping she would be able to escape as soon as either the space doors or a large enough hole in the hull opened up into the void of space.

Yeoman Carnell was sticking out, torso up, from the yacht's top hatch, arm extended toward the Chairman, as if to pull her in. "Hurry!" he yelled to the Chairman. At first, the Chairman was incensed that Carnell would dare to command her, but quickly forgave the transgression. *He's really so beneath me and my progeny,* she thought. *Like a pet. I can't expect him to really understand.* She would train him to show true respect without fail in time.

She landed on the roof and ignored Carnell's outstretched hand.

"Come on! Get in!" The Yeoman pleaded.

Her offended rage returned, and the Chairman slapped the young man harshly. "Do not order me, worm! Fetch me two oxygen breathers and a sleeping sedative injector before I have you airlocked.

This woman is sick crazy, the Yeoman thought as he looked around at the tempest that had formed in the hangar, but he said, "Yes, Madam Chairman," and called down into the bowels of the ship.

Moving through the weightless wind tunnel was challenging, and several times Jana almost slipped off her cable and into the ripped metal fissure. She bound North with a carabiner to her armor and drug him back toward the *Solar Flare.*

Alroy saw Amberly and called to her, but his voice was muted by the wind gusts. He put on his helmet, loaded his O2 and attempted to drag himself along the floor toward where Amberly had wrapped her arm in the docking cable to keep from being sucked into who-knows-what on the lower deck.

A screeching sound overpowered even the loud wind, as a small breach appeared near the trio of exterior windows. The polycarbonate framing around the windows buckled and popped out. Now in addition to atmosphere being funneled through the fissure, it was also being vented directly out into space. The new current pulled Alroy off the floor straight toward the windows into the void.

He knew he would be ripped apart soon after he hit the window, as his body would not fit through the 30-centimeter-wide portal. It would get crammed out. He readied himself, and as he hit the windowed wall, he kicked and rolled himself to the side. He was still pinned by the air current against the hull, but at least he wasn't ripped in two. *How can I get to Amberly now?* Once the atmosphere had evacuated entirely, assuming the waypoint was still holding together, he could just space walk over to her. But Amberly had no vacsuit on. Nothing. She would be dead before he reached his daughter.

"Hurry! Hurry!" Carnell called down into the yacht, and then started to push two emergency breathers and a packaged injector toward the Chairman. But instead of handing them to her, he tossed them away from the ship.

"Oops, sorry," he said. The Chairman was incensed at this tomfoolery as she started to leap to retrieve them, and in the second it took for her to understand Carnell's motivation, it was too late. "See you later, crazy old lady."

As he slammed the hatch closed, inside the ship, Carnell lied to his comrades on the yacht, "The Chairman said for us to evacuate and not wait for her. Direct order."

The Chairman snatched the injector, then got her fingers around the first breather as they floated away. She strained and touched the second one with the tip of her index finger, but was unable to secure it. It caught in a current and was sucked out the window into space.

My destiny must be fulfilled at all costs, the Chairman thought, a soft memory of a teenage Kimberly Macready unexpectedly surfacing in her head. She looked at Amberly, considered the wind current, and then plunged into the airstream and was swept toward the floor fissure.

Amberly saw the Chairman barreling toward her, and at the last minute, the Chairman snagged the anchor cable with her free hand. Amberly saw the injector and immediately knew the Chairman's intention. "No! I will not go with you. You cannot have me." As she spoke the threads in her mind considered the potential outcomes of a physical confrontation with the Chairman. Though she was much older than Amberly, Amberly knew the Chairman had years of strength and combat training. In the same millisecond, Amberly processed her only advantage was she had the superior grip.

A strong gust wildly flung the pair holding onto the cable away from the deck. They both clung for their life as the cable swung back down and slammed them hard onto the deck. Both held fast. Amberly had her arm looped around the cable, but the Chairman only had the grip of her fingers of her right hand — and still wasn't jerked off. Amberly mentally noted that she did not know the upward limit of the Chairman's strength.

It's now or never, Amberly thought. Amberly rewrapped her left arm under the cable, and slid down the length of the cable toward its end, where the Chairman gripped with only one hand, while she clutched the breather and injector with the other. Amberly reached out with her right hand and attempted to pry the Chairman's fingers off the end of the anchor cable. The Chairman grunted, her white hair whipping wildly, and with her free hand shoved the breather and injector into a pouch in her cloak.

As Amberly pried the Chairman's grip off the cable, as the old woman thrust her free hand out and grabbed Amberly's left shoulder, digging her hands deep into Amberly's flesh to keep from being sucked into the fissure. Amberly cried out in pain and jerked her torso to dislodge the fingers sunk into her flesh. The Chairman swung the pried-off arm back at the cable and achieved a more secure grip.

It was a stalemate.

"You think I am evil Amberly. Maybe you are right," the Chairman shouted over the maelstrom. "But what I am doing is greater than me. Greater than you. Even greater than your mother. It must endure. Please. I beg you."

"No! I'm done being hurt by you," Amberly said. As they spoke, both women's brains had multiple thought threads calculating thousands of tactics to figure out how to gain an advantage. The Chairman knew she couldn't get to the injector to subdue Amberly without making herself vulnerable to Amberly's attack. Amberly knew the Chairman had the strength advantage, but the Chairman was desperate to save her, not let her get sucked into the fissure. Amberly's multithreaded calculation returned that the most likely outcome for success, though the chance was small, was to wear the Chairman down, distract her, and hope that another variable — like a flying piece of rubble — would appear.

Amberly threw her clenched right fist into the Chairman's jaw. The Chairman's whole body bucked and flapped in the wind, but she held firm, her hand digging deeper into Amberly's flesh. Amberly punched her again, this time hitting the eye socket that held those evil eyes.

The Chairman cried out as Amberly hit her again and again.

The Chairman knew she could not take this beating indefinitely from Amberly. She loosened her grip on Amberly and slid down a yard toward the end of the cable, with just a dozen centimeters of slack before the end cap. The Chairman was calm. Her feeling of alarm was gone, replaced with profound sadness.

A grappling cable hit the floor near the anchor cable.

"Finally," the Chairman said, somewhat relieved.

Sliding down the grappling cable was Merwin One. She latched onto the anchor cable between the Chairman and Amberly, and turned to the Chairman, and helped to more securely wrap her arm around the cable.

"*Thank you*, chaperone," the Chairman said. The Chairman had used those words before, but this was the first time that Merwin felt true gratitude, not just generic positive reinforcement, from her master. *I am fulfilled,* Merwin thought. As Merwin helped the Chairman, Amberly forced herself against the wind flow, slowly retreating toward the base of the anchor cable. She knew she could not survive Merwin.

"I was on the yacht. Carnell meant to betray you," Merwin said.

"I know," the Chairman replied.

"He no longer is in possession of his head."

"Another weak man reaches his logical end," the Chairman said. "Help me get Amberly subdued. We will still prevail. This is a minor setback."

"No! Amberly will kill you the first chance she has. She must die so you can live, my Chairman."

The whole waypoint shook violently again, and the three women scrambled to keep their grips on the anchor cable. The fissures in the floor grew wider, and all three of the windows frames ripped out, merging into one big vent into space. The shaking stopped, and Merwin turned from the Chairman and began to pull herself toward Amberly.

"Merwin! Stop! Merwin!" The Chairman reached out to grab Merwin, but she was too far up the cable. "Amberly is everything... without her... my life is for nothing."

Amberly shook the cable to try to throw Merwin off. But Merwin impressively held fast with just one hand.

"I'm sorry, Raven Two, but this is the only way I know I can keep my glorious Chairman safe. It is my reason for being."

The wind had shifted the floating cable, so Amberly and Merwin were on the same plane. Merwin was downwind, but the gap was nearly closed. It didn't take Amberly's multivariate thoughts to realize there was no victory against Merwin. Desperate, Amberly punched at Merwin, but her untrained punches hit the hardened warrior like water over rocks. Merwin gripped the cable tightly with her left hand, and unsheathed her crimson-stained sword.

Merwin lifted the weapon high to power her swing. She wanted the kill to be clean, with no pain for the star-crossed daughter of Raven One. Amberly punched Merwin in the face, but the chaperone did not winch or flinch.

"Eternal rest now, Amberly," Merwin swung for the kill.

Unexpectedly, the warrior let her sword go, powerless to hold it as the weapon was swept away. Her eyes rolled back into her head, and she slowly, involuntarily, released the cable. The wind stream caught Merwin and tossed her toward the fissure. Instead of slipping through, her limp figure impaled on a shard of twisted support structure. The growing air current pushed her body further on the pike, until her body severed in two at the torso. Both pieces peeled off the shard and were sucked out of sight through the floor.

Shocked, Amberly looked back from the fissure, and the Chairman was closer to her now, having pulled herself up on the cable. In her hand, the Chairman had a discharged sedative injection.

"I... I... couldn't let her kill you," the Chairman said, her black eyes filled with dark sadness. "You must continue the work."

Amberly opened her mouth to reply, but was interrupted.

A broken klaxon warbled. "Warning. Space doors opening. Warning."

With Merwin gone, someone on the yacht had decided to not

wait for the Chairman. Both women knew if the doors opened, they would be dead in seconds from space exposure or suffocation or both. Both began to process thousands of outcomes.

"We have to jump into the fissure and take our chances," Amberly said. "If we could land on a subdeck, maybe we can keep from getting sucked out and find sanctuary." For an instant, Amberly considered abandoning the Chairman, but the Chairman likely had committed the layout of the whole waypoint to memory. Also, the Chairman would have access codes and other means to finding life-giving resources. With the Chairman, Amberly had a chance of survival. Without her, even if she successfully navigated the fissure, she had almost none.

"Yes," the Chairman said, proud of her granddaughter's obviously growing mental prowess. "My calculations have reached the same conclusion."

Amberly took her free hand and clasped the Chairman's free arm. "On the count of three, let go and hold onto my arm tight as you can. Grab onto anything, but be careful for your head. Three, two, one —"

The red and white locks of hair of grandmother and granddaughter whipped furiously and the pair, arm in arm, weightless in space, jumped and were pushed through the widening fissure.

On the *Solar Flare*, North opened his eyes. Pain shot through his body like forks of electricity, burning every nerve in his body. He gathered that he was in a small medbay, lying down. He forced himself to turn his head and saw a group of Marines surrounding Sparks, appearing to be in some sort of surgical procedure. He saw Sparks half-mask cast aside on the floor, covered in blood.

"Easy North," Master Sergeant Jana Smith was sitting on the other side of North, holding his hand. "Be still. We'll have you on the *Magnus* soon, and they can take care of you there."

"Sparks, is she…" North struggled to talk, every word made his chest feel like it was on fire.

"Shhh! The medics are hopeful that she'll make it. They are removing bullets now. You need to try not to speak or move," Jana said. "You only have a measly 24 breaks in your ribs. Don't worry, we'll pull Sparks through. You saved her life."

"Amberly!" North shouted and forced himself to sit up. He screamed from the pain. But the pain didn't matter. "Where's Amberly." North collapsed back down on the gurney.

"Whoa! Relax! She didn't make it out," Jana said. "I'm sorry, North, she didn't make it. The space doors opened... We've accounted for all our ships. She's not on any of them. Alroy, too. I'm so sorry, North."

"She could be on the waypoint still," North choked, spitting out blood, trying to get up. "Or in a life pod." He spasmed from the pain.

"North, you can't move! Medic," Jana shouted and looked to the team working on Sparks. "A little help. Sedative? Sedative!"

"I order you to take us back," North looked angry. "Take us back and look for her."

"North, there's no waypoint to go back to. *Marquette* is coming apart."

"We have to find Amberly, we have to—" One of the Marines attending Sparks injected North, and he fell asleep.

Amberly hit a flat surface on her back. There was still air, so she knew she wasn't out in space. She opened her eyes, and saw she and the Chairman had landed two decks down from the hangar deck, having successfully used their momentum to navigate out of the fissure's main current until they hit the floor.

They floated in a gaseous eddy. Amberly put herself upright to the ripped open corridor she had landed in. She underestimated the suction of current in the fissure, and the maelstrom pushed her toward the gap. The Chairman held onto a café table bolted to the ground with one arm, and with the other reached out and grabbed the shoulder strap of Amberly's dress, keeping her from tumbling down. Amberly put her foot down on the floor, creating enough friction to stabilize her in the eddy. She pulled herself into the relative safety of the eddy, and grabbed onto the edge of the table the Chairman held.

Amberly glanced down the fissure and saw the hull breach, and through the breach, about 300 kilometers below, the beautiful planet Arara. Amberly almost fainted from vertigo.

"Look at me! Amberly, look at me," the Chairman pulled Amberly's head to face her. Amberly looked hard into the

Chairman's eyes, and she saw the Chairman's resolve. "Focus. You must survive."

Amberly's mind snapped back on and began to fill her matrix with new variables. As she expected, the Chairman took action to protect Amberly. Now Amberly needed to take advantage of what was only in the Chairman's mind. "I assume you know where to go," Amberly said.

The Chairman pulled Amberly further into the corridor and away from the fissure. The capillary corridor traveled in a straight line for several hundred meters to the edge of the waypoint.

"There," the Chairman recalled deck schematics of the waypoint she had memorized. "After the bend, at the end of this hallway, is a door that opens to a foyer with an escape pod. Let's go."

Amberly looked in the direction the Chairman had pointed at the bend she indicated. Still weightless, the pair managed to pull themselves along the walls of the corridor, illuminated only by flickering emergency lights. Just a dozen meters in, they ran into a frozen, dead body of what looked like maybe a four or five-year-old girl. The girl had black hair, beautiful mocha skin, and her eyes were glassy and open.

Amberly grew red with anger. "You did this! Your maniacal obsession has killed tens of thousands."

"The price of perfection, Amberly," the Chairman said. "You don't have to agree with my moral calculus, but I was willing to do what had to be done. I will pay my own price soon. We must keep moving before it is too late. The atmosphere in this hall won't last."

Amberly felt like she couldn't just leave the child's body, but quickly concluded nothing could be done. She followed the Chairman, who had already proceeded down the dark, cold hall.

Amberly noticed the sound of rushing wind had abated significantly. "It's getting quiet."

"A bad omen," the Chairman said, still moving. "The waypoint is becoming a vacuum."

About 100 meters further down the corridor, Amberly felt short of breath and her lungs started to burn. When she exhaled, white wisps exited her mouth. Nothing in her matrix pointing to survival. "We can't make it. The air is almost gone. The temperature is plummeting." Amberly shivered and wished she was wearing something more appropriate than her mother's party dress.

Amberly looked back down the corridor, and again at the Chairman. The Chairman looked like she had aged 20 years in as many minutes. Even though she was literally floating, she seemed downtrodden and heavy. "The frigidity won't last. Once we hit the atmosphere, what's left of *Marquette* will start to cook. The whole of the waypoint must be nearly a complete vacuum now. Soon this air will be gone too," the Chairman waved her finger in a circle.

"Come on then," Amberly said, now feeling faint and a little panicked, "no time to waste."

"Wait, Amberly, wait," the Chairman pulled the respirator out of her cloak pouch. "You have to survive. Take this."

Amberly looked at the respirator that would give her air for several hours if she could survive the cold. She knew if she took it, she was dooming the Chairman to death. If she didn't take it, she would die. The Chairman saw Amberly's hesitation.

"You see, *I* am being selfish," the Chairman smiled. "You must survive for my legacy to survive. By saving you, I am saving myself. Take the mask. And take this."

The Chairman produced a data chit from the folds of her jumpsuit. "This is ... my life work, kept safe in my memory. I transcribed it for you ... the genetic sequencing protocol that made Kimberly, who made you. Take it. Take the mask. Promise me you'll finish what I started. Promise me!" The Chairman struggled for the air that was hardly there.

Amberly was filled with revulsion and compassion all at the same time. The Chairman was evil. So many had suffered for her vision. *She deserves to die,* Amberly thought. But in the Chairman, she saw the face of Kimberly Macready. Behind her mother's evil, there was some misguided sense of love. She knew in spite of it all, Kimberly had loved her. And she felt this was her moment to honor her mother's love. The Chairman was doomed. God or karma or the universe was about to snuff her out. Amberly was convinced the Chairman was wrong about people. Humanity will never be perfected.

We don't need to be perfect, Amberly thought. *We have forgiveness. And love.*

"I promise," Amberly said, struggling to breath at all. She started seeing stars in her peripheral vision. She grabbed the chit and the mask, and pulled the respirator over her nose and opened the O2 canister. Amberly breathed deeply and felt a wave of euphoria washed over her as the pure oxygen hit her bloodstream.

"My time is short," the Chairman gasped. "Stay with me … while I cross into the undiscovered country … no one else I'd rather be with here at the end."

Amberly pulled the suddenly frail woman into her arms and began to weep. The Chairman rested her head in Amberly's bosom.

"What's your name?" Amberly asked through the respirator.

"You mom named her firstborn after me."

"Kora?"

"Kora."

"I miss Kimberly," Kora said, almost inaudibly. "I loved her so."

"I miss her, too."

The Chairman, Kora, said nothing more.

Amberly wept for a brief moment as she clutched her grandmother, Kora, close to her heart. In her mind's eye, she saw the faces of the dead. Anderson. Eaton. Moreno. Thor. Skylar. Wong. Kato. Skip. Midas. Alfonsi. Kimberly. And Dek Tigona. And thousands more. Friends and lovers, allies and enemies, all sacrificed to fuel the Chairman's ambition.

The air was nearly non-existent. Amberly noticed the expansion and contraction of Kora's lungs had ceased.

The Chairman was dead.

I lied to North. I lied to Dek, Amberly thought. *One last lie for the greater good.* Amberly released the body of her grandmother and the dead woman floated parallel to the floor of the corridor. Amberly removed the Chairman's cloak and threw it over her own shivering body. Then Amberly took the data chit and placed it in the Kora's cold fingers, folding the dead woman's hand into a fist. She pulled the eyelids closed over those haunting, iris-less eyes.

She looked at the hand holding the chit and second-guessed herself. *I am a woman of science, dedicated to the pursuit of knowledge. What is on there will be lost forever, never known to mankind again*, Amberly thought. *Is that what I want? Haven't I always believed science will lift us up, that all knowledge has the power to edify humanity?*

Amberly closed her eyes, thought about the protocol on that chit and considered tens of thousands of outcomes in a few seconds. Her mind was never sharper.

No. Some things — including perfection – are best left as mysteries. Kora died believing the quest for perfection would continue, and that is good enough.

Amberly turned and began to hurry toward the end of the corridor.

Energized by the rich oxygen from the respirator, she pulled herself along the wall toward the waiting lifepod. She felt painfully cold, and figured the temperature was already negative.

She grasped at a window seal to pull herself forward, but her hand slipped on a thin layer of ice that had formed. Amberly saw where, a few meters ahead, a water pipe had burst, creating a cascade of icy formations.

Amberly imagined the waypoint falling into the atmosphere and heating from the intense friction, but she had done the math in her head and knew it could be hours or days before the orbit of the waypoint decayed enough to start heating things up. She'd be frozen dead long before that.

After another few minutes of elemental struggle, Amberly made it to the exterior portal of the staging chamber for the life pod. The power was out, so she had to manually slide the door. She reached out and grabbed the small handle, and quickly withdrew her hand, ripping epidermis that had freeze-bonded instantly with the metal. It stung, and she cursed.

She wrapped her hand in the corner of her cloak and yanked on the door.

It didn't open.

She wrapped both her hands, and yanked again, grunting loudly. The door was frozen shut.

She kicked the door with her flat-wearing foot as hard as she could. She was rewarded with a faint cracking heard over the thinnest air.

Amberly yanked again, and the door gave. A wisp of warmer air moved from the foyer into the hall. Amberly floated into the staging chamber, pulling the door shut behind her. Though frigid, she immediately noticed the temperature in this room was relatively warm compared to the death chill out in the corridor.

As the door latched, battery-powered emergency lights came on. Amberly quickly surveyed the room. She first saw a supply closet, door ajar, and spotted an environmental-controlled vac suit inside. She also saw a medkit and some glow rods. She kicked across the three-meter-deep room to the access portal to the life pod. The eject control was also battery powered. She keyed it on to check the pod status.

Gone.

Dammit. Of course, someone has already taken the pod, Amberly thought. Despair began to freeze her heart, but then she thought about everything North and Dek, and so many others, had done to save her. *There must be another way. I must keep trying.*

Amberly turned off the oxygen supply and pulled off her respirator. There was enough air trapped in this small room, so she didn't want to waste her portable supply.

She stripped down to her underclothes in the freezing room and pulled out the two-piece vacsuit. She stepped through the waistline of the lower piece. She hung the upper piece on a hook in the room designed for that purpose. She ducked under the waist opening and slid her arms and head up into the hanging top. She pulled back off the hook, reached down in the semi-bulky suit arms, and latched the upper and lower waist pieces together.

As soon as it was latched, a basic VI in the suit powered on. "Please attach helmet unit. Warning. Extreme low temperature detected. Activating heating units. Battery levels, 83 percent."

Amberly threw the closet door all the way open and didn't see the helmet. Frustrated, she pushed aside the medkit and saw the shiny dome of a helmet under some liquid rations and a pack of induction ports. She grabbed the helmet and placed it over her head, pushing a few locks of red hair out of the way of the magnetic seal.

"Welcome," the suit said to her in the helmet speakers. "Suit status report. Temperature control: Green. CO2 scrubbers, green. Oxygen supply, 100 percent. Induction port access, available. Short wave radio, available at 27.06501 and 27.06502 MHz"

Amberly already felt the suit's heating coils warming her body. She wanted to rest, but if she had hours or days before the waypoint hit the atmosphere or started breaking up even more. *I need to keep moving. There must be a ship or a pod off this waypoint.* Of course, a ship wouldn't do Amberly much good, as she was not a pilot. If she found a ship with a good AI, she might be able to at least get into an orbit. And then, maybe, just maybe, a waiting *Magnus* would come and pick her up.

Here goes nothing, Amberly thought, as she went to slide open the door. She couldn't budge it.

She yanked, and kicked. Nothing. The door had frozen shut again.

She tried to build a matrix to figure the best course of action, but she didn't have enough data. *The likely scenario is that it would take longer than not to fall out of orbit,* Amberly surmised. She was weary. *I should rest now,* Amberly thought, *considering the odds, it's going to be a while before I am able to open that door.*

The waves of heat from the suit also added to her drowsiness. Amberly let herself float in the weightlessness, closed her eyes and waited for sleep to take her. As she was literally drifting off to sleep, Amberly had a thought. "Turn on the short-wave radio emergency beacon."

The suit complied, and Amberly pushed her anxiety aside and willed her overwhelmed body to sleep.

For the first time in years, she did not dream.

L.S. ROEBUCK

CHAPTER TWENTY-FIVE

Tap. Tap. Tap.

Amberly woke stiff.

She had slept so hard, she needed a few moments to orient herself to remember where she was. Amberly noticed on the suit's heads up display eight hours had passed.

Then, she heard the tapping. Then, the cracking, like ice being busted. *Either the Marquette is disintegrating, or someone is out there. Is it friend or foe?* Amberly thought. *I guess it doesn't matter.*

She flipped herself upright and faced the door. She grabbed a glow rod and lit it, ready to use the hard cylinder as a makeshift weapon. "Radio, broadcast on both shortwave frequencies."

Amberly had no idea if whatever was breaking the ice was listening to the open radio channels. The suit spoke back. "Shortwave frequencies open."

"Who's there?" Amberly said. "This is Amberly Macready. I repeat, who is there?"

"Amberly! I heard the beacon. I hoped it was you," a man's voice said over the radio. "Oh, thank God it's you!"

"Dad!" Amberly said, as the door slid open. Less than a meter away, in a full Marine vacsuit sequestered from the *Tinkerbell,* was Alroy Macready."

"Dad! Dad!" Amberly repeated herself. Amberly floated forward and threw her bulbous vacsuit arms around her father's. "You came for me!"

"I would never leave you, not again," Alroy said, attempting to squeeze his daughter in an awkward space suit hug. "I was trying to rig some scanners to look for you when my suit received your generic beacon. It could have been anyone, but in my heart, I knew it was you. My daughter, Amberly," Tears ran down Alroy's cheeks. He instinctively felt like he should wipe them but couldn't because of his helmet.

"Dad, the Chairman's dead. This waypoint is doomed. We've won," Amberly said, also crying.

"I know. I ran into the Chairman down the hall. When I saw her frozen body, I feared the worst for you, but here you are,"

Alroy said.

"Here I am," Amberly smiled through her suit big enough that Alroy could see it. Amberly pressed her helmet up against her father's. She studied his red beard and green eyes with her green eyes.

"Dad, we have a lot of catching up to do."

"I know. My memory is coming back to me, slowly. But I need you to fill me in on everything that's happened to you in the past 10 years."

"Warning. Temperatures increasing rapidly," Amberly's suit said.

The waypoint shook violently. With the interior of the waypoint now in a complete vacuum, Amberly couldn't hear the sound of bulkheads failing, but she felt vibrations through her feet.

My feet. My feet! They are on the ground, Amberly thought. *Gravity.* Not the artificial gravity Amberly had known her entire life, but the light pull from the planet. Amberly realized they were close enough for Arara's gravity to hold onto enough atmosphere to create superheating friction.

"We don't have much time," Amberly told her father through the short-wave radio. "We have to locate a ship or lifepod." Amberly started processing every image she had mentally captured of the interior of *Marquette*, to see if maybe she missed a detail or could see a clue where they would find a way off the falling station.

"Ask and ye shall receive," Alroy smiled. "In the chaos, the Marines abandoned the *Tinkerbell*. Lucky for us. It's where I found this suit."

"You were on the *Tinkerbell*, and you didn't leave," Amberly felt loved. "You should have left when you had the chance... but now I am glad you didn't."

"Me too. The ship is connected by soft seal four decks up. Hopefully it's hanging on where I left it," Alroy said. "I left a grappling cable that can take us up to the secondary hangar. From there, it's just up one level to the temporary hatch."

The waypoint shook hard again, and Alroy and Amberly both nearly lost their footing.

"We better hurry," Amberly said, as she followed her dad

back down the capillary corridor. The Macready's ran as fast as their vacsuits allowed. Amberly came up to the body of Kora, now lying on the floor, and briefly paused.

Rest in peace, Kora, she thought.

The low gravity enabled them to cover the 300 meters to the edge of the fissure quickly.

"Don't look down," Alroy said, as he clipped his suit to the hanging grappling cable that led up to the secondary hangar through a maze of broken support pylons, ripped metal and polycarbonate panel shards.

Light atmosphere from the planet was being pushed up through the hole in the bottom of the waypoint. Amberly disobeyed her father to take a peek. Since she came by this way, the doomed *Marquette* had orbited past the terminator into the Arara night. The planet's surface was in darkness, with mostly ocean beneath them now.

The fringes of *Marquette*, however, which were exposed to the outer atmosphere were glowing red.

Alroy looped a carbon fiber cable between his suit and Amberly's. "Hold on, Amberly!" He activated a motorized ascender and the pair shot up the cable quickly. Alroy pulled his swagger stick off a belt attachment and swung it a few times to knock debris out of their path.

As they reached the hangar deck, Alroy climbed over the edge, hoisting Amberly up as well. Amberly stood on the deck, empty except for one corvette that was still anchored.

"What about that ship?" Amberly asked over the radio, as she followed her dad, sprinting toward the maintenance door.

"I don't know. Can you hack past the lock codes?"

Mom could, Amberly thought. Amberly closed her mind and visualized complex encryption algorithms. "I think I could, actually. But we don't have time. The *Tinkerbell* is our best bet."

As Amberly slipped through the maintenance door, she looked back at the hangar, space doors open. She watched the whole wall that framed the door tear loose and fly out into space, the edges glowing red from friction as it fell out of sight.

"Warning. Exterior temperature has reached critical levels," Amberly's suit told her. Sweat dripping down her forehead stung Amberly's eyes.

"Just up this hatch," Alroy ascended a ladder onto a small landing, where the soft seal had been cut through the hull. Amberly climbed up after her dad, having a little difficulty managing the ladder in her bulkier suit. She gripped tight as chaotic winds threatened to end her ascension. She mounted the landing, enveloped in the maelstrom, and through a circular portal, she saw the open airlock accessing the *Tinkerbell*.

Alroy grabbed Amberly by the suit and pushed her through the portal. Metal was warping all around them, shrieking vibrations through the tumultuous air.

Alroy jumped through the portal. "Disconnect us, Jules," he told his VI, now uploaded to the *Tinkerbell*.

The automated hatch shut, and the sound of a completed sequence of popping bolts told Alroy they were free. "Nice of the Marines to leave this runabout behind for us," he said as he flung off his helmet, paced the twenty steps onto the bridge and slid into the pilot's seat.

Amberly stepped in behind him on the bridge. "Take a seat, commander," he indicated the captain chair. "And strap in."

Amberly took the command station.

Alroy wanted to put as much distance between the *Tinkerbell* and *Marquette* as possible. He picked a vector to take them into a higher orbit and fired the main engines. As the ship ascended away from *Marquette*, the feeling of the inertial dampeners was like the feeling of home to Amberly.

Amberly watched in awe as she saw the waypoint was already a dozen or more separate fragments now, each glowing with a tail of fire. The number of fragments multiplied as the disintegration of *Marquette* continued.

"*Tinkerbell*, this is *Magnus*," the voice of Elizabeth Hawkins sounded from the comms. "Do you require assistance? Please transmit your passenger manifest."

Alroy looked at Amberly, and he extended his open hand toward her. "It's all you, Amberly."

"*Magnus*, this *Tinkerbell's* acting captain Amberly Macready. Only me and my dad on board. Would like to talk to the *Magnus* actual."

Over the comms, Amberly could hear cheers from the *Magnus* bridge. Alroy and Amberly traded smiles.

"Captain Macready, this is Captain North. Hallelujah! I can't believe it!"

"North, you made it!" Alroy said. "You took a nasty hit."

"Just a few broken bones. Medics wanted to keep me off the bridge, but I wasn't going to lie in bed this day."

"*Magnus* actual," Amberly asked, "permission to land?"

"Granted, Amberly. Report to the bridge immediately. Bring your old man. Alroy, thanks for bringing our bird home. We have you set to intercept in 42 minutes, confirm."

"That looks about right to me," Alroy said to North. "Thanks for your prayers. By the way, I like this ship. I think I'm going to keep it." Alroy flicked the comms off.

"I'm going back to get out of this suit," Amberly told Alroy as she walked toward the *Tinkerbell's* crew quarters. "I'm making you the captain now, dad."

Commander Bloom sat in a small clearing surrounded by tall grasses on the northernmost Lewis Island. She studied the star filled night sky, waiting, hoping. Suddenly, she saw dozens of meteors light up the night sky, flaming as they fell toward the horizon.

Please, Alroy, be safe. Come back to me, Nur thought, as her eyes watered with hope and fear.

She watched for three minutes until the remains of *Marquette* slipped over the horizon.

Her portable comm buzzed.

"I hope you saw the light show, Nur," Alroy said over the radio.

"Red!" Bloom replied, looking up in the night sky. "What happened? You downed a whole waypoint?"

"It's over. The Chairman is dead. We have Amberly. *Magnus* is the last man standing. We win."

"Thank God, Red. Thank God."

"Commander, we paid a high price for our victory. Alfonsi. Fiat. Rea. Ilam. Meganson. I'm sorry. They sacrificed for our freedom. I just wanted to let you know myself."

"Thank you. We've always known the price for freedom would be our dearest blood."

"I'll see you soon. We're landing on *Magnus* in a few minutes.

I can't wait to get back to my farm."

"I can't wait to meet Amberly."

Alroy remembered what it felt like to be a proud father.

A squad of Marines provided an honor escort for Amberly and her father to the bridge of the *Magnus*.

After her harrowing kidnapping and years of torture, Amberly hoped to find a peaceful normal. She just wanted to be. With her family. Wherever Kora and her father, Roy, and her nephew Al were, that was her home now. Her father was nervous to be reunited with his eldest child and meet his grandson for the first time.

The coming weeks and months would be an unknown transition into an uncertain future, Amberly thought. *But a good future.*

The bridge doors slid open. Standing to receive them were North, Kora, Lydia, the young Al and Alecia.

"Dad!" Kora ran to her father, weeping uncontrollably, throwing her arms around Roy. "I can't believe it. Dad, my God, it's dad." Kora turned and hugged her sister. "Amberly! I prayed for you every day for the last three years."

"I'm sorry about Trot," Amberly held her sister tight.

"I know. I know. Oh, but you are here now. Dad's here! We're going to fix everything. There's so much to be happy for, and so much to be sad about. Trot. Dek and … so much."

"Kora, I love you so much," Amberly stepped back and looked at her sister, and then she hugged her again. "We'll take our time celebrating and mourning. We'll take our time."

"Aunt Amberly!" Al ran to his aunt.

Amberly smiled through her tears, breaking from Kora to hug her nephew. "My, you've grown into quite the young man. I want you to meet your grandpa, Alroy."

"We have the same name," Al smiled. Roy took his grandson into his arms for the first time.

"I love you," Roy said.

Lydia put her hand on Amberly's shoulder, "I'm sorry about Dek."

"I'm sorry about Skip. We lost a lot of good people."

"But we saved some of them, too," Lydia said, choking up.

"You. I thought you were lost."

"Thanks for not giving up on me."

"I've spent the last three years, training to be a Marine. Me … a Marine. I wanted to be ready when we found you. I knew we would."

"You are the best sort of friend a person can have, Lydia. Did Sparks…?"

"North pulled her out of the fire," Kora said. "We think she'll pull through. She has a great nurse. *Moi.*"

Amberly looked over to North who was standing apart from the group, smiling his charming smile. His torso was wrapped in a stabilizing garment to protect his healing ribs. His hair was messy. His face was bruised. He looked like hell. Amberly suspected she didn't look much better.

But he looked like home.

North couldn't take his eyes off Amberly's fiery hair and piercing green eyes.

They slowly walked to each other and he took her hands in his.

"Hi, Red."

"I love you."

North pulled her head to his.

They kissed.

CHAPTER TWENTY-SIX

March 21, 2611, 13 months after the destruction of Marquette. The Alfonsi Peer, Williamston, Lewis Islands, Planet Arara.

Amberly, 27, couldn't imagine a more beautiful wedding. She had been to plenty of matrimonial ceremonies on *Magellan*, lovely affairs among the fruit trees at the Topside Garden Orchard, or military dress events on the waypoint's hangar deck. Those all paled in comparison to the affair here on the end of the peer named for the fallen Irregular corporal. Wooden posts held the large platform over the beautiful blue green ocean waters.

On either side of the peer, the Monet Sea splashed onto the rocky north shore of Williamstown. A warm wind blew through Amberly's hair, thrilling her. After nearly a year of living on a planet, the excitement of natural weather had not dulled. Viapos' rays warmed Amberly's face, bringing out an army of freckles. *This is so good,* Amberly thought. *The sun is everything Mom promised.*

She felt almost complete. Almost. Something was missing.

She looked to her side. There stood her father, the great Alroy "Red" Macready, war pilot, pirate, farmer and hero of Arara. The loving dad Amberly always remembered was back from the dead. He wore a simple brown suit that was the common formal dress for Lewis Island farmers. Arm-in-arm with Amberly, the two were quite the pair of redheads, though Alroy's was muted with new strands of white starting to show.

Amberly and Alroy walked slowly to the end of the procession, with eight-year-old Al in tow, carrying a white pillow with a large, reflective crystal shard ring tied on with a green ribbon. When they were at the front of the aisle, Amberly stopped and turned to her dad, took his hands, and kissed his cheek. "I love you, Dad."

Alroy beamed at his daughter as she went and stood next to North, 37, sharp in his Marine dress.

They all turned and faced the minister, the preacher from the church where Alroy's late protégé, Blaisé, attended. He called up the Bible on his infopad. "The word of the Lord, from the book of

Genesis. 'So God created man in his own image, in the image of God he created him; male and female he created them. And God blessed them. And God said to them, 'Be fruitful and multiply and fill the earth and subdue it and have dominion over the fish of the sea and over the birds of the heavens and over every living thing that moves on the earth.''

As the preacher read, Amberly thought about how Arara and hundreds of other planets, if mankind could ever reach them, were ready for humanity – beautiful, flawed humanity. To reach them was going to take waypoints, lots of them. The wedding was a welcome distraction from her work, but joyful as it was, she could not get her mind off her vocational obsession. Since the fall of *Marquette* and the defeat of Chasm a year ago, Amberly had committed to undoing the work of The Chairman. She would fill the chasm, building the waypoint bridges between the human worlds so they would be undying. Her gospel was a stellar manifest destiny.

"This is the Word of the Lord. Amen," the preacher continued. "Dearly beloved, we are gathered together to celebrate the union of this man, Captain Alroy Macready and this woman, Commander Nur Bloom, in Holy Matrimony."

Amberly looked at her dad and her soon-to-be step mother and smiled widely. The bride's nutmeg face radiated so much happiness. She glowed in her brilliant white dress. They were both going to be happy. *God knows Dad deserves some happiness after everything he has been through.*

The reception party for the Macready-Bloom wedding was held on the White Sands Hotel patio, overlooking the long west-facing beach. The hour was late; Viapos had long since sunk under the calm Monet waves on the horizon. Under the string of lights hung between tall reed poles, there was booze, music and dancing, in that order.

Rhodes, 24, wore the red dress Ryder had left behind, drawing the attention of many of war-veteran bachelor farmers. The just-promoted XO of the *Magnus*, Rhodes gladly spent her shore leave to celebrate with the Macready family. Dancing next to her was Sparks, 33, half-drunk, spinning in her manually-powered wheelchair. She wore an even tighter dress and was getting twice the attention Rhodes was.

During the retreat from *Marquette*, a bullet ripped Sparks' lower spinal cord, leaving her paralyzed from the waist down. She normally wore a powered, somewhat bulky exosuit on her lower body to provide decent mobility. But she didn't want to look like a robot for the wedding, and the dress didn't fit over the exosuit. She opted for the old-fashioned wheelchair.

Going out and being active without the support of her exosuit was discouraged by her physicians. The internal scarring was creating complications. Organ tissue damage meant frequent invasive therapy. Having never fully recovered from her latest war injuries, Sparks retired from her "consulting" work for the Marines. For most of the past year, Sparks lived on North's family farm on Ingram, keeping an eye on the operations for North. North was now Supreme Commander of the Arara Peace Forces, spending half his time on the main continent and the other in orbit on *Magnus*.

Amberly sat at the table alone, sipping tea and thinking about the people who weren't there. Lydia, seven months into a difficult pregnancy, was unable to travel from the main continent for the wedding. Having just quit her job as a research director in the Arara Science Corp, Lydia was one of many who believed starting a family on Arara was the best way to move past the trauma of the Chasm war. She wasted no time wooing and procreating with an Arara-born librarian from the capital. Lydia really only felt at home in the capital, where the skyline, streetlights and crowded marketplaces reminded her of the commons on a waypoint.

Amberly set her cup down and looked to the sea. Amberly remembered her visit to Lydia and her tall husband several months ago. Like her blonde friend, she felt a longing for the familiar confines of a waypoint. Arara was beautiful and enchanting, wild and untamed. But unlike Lydia, even the city didn't reduce her ache for *Magellan*, for home.

As Amberly held the tea cup, she thought about what Rita Moreno and Thor Rillio had taught her about leadership. She thought about Dek. North had recently given her the message Dek had recorded when he thought he was going to die during the self-destruction of *Magellan*. Dek had said that Amberly would "be all that is left of *Magellan*."

Maybe Dek was right. Lydia had a new husband and would soon be caring for a new baby girl. Kora and Al now lived in multifamily housing in Williamston, and they visited Grandpa Roy's farm every week. Kora had finally said goodbye to Trot in her heart, and had started dating the charming Charro, who had taken Bloom's old job as Williamston's chief of police. *Kora's always a sucker for a man in uniform*, Amberly thought.

North was still all duty. Amberly knew that although North desperately wanted to settle down to life on his dad's farm, he would keep serving as long as he was needed. North, Kora, Lydia – all her friends, her best people, had once been in love with *Magellan*, their shared home. But *Magellan* was gone. They had moved on.

But she had not.

Dek was right, Amberly thought. All that was left of *Magellan* was in her heart, and Amberly would never let that go. She felt no one understood that pain she carried.

Amberly felt bittersweetness clouding her brain. She loved seeing her friends enjoy a peaceful life, and nothing made her happier than seeing her father together with a good woman.

Amberly had been seeing North when she could over the past year, but both were focused on the common good. North was needed to give the new Arara government the stability only a powerful, moral military leader could provide. Amberly was obsessed with erasing the evil the Chairman had unleashed on world and waypoint. She wanted to make everything right again.

In this, Amberly felt alone. She realized that while she was working with a passion to rebuild the waypoints, everyone else had grown complacent with their new lives. *Magellan* could be brought back, Amberly believed. It could be rebuilt. But no one else was passionate about fixing what the Chairman had broken. Not Kora. Not Lydia. Not her dad. And not North.

No one else was holding on.

She wanted to *be* alone now, and she decided a walk on the beach would clear her head, and maybe, her heart.

Sparks looked over and saw Amberly walk out into the darkness toward the shore. "Hey... heeeyy. Sis... sis... ter." She tried to call out after her, but she was too intoxicated to put the words together. *I'll go see her in the morning. When I am sober. Or maybe that will be the afternoon*, Sparks thought.

On the patio, North was dancing with Bloom. "Alroy's a very lucky lad," North said, as he smiled at the beautiful bride. "I'm so happy for you both. And I'm sorry to hear you are retiring from the service."

Bloom and North mixed in the swaying crowd as they danced to Nat King Cole's L-O-V-E.

"Red and I are getting old. Farm life with him will be just the right speed. We are both accidental warriors anyway. Not like you."

"We are going to miss you. But your retirement is well-deserved."

"What about you, North?" Bloom asked.

"When am I going to retire?" North asked. "Well, I've thought about the old homestead... but... I, well, you know, someone has to run the military."

"I mean, when are you going to make Amberly a lucky lady?" Bloom winked at the younger man.

"Well, that's a good question," North said, "I've been wondering the very same thing myself."

"Hey, what's going on here," Alroy Macready joked as he tapped North on the shoulder. "Sorry, kid, cutting in. I want to dance with my wife."

"Of course, sir," North bowed.

North walked over to Sparks, and took his old friend's hands, and twirled her chair around. "Whoaa, tiger. Anymore and I'm ... Immmma ... going to share that whiiiiisky shots. Shots with... you."

"Which shots?" North asked, spinning her again.

"The four... I drank."

North stopped spinning the wheel chair. "Sorry."

"I'm too drunk to be...here," Sparks waved her hand at the party. "I'm gonna ... do something ... I regret. Put me away, Northy-North-man. Would you mind wheeling ... I said, said... would you mind wheeeeeling me to my ... room."

"Sure, Sparks," North said as he pushed the chair into the hotel lobby to the elevator.

"If you can ... just get me to the elevator," Sparks breathed deeply. "I can make... it... from here."

"Hey, North … she's gettin away. Too late."

"Getting away? Who?"

"Amberly, silly."

"I don't know what you are talking about?"

Sparks tried really hard to focus through her intoxication. "North, you have been good to me. To me. So Imma gonna shoot you straight. I love you tooooo much. Your redhead… she's not anchored anymore."

"What? Another guy? No way," North said confidently, but then began to wonder.

"Amberly's heart is up there… in the stars. You can't keep her grounded here."

A sense of alarm hit North. "What do you know? Why would you say that?"

"You don't have to believe meeeeee … if you don't want to. I… I've always been your friend. So I don't know why you d.. don't trust me. But that don't chaaaange the fact —"

Rhodes bounded into the lobby, not realizing she was interrupting the conversation. "There you are Sparks! I was worried about you. Oh no. I told them not to give you too many drinks. The doctors said be careful, it can —"

"Screw the doctors," Sparks said, feeling suddenly sober and bitter. "Screw the war. Screw Chasm."

"I'm sorry, Sparks, I didn't mean to —" North felt bad.

"Screw you, too, North. Just trying to be your friend. Asshole," Sparks hung her head down. "I need to go to bed."

Rhodes had seen versions of this fight before, and she held her tongue.

"Rhodes, can you?" Sparks asked.

"Of course," Rhodes pushed her friend into the elevator.

As the doors closed, Sparks called out. "She went …. a walk … on the beach. The beeeach."

North turned around and nearly ran into Kora and her new beau, Charro.

Charro saluted North sharply.

"At ease. This is a celebration, chief," North saluted back.

"Hey North," Kora smiled. "Have you seen Amberly? I wanted to get a vid of all of us together before the party died."

"I think the party just went up the elevator to go to sleep," North smiled weakly. "But Sparks said Amberly went for a walk on the beach."

Kora turned to Charro. "Hey, honey, I'm suddenly thirsty. Would you mind going and fetching me a Champagne cocktail? Take your time."

"Sure, dear," Charro kissed the elder Macready sister and went to the bar to fetch the drink.

"I hope he'll make you happy," North said.

"He's not perfect, but I think we all have learned what the quest for perfection will get us. But enough about me. You look unhappy."

"I'm fine," North waved her off.

"No, you are not. I've known you most of my life, North. I can see it in your eyes. Spill it."

"Sparks said that ... something ... is up with Amberly?"

"Oh, what did that nymph say now?"

"She said Amberly is, I don't know, pining for the stars. Do you know what that means?"

Kora looked away and said nothing.

"I've known you for a long time, too," North pressed Kora. "You're hiding something."

"I am," Kora admitted. "I promised Amberly. Oh, North, some things are not for me to say. I wish I understood my sister. I love her so much, but after her time as a prisoner of the Chairman, she's even harder to figure out. You can tell she's always thinking, processing, calculating something. Even when she is talking with me, I wonder if she is playing a game of chess against herself in her head. I never know if I should be offended or not."

"What is going on? What have I missed?" North said. He rubbed his chin. "I mean, we haven't had as much time together as I would like. But you can't blame us. I've been so preoccupied trying to keep civil war from breaking out. Amberly has been so busy working on Project Renascence."

"I'm worried about how obsessed she is with that project," Kora said.

"Still, I never thought I'd see a new waypoint in my lifetime," North mused. "The processes she has engineered just this year to build the next generation of waypoints — nothing short of miraculous. Maybe Renascence has changed everything right under my nose, and I have been too busy to see it?"

"I wish I could tell you North, but I am rooting for you," Kora reached forward and hugged the Marine. "I want the most powerful man on Arara as my brother-in-law! I know Amberly is an enigma. Keep fighting for her."

The beach was dark and abandoned. Amberly had removed her shoes several meters back and figured she'd have to wait for the light of dawn to find them.

The sound of the waves, driven by the now-cool winds blowing off the ocean, reminded Amberly of her mother's conch shell. Amberly remembered listening to that shell as a girl, dreaming of one day walking on a beach. Now that she was here, reality did not disappoint.

But now that she was here, she wanted to go back there.

Amberly looked up at the stars. Even in the dark sky, the stars seemed dim compared to their brightness when viewed from the observation deck on *Magellan*. Light was purer up there.

She recognized the star Alkaid, more than 100 light years away — 200 years of impossible travel. Then again, at one time, humans thought they would never reach Arara in a lifetime. Then came antimatter and the all-important waypoints. Humanity would get even to Ursa Major, someday, and she, Amberly Macready, would point the way.

"Amberly!"

North, I just need to be alone now. Please understand, Amberly thought, but instead she said, "North, over here."

North walked up to Amberly and took her shoulders in his hand. The romantic mood set by stars, sea and land coming together rivaled the atmosphere of Sonnet's shard caves. He leaned in to kiss Amberly.

Amberly turned her head away.

North let his arms drop.

"This isn't meant to be," Amberly said. "I'm going back. I'm going up there. I'm going home."

So, this is what Sparks and Kora were on about, North thought. "What do you mean you are going back? Home? *Magellan* is gone. Let it go, Amberly. The people who love you are right here. This is your home."

"I'm going to build *New Magellan* — and a hundred other waypoints."

"You're going to build...? Project Renascence? It's true your engineered brainpower has enabled the Corps of Engineers to accelerate waypoint construction in ways that no one ever thought possible. You're amazing. But we're still so far away from that end. I admit, I can't begin to understand—"

"That's just it, North," Amberly looked away from North. "You don't *understand*. You never will. You don't know what I know. You *can't* know what I know. And you haven't suffered like I've suffered. You haven't changed like I have changed."

"After all this time, after everything we've been through, are we really back to where we started?" North hurt.

"North, it's not like that," Amberly said.

"No, no, I get it. No one to shoot at anymore. I'm obsolete," North said. "But you. You. You've never been more important."

"Don't be so obtuse. Self-pity doesn't become you," Amberly snapped. "What did you think would happen when the war was over? You were so busy putting together the Peace Force to prop up our new government, and I was so busy leading waypoint reconstruction. If this... us... was really where our hearts were, we would have made time for us. Maybe something would be different now. If I love you, North, you wouldn't know it by my priorities. That's why we can't go on. We've followed our hearts to other places. My heart is going to take me back up there, where I belong," Amberly looked to the heavens.

"That's not fair. Just because we have our duties doesn't mean we can't have each other," North argued. "I love you. And what is this nonsense about going out there? The first waypoint won't be completed for at least five years."

"I've been running through my matrixes, and I believe I can have one done in three. But I can't wait that long. I'm going to Fuentes Station on the *Texas Star*. We leave within the month. My work requires ... solitude."

"The *Texas Star*? Is that old freighter even space worthy?"

"She'll get us there, and then we'll use the hull to expand the station. I'm leading a small mission. We'll start building the waypoint framework at the old *Magellan* anchorage and bring the components out piece by piece instead of as a whole unit. That will shave at least a year off of the time to get *New Magellan* operational." Reviewing the details of the project made Amberly perk up with excitement.

"This is what Kora didn't want to tell me. It's what Sparks was trying to tell me. You did all this behind my back," North pushed.

"Of course I did this behind your back. You would have tried to stop me. I *knew* you wouldn't understand, and I was right. I don't need to let *Magellan* go. You need to let *me* go."

North couldn't believe what he was hearing. "This is about you wanting to fix the sins of your mother and grandmother. Amberly, you could launch a hundred waypoints, and it won't bring back the people they killed. Can't you just stop and enjoy life and be happy?"

"No. I can't ignore my destiny. I won't."

"You sound like her."

"Like Kimberly Macready?"

"No, the Chairman."

Amberly turned from North. "How can you say I'm like her? She was ... evil." Amberly thought about the torture she endured by the hand of the Chairman, then she pushed away those dark memories. "Humanity *does* have a destiny. For good."

"Amberly, I'm sorry," North retreated. "I shouldn't have said that. I love you. Don't you believe that?"

"Dek loved me. It cost him his life. I choose to no longer bear that responsibility with you. I'm sorry."

North was quiet for a bit, his wisdom forcing his emotions to settle.

"What about your Dad? What about Kora?"

"Dad's thinking about joining the *New Magellan* crew if Bloom will come along. Kora has her family. She'll be married to Charro soon enough."

"I could come with you," North said, suddenly. "I *would* come with you."

"You can't, North," Amberly protested. "Arara needs you now more than ever. Without your strong leadership, your generals would inevitably bicker, and it would lead to civil war. I need you here. It has to be you. The waypoints have to be rebuilt. It has to be me. We must sacrifice our love to do what is right for the greater good."

"The greater good. Our love."

"You mean so much to me. You know that. Don't think I am not hurting, too. But my heart is high above these shores, as is my duty." Amberly was trying hard to hold back tears.

North melted for Amberly in her weakness. He placed his hand on her cheek gently. "Amberly."

"Please don't do this North," Amberly smudged a tear off her face. "Our happiness doesn't amount to a pile of ligrains in this world. There are bigger things than you and me and whatever this is. We have a job to do, for humanity. Your job is here. Mine is out there."

"It's not that simple," North was fighting his own tears now.

"But *it is* that simple. When I am quiet and honest with myself, I know I am meant to be out there. Back in the stars. You've been amazing to me. But it's time for me to go home now. My mother's heart was here at the edge of the sea — this very spot. Her biggest regret was never coming home. I will not live with that regret."

"If your happiness is on Fuentes Station, then I want to be there at your side."

"You would never forgive me for dragging you out to space, just like Kimberly never forgave Alroy."

"You don't know that," North said. "Sure, my heart is drawn to my farm, and I'd love to settle down there. But like you, something else has a stronger pull on my heart. It's you."

"You are just making this harder," Amberly sent a different message with her body, wrapping her arms around North and holding him tight. "We've been good for each other."

North slid his face into hers and they kissed slowly. The feeling of his warm body against hers in the cool breeze made her tingle. Amberly knew whatever North and she had, it was more than chemistry. North could sense powerful alchemy in Amberly's response to this kiss.

"Marry me," he said.

Amberly sharply pulled away from North. In the dim ambient light, she forced herself to look into his eyes, no matter how painful it would be.

"No. I won't."

After a moment of silence, North spoke. "I hope you find whatever it is you are looking for out there, Red."

"I'm so sorry. For everything."

"I'm sorry, too. Godspeed, Amberly Macready." North turned and started walking back to the hotel.

Alone, Amberly wept. She knew she could not let go of *Magellan*. She never would never be able to let go. She wanted everything how it was, in the beginning, on *Waypoint Magellan*. Before the flight of *Magnus* brought war to the waypoints. Before her home was sacrificed to destroy the Dark Armada.

But she couldn't go back. Time only moves forward.

EPILOUGE

May 12, 2621. Waypoint New Magellan, five years after becoming operational.

Captain Rhodes, 34, was as aware as anyone of the historical significance of the first visit of the *U.S.S. Magnus* to *New Magellan*. She had been on *Magnus* for both the Battles of *Magellan*. The old warship, now used primarily as a transport, carried a gift of fruit trees to create the Anderson Orchard in the waypoint's topside gardens.

Magnus was three years out from Arara, on its final mission: a second phase of Project Renascence to connect Arara to Tigona, a dry, but habitable planet only five light years from Arara and four from *New Magellan*, discovered and named by Amberly Macready. When *Magnus* arrived at Tigona in 2629, the aging warship would be decommissioned and repurposed to house the first settlement on the planet's surface.

Rhodes met the governor and Marine commander on *New Magellan* during a subdued Ship Day ceremony that morning, but the person she really wanted to connect with did not show up: the reclusive genius Amberly Macready.

The *Magnus* would spend three weeks at *New Magellan*, before making a brief stop at Fuentes Station and then off to Tigona. They would attempt the longest manned voyage ever without waypoint stops: Four lightyears covered in under a decade. In the meantime, Rhodes and her officers intended to enjoy their shore leave as much as possible.

Rhodes asked her VI, Condi, to see if it could find Amberly. North had given his beloved construct to Rhodes to help on the long trip.

"I've connected to Amberly's VI. Fortunately, after all these years, Verne and I still have our friendship protocol enabled. Verne reports she is reading stellar anomaly reports while enjoying a cup of tea in a booth at the Cantina," Condi said through Rhodes' infopad. "Do you want me to call her?"

"No, I'll just drop by," Rhodes replied as she excused herself from her group of officers and left them to pursue their own merriment.

The Cantina was the newest hotspot on *New Magellan*. Sultry music, flowing booze, vape sticks and other forms of entertainment were available.

Amberly was sitting alone in a dark faux-leather booth. Although she had a generous office suite attached to her large apartment, Amberly often took her work to the Cantina for a change of scenery. Her main occupation was still Executive Director of Project Renascence. She'd overseen the construction and launch of three waypoints, including *Waypoint Moreno*, *Waypoint New Magellan* and *Waypoint Macready*. The Arara Senate unanimously voted to name the waypoint that replaced *Marquette* in honor of Amberly over her protests. Amberly told everyone it was named for her father.

Amberly was more than good at her job managing the challenges of multiple waypoint construction projects happening over multiple construction sites light years apart. But sometimes, just for fun, she performed her old job of reading stellar radiation reports collected by passing ships.

"Amberly!" Rhodes said in a disproportionately loud voice.

"Captain Rhodes!" Amberly stood and gave the Marine from her old life a hug. "Let me buy you a drink. Have a seat."

"Wait," Rhodes hugged Amberly again, "that's from Kora. I'm glad I found you. I've got something else for you I brought from Arara. Very unique. Remind me to get it for you before we go."

"You shouldn't have. But sure, I'll remind you. Wow, captain of the *Magnus* now. Quite impressive. It looks good on you."

"We missed you at the Ship Day ceremony. We were all looking for you. Well, Caddo, Jana and I were. Jana is really excited to be taking over as Marine Commander here. I wish she'd come with us to Tigona."

"Sorry. I can't do Ship Days anymore. Too much baggage," Amberly admitted. "You understand."

"Of course," Rhodes smiled. "Wow, so it's been what? Ten years? I think I last saw you at your father's wedding. I was drunk as a skunk. So was Sparks."

"I remember that night well," Amberly thought about her old

friend North. "I was sorry to hear about Sparks. She died, what, five years ago?"

"Six. She was already going downhill when she and North were married," Rhodes explained. "North was amazing, taking care of her like he did. She made it for two more years with North on his farm."

"Must have been hard on them both," Amberly sympathized.

"Sparks had gone through too much and her body couldn't hold together anymore," Rhodes explained. "Some of the doctors blamed her body's inability to heal on defects in the cohort process. She was in so much pain, but she learned to love the peaceful life, and I think she died happy with North at her side."

"Dear North. How's he doing?"

"Well, he resigned his commission to take care of Sparks."

"I heard," Amberly said.

"His leaving the service was a big deal. After Sparks died, I visited often to make sure North was doing okay. He kept busy on the farm, but he was really in a funk until they called him up to help resolve the Ingram conflict. North took a lot of flak because a few dozen civilians died in that incident, but honestly, if North hadn't intervened, thousands would have died. The fires of war would have burned half of Arara. The battle gave him a new purpose."

"I miss him," Amberly said, sipping her tea. "It would be nice to see him again, but that's a six-year roundtrip I don't think I'll make. I won't live forever, and I have so much work to do. I'm not leaving this waypoint again."

"I understand. So how are you doing? Lydia says she hears about you on the news more than from you personally."

"I've been... preoccupied with my work," Amberly blushed. "I guess I'm not as good a friend as I should be."

"Don't be hard on yourself," Rhodes smiled. "It's difficult enough to keep up a friendship when you're on the same planet. You making good friends here? Any men in your life?"

Amberly chuckled to herself. "That ship has sailed. I'm married to Renascence. It's my life. My legacy."

Rhodes couldn't help but pity Amberly.

"Oh, don't look at me like that," Amberly sighed. "Life isn't bad. If I wanted a happily ever after, I would have married North when he asked me. I was 13 when I promised my mom that I would become the waypoint's greatest scientist and not be distracted by boys."

"And here you are!"

"And here I am. Promise kept."

"Do you wonder what life would have been like if you would have married North?"

"I wasn't really the marrying type. You remember how it went with Skylar. I suppose there's been some lonely nights. Still, *New Magellan* is my home, and this is the place I want to be."

"It's good to know where you belong. I feel the same way about the *Magnus*. So, I want your advice," Rhodes said, changing the subject. "You know what it's like to be so far away from the ones you love. Caddo and I have adopted Nora, and she's about to turn 18. She's a science nerd like you, and I just don't know if coming with us to Tigona to build a new colony is right for her. If she wants to come back, by the time she could, she'd be 38. That's a huge commitment."

"That's older than I am now!"

"Will you talk with her and give her some experienced advice on whether she should stay here, or go?"

"Of course. That's a hard choice. But harder for you to let her go, I think."

"Oh, if she doesn't come with us, my heart will ache. But it's what's best for her. Listen, Amberly, I have to go check in with my officers," Rhodes said. "But we'll be around for three weeks. Before we go, maybe we can find some time to —"

"Maybe."

Rhodes nodded her head and smiled tightly. "So long, Amberly Macready." The women stood and briefly clasped hands.

"Godspeed, Captain Rhodes," Amberly said as Rhodes walked away. "Wait. You said to remind you that you had something for me."

"Oh that," Rhodes tossed her dark hair and looked over her shoulder. "I'll have it delivered to your apartment tonight."

It was nearly 26:00 hours, and Amberly set her infopad down. She rubbed her eyes, sleepy from reviewing the task list for the new waypoint that was being assembled next to *New Magellan*.

Waypoint Destiny was built with modular components from Arara and raw resources harvested from the Spencer Belt. *Destiny* was the first waypoint to not be named after a person. *People die*, Amberly reasoned. *Ideas live forever.* Destiny was an idea Amberly believed in. Her grandmother Kora was right; she just had the wrong destiny in mind.

Amberly's waypoint apartment was luxurious. She had a hydrogen fireplace burning in her living area, framed by two white couches made from real leather imported from Arara. Over the fireplace hung a landscape painting of the White Sands hotel next to the enchanting Monet Sea. Amberly stretched out on her couch, enjoying the warmth of the fireplace. She wore her favorite nightshirt, modest sleepwear made from a fabric created from Arara marsh reed fibers.

Amberly yawned and considered just going to sleep on the couch instead of making the journey to her bedroom. The bedroom was situated flush with the outer rim of the waypoint. It was average sized, but unique in that the room had a floor-to-ceiling plexiglass wall, giving a magnificent view of the cosmos in all its glory. She glanced through the portal to the bedroom and could see the *Magnus* in the corner of her boudoir window.

The arrival of *Magnus* had stirred up old feelings in Amberly, memories of people and places she had abandoned years ago in the pursuit of her destiny. The feelings made her restless. She had multiple work problems processing in her multivariate brain, but she forced herself to shut down the plethora of thought threads going on in her head. She told Verne she wanted to hear some music, and the VI, familiar with her taste, brought up classics by Claude Debussy.

Some years ago, she realized that North was right. *Magellan* was gone. This new place she loved like her own child, but it wasn't *Magellan*. It wasn't really home. Home was lost forever.

Amberly made peace with that fact. *Loss is a part of life. At some point or another, we all lose something we love. Sometimes the choices we make bring loss; sometimes it's through no fault of our own.* Amberly pictured the faces of North and Dek in her mind's eye.

The main door chimed. *Who could that be?* Amberly thought, but then remembered. *Must be the delivery from Rhodes.*

"Do you want me to send him away," Verne said, sensing its master's unease.

"No, it's just a delivery, I think." Amberly threw on her emerald, Asian-floral patterned kimono robe and went to the door.

The standard pressure indicator was lit green. Amberly punched the door open.

"North! What ... how?"

In her doorway stood the 47-year-old ex-Marine. He looked more like a farmer than a soldier. He had a short greying beard that covered his scar. He was still solidly built, but only a hint of his boyish charm remained. The pair stood on either side of the open door for a moment, just looking at each other. His brown eyes looked tired to Amberly. His smile was hesitant.

North broke the silence. "I didn't know if you'd want to see me," North explained. "I thought after these years you might want to be left alone. But Rhodes convinced me to come."

That little sneak, Amberly thought as her face burst into a large smile. She reached forward and hugged North tightly. "I've missed you so much, old friend. Come in. Come in."

The pair walked in and sat down on separate couches. "Can I get you something to drink?"

"No, I'm fine, thanks," North said.

"Wow. What a surprise. It's so good to see you, North," Amberly said. "What are you doing here?"

"I'm a colonist now," North confessed.

"A colonist? For Tigona?"

"I didn't really have anything left on Arara for me," North said. "Kora and your Dad left for *Waypoint Moreno*. Lydia is busy with her four kids now. Rhodes and Caddo got married and volunteered to lead the Tigona colony. After Sparks went to be with the Lord, the farm was just memories of people gone. Mom. Dad. Sparks."

"I'm so sorry about Sparks," Amberly said. "She was truly a one-of-a-kind woman."

"The end was hard," North started to tear up a little. "She was in a lot of pain."

"I remember when I first saw her, almost 20 years ago. I was jealous because I thought she had a thing with Dek. I was so dumb.

I didn't really even know Dek yet."

"You were only, what, 18 or 19?" North smiled. "We were all pretty dumb back then."

Amberly shook her head as she remembered. "I almost shot Sparks on *American Spirit*. Glad I didn't. She became my second sister."

"She really did care about you. You'd be surprised how often the great Amberly Macready, daughter of the magnificent Raven One, was the topic of our conversations. I guess we were both a little obsessed with you."

"She was so weird, too, always changing the color of her hair. Collecting melee weapons. I miss her."

"She overcame so much. She deserved happiness," North looked down. "I tried."

"So, do you," Amberly said softly.

North responded with a familiar smile. After a moment, he took a breath and continued. "When Sparks passed, I didn't have any real purpose. I helped the Peace Force out for a while, but it wasn't the same. Rhodes convinced me to come with her and Caddo to Tigona. And now here I am."

"North the colonist."

"So, it seems."

"I didn't see that coming. I should have ... stayed in touch. I'm sorry I didn't reach out to you," Amberly said. "I didn't know how. I was broken... and I was trying to heal. I figured it was better for us both. And then so much time had passed. I'm sorry."

North waved Amberly off. "I know what it's like to be broken. You have nothing to be sorry for. You've done the most amazing things. I doubted you could pull off *one* waypoint. Now you've done *three*. I wouldn't believe it if I hadn't seen them with my own eyes. I'm so proud of you."

"That's kind of you to say," Amberly said.

"*Waypoint Moreno* is incredible. But then again, so is this," North waved his finger around at Amberly's apartment. "I got to see your dad and Bloom, Kora and her two boys when I was there."

"You know they came and visited about four years ago," Amberly said. "Such a gift for them to come. Her youngest boy is so cute. He's already six now. I was pleased she named him after you: North Trot Charro."

"A kid with three first names. And here I am with only one," North smiled. "And what about you? Is *New Magellan* what you always wanted it to be? Looks like you are very happy here."

"No, I was wrong," Amberly said too quickly. "Um… you sure you don't want a drink."

"Well, sure. That would be nice." North followed Amberly with his eyes as she stepped out of the living area.

"I have some cheap synth-Syrah," Amberly called from the attached kitchen area.

"Sounds good," North said.

Amberly brought two flutes filled with the red wine. She handed one to North and then sat down beside him. She pulled her legs up under herself, facing North.

North took a drink, but Amberly just set her flute on a nearby end table. "Hmmm… spicy."

"Yeah, it's not very good," Amberly confessed.

A long silence hung in the apartment.

"Want to get dinner sometime, Amberly? Chinese sounds good to me, for old time's sake? *Magnus* isn't leaving for another three weeks, so maybe —"

"Please don't go," Amberly interrupted, putting her hand on North's shoulder. North saw longing in Amberly's green eyes and wondered what it meant. He asked her with his own eyes.

Amberly took a deep breath. "North, listen. I've done so much thinking alone here on *New Magellan*. And believe me, I can do a lot of thinking."

"I've heard."

"I was wrong about us. I had grown so arrogant. I knew I was capable of so much, and it blinded me that evening at White Sands. I did want to come home. But you were right, the home that I wanted was gone. I wanted *Magellan*, but I really wanted the *Magellan* with you, with Skip, rest his soul, Lydia, Kora and the gang."

North offered a sad smile while he placed his hand on Amberly's. "I understand. Not a day goes by that I don't miss our lives before Chasm," North said. "But the memories, they are still here, a part of us. And having a glass of wine with an old friend and recalling those days, well, that's not bad."

"That's just it. The part of home I could have is sitting *right here*. It's not *Magellan*, it's you. By the time I realized that, I was a light year away, and you were with Sparks. I had to accept the fact I made the wrong choice, content with the consequences. I knew how to cope. I threw myself into my work. Pushed my feelings away, but wow, did I get a lot done for Project Renascence," Amberly laughed dryly.

North took a sip of his wine, then set his glass down on the end table.

"First I was angry at myself for letting you go. After a while I was just sad."

"What do you feel now, Red?" North touched Amberly's hair.

"What do I feel? Now? You're here," Amberly said, tears running down her cheeks, "and I don't ever want you to leave."

"Amberly, I'm an old man and a little slow on the uptake," North searched Amberly's eyes. "What are you saying?"

"Together, we're *home*," Amberly trembled, leaning into North. "Stay with me."

"Forever?" North ran his strong hands through Amberly's red locks.

"Don't you ever leave me. Marry me."

North answered Amberly with a long, soft kiss.

Fin.

ALSO BY L.S. ROEBUCK

Waypoint Magellan
Book one of the Project Waypoint Series

Flight of the Magnus
Book two of the Project Waypoint Series

To report errata in this book, please e-mail
editor@shadowlandspress.com

www.ingramcontent.com/pod-product-compliance
Lightning Source LLC
Chambersburg PA
CBHW060340260626
47160CB00006B/2148